THE LAND GOD GAVE TO CAIN

Hammond Innes's highly individual and successful novels are the result of travel in outback parts of the world. Many of them follow the central character to strange countries where the forces of nature, as much as people, provide the conflict. He has also written two books of travel and one of history. His international reputation as a story-teller keeps his books in print; they have been translated into over thirty foreign languages.

The land God gave to Cain is the Labrador, one of the most Godforsaken areas on earth. Hammond Innes was there in 1953 when Head of Steel was at Mile 250 as the iron ore railway was thrust into the heart of a land of muskeg, lake and jackpines. Few men had ever been there.

He was there again in 1956, and it was his meeting with a ham radio operator at Goose Bay that started him on this story of an expedition given up for lost beside an unknown lake. Prospectors, bush pilots, railway engineers – these are the men he writes about; and a young Scot, who hitch-hiked 3000 miles because he was convinced there was still hope.

Hammond Innes says of this novel – 'One of my most satisfying books. It took me four years to create a story that would bring the Labrador to life for those who will never go there, and I think I have succeeded.'

D1321887

HAMMOND INNES

The Land God Gave to Cain

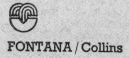

FONTANA / Collins

First published in 1958 by William Collins Sons & Co Ltd
First issued in Fontana Books 1961
Twenty-first Impression December 1978

© Hammond Innes 1958

Made and printed in Great Britain by
William Collins Sons & Co Ltd, Glasgow

This book is dedicated
to the memory of
my mother who died whilst I was
in Canada

CONTENTS

PART ONE

THE RADIO MESSAGE

I

"Your name Ian Ferguson?" The question was flung at me out of a cloud of dust and I straightened up from the theodolite to find one of the Company Land-Rovers had pulled in behind me. The engine was ticking over and the driver was leaning out so that his sun-reddened face was clear of the windscreen. "All right. Hop in, chum. You're wanted down at Company Office."

"What's it about?"

"I dunno. Said it was urgent and sent me up to get you. Probably you got your levels wrong and the runway's on the skew." He grinned. He was always trying to get a rise out of the younger engineers. I entered the figures in my notebook, shouted to my rodholder that I wouldn't be long and clambered in, and then we drove off across the rough ground, trailing a streamer of dust behind us.

The Company Office was just where the old runway finished and our new construction began. It was a large wooden hut with a corrugated iron roof, and as I went in the place was like an oven, for it was very hot in England that September. "Oh, there you are, Ferguson." Mr. Meadows, the chief engineer, came to meet me. "Afraid I've some bad news for you." The roar of an aircraft taking off shook the hut and through it I heard him say, "Telegram for you. Just came through on the phone." He handed me a shee. of paper.

I took it with a sudden feeling of foreboding. I knew it must be my father. The message was written in pencil. *Please come home at once. Dad taken very bad. Love. Mother.*

"When's the next train to London—do you know, sir?"

He glanced at his watch. "In about half an hour. You might just make it." His voice sounded undecided. "I find you had leave about three months ago on account of your father. You're quite certain it's serious? I mean——"

"I'm sorry, sir. I'll have to go." And then, because he remained silent, I felt I had to explain. "My father was badly shot up on a bombing mission during the war. He was a radio operator and he got a shell in the back of the neck. His legs are paralysed and he can't speak. The brain was damaged, too."

" I'm sorry. I didn't know." Mr. Meadows' pale eyes looked hurt. " Of course you must go. I'll have one of the Land-Rovers take you down."

I just caught the train and three hours later I was in London. All the way up I had been thinking of my father and wishing I could remember him as he had been when I was a kid. But I couldn't. The broken, inarticulate wreck that I had grown up with overshadowed all my early memories and I was left with the general impression of a big, friendly man. I had only been six when he joined the R.A.F. and went away to the war.

When I was at home I'd go and sit with him sometimes in that upstairs room where he had the radio. But he lived in a world of his own, and though he would converse by passing notes to me, I always had the impression that I was intruding. The neighbours thought him a bit balmy, and so he was in a way, sitting up there day after day in his wheel-chair contacting other " ham " radio operators. It was mostly Canada he contacted and once, when I was curious and wanted to know why, he'd got excited ; his shattered larynx had produced queer incoherent noises and his big, heavy face had reddened with the effort of trying to communicate something to me. I remember I had asked him to write down what he was trying to tell me, but the note he passed me simply said, *Too complicated. It's a long story.* His eyes had gone to the shelf where he kept his Labrador books and an oddly frustrated look came over his face. And after that I had always been conscious when I was up there of the books and the big map of Labrador that hung on the wall above the transmitter. It wasn't a printed map. He'd drawn it himself whilst in hospital.

I was thinking of this as I hurried down the familiar street, wondering whether there was any solid reason for his interest in Labrador or whether it was something to do with his mental state. A shell had ripped open his skull and the doctors had said the brain was permanently injured, though they'd done a good job of patching him up. The sun had set now and all our side of the street was black in shadow so that it was like a wall of brick. The uniformity of it all saddened me and unconsciously I slowed my pace, remembering that room and the morse key on the table and how he'd insisted on having the station's call sign painted on the door. Mother didn't really understand him. She hadn't his education and she couldn't see his desperate need of that radio room.

I think I knew I wasn't ever going to see him in that room again. Our house had its gate and door painted red, which was all that distinguished it from its neighbours, and as I approached I saw that the upstairs blinds were drawn.

My mother came to the door and greeted me quietly. " I'm glad you've come, Ian." She wasn't crying. She just looked tired, that was all. " You saw the blinds, didn't you? I would have told you in the telegram, but I wasn't certain. I got Mrs. Wright from next door to send it. I had to wait for the doctor." Her voice was lifeless and without emotion. She had come to the end of a long road.

At the foot of the stairs she said, " You'd like to see him, I expect." She took me straight up to the darkened room and left me there. " Come down when you're ready. I'll make you a pot of tea. You must be tired after the journey."

He was lying stretched out on the bed and the furrows of his face, that had been so deep-etched by years of pain, seemed to have been miraculously smoothed out. He looked at peace and in a way I felt glad for him. I stood there a long time, thinking of the fight he'd made of it—seeing him, I think, clearly for the first time as a brave and gallant man. Anger and bitterness stirred in me then at the rotten deal he'd had from life and the unfair way others get through a war scot-free. I was a little confused and in the end I knelt beside his bed and tried to pray. And then I kissed the cold, smooth forehead and tiptoed out and went down the stairs to join my mother in the parlour.

She was sitting with the tea table in front of her, staring at it without seeing it. She looked old and very frail. It had been a hard life for her. " It's almost a relief, Mother, isn't it?"

She looked at me then. " Yes, dear. I've been expecting it ever since he had that stroke three months ago. If he had been content to just lie in bed . . . but he would get up every day and wheel himself along to that room. And he'd be there till all hours, particularly lately. The last week or so, he couldn't seem to leave the wireless alone." She always called it the wireless.

And then, when she had poured my tea, she told me how it had happened. " It was very strange and I wouldn't dream of telling the doctor. He'd never believe me and he'd want to give me pills or something. Even now I'm not sure I didn't imagine it. I was sitting down here, sewing, when I suddenly heard your Dad call out to me. ' Mother!' he called. And then something else. I couldn't say what it was for he was up in that room and he had the door shut as usual. But I could have sworn he called out ' Mother,' and when I got up to the wireless room I found him standing up. He had forced himself up out of his chair and his face was all red and mottled with the effort he was making."

" You mean he was standing up on his own?" It was incredible. My father hadn't stood in years.

" Yes. He was leaning on the table and reaching out with his right hand. To the wall, I think. For support," she added quickly. And then she said, " He turned his head and saw me and tried to say something. And then his face became all twisted with pain. He gave a sort of strangled cry and all his body went suddenly limp and he fell down. I don't know when exactly he died. I laid him on the floor and made him as comfortable as possible." She began to cry quietly.

I went over to her and she clung to me whilst I did my best to comfort her, and all the time the picture of my father's struggle to stand stayed in my mind. " What made him suddenly make such a desperate effort?" I asked.

" Nothing." She looked up at me quickly with such a strange, protective look that I wondered.

" But it must have been something. And to find his voice like that—suddenly after all these years."

" I can't be certain. I may have imagined it. I think I must have."

" But just now you said you were positive he called out to you. Besides, you went up there. He must have called out. And to find him on his feet; there must have been some compelling reason."

" Oh, I don't know. Your Dad was like that. He never would give up. The doctor thinks——"

" Had he got his earphones on when you went in?"

" Yes. But ... Where are you going, Ian?" I didn't answer,

for I was already through the door and running up the stairs. I was thinking of the map of Labrador. She had found my father standing at the table, reaching out to the wall—and that was where the map hung. Or perhaps he had been trying to reach the bookshelf. It was below the map and it contained nothing but the books on Labrador. He was fascinated by the country. It was an obsession with him.

I turned left at the top of the stairs and there was the door with STATION G2STO stencilled on it. It was so familiar that, as I pushed it open, I couldn't believe that I wouldn't find him seated there in front of the radio. But the wheelchair was empty, swivelled back against the wall, and the desk where he always sat was unnaturally tidy, the usual litter of notebooks, magazines and newspapers all cleared away and stacked neatly on top of the transmitter. I searched quickly through them, but there was no message, nothing.

I had been so certain I should find a message, or at least some indication of what had happened, that I stood at a loss for a moment, looking round the small den that had been his world for so long. It was all very familiar, and yet it had a strangeness because he was no longer there to give it point. Only that had changed. All the rest remained—the school pictures, the caps, the wartime photographs, and the bits and pieces of planes with the scribbled signatures of the air crews who had been his companions. And over by the door hung the same faded picture of my grandmother, Alexandra Ferguson, her strong face unsmiling and yellowed above the tight-buttoned bodice.

I stared at it, wondering whether she would have known the answer. I had often seen him glance at the picture—or was it at the things that hung below it, the rusted pistol, the sextant, the broken paddle and the torn canvas case with the moth-eaten fur cap hanging over it? Alexandra Ferguson was his mother. She had brought him up, and somehow I'd always known those relics beneath the photograph belonged to the north of Canada, though I couldn't remember anybody ever telling me so.

I dug back in my memory to the vague impression of a grey, bleak house somewhere in the north of Scotland, and a terrifying old woman who had come to me in the night. The photograph didn't recall her to my mind, for all I remembered was a disembodied face hanging over me in the flickering flame of the night light, a cold, bitter, desiccated face, and then my mother had come in and they had shouted at each other until I had screamed with fear. We had left next morning and as though by common consent neither my mother nor my father had ever mentioned her to me again.

I turned back to the room, the memory of that scene still vivid. And then I was looking at the radio receiver and the morse key with the pencil lying beside it, and the memory faded. These were the things that now dominated all the bits and pieces of his life. Together they represented all that had been left to him, and somehow I felt that, as his son, I should have enough understanding of him to wring from them the thing that had driven him to such a superhuman effort.

I think it was the pencil that made me realise something was missing. There should have been a log book. He always kept a radio log. Not a proper one, of course ; just a cheap exercise book in which he jotted things down—station frequencies and their times of broadcasting, scraps of weather forecasts or ships' talk or anything from Canada, all mixed up with little drawings and anything else that came to his mind.

I found several of these exercise books in the drawer of the table, but they didn't include the current one. The latest entry in these books was for September 15, a page of doodling in which it was almost impossible to decipher anything coherent at all. Drawings of lions seemed to predominate, and in one place he had written: *C2—C2—C2 . . . where the hell is that?* The scrawled line of a song caught my eye—*LOST AND GONE FOREVER*—and he had ringed it round with a series of names—Winokapau—Tishinakamau—Attikonak—Winokapau—Tishinakamau—Attikonak—repeated over and over again as a sort of decoration.

Turning back through the pages of these old log books I found they were all like that—a queer mixture of thoughts and fancies that made me realise how lonely he had been up there in that room and how desperately turned in upon himself. But here and there I picked out dates and times, and gradually a pattern emerged. Every day there was an entry for 2200 hours, undoubtedly the same station transmitting, for the entry was nearly always followed by the call sign VO6AZ, and on one page he had written *VO6AZ came through as usual.* Later I found the name Ledder occurring—*Ledder reports* or *Ledder again*, in place of the call sign. The word *expedition* occurred several times.

It is difficult to convey the impression these muddled pages made. They were such an extraordinary mixture of fact and nonsense, of what he had heard over the air and the things that came into his mind, all patterned and half-obliterated with childish lines and squiggles and odd names and little drawings with the shape of a lion repeated and repeated in page after page. A psychiatrist would probably say that it was all symptomatic of cerebral damage, and yet most people doodle when they are much alone with their thoughts, and through it all ran the thread of these reports from *VO6AZ*.

I turned to the bookcase behind me, which housed his technical library, and took down the *Radio Amateur Call Book*. This I knew listed all the world's ham operators under their different countries, together with their call signs and addresses. He had explained the call sign system to me once. The prefix gave the location. G, for instance, was the prefix for all British hams. I started to look up Canada, but the book fell open almost automatically at Labrador and I saw that VO6 was the prefix for this area. Against the call sign VO6AZ appeared the names Simon & Ethel Ledder, c/o D.O.T. Communications, Goose Bay.

The knowledge that he had been in regular contact with Labrador drew me again to the map hanging above the transmitter, the names he had written on that last page running through my head—Winokapau—Tishinakamau—Attikonak. It was like the opening of Turner's poem and, leaning forward across the desk, I saw that he had made some pencil markings on the map. I was certain they hadn't been there when I'd last been in the room with him. A line had been drawn from the Indian settlement of Seven Islands on the St. Lawrence, running north into the middle of Labrador, and against it was pencilled the initials—Q.N.S. & L.R. To the right of it, about halfway up, an almost blank area of the map had been ringed, and here he had written *Lake of the Lion* with a large question mark after it.

I had just noticed *Attikonak L.* inked in against the outline of a large, sprawling lake, when the door behind me opened and there was a little gasp. I turned to find my mother standing there with a frightened look on her face. "What's the matter?" I asked.

She seemed to relax at the sound of my voice. "You did give me a turn—I thought for a moment——" She checked herself and I realised suddenly that this was how my father had stood, leaning on the table and reaching over towards the map of Labrador.

"It was the map, wasn't it?" I was excited by the sudden certainty that it was the map that had drawn him to his feet.

A shadow seemed to cross her face. Her gaze fastened on the log books strewn on the table. "What are you doing up here, Ian?"

But I was remembering something a Canadian pilot had told me at the airfield—something about a party lost in Labrador and Canadian Air Force planes searching for them. The references to an expedition in the log books, the map and my father's obsession with Labrador, and that sudden frightened look on my mother's face—it was all coming together in my mind. "Mother," I said. "There was a message, wasn't there?"

She looked at me then and her face went blank. "I don't know what you mean, dear, Why don't you come down and finish your tea. Try to forget about it."

But I shook my head. "You do know what I mean," I said, and I went over to her and took hold of her hands. They were cold as ice. "What did you do with his log book?"

"His log book?" She stared at me and I could feel her trembling. "Aren't they all there?"

"You know they aren't. The current one—it's missing. What have you done with it?"

"Nothing, dear. You don't understand—I was too busy. It's been a terrible day . . . terrible." She began to cry gently.

"Please," I said. "All the log books are there, except the current one. It should have been on the table beside the morse key. He always kept it there, and now it's gone."

"He may have thrown it away. Or perhaps he'd forgotten to keep it for a time. You know how your father was. He was like a child." But she wouldn't look at me and I knew she was hiding something.

"What have you done with it, Mother?" I shook her gently. "He received some sort of a message. Something to do with Labrador."

"Labrador!" The word seemed to explode out of her mouth. Her eyes widened and she was staring at me. "Not you, too, Ian. Please God. Not you. All my life . . ." Her voice trailed away. "Now come down and have your tea, there's a good boy. I can't take any more—not to-day."

I can remember the weariness in her voice, the note of pleading—and how cruel I was. "You never understood him, did you, Mother?" I said that to her, and I believed it. "If you'd understood him, you'd know there was only one thing would drive him to call out, struggling to his feet and reaching out for the map. It was the map he was reaching out to, wasn't it?" And I shook her gently whilst she just stared at me with a sort of fascination. I told her then about the planes searching for a geological party lost in Labrador. "Whatever Dad may have been during these last few years, he was still a first-class radio operator. If he picked up some sort of a message from them . . ." I had to make her see it my way —how important it could be. "Those men's lives might depend on it," I said.

She shook her head slowly. "You don't know," she murbured. "You can't know." And she added, "It was all in his imagination."

"Then he did pick up a message?"

"He imagined things. You've been away so much . . . you don't know what went on in his mind."

"He didn't imagine this," I said. "It made him suddenly find his voice. It forced him to his feet and the effort killed him." I was being intentionally brutal. If my father had killed himself in an effort to save other men's lives, then I wasn't going to have his effort go for nothing, whatever my mother's reason for concealing it. "Look—I'm sorry," I said, "but I must have that log book." And when she only stared at me with a sort of dumb misery in her eyes, I said, "He wrote the message down in it, didn't he? Didn't he, Mother?" I was exasperated by her attitude. "For God's sake! Where is it! Please, Mother—you must let me see it!"

A defeated look showed in her face and she gave a tired little sigh. "Very well, Ian. If you must have it . . ." She turned then and went slowly out of the room. "I'll get it for you."

I went with her because I had an instinctive feeling that if I didn't she might destroy it. I couldn't understand her attitude at all. I could literally feel her reluctance as I followed her down the stairs.

She had hidden it under the table linen in one of the drawers of the sideboard, and as she handed it to me, she said, " You won't do anything foolish now, will you?"

But I didn't answer her. I had seized hold of the exercise book and was already seated at the table, leafing through the pages. It was much the same as the others, except that the entries were more factual with fewer doodles and the word *search* caught my eye several times.

And then I was staring at the last entry on a page clear of all other jottings: *CQ—CQ—CQ—Any 75-metre phone station—Any 75-metre phone station—Come in someone please —Come in someone please—K.*

There it was in my father's laboured hand, and the desperation of that cry called to me through the shaky pencilled words in that tattered child's exercise book. And underneath he had written *BRIFFE—It must be.* And the date and the time— *September 29, 1355—voice very faint.* Voice very faint! And below that, with the time given as 1405— *Calling again. CQ—CQ—CQ, etc. Still no reply.* Then the final entry: *Calling VO6AZ now. Position not known but within 30 miles radius C2—situation desperate—injured and no fire—Baird very bad—Laroche gone—CQ—CQ—CQ—Can hardly hear him—Search for narrow lake (obliterated)—Repeating . . . narrow lake with rock shaped like . . .* The message ended there in a straggling pencil line as though the point of it had slipped as he made the effort to stand.

Injured and no fire! I sat there, staring at the pencilled words, a vivid picture in my mind of a narrow desolate lake and an injured man crouched over a radio set. *Situation desperate.* I could imagine it. The nights would be bitter and in the daytime they'd be plagued with a million flies. I'd read about it in those books of my father's. And the vital part was missing—the bit that had brought my father to his feet.

" What are you going to do?" My mother's voice sounded nervous, almost frightened.

" Do?" I hadn't thought about it. I was still wondering what it was that had so galvanised my father. " Mum. Do you know why Dad was so interested in Labrador?"

" No."

The denial was so quick, so determined, that I looked up at

her. Her face was very pale, a little haggard in the gathering dusk. "When did it start?" I asked.

"Oh, a long time ago. Before the war."

"So it wasn't anything to do with his being shot up?" I got up from the chair I had been sitting in. "Surely you must know the reason for it? In all these years he must have told you why——"

But she had turned away. "I'm going to get supper," she said, and I watched her go out through the door, puzzled by her attitude.

Alone, I began thinking again about those men lost in Labrador. Briffe—that was the name Farrow had talked about in the Airport Bar. Briffe was the leader of some sort of geological expedition, and I wondered what one did in a case like this. Suppose nobody but my father had picked up that message? But then they were bound to have heard it in Canada. If Dad had picked it up at a distance of over two thousand miles. . . . But, according to Dad, Goose Bay hadn't replied. And if by some queer chance he had been the only radio operator in the world to pick that message up, then I was the thread on which those men's lives hung.

It was an appalling thought and I worried about it all through supper—far more I think than about my father's death, for I couldn't do anything about that. When we had finished the meal I said to my mother, " I think I'll just walk as far as the call box."

"Who are you going to phone?"

"I don't know." Who did one ring? There was Canada House. They were really the people to tell, but they'd be closed now. "The police, I suppose."

"Do you have to do anything about it?" She was standing there, wringing her hands.

"Well, yes," I said. "I think somebody ought to know." And then, because I still didn't understand her attitude, I asked her why she'd tried to hide the message from me.

"I didn't know if you . . ." She hesitated, and then said quickly, "I didn't want your father laughed at."

"Laughed at? Really, Mother! Suppose nobody else picked up this transmission? If these men died, then you'd have been responsible."

Her face went blank. "I didn't want them laughing at

him," she repeated obstinately. " You know what people are in a street like this."

" This is more important than what people think." My tone was impatient. And then, because I knew she was upset and tired, I kissed her. " We shan't be bothered about it," I reassured her. " It's just that I feel that I must report it. It wouldn't be the first time he picked up a transmission that no other operator received," I added, and I went out of the house and back along the street to the Underground.

I had no idea who I should get on to at Scotland Yard, so in the end I dialled 999. It seemed odd to be making an emergency police call when we hadn't been burgled or anything. And when I got through to them I found it wasn't easy to explain what it was all about. It meant telling them about my father and the " ham " radio station he operated. The fact that he had just died because of his excitement over the message only made it more confusing.

However, in the end they said they had got it all clear and would contact the Canadian authorities, and I left the call box feeling that a weight had been lifted from my shoulders. It was their responsibility now. I needn't worry about it any more. And when I got back to the house, I put the log book away in my suitcase and went through into the kitchen, where my mother was quietly getting a meal. Now that the matter of the message was cleared up and the authorities notified, I began to see it from her point of view. After all, why should she worry about two men in a distant part of the world when my father was lying dead upstairs?

That night my mother had the little bedroom and I slept on the couch in the parlour. And in the morning I woke to the realisation that there was a lot to be done—the funeral to arrange, all his things to go through and the pension people to be notified. I hadn't realised before that death didn't end with sorrow.

After breakfast I sent a wire to Mr. Meadows and then went on to arrange things with the undertaker. When I got back it was almost eleven and Mrs. Wright was in from next door having tea with my mother. It was Mrs. Wright who heard the car draw up and went to the window to see. " Why, it's a police car," she said, and then added, " I do believe they're coming here."

It was a Police Inspector and a Flight Lieutenant Mathers of the Canadian Air Force. They wanted to see the log book, and when I'd got it from my suitcase and had handed it to the inspector, I found myself apologising for the writing. "I'm afraid it's not very good. You see my father was paralysed and——"

"Yes, we know all about that," the Inspector said. "We've made inquiries, naturally." He was no longer looking at the page on which the message had been written, but was leafing back through the log book, the Flight Lieutenant peering over his shoulder. I began to feel uncomfortable then. The pages were such a muddle and in the Inspector's hands the log looked exactly what it was, a child's exercise book. I remembered my mother's words—*I didn't want your father laughed at.*

When he had examined every page, the Inspector turned back to the one on which the message was written. "I think you said that your father died immediately after writing this?"

I explained to him what had happened—how my mother thought she heard him call out to her and went up to find he had somehow struggled to his feet. And when I had finished, he said, "But you weren't here at the time?"

"No. My job is near Bristol. I wasn't here."

"Who was here? Just your mother?"

"Yes."

He nodded. "Well, I'm afraid I'll have to have a word with her. But first we'd like to have a look at the room where your father had his radio."

I took them up and the Flight Lieutenant had a look at the radio whilst the Inspector prowled round, looking at the books and the map hanging on the wall. "Well, it's all in working order," the Flight Lieutenant said. He had switched on the receiver and he had the earphones over his head whilst his fingers played with the tuning dial. But by then the Inspector had found the old log books in the drawer and was glancing through them.

At length he turned to me. "I'm sorry to have to ask you this, Mr. Ferguson, but we've been on to the doctor and I understand your father had a stroke some three months ago. You were down here then?"

"Yes," I said. "But only for a few days. He made a very quick recovery."

"Have you been here since?"

" No," I told him. " We're on airfield construction at the moment. It's a rush job and I haven't had another chance——"

" What I'm getting at is this . . . can you vouch for your father's mental state? Could he have imagined this?"

" No. Certainly not." I felt suddenly angry. " If you're suggesting that my father . . ." I stopped then, because I realised what must have prompted the question. " Do you mean to say nobody else picked up that transmission?"

" Not as far as we know." He turned to the Flight Lieutenant. " However, there's no doubt he was following the progress of this expedition," he said. " There are dozens of references to it in these notebooks, but . . ." He hesitated, and then gave a little shrug. " Well, take a look for yourself." He passed the books across to the Canadian. I might not have been there as the Air Force officer bent down to examine them and the Inspector watched him, waiting for his reaction.

At length I could stand it no longer. " What's wrong with the message?" I asked.

" Nothing, nothing—except . . ." The Inspector hesitated. The Flight Lieutenant looked up from the log books. " We're not doubting he was in touch with Ledder, you know." His voice held a note of reservation, and as though conscious of this he added, " I checked with our people at Goose right away. Simon Ledder and his wife are both registered hams operating their own station under the call sign VO6AZ. They take on outside work and in this case they were acting as base station for the McGovern Mining and Exploration Company, receiving Briffe's reports by R/T and transmitting them to the Company's offices in Montreal."

" Well, then?" I didn't understand why they were still so doubtful about it. " The fact that nobody else picked up the transmission——"

" It's not that," he said quickly. And he looked across at the Inspector, who said, " I'm sorry, Mr. Ferguson. All this must be very trying for you." He sounded apologetic. " But the fact is that Briffe and the man with him were reported dead—almost a week ago, didn't you say, Mathers?" He looked across at the Canadian.

" That's so, Inspector." The Flight Lieutenant nodded. " On September twenty-fifth to be exact." He tossed the log books on to the table. " I don't want to seem unappreciative," he said, looking across at me. "Particularly as you say your father's excitement at receiving the message was the cause of his death. But the fact is that Bert Laroche, the pilot of the crashed plane, trekked out on his own. He reached one of the construction camps of the Iron Ore Railway on the twenty-fifth and reported that the other two were dead when he left them. He'd been five days trekking out, so they were dead by September twentieth. Now you come along with the information that your father picked up a radio broadcast from Briffe yesterday. That's nine whole days after Briffe was dead." He shook his head. "It just doesn't make sense."

"The pilot might have made a mistake," I murmured.

He stared at me with a sort of shocked look. "I guess you don't understand the Canadian North, Mr. Ferguson. Men just don't make that sort of mistake. Certainly not experienced fliers like Bert Laroche." And he added, "He crashed his Beaver floatplane into a rock trying to land on a lake in a snow storm. Briffe and Baird were injured. He got them ashore and the plane sank. That was on September the fourteenth. Baird died almost immediately, Briffe a few days later, and then he started to trek out."

"But the message," I cried. "How else could my father have known——"

"It was all in the news-casts," Mathers said. "The whole story—it was repeated over and over again."

"But not about the lake surely," I said impatiently. "How would my father know it was a lake with a rock in it? And how would he know about Briffe and Baird being injured and the pilot gone?"

"I tell you, Briffe and Baird were dead by then."

"Are you suggesting he made it all up?"

Mathers shrugged his shoulders and reached for the last of the log books, turning the pages until he came to the message. He stared at it for a long time. "It just isn't possible," he murmured. "If your father picked up a transmission, why didn't someone else?"

"You've checked, have you?"

"We're checking now. But, believe me, if anybody in Canada had picked it up, they'd have reported it immediately. The papers were full of the search when it was on."

"I can't help that," I said. "Maybe nobody else picked it up. But my father did. The message is there in that log book to prove it." He made no comment. He was looking back again through the old log books. " I remember once," I added desperately, " my father picked up a message from a yacht in the Timor Sea when nobody else did. And another time he made a contact——"

" But this is R/T. How could he possibly pick up Voice from an old set like Briffe's?" The Flight Lieutenant was still riffling through the pages of the logs, but now he suddenly closed them. " There's only one explanation, I guess." He said it to the Inspector, who nodded agreement.

I knew what he meant and I was furious. I'd done what I thought was right and here were these two strangers trying to make out that my father was crazy. I wished to God I'd never reported the matter. My mother was right. How could I possibly make them understand that a lonely man could scribble a lot of nonsense all over those log books and yet be reliable when it came to picking up a transmission? " Surely somebody else must have picked the message up," I said helplessly. And then, because they didn't say anything, but stood there looking uncomfortable, I let my feelings run away with me. " You think my father made it all up, don't you? Just because he had a head wound and was paralysed and drew little pictures in those books, you think he isn't to be relied on. But you're wrong. My father was a first-class radio operator. Whatever the doctors or anybody else may say, he'd never make a mistake over a message like that."

" Maybe," the Canadian said. " But we're two thousand five hundred miles from Labrador and Briffe wasn't on Key, he was on Voice transmission—in other words, radio telephone."

" That's what my father implies. He says it's Briffe's voice he's hearing."

" Sure. But I've already checked on this and all Briffe had was an old wartime forty-eight set. That's the Canadian equivalent of your British Army eighteen set. It had been modified to operate on the seventy-five metre phone band, but he was still using it in conjunction with a hand generator. Even with a line aerial instead of a whip, Goose would have been just about at the limit of his range—that's why he was reporting back to Ledder instead of direct to Montreal."

" I don't know about that," I said. " But I do know this. See all those books up there? They're about Labrador. My father was fascinated by the place. He knew what it would be like for those men lost out there. He knew that message was important. That's why he suddenly found his voice and called out. That's what forced him to his feet when he hadn't stood——"

"Just a minute," the Flight Lieutenant said. "You don't seem to understand what I've been trying to tell you. Those men are dead. They've been dead more than nine days."

"But that message . . ."

"There wasn't any message." He said it quietly, and then added, "See here, Ferguson. I'm sorry about your father. But let's be practical. We had four planes searching for almost a week. Then Laroche came out and reported the other two dead and we called off the search. Now you want me to advise a resumption of a full-scale search, involving machines and fliers in hours of duty over desolate country, just because your father wrote down a message in an exercise book before he died—a message that, even if it had been transmitted, it was technically impossible for him to pick up."

There wasn't anything I could say to that. "If it's technically impossible——"

"He was more than two thousand miles outside of normal range. Of course," he added, "there's always the chance of freak reception, even at that distance, and just in case, I'm having inquiries made of all ham operators in Canada. I've also asked for a full report from Ledder. I think you can be quite sure that if any transmission was made on the twenty-ninth, then we'll find somebody who picked it up."

The Inspector nodded. "If you don't mind, I'll keep these notebooks for the time being." He picked them up off the table. "I'd like to have them examined by our experts."

"No," I said. "I don't mind." It seemed useless to say anything more. And yet . . . My eyes strayed to the map of Labrador. He'd forced himself to his feet in order to look at it. Why? What had been in his mind?

"I don't think it's necessary for us to trouble Mrs. Ferguson after all," the Inspector was saying. They went down the stairs then and I showed them out. "I'll let you have these back in a day or so." The Inspector indicated the exercise books in his hand.

I watched them as they walked out to the police car and drove away. What had he meant by saying he'd like to have them examined by experts? But, of course, I knew, and I felt as though in some way I had let my father down. And yet, if the men were dead . . . I went back into the parlour to be faced with my mother's reproachful gaze and Mrs. Wright's eager questioning.

But there were other, more practical things to think about, and with the funeral the sense of grief pushed everything else into the background of my mind.

It wasn't until the morning I was leaving to return to Bristol that I was reminded of the strange message that had caused my father's death. The postman brought a registered package addressed to me, and inside were the log books. There was also a letter, impersonal and final: *I have to inform you that the Canadian authorities have been unable to obtain any confirmation of the message claimed to have been received by your father, Mr. James Ferguson, on 29th September. Our experts have examined the enclosed, and in view of their report, and the statement by the only survivor that the two remaining members of the party are dead, the Canadian authorities do not feel that any useful purpose can be served by resuming the search. However, they wish me to express their appreciation, etc., etc.*

So that was that. The experts—psychiatrists presumably—had looked at the log books and had decided that my father was mad. I tore the letter savagely across, and then, because I didn't want my mother to find the fragments, I slipped them into my suitcase, together with the log books.

She came to the station to see me off. Ever since that visit from the police she had never once referred to the cause of my father's death. As though by tacit consent we had avoided any reference to the message. But now, just as the train was about to leave, she gripped my hand. " You'll let that Labrador business alone, won't you, Ian? I couldn't bear it if you . . ." The whistle blew then and she kissed me, holding me close that way she hadn't done since I was a kid. Her face was white and tired-looking and she was crying.

I got in and the train began to move. For a moment she stood watching, a small, lonely figure in black, and then she turned quickly and walked away down the platform. I often wonder whether she knew in her heart that she wouldn't see me again for a long time.

II

I HAD forgotten to get anything to read and for a time I just sat there, watching the backs of the houses until London began to thin out and the green fields showed beyond the factory buildings. I was thinking about my mother and our parting and the way she had referred again to Labrador. She hadn't mentioned the message my father had picked up. She wasn't worried that the lives of those two men might be at stake. It was Labrador itself that was on her mind, which struck me as odd. And then I began thinking about my father again, wishing I had known him better. If I had known him better, I might have understood what it was about Labrador that had so fascinated me.

And then I got out the log books and looked through them again. It wasn't difficult to see why the authorities and the " experts " had decided to disregard the message. The books were such a mess. And yet, running through them, was this thread of the Labrador expedition.

My training as an engineer had taught me to break every problem down to its essentials, and before I knew what I was doing, I had got out pencil and paper and was jotting down every reference in the log books that could conceivably have a bearing on Briffe's expedition. Disentangled from all the jottings and drawings and scraps of other messages, the thread became stronger and more lucid. It told a definite story, though it was necessary to read between the lines to get at it, for it soon became clear to me that my father seldom took down anything verbatim ; a single line of comment or a brief note to give him the gist of the transmission was all he bothered about. This was not surprising since the forming of legible characters had always been a labour to him. Indeed, there were several jottings that it was quite impossible for me to decipher.

In all I found I had isolated seventy-three references. Twelve of these were unintelligible and seven I finally discarded as having no bearing on the subject. From the remaining fifty-four I was able, with the help of a little guess-work, to build up some sort of a picture of what had happened. Briffe had presumably started out on his survey sometime around end-July for the first reference to a location occurred on August 10. The note simply said *A2—where's that?* Three days later there was a reference to—*Minipi River area:* and on August 15 my father had noted: *Moved to A3.* Then followed B1, B2 and B3. Clearly these were code names for the areas under survey and as A1 would have been the first, my father must have been picking up Ledder's reports almost from the start. There was no indication of the purpose of Briffe's expedition—whether he was prospecting for gold or uranium or just a base metal like iron ore. He might simply be making a general survey, but this seemed unlikely since he was working for a mining company and was coding his areas and reports. The fact that the location code was dropped in later reports suggested negative results. This happened, not only in the case of A2, but in several other cases as well. Thus A3 later became *Mouni Rapids* and B2 *near old H.B. Post.* Against the reference to Mouni Rapids my father had written—*Winokapau! The right direction.*

By September 9, the expedition had reached Area C1. This was later referred to as *Disappointment,* and later still it became obvious that it was the name of a lake. These scraps of information were all apparently gleaned from the same source—VO6AZ. And always at the same time—2200 hours. An entry for August 3 appeared to be the first reference to the expedition. It simply said: *Interesting—some sort of code.* The next day's entry read. *2200. VO6AZ again. Survey report?* And he had scrawled in pencil: *EMPLOYED BY THE McGOVERN MINING AND EXPLORATION COMPANY OF MONTREAL?*

And on the top of the next page, again in pencil: *KEEP WATCH 20 METRE BAND 10 P.M.* Later in August was an entry *2200—VO6AZ. Code again! Why can't he report in clear?* And a note on the following page: *BRIFFE, BRIFFE, BRIFFE. WHO IS BRIFFE? 75 METRE PHONE. NET FREQUENCY 3.780 kcs. WATCH 2000.* But this was so fantastically scrawled over that I had difficulty in deciphering it. Two pages further on I found the name Laroche mentioned for the first time. He had written it in capitals, heavily underlining it and putting a question mark at the end, and had added a note: *QUERY LEDDER.*

Isolated from all the nonsense and doodles which disfigured

the pages of his log books, my father's notes confirmed what I already knew—that he had been picking up messages from Simon Ledder at Goose Bay to the McGovern Mining Company in Montreal and that these were daily reports in some sort of code passing on information received from Briffe at 2000 hours from somewhere in Labrador. I found one half-obliterated entry which appeared to read: *3.780—nothing, nothing, nothing—always nothing*. It suggested that my father was also keeping regular watch on Briffe's transmitting frequency. But I could only pick out for certain one entry a day at 2200 hours, until September 14. That was the day of the crash, and from then on the pattern changed and the entries became more frequent, the comments fuller.

Two days before that Briffe appeared to have called for air transport to move the party forward to C2, for on September 13 occurred an entry: *Plane delayed, W bad. B. calling for usual two flights, three in first wave and Baird and himself in second. If C2 NORTH OF C1 THEY ARE GETTING V. NEAR.*

The move apparently took place on September 14, but the first flight proved difficult for at 1945 hours he had made this entry: *In luck—Contact VO6AZ. Beaver floatplane not back.* Scrawled across these were the words *TROUBLE* and *KEEP CONSTANT WATCH ON 75-METRE BAND*. And then an hour later at 2045: *Fog cleared, but Beaver still missing*. VO6AZ was now apparently transmitting to Montreal every hour at 15 minutes to the hour, for the next time entry was for 2145. But nothing had been written against it and the time itself was barely decipherable amongst the mass of little drawings my father had made. In fact, the whole of this last page of the log book was an indescribable mess and it took me a long time to sort it out. The next entry, however, was only half an hour later—*2215: Advance party safe C2. Beaver back. Hellish W. report. B. going. . . .* The last part was completely unreadable. But the comment that followed was clear enough: *POOR HOLDING DISAPPOINTMENT—THAT THE REASON? BARELY AN HOUR. THE FOOL! WHAT'S DRIVING HIM?*

After that the entries were back to 15 minutes to the hour—2245, 2345, 0045, right on to 0345. They were all blank. There was a sort of finality about those blank entries, and though it was the soft, warm English countryside that slid past the windows of the train, I saw only the cold and fog and the desolate misery of Labrador, the night closing in on the little floatplane and my father sitting up half the night, waiting to find out whether they were safe or not.

The entries in the log book were, of course, for British Summer Time which is four and a half hours ahead of Goose Bay. Briffe's report that the plane was back must have been made shortly after 5 p.m. so that my father's reference to "barely an hour" obviously referred to the fact that Briffe was taking off with little more than an hour to go before nightfall.

The train stopped at Swindon and I sat staring down at that last page of the log book. I couldn't blame the authorities for regarding him as unbalanced. It had taken me almost a quarter of an hour to decipher that one page. I could see my father sitting in his wheel-chair with the earphones clamped to his head, waiting and waiting for the news of Briffe's safety that would never come, and passing the long, slow, silent hours by drawing. He had covered the whole of that page and all the cover of the exercise book with little pencil drawings—lions and fish with faces and canoes, as well as squares and circles, anything that his wandering hand and brain took a fancy to. It was here that he had written—*C2—C2—C2. . . . Where the hell is it?* and had scrawled the words: LOST AND GONE FOREVER and framed them with the names—Winokapau—Tishinakamau—Attikonak.

As the train started again I picked up the last log book, the one my mother had tried to hide from me. He could have had little sleep that night, for the first entry was for 0800 hours. *Ledder failed to make contact.* And an hour later—*No contact.* After that there were entries for every hour, but nothing against them. And by midday he was picking up odd scraps of news commentaries and transmissions from other stations. The word GREENWOOD occurred once. This appeared to be some sort of code word, like MAYDAY, for immediately afterwards there was a note: *Air search ordered.* There was a reference to bad weather and then, two days later: *Nova Scotia Air Rescue base.*

But this book, like the last, was a mass of doodles, on the front of the cover, inside and all over that first page, an indication of the long hours he had spent alone, huddled over the receiver. If I hadn't been so familiar with his writing I don't think I should ever have been able to decipher it.

I re-checked the entries against the notes I had made, and as I turned the pages the men involved in the disaster were revealed. There was Briffe, the leader of the party, and a man called Baird, and then a third man, the pilot. *Ledder keeps calling Laroche*. This was on the second page, and two days later he had written the name *LAROCHE* again in capitals, and underneath: *No, it can't be. I must be mad*. Nowhere could I find the names of the three men who had gone up to Area C2 on the first flight, though I did find a further reference to them amongst the jottings from news broadcasts—*Advance party evacuated from C2, all three safe*.

There were two other entries I thought might have some bearing on the disaster, one of which I could only partly decipher. On September 23 he had written *1705—Made contact VO6AZ—Query geologists*. And then two pages farther on: *1719—VO6AZ. SO THEY HAVEN'T FORGOTTEN ABOUT* . . . The rest was completely obliterated, though I could read my father's initials, J.F.F., written for some unknown reason into the middle of the sentence.

Excerpts from news broadcasts referring to the search continued until September 26. But on that date, against the time 1300 hours, he had written the one word: *Finis*. And then later the same day: *1714—Made contact Ledder. Briffe and Baird both dead. L. safe*. And he had added: *L-L-L-L-L— IMPOSSIBLE*.

Reading all this through as the train ran into Bristol, it was clear that my father had not only followed the story of the whole expedition with great interest, but he had even made direct contact with VO6AZ to clarify certain points. And bearing in mind that he was only making very brief notes for his own personal use and not transcribing messages in detail, it seemed to me there was nothing to indicate that there was anything wrong with his mental state. Some of the comments I didn't understand and, of course, these, if looked at amongst the jottings and drawings of the muddled pages in which they appeared, would give a different impression. If, however, the so-called experts had bothered to isolate the references to the expedition, as I had done, they would have seen how clear he was about it all.

All the way out to the airport I was thinking about this and how my mother had seen him standing on his two feet and reaching out to the map of Labrador. There must be something in that message. Whether the men were dead or not, I was convinced my father hadn't imagined it. He'd known it was important. And now all his effort was wasted because I hadn't had the sense to isolate the relevant passages for the police as I had done on the train.

It was after six when I reached the airport—too late to report to the Company office. I felt sad and depressed, and instead of going to my digs, I turned in at the Airport Bar. The sight of Farrow drinking with a bunch of charter pilots made me think that perhaps there was still something I could do that would convince the authorities. Farrow was the Canadian pilot who had told me about the search for the missing geologists and, flying trans-Atlantic charters, I knew he must land sometimes at Goose Bay.

I thought about it whilst I had my drink, and in the end I went over to the group and asked him if I could have a word with him. " It's about that survey party that was lost," I said as he moved down the bar with me.

" The search was called off over a week ago. Briffe was dead. Baird, too. Only the pilot got out."

" Yes, I know." I asked him what he'd have to drink.

" Fruit juice. I'm flying to-morrow." I ordered and when I turned to him again, I saw that he was watching me. He had baby blue eyes in a round, friendly face. But the eyes were shrewd. " What's biting you?"

" Do you ever land at Goose Bay?"

" Sure. Every time we do the west-bound flight—unless it clamps down."

" Do you know a radio operator called Simon Ledder?"

" Ledder?" He shook his head. " Where's he work— Control?"

" I don't know exactly. His address is care of D.O.T. Communications."

" That's the civilian radio station. D.O.T. stands for Department of Transport. They're over on the American side."

The drinks came and I paid, conscious that he was watching me as he sipped his fruit juice, waiting for me to tell him what it was all about. And now that I had him here alone with me, I didn't know quite how to put it to him. I didn't want to tell him what it was all about. And now that I had him here alone with me, I didn't know quite how to put it to him. I didn't want to tell him more than I had to. I didn't want to risk the look of disbelief that it would inevitably produce. "You're flying to-morrow, you say. Will you be landing at Goose?"

"Yes. Around twenty-one hundred hours our time."

"Will you have a word with Ledder for me—telephone him perhaps?"

"What about?"

"Well . . ." It was so damned difficult. "He's a ham operator," I explained, "and he was in touch with a British ham on three occasions—Station G2STO. There's a report, too. Could you ask him to let you have a copy of it?"

"What's the report about?"

I hesitated. But he had to know, of course. "It's about Briffe and his party. Ledder was the radio link between the survey party and the mining company they were working for. The authorities have asked him for a report of all his radio contacts with Briffe and also the contacts with G2STO."

"How do you know they've asked him for a report?" His voice was suddenly different, the softness gone out of it.

"Somebody told me," I said vaguely. But he was curious now and it made me nervous. "I'm sorry to bother you with this, but when I saw you in here I thought perhaps if you could have a word with Ledder . . ."

"You could write to him," he said. And then, when I didn't say anything, he added, "Hadn't you better tell me a little more—why you're so interested in this report, for instance?"

He was still watching me curiously, waiting for me to explain. And suddenly I knew it was no good. I'd have to tell him the whole story. "G2STO was my father," I said. And I told him about the wire I had received from my mother and how I'd gone home to find my father dead. I told it all exactly as it had happened to me, but when I came to my discovery of the message from Briffe, he said, "From Briffe? But Briffe was dead days before."

"I know." My voice sounded suddenly weary. "That's

what the police told me." And then I got out the notes I'd made in the train and handed them to him. " But if Briffe was dead, how do you explain that?"

He smoothed the sheet of paper out on the bar top and read it through slowly and carefully.

" They're all references from my father's radio log," I said.
He nodded, frowning as he read.

I watched him turn the sheet over. He had reached the final message now. " Does it sound as though he was mad?" I said.

He didn't say anything. He had read through the notes now and I watched him turn the sheet over again, staring down at it, still frowning.

" That's what the authorities think," I added. " They're not going to resume the search. I had a letter from them this morning."

He still didn't say anything and I began to wish I hadn't told him. The men were reported dead. That alone would convince him that my father had imagined it all. And then his blue eyes were looking straight at me. " And you think the search should be resumed—is that it?" he asked.

I nodded.

He stared at me for a moment. " Have you got the log books or do the police still hold them?"

" No, I've got them." I said it reluctantly because I didn't want him to see them. But instead of asking for them he began putting a lot of questions to me. And when he had got the whole story out of me, he fell silent again, hunched over the sheet of paper, staring at it. I thought he was reading it through again, but maybe he was just considering the situation, for he suddenly looked across at me. " And what you've told me is the absolute truth?" He was leaning slightly forward, watching my face.

" Yes," I said.

" And the log books look crazy unless all the contacts are isolated, the way they are here?" He tapped the sheet of paper.

I nodded. " I thought if I could find out a little more about the three direct contacts my father made with Ledder ... what Ledder's reaction to my father was ..."

" The thing that gets me," he muttered, " is how your father could possibly have picked up this transmission." He was frowning and his tone was puzzled. "As I recollect it, all Briffe had was a forty-eight set. I'm sure I read that somewhere. Yes, and operated by a hand generator at that. It just doesn't seem possible."

He was making the same point that the Flight Lieutenant had made. "But surely," I said, "there must be certain conditions in which he could have picked it up?"

"Maybe. I wouldn't know about that. But the old forty-eight set is a transmitter of very limited range—I do know that." He gave a slight shrug. "Still, it's just possible, I suppose. You'd have to check with somebody like this guy Ledder to make certain."

He had picked up the sheet of paper again, and he stared at it for so long that I felt sure he wasn't going to help me and was only trying to think out how to tell me so. He was my only hope of making effective contact with Ledder. If he wouldn't help, then there was nobody else I could go to—and I felt I had to settle this thing, one way or the other. If my father had made that message up—well, all right—but I had to know. I had to be absolutely certain for my own peace of mind that those two men really were dead.

And then Farrow put the sheet of paper down and turned to me. "You know," he said, "I think you ought to go to Goose and have a word with Ledder yourself."

I stared at him, unable to believe that I'd heard him correctly. "Go to Goose Bay? You mean fly there—myself?"

He half smiled. "You won't get into Goose any other way."

It was such an incredible suggestion that for a moment I couldn't think of anything to say. He couldn't be serious. "All I wanted," I murmured, "was for you to have a word with him . . . find out what he thought of my father, whether he considered him sane. You can take those notes and——".

"Look," he said. "If you're convinced your father was sane, then these notes"—he tapped the sheet of paper—"all the messages, everything—including that final message—are fact. They happened. And if that's what you believe, then you must go over there yourself. Apart from the question of whether Briffe's alive or not, you owe it to your father. If I go to this guy Ledder, he'll just answer my questions, and that will be that. You might just as well write him a letter for all the good it'll do." And then he added, "If you're really convinced that your father did pick up a transmission from Briffe, then there's only one thing for you to do—go over there and check for yourself. It's the only way you'll get the authorities to take it seriously."

I was appalled at the way he was putting the responsibility back on to me. " But I just haven't the money," I murmured.

" I could help you there." He was watching me closely all the time. " I'm checking out on a west-bound flight at O-seven hundred to-morrow morning. We'll be into Goose around four-thirty in the afternoon—their time. I might be able to fix it. You'd have about two hours there and I could radio ahead to Control for them to have Ledder meet the plane. Well?"

He meant it. That was the incredible thing. He really meant it. " But what about my job?" I was feeling suddenly scared. " I can't just walk out——"

" You'd be back on Friday."

" But . . ." It was all so appallingly sudden, and Canada was like another world to me. I'd never been out of England, except once to Belgium. " But what about the regulations and —and wouldn't the extra weight . . ." I found I was desperately searching for some sort of excuse.

He asked me then whether I had a British passport. I had, of course, for I'd needed one for my holiday in Bruges and Ghent the previous year, and it was at my lodgings, with the rest of my things. And when he told me that my weight wouldn't make any difference to the safety margin and that he was good friends with the Customs and Immigration people both here and at Goose, all I could think of to say was, " I'll have to think it over."

He gripped my arm then, and those baby blue eyes of his were suddenly hard. " Either you believe what your father wrote, or you don't. Which is it?"

The way he put it was almost offensive and I answered hotly, " Don't you understand—that message was the cause of my father's death."

" Okay," he said tersely. " Then it's time you faced up to the implications of that message."

" How do you mean?"

He relaxed his grip on my arm. " See here, boy," he said gently, " if Briffe really did transmit on September twenty-ninth, then either there's been some ghastly error or—well, the alternative doesn't bear thinking about." His words reminded me of the shocked expression on the Flight Lieutenant's face when I had suggested the pilot might have made a mistake. "Now do you see why you've got to go over and talk to Ledder yourself? What that message says"—and he jabbed his finger at the sheet of paper he had laid on the bar counter—"is that Laroche was wrong when he said Briffe and the other guy were dead. And I'm warning you, it's going to take a lot to persuade the authorities of that." He patted my arm gently and the blue eyes were no longer hard, but looked at me sympathetically. "Well, it's up to you now. You're the only man who's going to be really convinced about that message—unless they find somebody else picked it up. If you've the courage of your convictions . . ." And then he added, "I just thought you'd better be clear in your mind about what you're up against."

It was odd, but now that he'd put it to me so bluntly, I no longer felt out of my depth. I was suddenly sure of myself and what I should do, and without any hesitation I heard myself say, "If you can fix it, I'd like to come with you to-morrow."

"Okay, boy. If that's what you'd like." He hesitated. "You really are sure about this?"

In a sudden mental flash I saw my father as he had been last Christmas when I had been home, sitting up there in his room with the headphones on and his long, thin fingers with the burn marks playing so sensitively over the tuning dials. "Yes," I said. "I'm quite sure about it."

He nodded his head slowly. "Queer business," he murmured. A perplexed look had come over his face and I wondered whether, now that I had agreed to go—wanted to go—he was going to back down on his offer. But all he said was, "Meet me down at our freight office—that's the end of the block, next to Number One hangar—say, about a quarter before six to-morrow morning. Have your passport with you and an overnight bag. Better pack some warm clothes. You may be cold back in the fuselage. Okay?"

I nodded. "But what about the other end?" I murmured. "Surely it isn't as easy as that to fly somebody into another country?" It was an automatic reaction. Now that I'd said I'd go the difficulties seemed insuperable.

He laughed and patted my shoulder. "Canada isn't the

States, you know. It's still a Dominion—no fingerprints, no visa. I'll just have to clear you with Immigration and Customs, that's all." He stared at me a moment as though weighing me up and then he said, " Don't forget about the warm clothes." He turned then with a quick nod and walked slowly back to join his group at the other end of the bar.

I stood there, the drink I hadn't even started clutched in my hand, and a feeling of intense loneliness crept over me.

III

I DIDN'T sleep much that night and I was down at the Charter Company's freight office by five-thirty. Farrow wasn't there, of course, and I walked up and down in the grey morning light, feeling cold and empty inside. The office was locked, the tarmac deserted. I lit a cigarette and wondered, as I had done all night, whether I was making a fool of myself. A plane took off with a thunderous roar and I watched it disappear into the low overcast, thinking that in little more than an hour, if Farrow kept his word, I should be up there, headed west out into the Atlantic. I was shivering slightly. Nerves!

It was almost six when Farrow drove up in a battered sports car. " Jump in," he shouted. " Got to get you vaccinated. Otherwise it's all fixed."

We woke up a doctor friend of his and half an hour later I had got my certificate of vaccination, had cleared Customs and Immigration and was back at the freight office. I signed the " blood-chit " that absolved the Company of responsibility for my death in the event of a crash, and then Farrow left me there and I hung about for another twenty minutes, waiting for take-off. There was no turning back now. I was committed to the flight and because of that I no longer felt nervous.

Shortly before seven the crew assembled and I walked with them across the tarmac to a big four-engined plane parked on the apron opposite the office. Inside, it was a dim-lit steel shell with the freight piled down the centre, strapped down to ring bolts in the floor. " Not very comfortable, I'm afraid," Farrow said, " but we don't cater for passengers." He gave my shoulder a friendly squeeze. " Toilet's aft if you want it." The door of the fuselage slammed shut and he followed his crew for'ard to the flight deck. I was alone then.

We took off just after seven, and though I had never flown before I could sense what was happening—the sound of the engines being run up one by one on test at the runway-end and then the solid roar of all four together and the drag of the air-screws as we began to move, the dim-lit fuselage rocking and vibrating around me. Suddenly it was quieter and I knew we had left the ground.

The exhilaration of the take-off gradually faded into the monotony of the flight as we drove smoothly on, hour after hour. I dozed a little and now and then Farrow or one of his crew came aft. Shortly after ten the navigator brought me sandwiches and hot coffee. An hour and a half later we landed at Keflavik in Iceland and I clambered stiffly out, blinking my eyes in the cold sunlight.

The airport was a featureless expanse, the buildings modern utilitarian blocks without character. The whole place had the crisp, cold, lifeless air of outer space. But the cafeteria in the main building yielded eggs and bacon and hot coffee, and the echoing hall was full of transit passengers passing the time by sending postcards and buying Icelandic souvenirs from counters gay with northern colours. We had over an hour there in the warmth whilst the plane was refuelled and a quick check made on one of the engines which was running rough. They found nothing wrong with the engine and by twelve-thirty I was back in the hollow roar of the fuselage and we were taking off on the last lap.

We flew high to clear a storm belt off the Greenland coast and it was cold. I dozed fitfully, the monotony only broken by an occasional cup of coffee, the lunch pack and brief talks with the crew as they came aft. It was nine-twenty by my watch when the flight engineer finally roused me. " Skipper says if you want to take a look at Labrador from the air you'd better come up for'ard right away. We'll be landing in fifteen minutes."

I followed him through the door to the flight deck. To my surprise it was daylight and, because I could see out, the long, cold hours spent huddled amongst the freight in the fuselage were suddenly forgotten. Not that there was anything to see ... just the grey of cloud through the windshield and Farrow's head outlined against it. The wireless operator gripped my arm as I passed, pulling me down towards him. " I've radioed the Tower to have Ledder meet you," he shouted in my ear. " Okay?"

" Thanks."

Farrow half turned his head and indicated the flight engineer's seat beside him. " Going down now." He jerked his thumb downwards. The engines were already throttled back. " We'll come out of the cloud at eight thousand." He tapped the altimeter dial where the pointer was dropping slowly. And he added, " You'll have plenty of time to talk to Ledder. Another engine check. Port outer packed up a while back." He nodded towards the left-hand wing-tip where it wavered gently in the turbulent cloud mist. The outboard engine was lifeless, the propeller feathering slowly. " We'll be there the night. Get away sometime to-morrow—I hope."

I wanted to ask him whether we'd get down all right, but nobody seemed worried that we were flying on only three engines and I sat down and said nothing, staring ahead through the windshield, waiting for the moment when I should get my first glimpse of Labrador. And because there was nothing to see, I found myself thinking of my father. Had his flying duties ever taken him to Labrador or was I now doing the thing he'd wanted to do all his life? I was thinking of the books and the map, wondering what it was that had fascinated him about this country ; and then abruptly the veil was swept away from in front of my eyes and there was Labrador.

The grimness of it was the thing that struck me—the grimness and the lostness and the emptiness of it. Below us was a great sheet of water running in through a desolate, flat waste, with pale glimpses of sand and a sort of barren, glacier-dredged look about it. But what held my attention was the land ahead where it rose to meet the sky. There were no hills there, no mountain peaks. It rose up from the coastal plain in one black, ruler-straight line, utterly featureless—a remote, bitter plateau that by its very uniformity gave an impression of vastness, of being on the verge of land that stretched away to the Pole.

" There's Goose now." Farrow was shouting in my ear and pointing. But I didn't see it. My eyes were riveted by the black line of that plateau and I held my breath, strangely stirred as though by some old challenge.

" Sure is a pretty country," Farrow shouted to me. " You can get lost in there just like that." And he snapped his fingers. " Nothing but lakes, and every one the same as the next." He was suddenly grinning. " The land God gave to Cain—that's what Jacques Cartier called it when he first discovered it."

The land God gave to Cain ! The words mingled with my

thoughts to trickle through my mind in a cold shiver. How often I was to remember later the aptness of that description!

We were coming in now, the water of Goose Bay rising to meet us, the airfield clearly visible. The flight engineer tapped me on the shoulder and I clambered out of his seat and went back into the dimness of the fuselage. A few moments later we touched down.

When we had come to rest with the engines cut, the navigator came aft and opened the freight door. Daylight entered the fuselage, bringing with it warmth and the smell of rain, and through the open door I looked out across wet tarmac to a line of green-painted, corrugated iron buildings. A man stood waiting on the apron, alone, a tall, dark-featured man in some sort of a plastic raincoat.

I gathered my things together, and then Farrow came down through the fuselage. "I'll fix you up with a room at the T.C.A. Hotel," he said. "You can get a meal there. The time, by the way, is . . ." He glanced at his watch. "Five twenty-two. There's four and a half hours difference between Goose and England." And he added, "There'll be transport to run us down as soon as I'm through with the maintenance people and we've cleared Immigration." He had moved on to the door by then and I heard a voice say: "Captain Farrow? My name's Simon Ledder. I was told to meet your flight." It was a slow voice, puzzled and a little resentful.

And then I was at the door and Farrow said, "Well, here you are. Here's the guy you wanted to talk to." And as I jumped out on to the tarmac he was already walking away with a casual lift of his hand.

"Where will I find you?" I called after him. I didn't want to lose him. The place looked so vast and desolate.

"Don't worry, I won't forget you," he answered over his shoulder. His crew were waiting for him and when he had caught them up, they all went on together in a bunch. I heard the flight engineer's rather high-pitched laugh, and then they disappeared into the hangar.

"What did you want to see me about?" Ledder's voice was dull and flat and I turned to find him standing close beside me, his hands in his pockets and a bored look on his face.

I'd thought about this meeting all through the monotonous hours of the flight, but now that I was alone with him, I found myself at a loss for words. The references to him in my father's log books had given him an importance in my mind I couldn't reconcile with this morose-looking individual. " Do you recall the name Ferguson?" I asked. " James Finlay Ferguson. He's dead now, but——"

" The expedition of nineteen hundred. Is that what you mean?" There was a sudden flicker of interest in the eyes that peered at me through thick horn-rimmed lenses.

Intuition should have told me that a gap in the past was being bridged for me, but my mind was on Briffe and the things my father had written. " No, Station G2STO," I said. " It's about those radio contacts you had with him." But the momentary flicker of interest had vanished from his eyes and his face was blank. " Your call sign is VO6AZ, isn't it?" I asked him.

He nodded, waiting.

" G2STO contacted you three times in the past few weeks. Don't you remember?"

" Sure I do. It was six times to be exact." His voice sounded weary. And then he added, " What are you, Police or Air Force?-"

I didn't answer that. I thought maybe he'd talk more readily if he believed I had authority to question him. " Can we go somewhere where we can talk?" I said. It was beginning to rain again and an aircraft had started warming up its engines farther along the apron. " There are one or two questions——"

" Questions?" That seemed to touch him off. " I've had nothing but questions about this darned ham for the past few days. G2STO! I'm sick of him. The crazy bastard claims he picked up a transmission from Paul Briffe. That's what you've come about, isn't it?" His manner was openly hostile. " Well, I spent a whole day making out a report on him. The Station Commander here has a copy of it, if you want to see it. I've nothing to add. Nothing at all."

I was too angry to say anything. To come all this way and find that Ledder was completely unco-operative . . . it was what I'd feared the moment I had seen him waiting there, sullenly, on the apron.

" Well," he said, " do you want to see the report?"

I nodded and we began to walk across the tarmac.

" You know about Briffe?" He was looking at me. I think

he was puzzled by my silence. "He couldn't have made that transmission."

"How do you know?" I asked.

"How do I know? Why, the man was dead. How the hell can a man who's been dead a week suddenly start sending?"

"You don't *know* he's dead," I said.

He stopped then. "How do you mean?"

"He's been reported dead. That's all."

"That's all, you say." He was peering at me curiously. "What are you getting at?"

"Just that you can't be absolutely certain he didn't transmit," I told him. "Not unless you were listening in for him on his frequency that day." I was facing him then. "Were you listening in for him at two o'clock on the twenty-ninth?"

"The time I was given was nine twenty-five."

"Yes, of course." That was the four and a half hours difference. "It would have been nine twenty-five here. But you weren't listening for him then, were you?"

He shook his head. "Why should I? The search had been called off three days before, and I'd no reason to think——"

"Then you can't be absolutely certain."

"I tell you Briffe was dead." I had touched his professional pride and he said it angrily. "If I thought there'd been a chance of any transmission, I'd have kept constant watch. But there wasn't. He'd been dead since the twentieth."

Perhaps he wasn't so unlike my father when it came to radio. "You've only the pilot's word for that," I said.

He stared at me and his face had a startled look. "Are you suggesting . . . Look, for Chrissake, Laroche is all right." He was looking at me with sudden suspicion. "You're not the Police. You're not Air Force either. Who are you?"

"My name's Ian Ferguson," I said. "The crazy bastard you spoke of was my father, and I happen to believe that he did pick up some sort of a transmission." My words had shocked him and I didn't give him time to recover, but added quickly, "My father made several contacts with you." I pulled out the sheet of paper with the entries I had isolated. "The first time was on the twenty-third of September, and then again on the twenty-fifth of last month and again on the twenty-sixth. Did he seem crazy to you then?"

"No, but that was before——"

"He was perfectly rational, was he?"

"He asked some odd questions," he answered evasively.

I hesitated. But this wasn't the moment to find out what those questions were. "Forget for the moment that Briffe has been reported dead," I said, "and that my father ever picked up this transmission. Cast your mind back to the first time he contacted you. Can you remember what your reaction was?"

"I tell you, he asked some odd questions," he answered uncomfortably. "Otherwise there was nothing to it, I guess. He was just another ham."

"Look," I said, trying to get my own urgency across to him. "My father was a radio operator, like you." Surely there was some sort of freemasonry between these men whose world was the ether, some sense of brotherhood. "I know he was contacting you on W/T and that all you get is a lot of dots and dashes, but something must come through, some indication——"

"It's not the same as Voice, you know. And he always contacted me on Key—never Voice."

"Of course he did," I said angrily. "How else could he contact you? But even so," I added, "something must come through, surely—some indication of the sort of man he was, his mood, something?"

"I tell you, it was all on Key. If I'd had a QSO—a Voice contact—then maybe . . ." He gave a little shrug. "To tell you the truth I didn't think much about him—not then."

It was raining harder now, but he made no move to take shelter and I asked him again what he'd thought of my father. "You must have formed some impression." And when he didn't answer, I said impatiently, "Don't the men you contact on the air mean anything to you? Surely you must have got some impression——"

"He was just another ham, that's all." He said it irritably. "I pick up any number of hams."

I felt suddenly tired of the whole thing then. My father had meant nothing to this morose Canadian operator, nothing at all. There seemed to be no point in my having made the trip to Goose. In desperation I said, "At least you didn't think him irrational or irresponsible—at that time?"

"I tell you, I didn't think anything about him. I was puzzled by his questions. That was all."

Over two thousand miles, and I was no further forward. I

asked him about the questions then and he said it was all set down in the report he'd written. " All I could remember, anyway." And he added, " If you want to come back to the house I could show you the report there. I kept a copy."

I hesitated because the invitation had been made so grudgingly, but then he looked at his watch and said, " It's after five-thirty now. I guess the Station Commander will have left anyway."

" All right." I was thinking that perhaps I'd get more out of him at his home, and without a word he turned and led me back across the apron. As we passed the open door of the hangar, Farrow appeared and called to me. " If you come into the office now we can get the formalities completed." And then to Ledder: " Give you a lift down, if you like. The truck will be here any minute."

" Okay, thanks," Ledder said. " Save me a wetting. That's the worst of this dump," he added, turning to me with the ghost of a smile. " We're not allowed a car of our own. A question of gas, I guess. The bay's frozen half the year and then supplies have to be flown in."

We went into the office, and whilst my passport was being checked and my suitcase cleared, Farrow inquired about Ledder. " Got what you wanted?" he asked in a whisper.

" No," I said. " Not yet."

" Oh, well, you've plenty of time. Take-off won't be till seven in the morning, and that's presuming they work on that engine all night."

" You're here the night, are you?" Ledder said. And when Farrow nodded, he turned to me. " Then you'd better get some food and come over to my place afterwards. The D.O.T. houses are right across from the hotel."

The truck had already arrived. We piled in, and a moment later we were bumping along a dirt road overlooking the bay. The airport dropped behind us, desolate in the rain, and below us I caught a glimpse of a jetty with a steamer alongside and beyond that some seaplanes anchored close against the shore, small and indistinct in the fading light. Beside the road bull-dozers had exposed the gravel soil in raw slashes, the clearings littered with uprooted trees, and here and there the yellow wood of a new construction was reared up out of the naked land. The whole place had a lost feel about it, raw and ugly like a frontier settlement. It was a gauntlet flung in nature's face, the scrub spruce crowding it in so that I was conscious all the time of the infinite wastes that lay beyond it.

The hotel was a low, sprawling building made up of a series of wood-frame huts angled out in the form of a star. Thin dwarf scrub lapped round the sandy clearing. The rain had slackened and as we climbed out of the truck, I could see the hills across the bay again, dark and remote and very blue. It had become suddenly colder. Ledder pointed me out his house, just visible through a screen of trees. "Come over as soon as you've had your supper," he said. And then we left him and went inside to be greeted with the hot breath of steam heating turned full on. The place had a bare, barrack air, but surprisingly the rooms were neat and very modern, the food good.

It was almost seven-thirty before I'd finished eating and I came out into a biting wind. It was dark and the stars had a frosty look. A thin pale curtain of northern lights wavered across the sky and the silence was absolute. Through the trees the lights of Ledder's house had the warm glow of orange curtains.

He came to the door dressed in a vivid, short-sleeved shirt open at the neck. There was a little girl with him and in the room beyond his wife and another woman sat chatting through the blare of the radio. He introduced me and I stood there, feeling awkward because I wanted to talk to him alone. The room was overpoweringly hot, full of very new-looking furniture upholstered in brilliant colours. "Would you care for some coffee?" Mrs. Ledder asked.

I shook my head. "I've just had some."

She laughed. She was young and jolly, with broad features and fair hair, rather pretty except that she was a little too stockily built. But that may have been because she was going to have a child and was wearing a smock. "It's easy to see you're not a Canadian, Mr. Ferguson. No Canadian would ever refuse a cup of coffee because he'd just had one, that's for sure. Simon and the boys drink it all the time. Sure you won't change your mind?"

I shook my head, and Ledder said, "Well, if you don't want any coffee we'll go down below, shall we? It'll be quieter there." He pulled open a door under the stairs and switched on the light. "You must excuse the mess, but I'm just installing some new equipment."

I followed him down steps that led into a sort of cellar that was probably meant to house just the furnace and hot water boiler. But there was also a desk thrust close against one wall with a mass of radio equipment stacked round it like a barricade. Toys littered the floor, odds and ends of household gear, the remains of a Christmas tree, a pram, and over everything lay a sprinkling of tools and the insides of old radio sets. " Is this where you work?" I asked.

" Sure. Folk here are always asking me to fix something or other."

" I mean—is this where you send from?"

He nodded and went across to the desk. " I told you it was a mess."

I don't know what I'd expected. Something neat and tidy, I suppose. It seemed incredible that this junk room of a basement should be VO6AZ and that out of this muddle he could have made contact with my father on the other side of the Atlantic. " It doesn't look much I know, not all spick and span like the D.O.T. station." He was sitting down and rummaging amongst some papers in a drawer. " But I can tell you this, there's equipment here that Goose Radio hasn't got." He slammed the drawer shut. " Here you are," he said and held out a typed sheet of foolscap. I took it from him. It was headed: REPORT ON BRITISH AMATEUR RADIO STATION G2STO. " You must remember that when I wrote that I knew Briffe was dead," he said, his smile half-apologetic. " And I didn't know your father's name. If I'd known his name it might have made some sense."

Seated at his desk he seemed a different person, more alive, more vital—I suppose because this was his world, as it had been my father's. His hand strayed automatically to the key, the way my father's always had. It was a different key, an American side-operated pattern known as a bug key. But though the key was different, the gesture was the same. " As far as I was concerned G2STO was nuts and that's all there was to it." His voice was easy and natural, all the hostility gone out of it. " I'm sorry," he added. " But I guess I was pretty tired of the whole business by then. I should have checked his name in the book."

I stared down at the report, wondering why the name should have made any difference. He had detailed six contacts and two of the three that I didn't know about concerned Briffe's sending frequency. " I see my father first contacted you on August the eleventh," I said. " He asked for Briffe's transmitting time, and you gave it to him. The sending frequency, too."

" Sure I did. There was nothing secret about it."

" What was the frequency?"

" Three seven eight zero."

I got out my sheet of notes. *August 11: Briffe. Briffe. Who is Briffe?* " Is that it?" I asked, showing him the note I had made.

He leaned forward, looking at it. " Seventy-five meter phone band. Net frequency three point seven eight zero. Yes, that's it."

It explained the half-obliterated entry I had found. " Take a look at that," I said. " I couldn't read the date, but it was somewhere towards the end of August."

" Three point seven eight zero—nothing, nothing, nothing, always nothing." He read it out slowly and then looked up at me. " Well?"

" It means my father was watching on Briffe's frequency."

" It means he was curious, sure. But then so were several other hams. There were two Canadians, one at Burnt Creek and the other right up in Baffin Island, listening regularly. It doesn't mean anything. They were just interested, that's all."

" Then what about this contact on September 26? That was the day the search was called off. According to your report my father actually contacted you that evening to check Briffe's frequency and ask whether there was any other frequency he might use in an emergency. Doesn't that make it obvious that he was keeping watch for Briffe?"

" Paule Briffe only had an old forty-eight set. It was operated by a hand generator and a British ham would be more than two thousand miles outside normal range."

" Outside of normal range, yes," I said impatiently. " Nevertheless, my father was keeping watch. You knew that, and yet down here at the bottom of your report you give it as your opinion that G2STO couldn't possibly have picked up a transmission from Briffe. And you list your reasons—one of them, *that, granted freak reception and the transmission having actually been made, the odds against G2STO choosing that particular moment to listen in are too great.* What exactly did you mean by that?"

"Just what I say," he answered sharply. "Take all those points together—Briffe transmitting when he's known to be dead, freak reception and finally the remote chance that your father should be keeping watch at that precise moment. It just doesn't make sense."

"Why not? The odds are against it, I admit, but it's not impossible."

"Oh, for heaven's sake!" he exclaimed irritably. "The plane crashed on the evening of the fourteenth. We were on constant watch until the twenty-sixth when the search was abandoned—not only us, but the Air Force, Government stations, and a whole bunch of hams. We picked up nothing. And three days after we ceased watch G2STO reports contact. Suppose Briffe did transmit on the twenty-ninth as he says. To be certain of picking up that transmission he'd have had to be listening on net frequency for three whole days, twenty-four hours out of the twenty-four." He shook his head. "It just isn't credible."

"My father was paralysed," I said. "He had nothing else to do."

He stared at me. "I'm sorry," he said tonelessly. "I guess they didn't tell us anything about him."

"They didn't tell you then that he died immediately after picking up the transmission?"

"No. I guess that explains it—why you're here, I mean. I'd been wondering about that."

"That transmission killed him."

His eyes widened, looking at me curiously. "How do you mean?"

I told him then about my father calling out and how he'd somehow struggled to his feet. I told him the whole story, and when I'd finished, he said, "I didn't know about all this." His soft, slow voice was shocked, his tone apologetic. "They didn't give any details, not even his name. I been thinking about that over my supper. It was those questions he asked that started me thinking he was nuts. If they'd given me his name I might have understood what he was getting at. As it was those questions just seemed so Goddamned irrelevant." He nodded to the report in my hand. "Read 'em. They're all there. You'll see what I mean then. You'd have thought he was nuts if they'd come at you out of the blue, so to speak—anybody would."

I could see his point, for on the second occasion my father had contacted him he'd asked him if Briffe had ever mentioned Lake of the Lion. That was on September 10, and when Ledder had said No and had refused to give him the exact location of Area C1, he had requested details of the reports or at least the code so that he could follow the progress of the expedition for himself. Finally: *He asked me to question Laroche about Lake of the Lion and report his reaction.*

"Why did he want you to question Laroche about the lake?" I asked. "Did he say?"

"No, he didn't say. I tell you, they're damned queer questions, some of them."

On September 15, the day after the geologists had disappeared, my father had asked him a lot of questions about what had happened and why Briffe had been in such a hurry to reach C2. *Had I asked Laroche about Lake of the Lion and what was his reaction? Where was C2? My negative replies seemed to annoy him.* On September 23 my father had made contact again, asking for information about Laroche. *Could I find out for him whether Canadian geologists still remembered the expedition of 1900 into the Attikonak area?* And two days later he had asked about this again. *I told him that it was still talked about and added that if he wanted further details he should contact the Department of Mines in Ottawa.*

And then there was the final contact in which Ledder had confirmed Briffe's sending frequency.

I folded the report up and put it down on the desk beside him, conscious that he was watching me, waiting for me to tell him what those questions meant. He expected me to know, and the fact that I didn't made me feel uncomfortable, so that my throat felt suddenly constricted and my eyes moist. To gain time I asked him about C2. "Was it in the Attikonak area?"

He nodded. "Sure. The advance party were camped right on the river bank." And then he added, "What was his interest in the Attikonak River, do you know that? And this Lake of the Lion ne asked about?"

I shook my head. "I don't know." It was a confession that I'd never bothered to get very close to my father. "My mother might know," I murmured uncomfortably.

He was puzzled now. " But those questions make sense to you, don't they."

I didn't know what to say. It came down to this, that Ledder would only be convinced that the message was genuine if I could explain the motive behind my father's questions, and I didn't know the motive. That belonged to the map and the books and the relics of the Canadian North, all the secret world I'd never shared. *It's a long story.* That was the only reference he'd ever made to it. If only I'd persisted then. With a little patience I could have dug it out of him.

Ledder had picked up the report and was staring at it. " I could kick myself," he said, suddenly tossing it down amongst the litter of papers. " I'd only to look him up in the book. But I'd lent my copy to somebody in the D.O.T. and I just didn't bother to go and find him and get it back." He had misunderstood my silence. " It never occurred to me," he added, looking up at me apologetically.

" What never occurred to you?" I asked. There was something here that I didn't understand.

" That his name was important," he answered.

" Important? How do you mean?"

" Well, if I'd known it was James Finlay Ferguson . . ." He broke off abruptly, staring at me with a puzzled frown. " He was related, wasn't he?"

" Related?" I didn't know what he was getting at. " Related to whom?"

" Why, to the Ferguson that got killed up in the Attikonak area in 1900."

I stared at him. So that was it. The expedition of 1900. " Was there a Ferguson on that expedition?" I asked.

" Sure there was. James Finlay Ferguson." He was looking at me as though he thought it was I who was crazy now. " You mean you don't know about it?"

I shook my head, my mind busy searching back through my childhood to things I'd half forgotten—my mother's fears, my father's obsession with the country. This was the cause of it all then.

" But the name?" He said it almost angrily, as though he were being cheated of something that would add interest to the monotony of life in this distant outpost. " And him asking all those questions? You mean it's just coincidence that the names were the same? Was it just because of that your father was interested?"

"No," I said. "No, it wasn't that." And I added hastily, "It's just that my father never talked about it." I, too, felt cheated—cheated because he hadn't shared the past with me when it belonged to me and was my right.

"Never talked about it? Why ever not?" Ledder was leaning forward. "Let's get this straight. Are they related or not—your father and this Ferguson who went into Labrador?"

"Yes, of course they are," I answered. "They must be." There was no other explanation. It explained so much that I'd never understood. It was a pity that my grandmother had died when I was still a child. I would like to have talked to her now.

"What relationship?" Ledder was staring up at me. "Do you know?"

"His father, I think." It must have been his father for I hadn't any great uncles.

"Your grandfather, in fact."

I nodded. And it would have been grandmother Alexandra who would have given him the names of James Finlay. I was thinking it was strange that my father had been born in the year 1900.

"But how do you know it's your grandfather?" Ledder asked. "How do you know when you didn't even know there was an expedition back at the beginning of the century?"

I told him about the sextant and the paddle and the other relics hanging on the wall, and about my grandmother and the house in Scotland, and how she'd come to me in the night when I was barely old enough to remember. "I think she must have been going to tell me about that expedition." Talking to him about it, everything seemed to fall into place— my father's obsession, everything. And then I was asking him about the expedition. "Can you give me the details?" I said. "What happened to Ferguson?"

"I don't know," he answered. "In fact, I don't know very much about it—only what the Company geologist told me. There were two of them went in, from Davis Inlet. Two white men, no Indians. One was a prospector, the other a trapper, and it ended in tragedy. The trapper only just escaped with his life. The prospector—that was Ferguson—he died. That's all I know." He turned to the desk and picked up his log, searching quickly through it. "Here you are. Here's the geologist's reply: *Expedition 1900 well known because one of the two men, James Finlay Ferguson, was lost.*"

"And he was a prospector?"

"So Tim Baird said."

"Was he prospecting for gold?" I was remembering that my mother had once said I wasn't to ask about my grandfather . . . an old reprobate, she had called him, who had come to a bad end and wasted his life searching for gold.

"I don't know what he was prospecting for. Tim didn't say."

But it didn't matter. I was quite certain it was gold, just as I was quite certain that this was the past that had bitten so deep into my father in his loneliness. It was just a pity that I'd never bothered to get the story out of him.

"It's odd he never talked to you about it," Ledder said, and I realised that he was still uncertain about it all.

"I told you, he couldn't talk." And I added, "It's so long since he was wounded that now I can't even recall the sound of his voice."

"But he could write."

"It was an effort," I said.

"And he left no record?"

"Not that I know of. At least, I didn't find one when I looked through his things. I suppose it was too complicated or something. That's what he said, anyway. What else did the geologist tell you?"

"Just what I've read out to you—nothing else." He was sitting there, doodling with a pencil on the cover of his log.

"What about this man Tim Baird? Did he tell you anything else—the name of the other man, or where they went or what they were looking for?"

"No. I guess he didn't know much about it. I've told you all I know." He shook his head, frowning down at the pattern he was tracing. "Dam' queer him not telling you anything about it, and the thing an obsession with him."

"That was because of my mother," I said. "I think she must have made him promise. She didn't want me involved. I think she hated Labrador," I added, remembering the scene on the platform as the train was about to leave. And here I was in Labrador.

My mind switched back to the questions my father had asked and I picked up the report again. I was thinking of the map above the transmitter, the name Lake of the Lion pencilled on it. "Did you ask Laroche about Lake of the Lion?"

"No. I never had the chance." And then Ledder had stopped doodling and was looking up at me. "You know, it wasn't so much the strangeness of his questions that made me think him crazy. It was this obsession with an old story——"

"My father wasn't crazy," I said sharply. I was still wondering why he should have been so interested in Laroche's reaction.

"No, I guess he wasn't." Ledder's voice was slow, almost reluctant. "If I'd known his name was James Finlay Ferguson it would have made some sense." He was excusing himself again. But then, after a pause, he said, "But even so, if he wasn't crazy . . ." He left the sentence unfinished, staring down at the desk and fiddling with the morse key. "Did he keep a log?" he asked at length.

"Yes, of course," I said. And I gave him the sheet of notes, glad that I'd isolated them from the actual books. "Those are all the entries that concern Briffe, right from the time my father first picked up your transmissions until that final message." I tried to explain to him again that writing had been difficult for him and that my father usually just jotted down a note to remind him of the substance of each transmission, but he didn't seem to be listening. He was going carefully through the notes, sucking at a pencil and occasionally nodding his head as though at some recollection.

Finally he pushed the sheet away and leaned back, tilting his chair against the wall and staring across the room. "Queer," he murmured. "They make sense, and then again in places they don't make sense." And after a moment he leaned forward again. "Take this, for instance." He pulled the sheet towards him again and pointed to the entry for September 18 which read: *LAROCHE. No, it can't be. I must be mad.* "What's he mean—do you know?"

I shook my head.

"And this on the twenty-sixth, the day after Laroche

reached Menihek—L-L-L-L-L—IMPOSSIBLE." He looked up at me as he read it aloud, but there was nothing I could tell him. " Was he much alone?" he asked.

" There was my mother." I knew what he was getting at.

" But that room you described and the hours he spent there every day with his radio. He was alone there?" And when I nodded, he said, " We get men like that up here. The emptiness and the loneliness—they get obsessions. Bushed we call it." And then he asked me whether I'd brought the log books with me.

It was a request I had been dreading. One glance at them and he'd begin thinking my father was crazy again. But if I were to get him to help me he'd a right to see them. " They're in my suitcase," I said.

He nodded. " Could I see them please?" He was reading through the notes again, tapping at the paper with his pencil, his lips pursed, absorbed in his thoughts. He evidently sensed my hesitation for he said, " Do you want a torch?" He reached up to the high top of the desk and handed me one. " Just walk straight out. Ethel won't mind." And then he was staring down at the notes again.

The two women were still there in the room upstairs. They stopped talking as I came in and Mrs. Ledder said, " Ready for your coffee yet?" The room looked very gay and cheerful after the bare, untidy basement.

" I'm just going across to get something from the hotel," I explained.

She nodded, smiling at me, and I went out into the night. The stars were misting over and the cold had a harshness in it that I'd never experienced before.

I got the log books out of my suitcase and when I returned to the basement room, Ledder was hunched over the desk, writing. He had the radio on and through the crackle of atmospherics a voice was talking in a foreign language. " Brazil," he said, looking up at me. " Never have any difficulty getting South America." He switched the receiver off and I gave him the log books, trying to tell him that the drawings and doodlings were irrelevant. But he waved my explanations aside, and I stood and watched him work steadily back through the pages. " He was alone a lot, that's for sure," he muttered, and my heart sank.

" He just did it to pass the time," I said.

He nodded. " Sure. It means nothing." He reached out to one of the cubbyholes of the desk. " Look at my pad." And he showed it to me all covered with doodles. " You got to do something whilst you're waiting to pick up a transmission. It's like telephoning." He smiled at me, and that was when I began to like him.

" What sort of a person is Laroche?" It was the question that had been in my mind ever since Farrow had pointed out to me the implications of that transmission.

" Laroche?" He seemed to have to drag his mind back. " Oh, I don't know. A French Canadian, but a decent guy. Tallish, hair going slightly grey. I've only seen him once. He kept the Beaver down at the sea plane base and our paths didn't cross. It was Tim Baird I kept in touch with. Bill Baird's brother. He was base manager—looked after stores and all their requirements." He had turned to the page on which the final message had been written and he read it slowly, tapping his teeth with the pencil. " *Search for a narrow lake with a rock shaped like . . .*" He read it aloud slowly and looked up at me. " A rock shaped like what?"

I didn't say anything. I wanted to see if his mind would follow the track that mine had followed.

He was looking back through that last log book. " All these drawings of lions. I wonder if Laroche knows anything about that Lake of the Lion. Could that message have finished —a rock shaped like a lion? Here's a drawing that shows a lion set into a rock. And another here." He looked up at me. " You said something about a map of Labrador over his desk. Was Lake of the Lion marked on it?"

" He'd pencilled it in, yes," I said and explained how it had been enclosed in a rough circle covering the area between the Attikonak and the Hamilton.

He nodded. " And C2 was in that area." He was toying with the bug key and he suddenly slapped his hand on the desk. " Hell! No harm in telling them. Where's your plane going on to?"

" Montreal." I waited now, holding my breath.

" Okay. The Company offices are there." He hesitated a moment longer, frowning and shaking his head. " It's crazy," he muttered. " But you never know. There's crazy enough things happen all the time up here in the North." He pulled the paper on which he had been writing closer to the key, read it through and then reached over to the transmitter. The pilot light glowed red and there was a faint hum as the set warmed up. And then he put the earphones on and hitched his chair closer to the desk. A moment later and his thumb was tapping at the key and I heard the buzz of his morse signal as he began to send.

I lit a cigarette. I felt suddenly exhausted. But at the same time I was relaxed. I had achieved something, at any rate. I had persuaded a man who had been hostile at first to take action. But it was all to be done over again at Montreal—the story of how my father had died, the explanations. All to be told again, over and over again perhaps. I wondered whether it was worth it, conscious of the size of the country out there in the darkness beyond the airport—the wildness and the emptiness of it. They'd both be dead by now surely. They couldn't possibly have survived a whole week. But it was a chance, and because of my father and because of something in my blood, I knew I had to go on with it.

"Well, that's that, I guess." Ledder switched off the transmitter and pulled his earphones off. "That's what I told them." He handed me the slip of paper on which he'd pencilled his message. "It's up to the Company now." He seemed relieved.

Possibility G2STO picked up transmission. Briffe should not be ignored, I read. *Urgently advise you see Ferguson's son . . .* I looked across at him. "I can't thank you enough," I said.

He seemed suddenly embarrassed. "I'm only doing what I think right," he murmured. "There's an outside chance, and I think they ought to take it."

"The authorities don't think so. They think my father was mad." And I told him then about the expert's report. I'd nothing to lose now the message was sent.

But he only smiled. "Maybe I can understand him better than they can. They're a queer lot, radio operators," he added, and the smile extended to his eyes.

"And it's technically possible?" I asked. "He could have picked up that message?"

"Sure he could." And he added, "It would be freak reception, of course. But if a message was transmitted, then he could certainly have picked it up. Look." And he drew a little diagram for me, showing that, however faint the signal was, the waves would still rebound from the ionosphere to the earth and back again to the ionosphere. "They'd travel like that all the way round the earth, and if your aerial happened to be set up at one of the points of rebound, then it would be possible to pick up the transmission, even if it were six thousand miles away. It's just one of those things."

"And the transmitter was with Briffe in the aircraft when it crashed?"

"Yes. But the plane sank and they didn't salvage anything. Laroche came out with nothing but the clothes he stood up in. That's what I've heard, anyway."

Possible, but not probable! And always there seemed to be the blank wall of Laroche to block any credence being given to my father's message. "You'll see I've asked them to meet you at Dorval Airport and I've given them your flight number," he said. "I've also asked them to confirm through D.O.T. Communications. I don't expect we'll get a reply to-night, but it should come through fairly early in the morning."

I nodded. He couldn't have done more. And at that moment his wife called down the stairs to say that Mrs. Karnak had gone and she'd made some fresh coffee for us.

We went up then, and over coffee in the bright warmth of their living-room, he gave me the first detailed account of Briffe's disappearance. He told it, of course, from the point of view of a man whose contact with the outside world was exclusively by radio. Like my father, he was confined to scraps of information plucked from the ether, to news broadcasts and messages from planes flying to search. But he was much closer to it. He had even met the men who figured in the disaster—Briffe twice, Laroche once, and he knew a good deal about Bill Baird from talks with his brother, Tim, the Company's base manager.

On September 12, Briffe had called for an air lift from Area C1, which was Lake Disappointment, up to C2, on the banks of the Attikonak River. This request was made in the course of his usual daily report. He had completed the survey at Disappointment. "Aptly named was how he described it." Ledder smiled. And then he went on to explain that the survey party consisted of five men and the procedure in making the hop forward to the next area was always the same —three of the five men, Sagon, Hatch and Blanchard, would go forward as an advance party to establish the new camp, together with as much of the stores as the floatplane would carry and one canoe ; Briffe and Baird would move up on the second flight with the transmitter, the other canoe and the rest of the stores.

This was the procedure adopted on September 14, and Ledder was now more or less amplifying my father's notes for me. The air lift was actually called for September 13, but the weather had been bad and Laroche had decided to wait. However, the following day it was better and he took off early in the morning. Ledder had actually seen the little Beaver floatplane scudding a broad arrow out across the still waters of the bay, had watched it take off, circle and disappear into the haze beyond Happy Valley, headed west. He was off duty that day and after about an hour he tuned in on the 75-metre band. But Briffe didn't come through until 1133. Laroche had arrived, but thick fog had closed in on the camp and was preventing take off for C2. The delay in transmission had been due to condensation on the terminals of the hand generator.

He immediately reported the delay in the flight to Montreal. It was apparently the normal procedure for either himself or his wife to keep a radio watch and report regularly to Montreal whenever a supply flight was made or the party were being air lifted to a new location. He reported again at 1230, Briffe having come through with the news that the fog had lifted and the Beaver had taken off with the advance party.

After that he heard nothing from Briffe until 1500 hours when the survey party leader came through with the information that the Beaver had not returned and the fog had clamped down again. It was Ledder's report of this information to Montreal that my father had picked up. " I began to get worried then," Ledder said. " We had started picking up reports of a storm belt moving in from the Atlantic and things didn't look so good. I asked Briffe to report every hour."

At 1600 Briffe came through again. The fog had cleared, but the Beaver had still not returned. And then, at 1700, Briffe reported the plane safely back. Laroche had come down on a lake about ten miles short of C2 just before the fog closed in and had taken off again as soon as it had lifted. The advance party were now at C2 and Briffe's only concern was to get himself and Baird and the rest of the equipment up there before nightfall. " I told him," Ledder said, " that I didn't think it a good idea on account of the weather. He then asked me for a met. forecast." He was turning over the pages of his log which he had brought up with him. " Here you are." He passed it across to me. *Weather worsening rapidly. Ceiling 1,000, visibility 500, heavy rain. Expect airfield close down here shortly. In-coming flights already warned and west-bound trans-Atlantic traffic grounded Keflavik. Rain will turn to snow over Labrador plateau. Winds to-night easterly 20 knots plus. To-morrow reaching 40 knots; rain, sleet or snow on high ground. Visibility nil at times.*

" And he decided to go on?" I asked.

" Yes, it was either that or stay at Disappointment, and the lake had poor holding ground, so that it meant the possible loss of the floatplane. In the end he decided to take a chance on it and make the flight."

I remembered my father's comment. He had called Briffe a fool, and he added: *What's driving him?* Had there been something besides concern for the floatplane? " The pilot has the final word, surely?"

" I guess so," Ledder said. " But by all accounts, Laroche isn't frightened of taking a chance."

" He could have returned to base here."

He shrugged his shoulders. " A twenty knot head wind and the risk that he'd be short of gas and unable to locate Goose. Maybe he thought going on to C2 the lesser of the two evils." And then he went on to tell me how Briffe had failed to come through as arranged at 2200 and how he and his wife had kept watch all that night. " But he never came through," Ledder said.

And in the morning conditions had been so bad that nothing could get in to Goose, let alone fly a search over the Labrador plateau. It had been like that for two days, and then one of the floatplanes from the base had flown in to C2 and had come back with confirmation that Briffe and his party were missing. The search was on then, with the R.C.A.F. contributing four Lancasters out of the Nova Scotia Air Rescue Station and the Iron Ore people flying a search out of Menihek.

He was giving me details of the search when his wife reminded him that they had promised to be at the Officers' Mess at nine. " Perhaps Mr. Ferguson would like to come with us," she suggested. But I hadn't any Canadian money and, anyway, I wanted time to myself to think over what he had told me. I excused myself by saying I wanted to turn in early, finished my coffee and got up.

"I'll get the Company's reply to you as soon as it comes through," Ledder said as he saw me to the door. "If there's anything else I can do, let me know."

I thanked him and went down the wooden steps, out into the night. "Good luck!" he called after me, and then the door closed and I was alone in the darkness. The stars were gone now and it was snowing. It was so still I could almost hear the flakes falling, and without a torch it took me some time to find my way back to the hotel.

Actually I didn't get to bed till almost midnight, for I sat up in the warmth of my room, making notes and thinking about what I should say to the Company officials. I suppose I was tired. At any rate, I didn't wake up in the morning until a quarter to seven and I jumped out of bed in a panic, convinced that I had missed my flight. I hurried into my clothes and went along to Farrow's room. To my relief he was still there, lying on his bed in his shirt and trousers. "I was afraid I'd missed you," I said as he opened his eyes, regarding me sleepily.

"Relax," he murmured. "I won't go without you." And he added, "Take-off won't be till nine-thirty or later. There was no point in waking you." He turned over then and went to sleep again.

The truck called for us at nine and we hung around on the airfield until almost ten-thirty whilst the maintenance crew, who had been working most of the night, finished fixing the engine. The snow had gone and the air was cool and crisp, the hills across the bay sharply defined under a cold, grey sky streaked with cloud. There was a steely quality about Goose that morning, the menace of winter in the air. The country round was all greys and blacks, the scrub spruce unrelieved by any colour. The harshness of it was almost frightening.

And there was no word from Ledder. I told Farrow how Ledder had reacted when I had shown him my father's log books, and he phoned Communications for me. But Ledder wasn't there and there was no message for me.

We took off at ten-twenty and I had still heard nothing. I stood in the alley of the flight deck, watching Goose drop away from us below the port wing as we made a climbing turn. All ahead of us was a desolate waste of spruce with the thread of the Hamilton River winding through it. Then we were in cloud, and when we came out above it there was still no sun and the cloud layer below us was flat like a grey mantle of snow.

Later, watching from the flight engineer's seat, there were rifts in the cloud layer and I could see the ground below, looking strangely close, though I knew it couldn't be for we were flying at 6,600 feet. It was all ridged the way sand is when the tide is out, but the ridges were dark and grim-looking, with patches of exposed rock worn smooth by the tread of Ice Age glaciers, and all between was water, flat like steel and frosted white at the edges.

We flew on and on and the country below never changed. It was the grimmest land I had ever seen. The land God gave to Cain! It seemed as though it could never end, but would run on like that for ever, and after a while the flight engineer tapped me on the shoulder and I went back into the fuse-lage and sat down on the freight, feeling cold and depressed.

I had been there about an hour when the radio operator came aft to say that Farrow wanted a word with me. "We just got a message from Goose."

Back in the flight deck alley, Farrow handed me a message slip. On it was written: *Presd. McGovern Mng & Ex now at Iron Ore Terminal. Wishes question Ferguson earliest. Can you land him Seven Islands?* "Well, what do you want me to do?" Farrow shouted to me.

"Seven Islands? But that's just an Indian fishing village," I said.

"You think so?" He laughed. "Then I guess you're in for a shock. It's quite a town. The Iron Ore Company of Canada is building a railway north from there to get at the ore in the centre of Labrador. Worth seeing since you're an engineer. About the biggest project on this continent right now."

So the line my father had pencilled on his map was a rail-way. "But can you land there?" I asked doubtfully.

"Sure. They got a good airstrip. And they need it. They're supplying their forward camps entirely by air lift, flying every-thing in—even cement for the dam at Menihek and bull-dozers for the Knob Lake ore deposits." He glanced back at me over his shoulder. "But I won't be able to wait for you there. You understand that? You'll be on your own from then on."

I didn't know what to say. The plane was suddenly immensely precious to me, a familiar, friendly oasis in the immensity of Canada that was beginning to roll itself out before me. To abandon it would be like abandoning a ship in mid-Atlantic. "Better make up your mind," Farrow shouted. "We got to alter course right now if we're to drop you off at Seven Islands." He was watching me curiously. I suppose he saw my dilemma, for he added, "It's what you wanted, isn't it? You've stirred 'em up, and you can't go higher than the president of the Company."

There was nothing for it. I'd known that as soon as I had read the message. "All right," I said. And then, because that sounded ungrateful, I added, "You're sure it's all right for you to land there?"

"Who's to know?" He grinned and pointed ahead through his side windows to where a pale glimmer like a cloud or mist showed along the horizon. "There's the St. Lawrence now. Another hour and we'll be very close to Seven Islands. Okay?"

I nodded.

He called back instructions to the navigator and the radio operator, and then looked at me with a grin and added, "Who knows—I may even get a mention in despatches if those poor devils are lifted out alive."

A mood of optimism swept over me then and, as I went back into the fuselage, I was thinking that some divine providence must be guiding me.

The mood was still with me more than an hour later when we began to descend. I felt the check as the flaps went down and then the engines were throttled back and a moment later we touched down. We taxied for a while, bumping heavily over rough ground, and then we stopped, the engines quietly ticking over.

Farrow himself came back down the fuselage and opened the doors for me. "Good luck," he said. "And see they look after you. We'll be in Montreal until midday to-morrow if you want a ride back."

"Of course I want to go back with you," I shouted. I was

appalled at the thought that he might return to England without me.

He clapped me on the shoulder and I jumped out into the backwash of air from the slowly turning props.

" I'll be there," I shouted up to him.

The door slammed shut and I hurried clear, to stand a little way off, watching, with my suitcase gripped in my hand. Farrow was back at the controls. He waved to me through the windshield. The engines roared, kicking up a great swirl of dust, and then the machine that had brought me across the Atlantic went lumbering away over the hard-baked dirt of the airfield, out to the runway-end.

I watched it take off—watched it until it was a speck in the sky. I hated to see Farrow go. I was alone now, and there was nobody here I knew. I stood there for a moment, waiting and turning the loose change over in my pocket. I'd a few pounds in my wallet, but that was all. Nobody came out to meet me.

PART TWO

THE LABRADOR RAILWAY

I

WHEN I could no longer see the plane I walked slowly towards the line of pre-fabricated huts that were the airport buildings. I felt abandoned, almost lost now, for there was nothing about Seven Islands to give me a sense of ease.

The bull-dozed road, the dust, the maple leaf in the last flush of autumn, and the distant glimpse of new construction and heaped-up stores and equipment; it had a barbaric newness, an alien quality like the supply point for a battlefield. There were open hangar-like sheds piled with crates and sacks of foodstuffs, pieces of machinery, tyres, and a fork lift trundling the stuff out to a battered Dakota where a group of men stood smoking. They were a wild, mixed lot in strange headgear and gaily coloured bush shirts, and their kit stacked about them included bed rolls and thick, quilted jackets.

The place had an edge-of-the-wilds smell about it, and in the despatch office they knew nothing about me. There was nobody to meet me, not even a message, and when I asked for the offices of the McGovern Mining & Exploration Company, they had never heard of it. "You a geologist?" the despatcher asked.

"No." I didn't want to start explaining myself here.

"Well, what's your job then?"

"I'm an engineer," I said. "But that's got nothing to do——"

"You better report to Q.N.S. & L. then." He went to the door and shouted to a truck driver who was just moving off. "He'll take you down. Okay?" He was back at his desk, checking a despatch list, and because there seemed nothing else to do I went out to the truck and got in. An office would know where I ought to go or at least I could phone. "What's Q.N.S. & L. stand for?" I asked the driver as we lurched out through the wire on to a dirt road. I was thinking of the pencilled line my father had drawn in on his map.

"Quebec North Shore and Labrador Railway." He looked at me, his battered, sun-reddened face softened by a smile.

"You from the Old Country?" He wore a scarlet-patterned woollen bush shirt and the open neck of it showed the hair of his chest grey with road dust. He asked about England. He'd been there with the Canadian Army. And then we crossed the track and he talked about the railway. "I worked on the Tote Road when we started two years back. Boy, that was real tough. Now the Americans are in and they got all the equipment they need to build the grade. You going up the line?"

I shook my head. I was looking at the skyline ahead, staggered by the mushroom growth of buildings. And all to the left of us were acres of piled-up railway equipment—great stacks of rails and sleepers, and store sheds as big as hangars, and in between were the solid, powerful shapes of big diesel electric locomotives, their paintwork factory-new.

"Guess I wouldn't mind going back up the line again," he said. "Drive, drive, drive; but it's good to see a thing take shape and be a part of it. You oughter go up there, just to tell 'em back in the Old Country how we built a railroad slap into the middle of nowhere." And he went on: "Gee, you oughter see it now the heat's on. Not more'n a month to go before the big freeze-up and Head of Steel pushing forward near on two miles a day." He shook his big bullet head. "You oughter see it." He jammed his foot on the brake pedal and the truck stopped with a jerk. "Okay, fellow. There's the office." He jerked his head at a group of wooden buildings and there was a board with Q.N.S. & L. R. on it.

The airport despatcher must have phoned them, for the man in the office took me for a newly-arrived engineer. And when I told him I had just stopped off to see the president of the McGovern Mining & Exploration Company, he said, "Hell! I thought it was too good to be true."

"If you could direct me to the Company's offices," I suggested.

He scratched his head. "There's no company of that name here. There's just ourselves and the Iron Ore Company and the construction combine." He tipped his chair back, looking at me. "What's this fellow's name?"

"I don't know," I said. "I was just told to meet him here in Seven Islands."

"There was a guy called McGovern at breakfast this morning. Came in last night from Montreal—big man with a voice like a nutmeg grater. That him?"

"Couldn't you ring somebody and find out for me?" I asked. "The plane landed me here specially. There must be a message for me somewhere."

He sighed and reached for the phone. "Maybe the Iron Ore Company will know something about you. They handle all the mining and exploration side. We're just the railroad here." He got through to somebody and told him my name and who I'd come to see, and after listening for a bit, he put the receiver down. "Well, McGovern's your man all right. But he's busy right now. A conference." His chair was tilted back again and he was looking at me with renewed interest. "That was Bill Lands I was on to. He keeps tabs on Burnt Creek and all the geological parties. He'll be right over. I'm Staffen, by the way. Alex Staffen." He held out his hand to me. "I'm the personnel manager. Bill said something about your being here in connection with this survey party that crashed?"

I nodded.

"Bad business." He shook his head, sucking in air between his teeth. "Briffe was a nice guy. Did you ever meet him?"

"No," I said.

"French-Canadian, but a fine guy. A throw-back to the *voyageurs*." He stared at his desk. "It's tough on his daughter." He looked up at me suddenly. "You reckon there's hope?" he asked. And when I didn't answer, he said, "There's talk about a transmission having been picked up in England." His eyes were fixed on mine. "You know anything about that?"

"That's why I'm here," I said.

I suppose he sensed that I didn't want to talk about it, for he just nodded and looked away towards the window which gave on to a drab view of sand and gravel and huts. "Well, Paule's lucky, I guess, to have one of them come out alive."

He meant the pilot presumably and I asked him if he knew where Laroche was now.

"Why, here of course." He seemed surprised.

"You mean he's here in Seven Islands?"

"Sure. He and Paule Briffe . . ." The phone on his desk rang and he picked it up. "Harry West? Oh, for God's sake!" he exclaimed. "A gas car, you say? Hell!" He made

a note on his pad. " Okay, I'll have Ken Burke take over at
Two-two-four. No, I'll arrange for him to be flown up." He
slammed the receiver down. " The damn' fool got his foot
crushed by a gas car. You'd think after six months up the line
he'd know how to handle a speeder."

The door swung open and a big hustling man came in. He
had a tanned face and his calf-length boots were all caked with
mud. " Here's Bill now." My hand was gripped in a hard fist
as Staffen introduced us. " I was telling him how Briffe was a
real *voyageur* type."

" Sure was. Knew the North like city folk know their own
backyard." Bill Lands was looking at me, mild blue eyes in a
dust-streaked face summing me up. " Okay," he said abruptly.
" Let's go across to my office, shall we? Mr. McGovern should
be about through now, I guess." He gave an off-hand nod to
Staffen, and as we went out through the door, he said, " I've
sent for Bert Laroche, by the way."

" For Laroche—why?"

He gave me a flat, hard look. " If a man's going to be called
a liar, it better be to his face." He left it at that and led me
down a concrete path to another hut. " Ever meet McGovern?" He tossed the question at me over his shoulder.

" No," I said. " I'm from England."

He laughed. " You don't have to tell me that." At the
door of the hut he paused and faced me. " I think, maybe, I'd
better warn you. Mac's tough. Spent most of his life in the
North-West Territories. He reckons this about the damnedest
thing he ever struck." He strode ahead of me into his office
and waved me to a seat across the desk from him. " So do I,
if it comes to that. Smoke?" He tossed a pack of American
cigarettes into my lap. " Bert's flown me thousands of miles.
We've been in on this thing from the start, since back in forty-
seven when they decided to establish a permanent survey base
at Burnt Creek and really go to work on this iron ore project."
He took the pack from me and lit himself a cigarette. " Bert's
a fine guy."

I didn't say anything. It was McGovern I'd come to see.

" And there's Paule, too," he added. " That's Briffe's
daughter. How do you think she's going to feel when she
learns why you're here?" He was leaning back, looking at
me through eyes half-closed against the smoke of the cigarette

stuck in the corner of his mouth, and I could feel him holding himself in. " Did Alex tell you about Bert and Paule?"

He didn't wait for me to answer. " They were planning to be married this fall." He stared at me and I knew he was hating me and wishing I were dead. But whether for the sake of his friend or because of the girl I didn't know. And then he said, " Paule works right here in this office—has done ever since her father took this job with McGovern and they moved down from Burnt Creek." He took the cigarette out of his mouth and leaned forward. " What happens when she hears about this? Her father was all the world to her. She grew up in the North, camping and trekking and canoeing with him through the bush like a boy. He was her hero. And now he's dead. Why raise false hopes?"

" But supposing he isn't dead?"

" Bert was there. He says he's dead." He was jabbing the cigarette at me. " Leave it at that, why can't you?"

He was against me. And I knew then that they'd all be against me. I was an outsider and they'd close their ranks. . . . " Anyway, I just don't believe it," he was saying, leaning back and stubbing out his cigarette. " If Bert says they're dead, then they're dead and that's all there is to it. It's not his fault he was the only one got out. It happens that way sometimes." And he added, " He's one of the finest bush fliers in the North. I remember one time, back in forty-nine: we were flying out of Fort Chimo and the weather clamped right down . . ."

He was interrupted by the slam of a door in the corridor outside and a harsh voice saying, " I agree. No point in hanging on to those concessions."

" That's Mac now." Lands rose from his chair and went to the door. " We're in here, Mac."

" Fine, Bill. I'll be right with you." And then the voice added, " Well, there it is. Sorry it didn't work out."

Bill Lands turded away from the door and he came across to where I was sitting. " I've read the reports," he said. " I know what they say about your father." His hand gripped my shoulder. " But he's dead and nobody can hurt him. These others, they're alive." He was staring at me hard, and then he added, " Don't crucify Paule just to try and prove a point."

It was said very quietly, but grim-faced, so that I caught my breath, staring up at him. And then McGovern's harsh voice came from beyond the door again: " But don't expect too much from us on the northern concessions. There's a bare month before freeze-up—maybe less." And another voice said, " Okay. Do the best you can, Mac. But we've got to know what we hang on to and what we give up." The outer door slammed, and then McGovern was in the room.

He was a broad, chunky man, hard-jawed and tight-lipped, and the battered face was weathered with a thousand wrinkles. Eyes clear as grey stone pebbles looked me over. " You a ham operator, too?" The voice grated on my nerves, the tone hostile. Or was that my imagination?

" No," I said. I had risen to my feet, but he didn't come across to greet me. Instead he went over to the desk, slammed a bulging briefcase on top of it and sat down in Bill Lands' chair. The briefcase didn't seem to fit the man any more than his city suit. There was something untamed about him— an impression that was enhanced by the mane of white hair that swept back from his low, broad forehead. It was as though a piece of northern wild had moved into the office, and I think I was scared of him before ever he started to question me.

Bill Lands gave a little cough. " Well, I'll leave you two to——"

" No, no. You stay here, Bill. I'd like you to hear what this young man has to tell us. Has Bert arrived yet?"

" No, but he should be here any minute."

" Well, pull up a chair. Now then." McGovern fastened his eyes on me. " I take it you've got some new information for us . . . something that proves Briffe's still alive?" He phrased it as a question, his shaggy eyebrows lifted and his flinty eyes boring into me. " Well?"

" Not exactly new information, sir," I said.

" Then what's this guy Ledder all steamed up about? You saw him at Goose and he radioed a message to our office. You wouldn't have come all this way without something new for us to go on. What did you tell him?"

My mouth felt dry. McGovern was a type I'd never met before and his domineering personality seemed to bear down on me and crush me. " It wasn't exactly anything new," I murmured. " It was just that I convinced him that my father really did pick up a transmission."

"It doesn't say that here." He tugged at the straps of his briefcase and pulled out a message form. "This is how his message reads." He pushed a pair of steel-rimmed glasses on to his blunt nose. "*Possibility G2STO picked up transmission Briffe should not be ignored. Urgently advise you see Ferguson's son.* Why?" he said. "What did you tell him?" He was looking up at me over the top of his glasses. "What made Ledder advise us to have a talk with you?"

"It wasn't so much what I told him," I said. "It was more the background I gave him to my father's reception of Briffe's message. You see, my father died, virtually as a result of receiving——"

"Yes, we know all about your father's death," he cut in. "What I want to know is what you told Ledder that made him radio this message?"

"I merely filled in all the background for him." I felt at a loss how to break through and explain my father to this man. "It's not so much the facts," I said, "as the story behind the reception. If you'd known my father——"

"So there's nothing new?"

What could I say? He was watching me and it seemed to me that he was challenging me to produce something new. And all the time his eyes remained wide open, not blinking. It disconcerted me and in the end I said nothing. He seemed to relax then and looked away, glancing down at the papers he had spread out on the desk. "Your name's Ian Ferguson, I believe?"

"Yes." My voice sounded a stranger to me.

"Well, now, Ferguson, I think I should tell you, before we go any further, that the report of this transmission your father was supposed to have picked up was given immediate and most serious attention, not only by myself, but by the Air Force authorities and others. If we could have found one single radio operator anywhere in the world who could confirm it, the search would have been resumed. But we couldn't, and when we got the police reports of the full circumstances . . ." He gave a slight shrug that dismissed my father entirely.

I found my voice then. "If it's facts and nothing else that interest you," I said angrily, "then perhaps you'll appreciate the significance of what I learned at Goose. You say you couldn't get confirmation of Briffe's transmission. Of course you couldn't. Every other operator had given up listening for him. Every operator, that is, except my father. If you'd read Ledder's report you'd know that my father contacted him again on the twenty-sixth, the day the search was called off, to ask whether there was any other frequency Briffe might use in an emergency. Ledder told him No, and repeated Briffe's transmitting frequency. Surely that's proof enough that my father was keeping a constant watch?"

" I see. And you expect me to believe that your father was keeping a twenty-four hour watch for a transmission that he couldn't possibly expect to receive, and from a man who was dead anyway?" He was looking at me as though to say, *If you tell me Yes, then I'll know your father was crazy.* " Well, was he?"

" He had Briffe's sending frequency," I said. " He'd nothing else to do and he was obsessed . . ."

" Was the receiver tuned to that frequency when you got home the evening of the day he died?"

I should have checked that, but I hadn't. " I don't know." I felt angry and helpless. And then footsteps sounded in the passage outside and Bill Lands went to the door. " Here's Bert now."

" Tell him to wait," McGovern said. And then he was looking at me again. " So you believe your father really did pick up a transmission from Briffe? And you've come all this way in order to convince us—without a single item of fresh information. Correct?"

" But I've just told you——"

" You've told me nothing. Nothing that I didn't know already." He pulled a stapled sheaf of papers from his brief-case and after removing two of the pages, he passed the rest across to me. " Now I want you to read these reports through. Read them carefully, and then if there's anything you can add to them or any new light you can throw on the situation, I'll be glad to know about it." He had risen to his feet. " But," he added, " I think you should understand this. The man waiting outside is Bert Laroche, the pilot of the floatplane that crashed, and he says Briffe is dead."

" I'm not interested in what Laroche says." My voice sounded a little wild. " All I know is that my father——"

" You're calling Bert Laroche a liar. You're doing more than that. You're accusing him——"

"I don't care," I cried. "I'm not concerned with Laroche."

"No," he said. "Why should you be? You never met the guy and you don't understand his world." He was staring at me coldly.

"It's Briffe I'm concerned about," I murmured.

"Yeah?" His tone had contempt in it. "You never met him either, or the other guy—Baird. They mean nothing to you, any of them. All you're concerned about is your father, and for his sake you're prepared to make a lot of trouble and smear a decent man with the mud of your accusations." He had come round the desk and was standing over me, and now his hand reached out and gripped hold of my shoulder, stilling my protest. "You read those reports. Read them carefully. And just remember that, afterwards, you're going to meet Laroche, and anything you have to say will be said in his presence." He was staring down at me, the eyes stony and unblinking. "Just remember, too, that his story says your father couldn't have picked up a transmission from Briffe on the twenty-ninth. Okay?" He nodded to Bill Lands and the two of them went out.

His greeting to Laroche outside in the passage was in a softer tone, and then the door closed and I was alone. The voices faded and the walls of the office closed in around me, unfamiliar and hostile—isolating me. Was it only two days since I'd run into Farrow in the Airport Bar? It seemed so long ago, and England so far away. I was beginning to wish I'd never come to Canada.

Automatically I started to look through the papers. It was all there—a summary of the notes my father had made in his log books, my statement to the police, the description of the room and his radio equipment, technical information about the possibility of R/T reception at that range, Ledder's report, everything. And then I came to the psychiatrist's reports: *It is not unusual for physical frustration to lead to mental un-balance, and in those conditions a morbid interest in some disaster or human drama may result in the subject having delusions that attribute to himself an active, even prominent role, in the events that fill his mind. This occurs particularly where the subject is overmuch alone. In certain unusual cases such mental unbalance can give rise to extraordinary physical effort, and in the case under review . . .*

I flung the sheaf of papers on to the desk. How could they

be so stupid? But then I realised it wasn't their fault so much as my own. If I could have told them about that earlier expedition, they might have understood my father's obsession with the country. All those questions that had puzzled Ledder. . . . I couldn't blame them really. They hadn't meant anything to me until Ledder told me what had happened to my grandfather. Even now I didn't understand all the references.

I got out the list of jottings I'd made from his log books and went through them again, and the name Laroche stared me in the face. Why had my father been so interested in Laroche? Why was his reaction important? I picked up the sheaf of papers McGovern had given me and searched through it again. There was a list of all the radio stations—service, civilian and amateur—that had been contacted, and three solid pages of reports from pilots flying the search. But the one thing I wanted wasn't there and I guessed that the pages McGovern had detached before giving it all to me were those containing Laroche's statement.

I sat back then, wondering what Laroche would be like and whether his story would help me to decide what I ought to do now. McGovern wasn't going to do anything—of that I was certain. But if Laroche had been able to satisfy Briffe's daughter that her father was dead. . . . I didn't know what to think. Maybe Lands was right. Maybe I should just leave it at that and go home.

The door behind me opened and McGovern came in. " Well?" he said, shutting the door behind him. " Have you read it all through?"

" Yes," I said. " But I didn't find Laroche's statement."

" No. He'll tell you what happened himself." He came and stood over me. " But before I call him in, I want to know whether there is any material fact that's been omitted from these reports. If there is, then let's have it right now, whilst we're alone."

I looked up at him and the hard grey eyes were watching me out of the leathery face. His hostility was self-evident, and I was conscious of the limitations of my background. I hadn't been brought up to deal with men like this. " It depends what you call material facts," I said uncertainly. " That psychiatrists' report—it's based on the supposition that my father was simply a spectator, that he wasn't involved at all. They didn't have all the facts."

" How do you mean?"

" They didn't know his background, and without that the questions he asked Ledder and many of the jottings he made couldn't possibly make sense to them."

" Go on," he said.

I hesitated, wondering how to put it when I knew so little. " Did you know there was an expedition into the Attikonak area in nineteen hundred?" I asked.

" Yes." And it seemed to me his tone was suddenly guarded.

" Well, it appears that the leader of that expedition was my grandfather."

" Your grandfather?" He was staring at me and it was obvious that the revelation meant something to him, had come as a shock.

" Now perhaps you'll understand why my father was so interested in anything to do with Labrador," I said. " It explains all those questions he asked Ledder—questions that the psychiatrists couldn't understand. And because they couldn't understand them, they thought he was mad."

" So James Finlay Ferguson was your grandfather, eh?" He nodded his head slowly. " I thought maybe it was that. As soon as they told me your father's name I guessed we'd be back to that expedition. So did Bert. My God!" he said. " This is the third generation. And it was never more than gossip. Nothing was proved. Not even that woman could prove anything. And now you come over here with a lot of wild accusations that are based on nothing more substantial than this." He stared at me stonily, the veins of his face corded with anger. " Why the hell didn't you tell the authorities that your father was living in a world of the past—or didn't you dare? Did you think that would make him appear even more crazy?"

" He wasn't crazy," I almost shouted at him. I didn't understand half of what he'd been saying. " As for telling the authorities—I'd never heard about my grandfather's expedition until last night."

" Never heard about it?" He stared at me with obvious disbelief.

I told him then how I'd heard of it first from Ledder and how he'd only got the briefest information about it over the air from one of the geologists.

" Good God!" he said. " So you don't know the details. You don't know who was with your grandfather on that expedition——"

" No," I said. " I didn't come here because of that. I came because my father was a first-rate radio operator and I'm convinced . . ."

" Okay," he said. " I admit that puts a different complexion on it. But only as far as your motive in coming over is concerned," he added quickly. " It doesn't mean Briffe is alive. You may have known nothing about the Ferguson Expedition, but your father did."

" What's that got to do with .it?" I demanded.

" Everything," he said. " In my opinion, everything. His motive is obvious." And he added darkly, " There are more ways than one of being unbalanced."

I didn't understand what he was getting at, and I told him so.

" All right," he said. " Forget it. You're not involved, and I accept that. But I can't accept the rest—that your father really did pick up a transmission." And when I started to protest, he silenced me with an impatient movement of his hand. " Wait till you've heard what Bert Laroche has to say."

He left me then and went out, closing the door behind him. Through the flimsy wood partitioning I heard the whisper of their voices. What was he telling them? Was he briefing Laroche what to say? But I couldn't believe that. It was something else—to do with that expedition. If only I knew all the facts! I twisted round in my chair, watching the door, wondering what Laroche would be like. If my father were right, then the man had made a terrible, unbelievable mistake.

The door opened again and McGovern entered. " Come in, both of you," he said, and went over to the desk and sat down. Lands followed, and then a third man, tall and lean with the sort of face I'd never seen before. A gleam of sun threw a dusty shaft across the office and he walked right into it, his face dark and angular, almost secretive, with high cheekbones and the eyes laced with little lines at the corners so that they seemed constantly screwed up to peer at some distant horizon. A great gash ran from the top of his head down across his forehead to finish above his right eye. It was part-healed now, a black scab of dried blood, and the hair that had been shaved away on either side of it was beginning to grow again like black fur against the white of the scalp. The eyebrow had also been shaved away and this gave his features a strangely twisted look.

McGovern told him to pull up a chair and as he sat down he darted a quick glance at me. His eyes were brown and deep-sunk in sockets darkened by strain. It was obvious that he'd been under tension for a long time and there was a pallor beneath the dark skin that suggested exhaustion. And then he smiled at me, pulling a pipe from his pocket and relaxing. His teeth were very white and the smile somehow altered the balance of his face so that it suddenly had a boyish, almost debonair look; the same sort of look that I'd seen on the faces of Farrow and his friends—careless and yet concentrated. He seemed younger then, though his dark hair was turning grey at the temples.

Lands had shut the door and he pulled a chair up and sat down. McGovern leaned forward across the desk. " Now then, let's get this over with," he said to me. " I gather you still think your father may have picked up some sort of message from Briffe?"

I nodded, my mind concentrated on Laroche. I was trying to be honest with myself, to see him as he really was—an experienced bush flier. It didn't seem possible that he could have made a mistake, not over a thing like that, and not when he was engaged to Briffe's daughter.

McGovern had been saying something and he suddenly hit the desk in front of him. " Don't just sit there, man," he shouted at me. " Tell us why you're still convinced." And then in a quieter tone, he added, " You don't seem to realise that we knew Paul Briffe. He was a friend of mine, of Bill's, too. Bert was going to be his son-in-law. We've all of us every reason in the world to wish him alive." He leaned back in his chair with a little sigh. " But we don't think he is." And he went on: " When I had the first report of this alleged transmission, I thought for a moment Bert had made a mistake. Sometimes in the bush it's difficult to be sure. . . ." He let it go at that. " But then we got the full report, and when it was clear that nobody else had picked up the transmission, I knew it was no good calling for the search to be resumed. Now you come here and after reading those reports, you say you're still convinced your father did pick up a transmission. Why?"

I stared at him, sitting squat like a rock behind the desk. How could I explain to him how I felt about my father? The sense of helplessness came back to me, stronger than ever. " I'd like to hear what Laroche has to say," I said obstinately.

" Sure. But first, you tell us what makes you so damned sure."

" Because I know the sort of man my father was," I answered.

" You read the psychiatrists' report?"

" Do you expect me to agree with it?" I stared at him, anger flaring up inside me. " He wasn't unbalanced. And he didn't suffer from delusions."

" Did you live in the same house with him?"

" No."

" Then how can you be sure about his mental state?"

" Because I'm his son." McGovern's attitude was that of a brick wall. I could feel myself battering against it. " A son should know if his father's mad or not. And Dad wasn't mad. He knew it was Lake of the Lion and he knew it was Briffe. Why else do you think——"

" What's that you said?" The question was slammed at me by Laroche and there was a sudden stillness in the room. He was staring at me, and then he glanced across at McGovern who said quickly, " We'll leave the matter of your father for the moment." He leaned forward, holding my attention with his eyes. " Right now I want you to hear what actually happened. When you've heard it, I think you'll agree with us that there can be no room for doubt." He turned to Laroche. " Go ahead, Bert. Tell him what happened."

Laroche hesitated, glancing at me and running his tongue along the line of his lips. " Okay," he said. " I guess that's best. Then he can sort it out for himself." He shifted his gaze, staring down at his hands. I thought—he's nervous. But then he began to talk and I wasn't sure. He had a slight accent, and, though he was hesitant at times, it was mostly because he was searching for the word he wanted. His voice was flat and without emotion ; he had been through it all many times before.

They had taken off at approximately six-thirty on the evening of September 14. They had abandoned part of the stores and one tent and one canoe and cleared out of Disappointment in a hell of a hurry, for the storm was already upon them and the waters of the lake were being kicked up by a twenty-knot wind. Area C2 was about half an hour's flying time away, but before they had covered half the distance, the cloud base had come down very low with driving sleet and poor visibility.

" I should have landed whilst I had the chance," Laroche said. He wasn't looking at me. He wasn't looking at anybody He just sat there, telling what happened in that flat, slightly foreign voice.

He had been forced down until the floats were skimming the tops of the jackpine and he was lake hopping from one expanse of water to the next. " At that level things come up very fast. And the lakes take on a different shape. It was only the small ones that I could see as a whole. The rest were just scraps of water, blurred in the sleet and the poor light." He thought he might have underestimated the wind strength. Coming up with the advance party the fog and his forced landing had made it impossible for him to memorise the ground. Anyway, it wouldn't have helped with dusk falling and poor visibility. He flew a compass course, and when he'd flown the estimated time distance, he began to search, flying in widening circles, still held down to tree-top level. He flew like that for almost fifteen minutes with the light fading all the time and no sign of the Attikonak River or any feature that would give him his bearings.

And then the snow came. It came suddenly in a blinding squall that blotted out everything. " I had no choice," he said. " I had been crossing a lake and I did a tight turn and put the nose down." He had ripped the floats as he crashed through the trees at the water's edge and had hit the surface of the lake hard, bounced twice and then smashed into a rock that had suddenly loomed up in front of him. He had hit it with the starboard wing so that the plane had swung round, crashing into it broadside and shattering the fuselage. The impact had flung him head-first against the windshield and he had blacked out.

When he came to, the plane was half in, half out of the water with the rock towering above it. Dazed, he crawled back into the fuselage to find Baird unconscious, pinned there by a piece of metal that had injured his right hand and opened up all one side of his face. " Paul was injured, too."

Laroche's eyes were half-closed as he talked and I couldn't doubt that this was how it had happened. His voice and the details carried conviction.

He had done what he could for them, which wasn't much for there was no wood on the rock with which to make a fire. He was there two days until the storm had passed, and then he hacked one of the floats clear, patched it and ferried the two injured men ashore. He had got a fire going and had rigged up a shelter of branches, and had brought some supplies from the plane. Two days later another storm had come up. The wind had been north-westerly and the following morning the plane had vanished. It had killed the fire, too, and he hadn't been able to light another because all the matches were soaked and he had lost his lighter, which was the only one they possessed. Baird had died that night; Briffe the following night. After that he had started trekking westward. " I knew that as long as I kept going west I must arrive at the line of the railway sooner or later. . . ." He had kept going for five days and nights with almost no food, and on the afternoon of the twenty-fifth he had reached Mile 273 where a construction gang with a grab crane were working on the grade. " I guess that's all," he said, looking at me for the first time. " I was lucky to get out alive."

" Well, there you are," McGovern said, and the finality of his tone made it clear he considered I ought to be satisfied.

" That trip you made out to the plane," I said. " Did you bring the radio ashore?"

" No," he said. " It went down with the aircraft."

" And you're sure Briffe was dead when you left him?"

Laroche looked at me, his eyes wide in his tanned face. And then he glanced quickly at McGovern. It was as though he had turned to him for help. But it was Lands who said, " He's just told you so, hasn't he?" His tone was angry. " What more do you want?"

And then McGovern said, " You'd like to see the bodies, I suppose?" He was glaring at me.

" Did you bury them?" I asked Laroche. I thought if I dug hard enough . . .

" For God's sake!" Lands said.

" No," Laroche answered me. " I didn't bury them. I guess I didn't have the energy." His voice was flat. And then he added quickly, " I tried to locate them afterwards. I flew twice with a pilot out of Menihek. But there are thousands of lakes —literally thousands." His voice trailed away.

" Thousands, yes," I said. " But only one Lake of the Lion." And again I was conscious of a tension in the room. It wasn't only Laroche, who was staring at me with a shocked expression on his face. It was McGovern, too. " What the hell's the name of the lake matter if he couldn't locate it again?" he said angrily.

But I was looking at Laroche. " You knew it was Lake of the Lion, didn't you?" I was so sure it was important that I pressed the point. " That rock in the middle——"

" It was snowing," he muttered.

" When you crashed. But later . . . Didn't you see the rock later? It was shaped like a lion, wasn't it?"

" I don't know," he said. " I didn't notice."

" But you've read those reports? You know the message my father picked up?"

He nodded.

" That transmission of Briffe's—it was from Lake of the Lion."

" You don't know that," McGovern cut in.

" Then why did he say— *Search for narrow lake with a rock shaped like . . .* ?" I demanded. " There's only those two words—*a lion*—missing."

" You're just guessing," McGovern said. " And, anyway, your father was simply inventing on the basis of what he knew of the Ferguson Expedition."

" Do you really believe that?" I cried. " Those were the last words he wrote before he died."

" That doesn't make them true. He couldn't have known he was going to die."

I stared at him, appalled. " I tell you, he struggled to his feet to look at that map. Lake of the Lion was marked on that map; his log books, too—they were littered with drawings of lions. . . ."

" All right," McGovern said heavily. " Suppose Briffe did send and those were the exact words he transmitted. Do you know where this lake is?"

" It's in the Attikonak area," I replied. " East of the river."

" Hell! We know that already. We know to within thirty miles or so where it was Bert crashed, but we still haven't

located the lake. But of course if you know the exact location of this lake you keep talking about . . . But your father
didn't pin-point it, did he?"

"No," I was still looking at Laroche. He was busy filling
his pipe, his head bent.

"Then it doesn't help us very much." Was there a note of
relief in McGovern's voice? I glanced at him quickly, but the
grey, stony eyes told me nothing. "As Bert says, there are
thousands of lakes out there."

"But only one with a rock shaped like a lion," I said obstinately.

And then Laroche said quietly, "You don't know what it
was like out there." It was as though he had been following
some train of thought of his own. "It was snowing, and later
there was fog. And there was so much to do. . . ." His voice
tailed off again as though he didn't want to think about it.

"This isn't getting us anywhere." McGovern's voice was
suddenly brisk and business-like. "Lake of the Lion is mentioned in Dumaine's book and in the newspaper reports of—
the survivor." He had glanced quickly at Laroche. And then
he was looking at me again. "Your father would have read
the name they gave to that lake—their last camp. That was
the place where your grandfather died, and as far as I'm concerned it only proves that your father was living in the
past."

I stared at him, unbelievingly. "Won't you even try to
understand?" I said. "My father was a radio operator. The
ether was his whole world. He'd never have invented a transmission that didn't take place—never." And I went on to
explain what it must have cost him in effort to force himself
to his feet. But, even as I was telling it to him, I knew it was
no good. The hard lines of his face didn't soften, the eyes held
no sympathy.

He heard me out, and when I'd finished, he glanced at his
watch. "I'm sorry," he said. "But all this doesn't really help
us. If you'd been able to tell us something new—give us
something positive to work on . . ." He got to his feet. "I've
got to go now." He came round the desk and stood over me.
"Don't think I don't appreciate it that you've come a long way
to tell us this. I do. But you must understand that yours is a
personal point of view—a very personal one."

"Then you're not going to do anything?" I asked.

" What can I do? Call for a resumption of the search? I'd have to convince the authorities first." He shook his head.

I jumped to my feet then. " But before you were searching blind," I told him. " Now you'd have something to go on. If you searched for this lake. . . ." I turned to Laroche. " For God's sake try to make him see it," I cried. And when he didn't answer, but remained staring down at his pipe, I burst out wildly, " Don't you want them to be found?" And at that his head came up with a jerk and he stared at me with a sort of horror.

" Bert flew in twice," McGovern reminded me quietly. " Twice when he should have been in hospital. And he couldn't find the lake." He paused and then added, " I understand your disappointment. It's natural after coming so far. And I may say I'm disappointed, too. We all are. When I got Ledder's message I had hoped . . ." He turned away with a little shrug that was a gesture of finality. " I gather your aircraft has gone on to Montreal. That correct?" he asked me.

I nodded, feeling suddenly drained of the will to fight them any more.

" I'm told there's a flight going out to Montreal to-night," he said to Lands. " Do you think you could fix him a ride on it, Bill?"

" Sure."

McGovern glanced at his watch again and then turned to Laroche. " You got your car with you? Then perhaps you'd drive me down into town. I'm late as it is." He picked up his briefcase. " I'm grateful to you, Ferguson—very grateful indeed. If there's anything I can do for you let me know." And with that he strode out of the room. Laroche hesitated, glancing quickly at me as though he were about to say something. And then he hurried after McGovern.

The door slammed behind him and I stood there, feeling numbed and exhausted. I should have stopped him, made one final effort. But what was the good? Even if he'd known the name of the lake all along, it didn't mean he could find it again. And the world had got used to the idea that the men were dead. That was the thing I was up against—that and the stubbornness of men like McGovern who couldn't see a thing unless it was presented to them as hard fact. " Damn them! Damn them to hell!"

A hand gripped my arm. I'd forgotten Bill Lands was still

there. "What did you expect?" he said in a kindly voice. "We don't abandon men easily up here in the North."

I swung round on him. "But don't you see . . ." And then I stopped because I realised that he'd sat through it all and he still believed that Briffe was dead. He wasn't involved. He was outside it and if I hadn't convinced him, what hope had I of convincing anyone else?

"I'll just go and check this Montreal flight, and then I guess you'd like some food."

He was gone about ten minutes, and when he came back he told me it was all fixed. "Flight leaves at around twenty-thirty hours." He took me out into the slanting evening light, across flat gravel that had the silt look of a river bed, and in the distance a locomotive hooted an inexpressibly mournful note. "Supply train going up the line to Head of Steel," he said. "Going up myself to-morrow." There was pleasure in his voice and he smiled at me. He had warmth, this big American with his eyes screwed up against the westering sun.

We entered a hut similar to the one we had just left, to be greeted by a murmur of voices, the rattle of crockery, and the smell of food. It was good, that smell of food, for I was hungry, and I sat down with Lands at a table full of strangers, who took no notice of me and ate with concentration. What talk there was centred around the line and it carried with it the breath of railway engineering. They were blasting rock at one point, bearing down on the muskeg at another, and the rail-laying gang at Head of Steel were driving forward at the rate of a mile and a half a day. Dozens of construction camps, thousands of men, even an air lift to supply them—a whole world in itself, thinking, dreaming, eating, sleeping nothing but this railway. I felt myself being sucked into it mentally, so that it was difficult, whilst I sat there eating with them, not to feel a part of it.

And then somebody asked me whether I was going up the line. When I told him No, that I was going back to England, he stared at me as though I were some creature from another planet. "Well, well—and we got such a good climate up here." They laughed, and their laughter made me less of a stranger.

Lands waited for me to finish eating, and then we went outside and all the western sky was aglow with the setting sun. "You'll see a sight before you leave to-night, I reckon," he said. " The northern lights should be real good." He glanced at his watch. " It's early for your flight yet, but I got to go down town. Don't mind if I drop you off at the airstrip right away, do you?"

I shook my head and he went off to change and get his car. I was to pick up my suitcase and meet him at the Q.N.S. & L. Office. I moved out across the flat gravel space, feeling conspicuous and alone. All the purpose seemed to have been drained out of me. Glancing back, I saw that Lands had stopped to chat to a woman down by the farthest hut. I could see them looking at me and I went quickly on towards the office, conscious that others must know by now what had brought me here. Staffen would have told them, and the knowledge made the sense of failure overwhelming. If only I could have convinced Lands. I liked Bill Lands.

I reached the office and found my suitcase, and I went out and stood looking at the western sky, which had flared up into a violent furnace red. And now that I was leaving, I felt again the strange pull of this country.

Footsteps sounded, quick and urgent on the gravel behind me, and a voice that was soft and slightly foreign said, " Are you Mr. Ferguson?"

I turned and found it was the woman who had been talking to Lands. Or rather, it wasn't a woman, but a girl with black hair cut short like a boy and a dark, full-lipped face that had no trace of make-up. I remember, even in that first glimpse of her, she made a deep impression on me. It was her vitality, I think, and a sort of wildness, or perhaps it was just that her eyes caught and reflected the strange, wild light in the sky. Whatever it was, I was immediately aware of her in a way that was somehow personal. " Yes," I said. " I'm Ian Ferguson."

She didn't say anything, just stared at me, her nostrils aquiver and her eyes blazing with the reflected glare. Her wrists were very slender and her hands gripped the edge of her leather jacket so that she seemed to be holding herself in.

And then she said, " I'm Paule Briffe."

I think I'd known that from the first moment, the sense of emotion dammed up inside her had been so strong. " I'm sorry," I murmured awkwardly. I didn't know what else to say.

" Bill told me your father is dead, that that is why you

come." She spoke in a tight, controlled little voice that trembled on the edge of hysteria. " I can understand that. Believe me, I can understand that." And then, suddenly losing the grip she had on herself, she cried out, " But it doesn't help him. It cannot do any good." The words came in a rush. " Please. Go back to England. Leave us alone."

" It was because of your father that I came," I said.

I thought that would steady her, but she didn't seem to hear. " You came here and you hurt people and you do not care. Please, please, leave us alone."

" But your father——" I began.

" My father is dead," she cried. " He is dead—dead ; do you hear?" Her voice was wild, unrestrained, her eyes wide and scared.

" But suppose my father was right," I said gently. " Suppose that transmission——"

" Your father! *Mon Dieu!* You do not care about us— what we feel. You are afraid to admit that your father is mad so you come here to make trouble." Her small fists were clenched and her tight breasts heaved against the leather of her Indian jacket. And then, whilst I stared at her, appalled, she reached out her hand with her breath caught and said, " No. That was wrong of me." She was staring at me. " But it is so horrible," she breathed. " So very horrible." She turned away then, her face towards the sunset. " I do not mind so much for myself—father is dead. There's nothing to do about that. But for Albert "—she pronounced his name in the French way—" it is driving him out of his mind. I have just been talking to him. It is a terrible thing you are saying." This last in a voice scarcely above a whisper.

" But suppose he *has* made a mistake?" I said.

She rounded on me then, her eyes blazing. " You don't seem to understand," she cried. " He is with my father when he died, and it is because of him they stop the search. And now you come here and try to tell us that my father transmit on the radio, not when they crash, but two whole weeks after. That is what is terrible." She was crying now—crying wildly in a terrible flood of feeling. " It isn't true. It can't be true."

What could I say? What did you say when what you'd come to believe tore another human being in half? And because I didn't know, I stood in silence, scared by the sight of a passion that was quite foreign to me.

" You say nothing. Why?" She made a quick movement and caught hold of my arm. " Tell me the truth now. Please. The truth."

The truth! What was the truth? Did I really know it? Was it really what was written on the pencilled page of that log-book? " I'm sorry," I murmured. " I don't know the truth." And I added, " I wish I did. All I know is what my father wrote. He believed your father was alive and that he was transmitting from a place called Lake of the Lion."

She caught her breath then. " Lake of the Lion!" She was staring at me and now there was intelligence as well as passion in her eyes. " You say Lake of the Lion. How do you know?"

" The transmission," I said. " It was implied in the transmission my father picked up."

" It only said a narrow lake with a rock in it." Her voice trembled slightly. " That was all. I read it myself. Albert showed it to me."

" Did he show you Ledder's reports, too?"

She shook her head.

" Lake of the Lion was mentioned in that." I spared her the context and went on to tell her about the map in my father's room and the log books and how my father had been obsessed with Labrador because of the Ferguson Expedition. And all the time I was talking she was staring at me, her eyes wide, almost shocked. " So you see," I finished, " I felt I had to come."

She didn't say anything for a moment and her face had gone quite white. " Lake of the Lion." She murmured the name to herself as though it were something she'd dreamed about. " My father talked about it—often . . . over camp fires. He knew the story, and always he thought he would find it some day—always he was searching. All my life I hear that name on his lips." She had turned away from me, staring at the sunset. " *Dieu me secourrait!*" she breathed. God help me! Her hands were gripped together as she said it, as though she were kneeling before an altar. She looked at me slowly. " You are honest. At least you are honest. And I thank God for that." Her eyes held mine for a long moment and then she whispered, " I must think. I must pray to God." And she turned and walked slowly away, and there was something so forlorn about her, so matching my own mood of loneliness that I started after her.

But I stopped, because with a sudden perception that I scarcely understood, I realised that I could do no good. This was something that she had to discover for herself. It was a terrible choice, striking as it did at the roots of her relationship with Laroche, and I felt her dilemma as though it were my own. And in some strange way it strengthened my resolve. It was as though this other human, whom I had never met till now, had reached out to me for help. I knew then that I couldn't give up, that I must go on until I'd found the truth.

It was strange, but the past and the present seemed suddenly inextricably mingled, with Lake of the Lion the focal point, and I turned my face towards the north, feeling the chill of the faint wind that blew from the Labrador plateau.

This was my mood when Bill Lands drove up in his mud-spattered station wagon and told me to jump in. " I'm not going," I said.

He stared at me, still leaning across the passenger seat with his hand on the door he'd thrown open for me. " What do you mean, you're not going?"

" I'm staying here," I told him. " I'm staying here till I've discovered the truth."

" The truth? You've had the truth. You had it from Bert Laroche this afternoon." He was frowning at me. " Did Paule find you? Did you talk to her?"

" Yes."

" What did you say to her?" His voice was trembling with anger and his fist was clenched as he slid across the passenger seat and out on to the gravel beside me. " Did you try and tell her that her father was still alive out there?" He stood over me, his eyes narrowed and hard, looking down into my face. " Did you tell her that?" I thought he was going to hit me.

" No," I said.

" What did you tell her then?"

" She asked for the truth and I said I didn't know what the truth was."

" And that set her mind at rest, I suppose? Why the hell Bert had to tell her about you, I don't know." He gripped hold of my suitcase, wrenching it from me and tossing it into the back of the wagon. " Okay. Let's go. You've done enough damage for one day." His voice still trembled with anger. " Go on. Get in."

" But I'm not going," I repeated, my voice childishly stubborn.

" You're going, son, whether you want to or not." Then he caught hold of my arm and literally flung me into the seat and slammed the door.

There was no point in arguing with him—he was a big man, powerfully built. But as he got in behind the wheel and we drove off, I said, " You can take me down to the airstrip, but you can't make me board the plane."

He looked at me, frowning. " I don't understand you," he said. " Why the hell don't you accept Bert's statement and leave it at that?" And when I didn't say anything, he asked, " How much money you got—Canadian money?"

" None," I said.

He nodded. " That's what I thought." He was smiling. " How the hell do you expect to stay on here? This is a boom town. It costs money to live here."

" Staffen's short of engineers," I said quietly. " And I'm an engineer."

We had swung out on to the dirt road and he headed east, his foot hard down on the accelerator. " Alex won't give you a job, and nor will anybody else when they know you're just here to make trouble."

" I'm not here to make trouble," I said. " I just want to find out the truth. And if it's the girl you're worrying about," I added, " then don't you think she's entitled to the truth too? She knows I'm here and she knows why. She knows about that transmission, and if she never learns the truth of it, she'll wonder about it all her life." He didn't say anything and I went on: " You say her father was a hero to her. Well, she knows there's one person who doesn't believe he's dead, and if it's left at that she'll worry about it till the day she dies."

We had come to the airstrip and he turned in through the wire and pulled up at the despatch office. " All the more reason why I should get you out of here to-night." He flung open the door. " You leave to-night and she'll know there was nothing to it. Okay?" He sat there, looking at me, waiting for me to say something. " Well, it doesn't much matter whether you agree with me or not. You're taking this plane out of here to-night and that's the end of it. And don't try anything clever," he added menacingly. " If I find you still here to-night when I get back from town, Goddammit, I'll half-kill you. And don't think I don't mean it. I do." He got out then and went into the despatch office.

The sky was a darkening splurge of colour, lurid red down by the horizon, but fading to purple as night spread across it from the east. An old Dakota stood in black silhouette, a fork lift trundling supplies out to it and a little knot of men standing waiting. They were all types, men waiting to be flown up the line. I wished I were going with them. I was feeling the need for action. But maybe I could do something down at Montreal, see the authorities, something.

The door beside me was jerked open. " Okay," Lands said. " It's all fixed. That's your plane over there." He nodded towards a small, twin-engined aircraft parked behind us. " Take-off is at twenty-thirty hours. If you'll come into the office now, I'll hand you over to the despatcher."

I got out, feeling suddenly tired—glad to be going, to be getting out of Seven Islands.

" Can you lend me some money?" I asked as he handed me my suitcase.

" Sure. How much do you want?"

" Just enough to see me through till midday to-morrow," I said. " That's when my plane leaves Montreal."

He nodded. " Twenty bucks do you?" He pulled his wallet out of his hip pocket and handed me four fives.

" I'll send you the sterling equivalent as soon as I get home," I said.

" Forget it." He patted my arm. " To be honest, I'd have paid that and more to get you out of here. I guess I'm a sentimental sort of guy. I just don't like to see two people's lives busted up for the sake of something that nobody can do anything about." He took my suitcase and led me across to the despatch office. The despatcher was the same man who had been on duty when I arrived. " Ed, this is Mr. Ferguson. Comes from England. Look after him for me, will you? And see he doesn't miss his flight."

" Sure. I'll look after him, Mr. Lands."

" Here's his flight pass." Lands handed over a slip of paper. And then he turned to me. " I've got to go now. Ed will see you on to your plane." He held out his hand. " Glad you saw it my way in the end." He hesitated as though he wasn't sure whether he ought to leave me there on my own. But then he said, " Well, s'long. Have a good flight." And he went out and climbed into his station wagon and drove out through the wire.

" You've got about an hour to wait," the despatcher said, writing my name on a despatch sheet. Then he slapped my pass on to a spike with a lot of other papers. " Flight leaves twenty-thirty hours. I'll call when they're ready for you."

" Thanks," I said, and walked out into the hangar that adjoined the office. It was full of stores, and outside it was dark. The last patch of red had gone from the sky and the arc lights had been switched on, flooding the apron, and the Dakota was still there, waiting. The last of the freight was being loaded into it by hand, the fork lift standing idle beside the hangar door. A starter motor was wheeled into position under the port engine and there was a sudden surge amongst the waiting men as they crowded close around the open door of the fuselage.

Maybe the idea had been at the back of my mind all the time. At any rate, I found myself walking out across the apron to mingle with the construction men who were waiting to board the plane. I hadn't thought it out at all. It was just that this plane was going up the line and I was drawn to it by a sort of fascination. " Gonna be cold in that rig, ain't yer?" said the man next to me. He had a dark, wizened face half-hidden by a large fur cap with ear flaps. " First time you bin up the line?"

I nodded.

" Thought so." And he spat a stream of tobacco juice out on to the ground. " Where you bound for?"

I hesitated, but he was looking at me, expecting an answer. " Two-two-four," I said, remembering that a replacement engineer was being sent up there.

The little man nodded. " Be snowing up there I wouldn't wonder." He said it with a grin, as though he relished the thought that I should be cold.

I moved away from him, edging my way in amongst the rest of the men. " You on this flight?" A man in a long-visored cap standing in the door of the fuselage was staring down at me.

" Yes," I said, and it was only after I'd said it that I realised

I'd committed myself to something I was by no means certain I could see through.

"Well, just wait till I call your name." He turned to the others. "Okay, boys. Let's get started." And he began to call their names one by one and tick them off on the list in his hand as they climbed aboard.

I hadn't reckoned on them having a passenger list just like an ordinary airline. The crowd was dwindling fast, and I wondered how I was going to explain that I'd tried to board a plane going up the line when I was booked out on a flight to Montreal? Unless I could bluff my way on to it! I was thinking of Staffen and his need of engineers.

"What's your name?" The last man had climbed up into the plane and the man with the list was staring down at me.

"Ferguson," I said, and I could hear the tremor in my voice.

He ran his finger down the list. "Your name's not here. What's your job?"

"Engineer."

"This plane's going to One-three-four." He jumped to the ground beside me. "You work there?"

"No," I said. "I'm going on up to Two-two-four." And I added quickly, "The engineer there had an accident and I'm replacing him."

"Yeah, that's right." He nodded. "West. They flew him down this evening." He was looking at me and I could see him trying to make up his mind. "Did you have a flight pass?"

"Yes," I said. "The despatcher has it. Mr. Lands drove me down and asked him to be sure I didn't miss this plane."

"Ed didn't say anything to me about it." He hesitated, glancing down at the list again. "Okay, let's go over to the office and sort it out. Hold it!" he shouted to the man with the starter motor.

"What's the trouble, Mike?" asked the pilot, who was now standing in the entrance to the fuselage.

"Won't be a minute. Leave your bag here," he said to me. "We got to hurry."

We ran all the way to the despatch office. There was no turning back now. I'd just got to make the despatcher believe me. I remember a car drove up just as we reached the office, but I had other things to worry about, and in the office I stood silent whilst my companion explained the situation to the despatcher.

"You're booked out on the Beechcraft," he told me. "Twenty-thirty hours for Montreal."

"There must be some mistake," I said.

"No mistake, mister." He had got hold of my flight pass now. "There you are. See for yourself. Montreal. That's what it says."

I repeated what I'd said before, that I was bound for Two-two-four, and I added, "You were here when I arrived this afternoon. I came to get a job, and I got it."

He nodded. "That's right. I remember. Came in on that freighter and didn't know who you wanted to see." He scratched his head.

"Maybe I got the wrong pass or it was made out incorrectly," I suggested. "Mr. Lands was asked to drive me down specially so that I wouldn't miss this plane." I pulled my passport out of my pocket. "Look, if you don't believe I'm an engineer . . ." I opened it and pointed to where it gave Occupation.

He stared at the word Engineer. "Well, I don't know," he said. "On whose instructions was the pass made out?"

"Mr. Staffen's."

"Well, I won't be able to get Mr. Staffen at this time of night. They pack up at six."

"Is there room for me on this flight up to One-three-four?"

"Yeah, there's room all right." ·

"Then can't you just alter the flight pass? Look!" I said. "I'm not taking a plane down to Montreal. That's certain. Why would I want to leave when I've only just arrived?"

He laughed. "You got something there."

"And just when I've got the job I came to get. Besides, Mr. Staffen said I was to get up there right away. He's short of engineers."

"Sure. They're having to move them about all the time." He looked at me and I saw he was making up his mind and said nothing more. "Okay," he said. "I reckon it's a mistake, like you said. After all, I guess you're old enough to know where you're supposed to be going." And he chuckled to himself as he put a line through Montreal on the pass, wrote in One-three-four and altered the despatch sheet. "Okay," he said. "You're on the list now. Lucky you found out in time

or you'd have been back in the Old Country before you knew
where you were." And he laughed again, good-humouredly, so
that I hoped he wouldn't get into too much trouble for alter-
ing the pass.

But I didn't have time to think about that, for I was hustled
back to the plane. The port motor started up as we ran across
the apron and I was hauled aboard through the cold backwash of air from the turning propeller. My suitcase was tossed
up to me and, as I grabbed it, I saw a man come out of the
despatch office and stand there, hesitating, staring at the plane.
The headlights of a truck swinging in at the gates caught him
in their blaze and I recognised Laroche. The starboard motor
came to life with a roar and at the sound of it he began to run
out on to the tarmac. " Mind yourself!" A hand pushed me
back and the door was swung to with a crash, and after that
I could see nothing but the dim-lit interior of the fuselage with
the freight heaped down the centre and the construction men
seated in two lines on either side of it.

There was still time for the plane to be stopped. If Laroche
had checked with the despatcher and told him I was really
bound for Montreal. . . . The engines suddenly roared in
unison and the plane began to move, swinging in a wide turn
towards the runway-end. And then we were moving faster, the
fuselage bumping and shaking as the wheels trundled over the
rough ground.

I squeezed myself in between two men on the seat-line opposite the door and sat with my hands gripped round my knees,
waiting. Nobody was talking. The noise of the engines made
it impossible and there was that sense of strain that always
seems to precede take-off.

The plane turned at the runway-end. Only a few seconds
now. I held my knees tight as first one engine and then the
other was run up; and then suddenly both engines were roaring and the fuselage shuddered and rattled. The brakes were
released. The plane began to move. And in a moment we were
airborne and the nerves and muscles of my body slowly
relaxed.

It was only then that I had time to realise what I'd done. I
was on my way into Labrador.

II

WE CLIMBED for what seemed a long time and it grew steadily colder. I put my coat on, but it hardly made any difference. The plane was a relic of the war, the parachute jumping wire still stretched down the centre of the fuselage, and a bitter draught of air blew in through the battered edges of the badly-fitting door. The dim lighting gave to the faces of the men flanked along the fuselage a ghostly, disembodied look. They were types of faces that I'd never seen before, faces that seemed symbolic of the world into which I was flying—old and weather-beaten, and some that were young and dissolute, a mixture of racial characteristics that included Chinese and African.

The battering of the engine noise dropped to a steady roar as the plane flattened out. The cold was intense. " We'll be going up the Moisie River now," the man next to me said. He was a small squat man with the broad, flat features of an Indian. " Been up here before?" I shook my head. " I work on the line two winters now—all through the Moisie Gorge and up to the height of land." There was pride in the way he said it.

" How long before we get to One-three-four?" I asked him.

" One hour, I think." And he added, " Once I do it by canoe, all up the Moisie and across to the Ashuanipi. Six weeks. Now, one hour." He nodded and relapsed into silence, and I sat there, feeling a little scared as we roared on through the night into Labrador.

I had some idea of the country. I'd read about it in my father's books. I knew it was virtually unexplored, a blank on the map which only four thousand years ago had been covered by the glaciers of the last Ice Age. And I got no comfort from the men around me. They were all a part of an organisation that I was outside. And their hard-bitten, dim-lit features, their clothes, everything about them, only served to emphasise the grimness of the country into which I was being flown.

I was unprepared, inexperienced, and yet I think the thing that worried me most was that Laroche would have radioed

ahead and that I should be stopped at One-three-four and sent
down by the next plane.

But gradually the intense cold numbed all thought, and
when the chill ache of my body had so deadened my mind that
I didn't care any longer, the sound of the engines died away,
and a moment later we touched down.

We scrambled out into another world—a world where the
ground was hard with frost and a few shacks stood against a
starlit background of jackpines. Away to the left a solitary
huddle of lights illuminated a line of heavy wagons. There was
the sound of machinery, too. But the sound seemed small and
insubstantial against the overwhelming solitude, and over-
head the northern lights draped a weird and ghostly curtain
across the sky, a curtain that wavered and constantly changed
its shape with a fascination that was beyond the reach of
explanation.

I stood for a moment staring up at it, enthralled by the
beauty of it, and at the same time awed. And all about me
I was conscious of the iron-hard harshness of the North, the
sense of a wild, untamed country, not yet touched by man.

Stiff-jointed and cold we moved in a body to the wood-frame
huts that were the airstrip buildings, crowding into the despatch
office where the warmth from the diesel heater was like a
furnace. Names were called, the despatcher issuing instructions in a harsh, quick voice that switched from English to
French and back again as though they were the same language. The men began filing out to a waiting truck.
" Ferguson."

The sound of my name came as a shock to me and I moved
forward uncertainly.

" You're Ferguson, are you? Message for you." The despatcher held it out to me. " Came in by radio half an hour
back."

My first thought was that this would be from Lands, that I
wouldn't get any farther than this camp. And then I saw the
name Laroche at the end of it. *Urgent we have talk. Am
taking night supply train. E.T.A. 0800. Do not leave before
I have seen you. Laroche.*

Staring at that message, the only thought in my mind was
that he hadn't stopped me. Why? It would have been easy
for him to persuade the base despatcher to have them hold me
here. Instead, he was coming after me, wanting to have a

talk to me. Had I forced his hand? Did this mean . . . ? And then I was conscious of an unmistakably Lancashire voice saying, " Has Ferguson checked in on that flight, Sid?"

" He's right here," the despatcher answered, and I looked up to find a short, rather tired-looking man standing in the door-way to an inner office. He wore a khaki shirt with the sleeves rolled up and he had a green eye-shade on his head, and over his shoulder I caught a glimpse of radio equipment. " You got the message all right then?"

" Yes," I said. " Yes, I got the message, thanks."

" You a friend of Laroche?" I didn't know quite how to answer that, but fortunately he didn't wait for a reply, but added, " You're English, aren't you?"

I nodded and he came towards me, holding out his hand. " That makes two of us," he said. " My name's Bob Perkins. I'm from Wigan. Lancashire, you know."

" Yes, I guessed that."

" Aye," he said. " Not much fear of your mistaking me for a Canuk." There was a friendly twinkle in his tired blue eyes. " Two years I been up in this bloody country. Emigrated in fifty-one and came straight up here as Wireless Op. They still think I talk a bit peculiar like." And then he added, " That message—it's from that pilot who crashed, isn't it?"

I nodded.

" Aye, I thought there couldn't be two of 'em with a name like that." He looked at me hesitantly. " Would yer like a cup of tea?" he asked, and, surprised at anything so English up here in the middle of nowhere, I said Yes. As he led me into the radio room, he said, " I only been here a week. Five days to be exact. I was up at Two-ninety before that. I remember when they picked this Laroche up. Proper hulla-baloo there was." He went over to a kettle quietly steaming on the diesel heater. " Newspapers—everybody. Hardly had time to deal with the air traffic."

" Who found him, do you know?" I asked. If I could find out something more before I met Laroche. . . .

" Oh, some construction gang. By all accounts he stum-bled out of the bush right on top of a grab crane. The fellow that brought him out though was Ray Darcy, engineer up at Two-sixty-three. Radioed us to have a plane standing by and then drove him the twenty odd miles up the old Tote Road in one hour flat. Or that's what he said. It'd be some going on that road. Would you like milk and sugar? Trouble is you never know with a man like Ray Darcy." He handed me a battered tin mug. " Proper character he is and all. Came up to Labrador for a month's fishing an' stayed two years. You a fisherman?"

" No," I said.

" Wonderful fishing up here for them as likes it. Me, I haven't the patience like. You got to have patience. Not that Ray Darcy's got much. He's an artist really—paints pictures. But he's a proper fisherman when it comes to stories. Twenty miles an hour he'd have to've averaged, and on the Tote Road. Aye, and you should see his jeep. Proper mess—glued together with the mud that's on it, that's what I say. . . ."

And so it went on. I sat there and drank my tea and listened to him talking, basking in the warmth of his friendliness and the knowledge that he was English. That fact alone meant a lot to me. It gave me confidence and drove out the sense of loneliness.

Bob Perkins was the first friend I made on my way up into Labrador. And though he couldn't tell me much about Laroche—he had just seen him that once as they carried him out on a stretcher to the waiting plane—he had given me the name of the man who could.

I gleaned a lot of useful information from him, too. Camp 224 was a big place, highly organised, with a large engineering staff sending daily reports back to the Seven Islands base by teleprinter. Obviously no place for me. They'd know immediately that I'd no business to be up the line. Some twenty miles beyond 224 was Head of Steel. And after that there was nothing but the newly-constructed grade gradually petering out into isolated construction units slicing into virgin country with bulldozer and grab crane. No railway, no telephone link —nothing but the old Tote Road and the airstrips to link the camps with Base. Camp 263 he described as growing fast, but still just a clearing in the jackpine forest, primitive and pretty grim. " The only decent camp between Two-two-four and the permanent camp at Menihek Dam is Two-ninety," he said. " It's right on the lake with a big airstrip on a hill. Mostly C.M.M.K. personnel—that's the construction combine that's building the grade. They even got a helicopter stationed there for the use of the grade superintendent."

" A helicopter!" But even if I could persuade the pilot to

take me up in it, I didn't know where Lake of the Lion was. Laroche had said there were thousands of lakes and, remembering what the country had been like flying down from Goose, I could well believe it. Had my father known where the lake was? And if my father had known, would my mother know?

Perkins was explaining that they'd used the helicopter to try and bring out the bodies of Briffe and Baird. "He had two tries at it. But it wasn't any good. He couldn't find the place."

"Who couldn't—Laroche?" I asked.

"Aye, that's right. Like I said, he came back just two days after he'd been flown out. Proper mess he looked, too—a great gash in his head and his face white as chalk. They shouldn't have let him come, but he said he had to try and locate the place, and Len Holt, he's the pilot, flew him in twice. It didn't do any good, though. He couldn't find it. I saw him when he came back the second time. They had to lift him out, poor chap, he was so done up."

"Did a man called McGovern come up with him?" I asked. But he shook his head. "No, Laroche was on his own."

I asked him then about Camp 263. But he couldn't tell me anything more than he'd told me already. He'd never been there. He'd just heard men talking about it. "They say it's pretty rough. And the grub's bad. It's a new camp. All new construction camps are rough." And he looked across at me curiously and said, "You're not going there, are you?"

I'd made up my mind by then. I wasn't waiting for Laroche. I wanted to see Darcy first. "Yes," I said. "I've got to get up there as soon as possible." And I asked him whether there was any way of getting north that night. "It's urgent," I added.

"What about Laroche?" He was looking at me curiously. "He says to wait for him."

"Tell him I'll contact him from Two-sixty-three."

"But——"

"Laroche isn't employed by the Company," I said quickly. "I've been told to get up there as fast as I can and I'm sticking to my instructions. West has been injured and there's been a switch of engineers."

He nodded. "That's right. Got his foot crushed by a gas car." I thought for a moment he was going to pursue the subject. But all he said was, " Aye. Well, you know your business best."

" Is there a flight going up from here to-night?" I asked him.

He shook his head. " Northbound flights don't stop here any more. This camp's pretty well finished now. Another month and it'll close down altogether, I wouldn't wonder." And then he added, " Your best bet is the supply train. You'd see your friend Laroche then and still be up at Head of Steel before dark to-morrow."

So I was stuck here. " You're sure there's nothing else?" And then, because I was afraid he might think I was trying to avoid Laroche, I said, " I'm supposed to be at Two-sixty-three to-morrow."

He shook his head. " No, there's nothing . . ." He stopped then. " Wait a jiffy. I got an idea the ballast train's been held up to-night." He went out into the despatch office and I heard him talking to the despatcher and then the sound of the phone. After a while he came back and said, " It's okay if you want to take it. Usually it's left by now, but the ballast got froze going up the line last night, so she was late back and they're still loading."

" When will it leave?" I asked.

" Not before two. They've still quite a few wagons to load. That's what the foreman told me anyway."

I asked him how far it would take me and he told me they were ballasting right up behind Head of Steel. " And it doesn't stop anywhere, like the supply train," he added. " You'll be up there in a matter of four hours." He poured himself another mug of tea. " Well, shall I tell Sid you'll take it?" And he added, " It won't be all that comfortable, mind."

" It doesn't matter," I said. All I wanted was to see Darcy before Laroche caught up with me.

He nodded and went out again, carrying his mug carefully. It was intensely hot in the radio room and I began to feel drowsy. " Okay," he said when he came back. " You'll ride up in the caboose with Onry Gaspard. He's the train conductor. He'll look after you." He glanced at his watch. " You've got four hours before the train leaves. You'd better hit the hay for a bit. You look proper played out."

I nodded. Now that it was all fixed I felt very tired. " I was flying all last night," I explained. And then I remembered that

Farrow was expecting me at Dorval Airport in the morning. There was Mr. Meadows to notify, too—and my mother. I ought to tell her where I was. " I'll have to write some letters," I said. And I explained that people back home didn't even know I was in Canada.

" Why not cable them then?" He went over to the radio and tore a sheet off a message pad. "There you are. Write your message down on that and I'll radio it to Base right away."

It was as easy as that, and I remembered how small the world had seemed in that little basement room of Simon Ledder's house. I hesitated. " I suppose you couldn't contact a ham radio operator at Goose for me?"

He looked doubtful. " I could try," he said. " Depends whether he's keeping watch or not. What's his call sign?"

" VO6AZ," I told him. And I gave the frequency.

" VO6AZ!" He was looking at me curiously. " That's the ham who was acting as contact for Briffe's party."

I nodded, afraid that he'd start asking a lot of questions. " Will you try and get him for me?"

He didn't say anything for a moment. He seemed to be thinking it out. " Okay," he said finally. " It may take a little time. And I may not be able to get him at all. Do you want to speak to him personally or would a message do?"

" A message," I said. " That's all."

" What's his job at Goose? Is he with the Air Force?"

" No," I said. " He's with D.O.T. Communications."

" Goose Radio. Well, suppose I send it to them? I can always get Goose Radio."

" That would do fine," I said.

" Aye, well, you write the message and I'll let you know whether I've been able to send it when I come off watch." He pulled a pencil from behind his ear and handed it to me.

I sat there for a moment, uncertain what to say, conscious that he was standing over me, watching me curiously. Twice I started to write and then crossed it out. My brain was sluggish with lack of sleep and I wasn't certain how much I dared say. At length I wrote: *Company refuse take seriously. Going north into Labrador to try and find Lake of the Lion. Please notify Farrow. Request him on return Bristol to notify Meadows, Runway Construction Engineer, also my mother, Mrs. Ferguson, 119 Lansdown Grove Road, London, N.W.1. Would he telegraph her and ask her did my father ever tell her exact location of Lake of the Lion. Reply c/o Perkins, radio operator, Camp 134, Q.N.S. & L., Seven Islands. Thanks for all your help. Ian Ferguson.* I read it through and handed it to him. " I hope you don't mind me using you as a post box?" I said.

" That's okay." He stood, reading it through, and then he was looking at me and I knew there were questions he wanted to ask. But in the end he stuffed the message in his pocket. " Well, if you're going to get any sleep to-night you'd better get down to the camp," he said. " There's a truck outside will take you down. You can have the spare bed in my room."

I thanked him. " I'd appreciate it," I added, " if you'd regard that message as confidential."

" Aye," he said slowly. " I won't talk." He gave me a side-long glance. " But if you weren't English and I didn't like you, I might act different." And I knew he'd guessed why I was here. He couldn't very well help it with Laroche radio-ing for me to wait for him. " Come on," he said. " I'll get the driver to run you down to our bunkhouse. And I'll let you know what luck I've had with this message when I come off duty at midnight."

He took me out to the truck then and told the driver where to take me. " Call him at one-thirty," he said. " He's taking the ballast train north."

The northern lights were gone now. The night was black with just one star low over the jackpines. A bitter wind sifted a light dusting of powdery snow along the ground. " If I don't wake you when I come in, you'll know your message has gone off all right," Bob Perkins called up to me. " And I'll tell Laroche when he gets in that he'll find you up at Two-sixty-three. Okay?" He grinned up at me as the truck lurched forward.

We swung round the end of the airstrip buildings and out on to a dirt road where ruts stood out like furrows in the head-lights. It was like that all the way to the camp, the ruts hard like concrete, and then we stopped outside the dim bulk of a wooden hut. " Okay, feller. This-a your bunk'ouse." The driver was Italian. " You want me call you 'alf-past one, eh?"

" Half-past one," I said. " Don't forget, will you? The train leaves at two."

" Okay. I don't forget."

He gunned the engine and the truck bumped away over the

ruts, the swinging beam of its headlights shining momentarily on the little cluster of huts that was Camp 134. Somewhere in the darkness an electric generator throbbed steadily. There was no other sound. A few lights glimmered. The place had a loneliness and a desolation about it that was almost frightening.

I went into the bunkhouse and switched on the light. The naked bulb lit a small passage with a shower and lavatory at the end. The bare floorboards were covered with a black, glacial sand that was gritty underfoot. A diesel stove roared in the corner, giving out a great blast of heat. There were three rooms, two of them with the doors wide open so that I could see that the beds were occupied. I opened the door nearest the shower. It was cooler there and both beds were empty. On the table between them stood a leather-framed photograph of my Lancashire friend and a girl holding hands. There was a litter of paper-backs, mostly westerns, and a half-completed model of a square-rigged sailing ship. There was a bed roll parked in one corner and the cupboard space was full of cold-weather clothing.

Two canvas grips marked with the name Koster lay on top of one of the beds. I put these on the floor beside my own suitcase, switched off the light and turned in, not bothering to remove anything but my jacket and trousers. There were no sheets and the blankets were coarse and heavy with sand. Their musty smell stayed in my nostrils a long time, for sleep did not come easily. I had too much to think about. And when I did doze off, it seemed only a moment before I was dragged back to consciousness by somebody shaking my shoulder. " Is it time?" I asked, remembering the ballast train. The light was on and as I opened my eyes I saw the empty bed opposite and the alarm clock hanging on the wall. It wasn't yet midnight. And then I looked up at the man who had woken me, saw the half-healed wound running down through the shaved hair of the scalp and sat bolt upright in the bed. " You!" I was suddenly wide awake, filled with an unreasoning panic. " How did you get here?"

" I came by plane." Laroche had let go of my shoulder and was standing there, staring down at me. " I was afraid I'd miss you if I waited for the supply train." He unzipped his parka and sat down on the foot of the bed, tugging at the silk scarf round his neck. " It's hot in here," he said.

The diesel heater in the passage was going full blast and the boarded and papered window gave no ventilation. I could feel the sweat clammy on my face and lying in a hot, uncomfortable pool round my neck. The atmosphere was stifling. But that wasn't the reason why my heart was pounding.

"Sorry to wake you. Guess you must be pretty tired."

I didn't say anything. I couldn't trust myself to speak. The truth was, I was scared of the man. I can't really explain it, even now. I don't think it was the scar, though it stood out as a livid disfigurement in the white glare of the naked light bulb; and it certainly wasn't anything to do with the cast of his features or the expression of his eyes. There was nothing about him, except the unexpectedness of his arrival, to make me afraid of him. But that was my instinctive reaction and I can only think that, in the instant of waking, something of his mental state was communicated to me.

He had taken off his silk scarf and was wiping his face with it, and I wondered what he was going to do now that he'd caught up with me. I watched him remove his parka, and then he was sitting there in a thick woollen bush shirt buttoned at the wrist, staring at nothing. He looked desperately tired, the high cheek-bones staring through the sallow, tight-drawn skin and the shadows deep under the eyes.

"Have you told Lands I'm here?" I asked him, and my voice sounded dry and hoarse.

"No." He reached into the pocket of his parka and produced a packet of cigarettes and offered it to me. It was an automatic gesture and when I shook my head, he put a cigarette in his mouth and sat there, staring at the floor, as though too tired to light it. "I wanted to talk to you first," he said. And then after a while he reached into his trouser pocket for a match and struck it with a flick of his thumb nail against the head. The flare of it as he lit the cigarette momentarily softened the contours of his face and showed me the eyes withdrawn into some secret pocket of thought. His hands trembled slightly and he drew the smoke into his lungs as though his nerves were crying out for it. And then, abruptly, he said, "Why did you jump that plane and come up here? Didn't you believe what I told you?" He was still staring at the floor.

I didn't say anything and silence hung over the room so that the metallic ticking of the alarm clock sounded unnaturally loud and I could hear the murmur of breathing from the next room. The stillness of the world outside seemed to creep in through the flimsy wooden walls, and all the time I was wondering why he hadn't told Lands, why he had needed to see me first.

"Why didn't you believe me?" he demanded sharply, as though the silence were getting on his nerves. "You didn't believe, did you?"

"It's not a question of whether I believed you or not," I said.

He nodded. "No, I guess not." His hands gripped the silk scarf as though he wanted to tear it in shreds. And then he muttered something that sounded like "Fate" and shook his head. "I still can't believe it's true," he breathed. "That old man's son, sitting there at his radio, listening to the reports, waiting for it to happen."

"Do you mean my father?"

But he didn't seem to hear. "It's like a nightmare," he whispered. And then he turned his head, looking straight at me, and said, "I suppose you think I killed them or something?" He gave a quick, harsh laugh.

It wasn't said jokingly, but with sudden violence, and the harshness of that laugh shocked me as much as the words.

"Because my name is Laroche, eh?" he added, and there was bitterness in his voice. "Oh, you needn't look so startled," he said. "I knew what your father had been thinking as soon as I read Ledder's report." He dropped the scarf, reached forward and gripped hold of my wrist, speaking very earnestly. "You must believe this. I'm not responsible for their death. That's the truth. It's nothing to do with me." And he repeated it. "I'm not responsible."

"It never occurred to me you were." I was staring at him, appalled that he'd found it necessary to make such a declaration.

"No?" He stared at me, his eyes searching my face. "Then why are you here? Why, when nobody believes you, do you tell Paule that I'm a liar and that her father is still alive. *Mon Dieu!* And then to say you are employed by Staffen and come up the line when you are booked out to Montreal. . . . Do you think I don't know what's been planted in your mind? *C'est incroyable!*" he breathed, and he reached out to the table between the beds and stubbed his cigarette out viciously in the tobacco tin that served as an ash tray.

He picked up his silk scarf and wiped his face again. I think he was sweating as much with exhaustion as the heat of the room. "It would have been better if you'd told Mack the truth this afternoon," he said wearily. "Then we could have had it out, there in that office, just the three of us. If you'd told him the reason you were here . . ."

"But I did tell him," I said. Surely he couldn't have sat there in that office and not heard a word I was saying? "I came because my father picked up a message from Briffe and I——"

"That's not the reason." He said it impatiently, brushing my explanation aside with an angry movement of his hand.

"But it is the reason," I insisted.

"Oh, for God's sake!" he cried. "I'm not a fool. You couldn't be that much concerned about a man you'd never met before. How old are you?" he asked abruptly.

"Twenty-three," I told him.

"And I bet you've never been out of England before in your life."

"Yes, I have," I said. "Once. A holiday in Belgium."

"A holiday in Belgium!" He repeated it in a way that made me feel small, remembering that he must have flown thousands of miles over unmapped territory. "And you expect me to believe that you hitched a ride in a trans-Atlantic flight and came all the way over to Canada, where you don't know a soul, just because of a man you'd never met, never even heard of till your father told you about him. You'd reported the matter to the authorities. You'd have left it at that if you hadn't been driven by something more personal."

"But if they're still alive——"

"They're dead." He said it harshly.

"Then how could my father have picked up that transmission?"

But he didn't seem interested in the fact that Briffe had made contact with the outside world. "Why did you lie to him?" he demanded.

"Lie to him?"

"Yes, to McGovern."

"But I didn't lie to him," I cried. "I told him the truth. My father died because——"

"You lied to him," he almost shouted at me. "You told

him you didn't know the name of the man who'd accompanied your grandfather."

"Well, it's true," I said. "I'd never heard of the Ferguson Expedition until I talked to Ledder at Goose."

"You'd never heard of it!" He stared at me as though I'd said the earth was flat. "But that's absurd. You've admitted your father was obsessed by Labrador. You couldn't have grown up not knowing the reason for that obsession. And then, when you heard about that transmission—you must have known the reason he invented it otherwise you'd never have come all this way. . . ."

"He didn't invent it," I declared hotly.

"Well, imagined it then."

"He didn't imagine it either." I was suddenly trembling with anger. Couldn't he understand that this was real, so real that it had brought about my father's death? "He picked up a transmission and recorded it in his log. And that transmission was from Briffe. I don't care what you or anybody else says——"

"He couldn't have." His voice was pitched suddenly higher. "The radio was in the aircraft when it sank. I told you that before. He couldn't possibly have transmitted." It was almost as though he were trying to convince himself, and I stared at him, the sweat suddenly cold on my body. He hadn't said because Briffe was dead. He'd simply said that the radio was in the plane when it sank. "And what about Briffe?" I said.

But he only repeated what he'd said already. "He couldn't have transmitted that message." It was said softly this time, to himself. He was so wrought up that he hadn't even understood the significance of my question. And then his mind switched abruptly back to the Ferguson Expedition. It seemed to worry him that I hadn't known about it. "I don't believe it," he murmured. "You couldn't possibly have grown up not knowing about your grandfather and what happened to him."

"Well, I did," I said. It seemed so unimportant. "What difference does it make anyway? All I'm concerned about——"

"What difference does it make?" He was staring at me and the perspiration was gathering on his forehead again. "It means . . ." He shook his head. "It's not possible," he murmured. "It's too much of a coincidence." And then he looked at me and said, "Why didn't they tell you?" He seemed unable to leave the subject alone.

And for some reason it seemed to me important at that moment to convince him. "I think it was my mother," I said. And I told him how she'd tried to keep the final log book from me. "She was afraid of Labrador. I think she didn't want me involved and made my father promise——"

"But that woman," he said impatiently. "There was the diary . . ." He checked himself. "When did your grandmother die?"

"I was ten, I think."

"Then you were old enough . . ." He stared at me. "Didn't she ever talk to you about your grandfather? She must have. A woman so determined, so full of hate. . . . Well, didn't she?"

"Once, when I was very small," I said. "She came to my room and talked to me. But I was frightened and my mother found her there, and after that we never visited her again."

That seemed to convince him finally, for he said quietly, "So you came over here without knowing anything about the Expedition." There was a note of weariness in his voice.

"Yes," I said. "The first I heard of it was from Ledder." And I added, "Why is that so important to you?"

But his mind had leapt to something else. "And yet you know it was Lake of the Lion. How? How could you possibly know unless . . ." He stopped there and brushed his hand over his eyes. "The entry in the log, of course—the map, Ledder's report. You were guessing. Just guessing." His voice had dropped to a murmur; he looked suddenly smaller, his shoulders hunched. "*Mon Dieu!*" he breathed. "So it is true." He wiped his face again, slowly, and his hands were trembling.

"What's true?" I asked.

"About the transmission." He must have answered without thinking, for he added quickly, "That that's the reason you are here. I had to be sure," he mumbled. And then he got quickly to his feet. "I must get some sleep," he said. Again that movement of the hand across the eyes. "My head aches." He seemed suddenly to want to escape from the room. But by then my mind had fastened on the implications of what he had said. "Then it was Lake of the Lion," I said. "You told me you hadn't noticed . . ."

The sudden wild look in his eyes silenced me. He was standing at the foot of the bed, staring down at me. "What difference does it make to you whether it was Lake of the Lion or not?" he asked, his voice trembling. "You say you know nothing of what happened there before. So what difference does it make?"

"None," I said quickly, my skin suddenly chill. And then I added because I had to: "Except that if you knew where Briffe was transmitting from . . ."

"He didn't transmit," he almost shouted at me. "Nobody transmitted from that place."

"Then how did my father manage to pick up——"

"I tell you there was no transmission," he cried. His face was quite white. "Your father imagined it. He was mad—obsessed with Labrador—the whole thing locked up too long inside of him. It was what he saw in his mind—nothing more." He was breathing heavily, so wrought up that the words poured out of him. "It must be that. It must be," he reiterated as though by repetition it would become reality. "Briffe had nothing to transmit with. And that bit about Baird. . . . Bill Baird was dead. I'm sure he was dead."

"And Briffe?" I said in a whisper. "Was Briffe dead?" His eyes focused on me slowly and I saw them dilate as he realised what he'd been saying. He opened his mouth, but no words came, and it was then that I knew for certain that he'd left Briffe alive. He couldn't bring himself to repeat the lie he'd told so glibly in Lands' office, and I sat there, staring at him, unable to hide the feeling of revulsion that had suddenly enveloped me.

"Why are you staring at me like that?" he cried suddenly. And then he got a grip on himself. "That damned scar, of course. Makes me look odd." He laughed uneasily and reached for his parka.

He was leaving and I sat there, not daring to ask why he hadn't reported my presence up the line or why he was so concerned about the Ferguson Expedition. I just wanted to be rid of him.

"I must get some sleep." He had pulled on the parka and was muttering to himself. "It's sleep I need." He turned blindly towards the door. But then he stopped as though jerked back by the string of some sudden thought. "What are you going to do now?" he asked, turning to face me again. "You should go home. Nobody believes you."

I kept still and didn't say anything, hoping he'd go. But he came back to the foot of the bed. "You're going on. Is that it? Into the bush? To try and find them?" It was as though he were reading my thoughts and I wondered whether that was what I was really going to do, for I hadn't dared think beyond Darcy and Camp 263. "You'll never get there," he said. "Never." He swallowed jerkily. "You don't know what it's like. There's nothing. Nothing at all. Jackpine and muskeg and reindeer moss and water—lake after lake. You're crazy to think of it. You'll die. You don't know what it's like."

I heard the door of the hut open and footsteps sounded on the bare boards. And then Bob Perkins was there, stopped in the doorway by the sight of Laroche. "Sorry," he said, looking uncertainly at the two of us. "Thought you'd be asleep." He hesitated, and then said, "If you two want to talk . . ."

"No," I said quickly. "No, we've finished." I was intensely relieved to see him.

Laroche hesitated, staring at Perkins. "I must think . . ." he murmured. And then he turned to me. "The supply train doesn't get in till eight to-morrow. I checked. And there are no planes. I'll see you again in the morning . . . when I've had some sleep." He was fumbling with the scarf which he was tying round his neck. "I'll talk to you again then." And he pushed past Perkins, walking slowly like a man in a daze so that his footsteps dragged on the boards, and then the outer door closed and he was gone.

I felt the sweat damp on my face then and realised I was trembling. "That was Laroche, wasn't it?" Perkins asked.

I nodded, feeling suddenly limp.

"Thought so." He was looking at me curiously. "He hopped a northbound flight and persuaded the pilot to land him here." I thought he was going to question me, but in the end he went over to his bed and began to undress. "By the way," he said, "I got your message through to Goose."

"Thanks."

"I couldn't get Ledder. But they'll give it to him."

"Sorry to have been a nuisance."

"Oh, that's all right." He hesitated, unwilling to leave it at that. But when I didn't say anything, he switched off the light and got into bed. " You've another hour and a half before Luigi calls you." And then he added. " You don't want Laroche to know where you've gone, do you?"

" No," I said.

" Okay, I won't tell him. And I won't tell him about the message either."

" Thank you." And I added, " You've been a good friend."

" Aye, well, I like to help anybody from the Old Country. Good night and *bon voyage,* as the French say."

A moment later he was snoring peacefully. But I couldn't sleep, for my mind was too full of Laroche's visit. His manner had been so strange, and the tension in him ; there was something there, something I didn't understand, some secret locked away inside him. The way he had said: *I suppose you think I killed them.* And that interest in the Ferguson Expedition— it was almost pathological. Or was his manner, everything, the result of his injury? All I knew was that he'd left Briffe alive and that I had to find somebody who would believe me—or else locate this Lake of the Lion myself.

It seemed an age before the truck came. But at last I heard it draw up outside and then the light in the passage went on and the driver poked his head round the door. " If you want the ballast train, mister, you better hurry."

Perkins didn't stir. He lay on his back with his mouth open, snoring. I slipped into my clothes and went out to the truck with my suitcase. The night was bitterly cold—no stars now, not a glimmer of light from the sleeping camp. We took the same road with its iron ruts, bumping and lurching out past the airstrip buildings to the ballast pit where the train stood black in the headlights on the top of an embankment.

The driver set me down right below the caboose. It was an old-fashioned guard's van with an iron chimney poking out through the roof, and as the truck drove off, a torch flashed above me. " Who's that?" a voice called out of the night. And when I explained, he shouted, " Henri ! Passenger for you."

An oil lamp flickered beside the ballast wagons and a voice answered, " *Bon, bon.*" He was there waiting for me when I reached the track. " *Bonjour, M'sieur.*" The lamp was flashed on my face. " Ah, but of course. You are Eenglish, no? I am Henri Gaspard." As he shook my hand his face showed in the glow of the lamp he held. It was a sad, lined face with a little waxed moustache. Incredibly he wore an old C.P.R. pillbox hat complete with gold braid. The effect in this desolate place was strangely old-world, as though he had stepped out of a print illustrating the dress of a soldier of the *Grande Armée*. " You are only just in time, *mon ami*. We are leaving now." He led me to the caboose and waved me in. " My 'ome," he said. " *Entrez, M'sieur.*"

He left me then and I swung myself up into the van. Inside it was spotlessly clean and surprisingly cosy. There was a cabin with lower and upper berths on either side, and beyond that a sort of saloon with leather-cushioned seats and a table, and right at the end a wood-fired stove as big as a kitchen range. Mahogany panels and the oil lamp swung from the roof completed the Edwardian atmosphere.

I sat down, suddenly exhausted. Lying in that dark room in the bunkhouse, thinking of Laroche, I had been afraid I should never make this next stage, and now I was here.

For a long time nothing happened, and then suddenly there were shouts and a whistle blew. I went out on to the platform at the back. Torches flickered along the line and the black silence of the night was suddenly broken by the mournful hoot of the locomotive. Couplings clashed in a rising crescendo of sound that culminated in the caboose being jerked into motion. Henri swung himself up on to the platform beside me. " *Alors, n'marchons.*"

I stayed there, watching the single lit window that marked the airstrip buildings slide past. After that there was nothing, no glimmer of light, no sign of the camp. The jackpine forest had closed round us and there was only the rattle of the wheels on the rail joints and the cold and the black night. I went back into the warmth of the caboose where the oil lamp danced on its hook and Henri stood at the stove brewing coffee.

I had a cup of coffee and a cigarette with him, and then excused myself and went to bed in one of the upper bunks. This time I fell asleep at once and lay like a log, only dimly conscious of the stops and the sound of movement and voices. And after a long time there were shouts and the clash of couplings and I woke up, feeling cold and cramped and sweaty with sleeping in my clothes. And when I rolled over to face the grimy window, I found myself staring out into a cold grey world of Christmas trees all dusted white with snow, and I could hardly believe it.

I clambered slowly down from the bunk and went out to the rear of the caboose. Men were walking along beside the train, winding open the double floor doors of the wagons so that they spilled ballast out on either side of the track as they trundled slowly forward. The rails ran out behind us in two black threads that were finally swallowed up in the white of the jackpine, and when I dropped to the ground so that I could look ahead, it was the same . . . there was nothing anywhere in that cold, harsh world but the train, a black and lonely intruder.

I climbed back into the caboose, for I wasn't dressed for this sort of cold. There was nobody else there now and I sat on the lower berth, shivering and looking out through the window. A board with 235 painted on it slid past and shortly afterwards the train clanked over some points and stopped. We shunted backwards then, switching on to another track, and finally came to rest. "*Le fin du voyage*," Henri called to me from the rear platform. "Come. I give you to my friend Georges."

I followed him out of the caboose to find we were on a section of double track. Parked close behind us was a line of old coaches with smoke rising from their iron chimneys. "Bunk-'ouse train," Henri said as we trudged through soft snow already more than an inch deep. "You get brekf'st 'ere." He looked down at my shoes. "*Pas bon*," he said, and shook his head. "You get clothes from store queek, *mon ami*—or you die, eh?" And he smiled at me. "*C'est le mauvais temps*. The snow, she come too soon this year."

We clambered up into the fourth coach. A bare trestle table with wooden benches on either side ran the length of it, and from the far end came the smell of coffee and the sizzle of frying. It was hot like an oven after the cold outside. "Georges!" A big man in a dirty white apron emerged. I was introduced and then Henri shook my hand and left. "Breakfast in quarter of an hour," Georges said and disappeared into the cookhouse.

A little later men began to pile in, a mixed, half-dressed crowd who filled the benches and sat there, still red-eyed with sleep and not talking. A boy heaped food on the table—steaks and bacon and eggs, great piles of bread, pots of coffee and tea and tin bowls full of cornflakes. It was a gargantuan breakfast eaten hurriedly, the only conversation shouted demands to pass this or that. And then they were gone as quickly as they had come, like a plague of locusts, leaving behind a table full of scraps and the swill bin at the end half full, with their plates piled and their knives and forks in a tub of hot water.

What did I do now? I sat there, finishing my coffee, whilst the boy cleared the debris from the table. Outside the snow was thicker than ever, big wet flakes swirling softly. There was the hoot of a diesel and then the empty ballast train went clanking past the windows. And when it was gone there was nothing but the empty track and beyond that a dreary view of stunted jackpine growing reluctantly out of flat, swampy ground, and everything white with snow. I hadn't expected the winter to be so early.

And then Georges came in and I asked him how I could get up to Head of Steel. " Is anybody going up from here, do you think?" I asked him.

He shook his head. " The boys 'ere are ballast gang. They're rail lifting and packing the ballast you just brought up. They ain't going to Head of Steel. But I guess there'll be somebody come through with a gas car during the day." And he added, " You want some clothes? It's cold riding them little speeders."

" Can I get some here?" I asked. " I had to leave in a hurry. . . ."

He nodded. " Guess I can fix you up. The boys are always leaving stuff behind. But they'll be cast-offs mind."

He went out and a few minutes later came back with a sordid looking bundle. " Sort those over an' take anything you fancy." He dumped them on the table. " There's a parka there ain't at all bad, an' there's a pair of boots look all right." He nodded and left me.

The parka was a padded waterproof jacket, black with grease and dirt, and its hood was torn. There was an old fur cap with ear flaps and a pair of gloves with the fingers worn through and waterproof trousers stiff with grease. The trousers were tight and the parka too big, but there was a pair of boots that were a reasonable fit. I went into the kitchen and tried to buy them off him with the twenty dollars Lands had given me, but he said they weren't worth anything anyway; and after that I went back to the diner and sat there, staring out of the window, watching the track.

But the track remained empty. Nothing came. And now that I was equipped to withstand the weather, the snow stopped and the sun came out.

I was still there when the ballast gang returned for lunch. Halfway through a large steak I thought I heard the hoot of a locomotive. It was a faint, far-away sound, scarcely audible above the noise of fifty men shovelling energy back into their bodies, but I jumped to my feet and went to the door, peering out along the line of the through track.

At first I thought I must have been mistaken. North and south the track was empty, the black lines running out into the nothingness of Labrador. Then it came again, a sad sound carried by the wind, and far down the track to the south my eyes became focused on a small blob that didn't seem to move, but yet grew steadily larger.

I jumped down and stood beside the track, watching it grow until I could see the yellow of the diesel's paintwork against the drab white background of melting snow. It passed the points into the double track and as it came thundering down on me, I could feel the weight of it beating at the ground under my feet.

The track in front of me was leaping under the vibration, and then it was on me with a rush of air, pressing me back against the dining coach. There was a smell of hot oil, a glimpse of huge driving wheels, and behind it clattered a long line of steel transporters, their specially-constructed bogies beating a rapid tattoo. Wagons full of sleepers followed and, behind them, two coaches, and finally the caboose.

I clambered back into the diner and sat down again at the table. "Was that the supply train?" I asked the man next to me.

He nodded, his mouth full, and I finished my steak, wondering whether Laroche had been in one of the coaches.

The men were beginning to drift back to work and I went with them. Their transport, parked at the tail-end of the bunk-house train, consisted of small rail cars, hitched together in trains of three. With their upright coachwork, they looked like the rolling stock of an old-fashioned mountain railway. "Are you going up towards Head of Steel?" I asked the foreman. But he shook his head. He had a small, open speeder with a Perspex windshield and I stood and watched him as he put it in gear, eased forward the belt drive clutch and went trundling down the track behind his gang. He paused just clear of the points to switch them back to the through-track position and then ran on down the line, the fussy putter of the engine dwindling rapidly.

The brief interlude of sun was over. The world was cold and grey and I went back to the warmth of the diner, wishing now that I'd come up on the supply train. The tables had been cleared, the benches pushed back against the sides of the coach. It was nearly one-thirty. Farrow would be headed for home now. But it was difficult to believe in England up here in this wild country. I sat down by one of the windows, staring out across the empty main track to the solid wall of jackpine beyond. I'd give it until three. If I didn't get a lift by three I'd start walking. Ten miles . . . say, four hours. I'd be at Head of Steel about dusk. Nobody would see me then and I could slip past the supply train and head north.

Time passed slowly and nobody came up the line. And then, when it was almost three and I was getting ready to leave, voices sounded below the window, and a moment later the door at the end slid back with a crash, and two men entered, shouting for Georges and demanding coffee and doughnuts. "Mr. Lands been through here yet?" the elder of the two asked.

"Sorry, Mr. Steel, I don't see him for two weeks or more," Georges answered. Steel came on into the diner, pulling off his fur-lined gloves and throwing them on to the table. He was dressed entirely in olive green with a peaked ski cap, and his thin, lined face looked pinched with cold. "You here about this esker that's been located?" he asked, looking straight at me.

"No," I said. I didn't know what an esker was and all I wanted was to get out of there before Lands arrived. I picked up my gloves and fur cap.

But his companion stood between me and the door, a big, broad-shouldered youngster in a fur cap and scarlet-lined hunting parka. "What's your job?" he demanded. He had an Irish accent.

"Engineer," I answered without thinking. And then I checked, for I knew I'd made a mistake. These men were engineers themselves.

"Then you can probably tell us something about it," Steel said. "All we've heard is that there's talk of pushing a spur line in and starting a new ballast pit."

"I'm new here," I said quickly. "I don't know anything about it."

He nodded, his eyes fixed on my face. "Thought I hadn't seen you before. Straight up from Base, are you?"

"Yes." I didn't know quite what to do. I felt that if I left now he'd be suspicious. And then Georges came in with the coffee and a heaped plate of doughnuts. "You like coffee, too?" he asked me, and I saw that there were three mugs on the tray.

"You staying here or going on up the line?" Steel asked me, his mouth already full of doughnut.

"Going on," I said, gulping the coffee though it was scalding hot. I had to get out of here somehow before Lands arrived.

"We can probably give you a lift as far as Head of Steel. Where are you bound for?"

I hesitated. But it didn't seem to matter. "Two-six-three," I said.

"Crazy Darcy, eh?" His companion gave a loud guffaw. "Jesus Christ! So they haven't rumbled him yet, the old devil."

"What Paddy means," Steel said, dunking his doughnut, "is that Ray is one of the old-timers on this railroad."

"What I mean is that he's an old rogue and you'll do all the work for him whilst he takes the credit—if you're a hard-working, sober, God-fearing engineer, which is what we all are seeing this is the Wilderness and no Garden of Eden running with the milk of human kindness that comes from my native land."

"There's no liquor allowed up here," Steel said. "That's what he means. It's a subject of conversation that gets kind of boring after you've been up here a while." He was looking at me curiously. "Your name wouldn't be Ferguson, would it?"

I nodded, my body suddenly tense, wondering what was coming.

But all he said was, "Somebody was inquiring for you just as we left Head of Steel."

"Laroche?" The question seemed dragged out of me.

" That's the guy, yes. The pilot of that plane that crashed. You know him?"

I nodded, thinking that now he was between me and Two-six-three.

" Bad business, that crash," Steel said. " Did he ever talk to you about it?"

But all I could think of was the fact that Laroche had been on the supply train. " What did he want?" I asked. " Did he tell you what he wanted?"

" No. Just asked if we'd seen you. But it seemed urgent." And then he went back to the subject of the crash. " I guess it must've been a hell of a shock to him, both his passengers dead and then struggling out alone like that. Makes you realise what this country's like soon as you get away from the grade." And he added, " I heard he was engaged to Briffe's daughter. Is that true?"

The sound of a speeder came from the track outside and the Irishman jumped to his feet and went to the window. " Here's Bill now."

Laroche at Head of Steel and now Lands. I felt suddenly trapped. The speeder had stopped outside the diner, the engine ticking over with a gentle putter that was muffled by the thick glass of the windows. Boots sounded on the iron grating at the end of the coach and then the door slammed back. I only just had time to turn away towards the window before Bill Lands was there.

" You got my message then, Al." His voice was right behind me as he came down the coach. " And you brought Paddy with you. That's swell."

He was down by the stove now and I glanced at him quickly. He looked even bigger in his parka and the fur cap made his face look tougher, a part of the North. " You want some cawfee, Bill?" Steel was standing to make room for him.

" Sure," Lands said, his hands held out to the hot casing of the stove. " And some doughnuts. You know why I asked you and Paddy to meet me here?"

" There was some talk about an esker——"

" That's it. Williams found it." His voice was muffled by the doughnut he was wolfing down. " Thought it might solve our problem. That ballast coming up from One-three-four is start-ing to get froze. But if we could open up a ballast pit here, right behind Head of Steel . . ." He checked suddenly and said, " Hell! My speeder's still on the track. Hey, you!"

I knew he'd turned and was staring at my back. I couldn't ignore him and at the same time I didn't dare turn to face him. " Can you drive a speeder?" he demanded.

It was the opportunity I'd been wanting, the excuse to get out without raising their suspicions. But I hesitated because the door seemed a long way off and I was afraid my voice might give me away.

" I asked you whether you could drive a speeder." His voice was impatient.

" Sure," I said, and started for the door.

Maybe it was my voice or maybe I moved too quickly. I heard him say, " Who is that guy?" But he didn't wait for an answer. He was already coming down the coach after me. " Just a minute!"

I had almost reached the door where my suitcase stood and I might have made a dash for it then, but I hadn't had time to think what the use of a speeder could mean to me. I just felt it was hopeless to try and get away from him, and so I turned and faced him.

He had almost caught up with me, but when I turned and he saw my face, he stopped abruptly. " Ferguson!". There was a look of blank astonishment in his eyes as though he couldn't believe it. " How the hell . . ." And then his big hands clenched and the muscles of his jaw tightened.

It was the knowledge that he was going to hit me that made my brain seize on the one thing that might stop him. " Briffe is alive," I said.

He checked then. " Alive?"

" At least he was when Laroche left him. I'm certain of that now."

" And what makes you so damned certain?" His voice was dangerously calm.

" Laroche," I said. " He came to my room last night and he virtually admitted——"

" What room? Where?"

" At One-three-four."

" One-three-four. That's a lie. Bert's at Seven Islands."

" No," I said. " He's at Head of Steel right now. Ask them." And I nodded at the two engineers.

That seemed to shake him for he said, " He followed you, did he?"

" Yes," I said. " He's scared and——"

" So would I be scared. I'd be scared as hell if I knew some crazy fool——"

" It's not me that's crazy," I cried.

He stared at me. " What do you mean by that?" His voice had suddenly gone quiet again.

" It's Laroche," I said quickly. " For some reason he can't get the Ferguson Expedition out of his mind. He crashed at Lake of the Lion and something happened there that's driving him" He had taken a step forward and my voice trailed away. away.

" Go on," he said ominously. " You think something happened there? What do you think happened?"

" I don't know," I murmured. " But it's preying on his mind."

" What is?"

" I don't know," I repeated. " That's what I've got to find out. But he asked me whether I thought he'd killed them and then he said he was sure Baird was dead. He didn't say——"

" You damned little liar!" He had suddenly lost his temper. " First you say he left Briffe alive. Now you try to suggest he killed Baird. My God!" he cried, and I backed away from him into the open doorway. I was out on the steel platform then and below me was the track with the speeder standing there, its engine ticking over. " You slip up the line," he was saying, " and try to make people believe a lot of wild, lying accusations. Well, you're not going any farther. Goddammit!" he added. " If you weren't just a kid——"

That was when I slammed the door in his face and leapt down on to the track and straight on to the speeder. I let go the brake and thrust it into gear, revving the engine, the way I'd seen the gang foreman do it, and I was just easing the belt on to its drive when he hit the ground beside me. He reached out and grabbed at the hand rail just as I got the speeder moving. He missed it and I heard him swear, and then his feet were pounding after me. But by then I was gathering speed, and after that I couldn't hear anything but the sound of the engine and the beat of the wheels on the rail joints.

I was clear of him. That was what the wind sang in my ears. Clear of him, and I had transport. I glanced back over my shoulder as I ran clear of the bunkhouse train. He was standing in the middle of the track shouting something and waving his arms. I didn't know he was trying to warn me and I waved back out of sheer bravado, and then I pushed the throttle wide open, crouched low and riding the speeder like a motor-bike.

The switch to the double track clattered under the wheels and beyond there was nothing but the twin rails streaming out ahead of me to a long curve where the speeder bucked and swayed. When I looked back again the double track and the bunkhouse train had vanished. I was riding alone, with nothing behind or in front but the track with the snow-spattered jackpine crowding it on either side.

III

FOR THE first mile or two I was swept forward on a tide of exhilaration—the sense of speed, the illusion of power. I felt that nothing could stop me from reaching Lake of the Lion and finding Briffe still alive, and I drove the speeder full out, the wheel flanges screaming on the curves and the virgin country streaming past on either side.

But the mood didn't last. My fingers stiffened with cold where the gloves were worn, my feet became deadened lumps inside the chill casing of my boots and the wind on my face was a biting blast. I hit a bad patch, where the track had recently been ballasted and the steel was half buried in gravel, and I had to throttle down. I became conscious of the country then, the difficulties that faced me; Lands would phone Head of Steel and the whole organisation would be against me.

I must have passed dozens of telegraph poles lying beside the track before it dawned on me that the linesmen hadn't yet reached this section of the track. Lands couldn't phone them. He'd have to get another speeder and come after me. I opened the throttle wide again, and as I did so there came the crack of a rifle and I ducked my head. But when I looked back over my shoulder, the track behind me was empty.

I thought maybe it was a stone then, thrown up from the track. But the rifle cracked again, unmistakable this time, and suddenly I could hear wild human cries above the noise of the engine. They came from away to my left where a lake glimmered like pewter through a screen of trees. There was a canoe there and an Indian stood in the bows, a rifle to his shoulder, and close inshore a head and antlers thrust towards the shallows. There was a crashing in the undergrowth and the caribou broke cover a hundred yards ahead of me. It hesitated a moment, pawing at the steel of the track, and then with a quick terrified leap it was across and had vanished into the bush on the other side.

I didn't catch sight of the Indians again, for the track went into a long bend. There were levelling stakes beside the track here and in the stretch beyond I found the engineers who had put them there. They stood in a little group round their speeder, which had been lifted clear of the track, and as I rattled past them one of them shouted what sounded like " *Attention!* "

He was a French Canadian with a round fur cap like a Russian and before I had worked out that it was a shout of warning I was into the next bend. It was ballast again and the speeder bucked violently as the gravel flew, and through the rattle of the stones came the lost hoot of an owl. And then I was round the bend, clear of the gravel, and there was something on the line ahead. I slammed on the brake as the weird owl-hoot sounded again, louder and clearer, suddenly unmistakable.

Before the speeder had jerked to a halt I could see the yellow paintwork of the locomotive, could feel the rails trembling under me. There was no hope of getting the speeder off the track in time, not by myself. I did the only thing I could and flung the gear lever into reverse, opening the throttle wide and tearing back down the track, round the bend to where the little knot of engineers stood waiting.

The instant I stopped they crowded round, the lifting bars were pulled out and then they dragged it clear just as the train came rumbling round the curve. The hooter wailed again, loud as a trumpet note between the enclosing walls of the jackpine, and then the heavy locomotive was on top of us, sliding by at walking pace with a smell of hot engine oil and a slow piston-beat of power. The driver leaned out and shouted down: " You want to commit suicide, just jump in the muskeg. Don't pick on me." He spat into the slush at my feet and went back to the controls. The beat increased with a roar like a power station and the diesel gathered way again, clanking a long line of empty rail flats. And behind the flats came two wooden coaches with men looking down at us incuriously from the windows.

That was when I saw Laroche again. He was in the second coach and for an instant our eyes met. I saw him jump to his feet, and then the coach was past. The caboose followed and as it rattled by Laroche swung himself out of the coach doorway. I thought for a moment he was going to jump. But the train was light, gathering speed quickly. He hung there for a moment and then he thought better of it and disappeared into the coach again.

I watched the train as it dwindled down the track and the only thought in my mind then was that the way was clear for me to get to Camp 263. Laroche was behind me now, and Lands, too, and as long as I kept ahead of them there'd be nobody who knew me at Head of Steel. I turned to the engineers and asked them to get my speeder back on the track.

The French Canadian with the fur cap was looking at me curiously. "Why don't you check when you enter this section?" he asked.

"I was in a hurry," I said, my voice a little unsteady because I was feeling badly shaken now.

"You might have killed yourself."

"I was in a hurry," I repeated. "I still am."

"Sure. So is everybody else. But Mr. Lands won't thank you if you wreck his speeder."

I thought he was going to ask me why I was riding it then, but after staring at me a moment, he turned to his men and told them to get the speeder back on the track. "That's the trouble with this outfit," he grumbled. "Too much dam' hurry."

Three miles farther on I was stopped by a ballast gang. Their gas cars had been dumped beside the track to let the supply train through, but the track-lifting and ballast-tamping machines were already back at work on the track and there was nothing for it but to abandon my speeder and continue on foot. Head of Steel, they told me, was two miles up the line.

It was all new grade here, a long fill that ran out across a muskeg swamp. The line sagged in shallow waves where the muskeg sucked at the gravel embankment and the ties were covered with fresh ballast. It was hard walking, and the wind had swung into the north, so that it cut through my borrowed clothing and chilled the sweat on my body. Out across the marsh, where the black line of the scrub joined the iron-grey sky, I caught a glimpse of hills that were long-backed and bare, as though ground down to the bone by ice.

It seemed a long time that I trudged across that desolate area of swamp, but at last I reached the shallow gravel rim that enclosed it, and round a bend I came on a gang of men working with drills and machine-operated spanners, bolting the rails together and driving spikes. The detached chassis and wheels of dismantled rail transporters lay beside the track, and up ahead were more men and machines, and beyond them the steel-laying train. Everywhere about me now there was a sense of movement, of drive and thrust and effort, so that Labrador seemed suddenly crowded and full of life. The track, laid on the bare gravel without ballast, like toy rails in a sandpit, had a newness about it that showed that it hadn't been there yesterday, and walking beside it, through all these gangs of men, I felt conspicuous.

But they took no notice of me, though as I went by them, my gaze fixed self-consciously on the steel or the machines they operated, I felt that each one of them must know I'd no right to be there. I wondered who was in charge at Head of Steel and what Laroche had told him.

It was better when I reached the train itself. There were no gangs working there, just the wagons full of ties and plates and bolts which men threw out beside the track each time the train moved forward. The train was in a steep cut and I was forced to walk close beside it, so that when I reached the bunkhouse section I was conscious of men lounging in the open doorways of the coaches, staring down at me. But nobody stopped me, and I went up past the engine and the rail transporters until at last I could see the steel-laying crane swinging with a length of rail. A whistle blew and the crane swung back, its claw empty. The train hooted and then moved forward a few yards. Another length of track had been laid.

There was something so fascinating about the rhythmic thrusting of this train into the unknown that for the moment I forgot everything else and climbed half-way up the side of the cut to watch it. Each time, before the train had stopped, the crane was already swinging, another length of steel balanced in its claw grip. A man stood signalling with his hands to the crane-driver and shouting instructions to the steel-laying gang, and as the rail came down on to the grade, they seized hold of it, thrusting it into place on the ties and spiking it there with the balanced swing of sledge hammers.

This was Head of Steel and I stood and watched with a sort of awe. And then I saw the bare grade stretched out ahead, naked except for the few ties laid at regular intervals, and my gaze lifted to the black line of the jackpine. The yellow slash of the bulldozed grade ran into it and was abruptly swallowed.

I don't know what I had expected at Head of Steel. Obviously there could be no railway beyond this point. But I had travelled more than a hundred miles of the line, feeling close to the steel all the time, so that in a sense I had felt it to be an integral part of Labrador. And now, suddenly, it ended.

Until that moment I don't think I had faced up to the reality of what I had set out to do. Lake of the Lion somewhere to the north-east—fifty, at most a hundred miles. But looking at the slender line of the grade and the desolate emptiness of the country ahead, it might have been on another continent, so remote did it seem. Even to reach Darcy at Camp 263 appeared suddenly as a journey into the unknown.

"Hey you!" A man stood looking up at me from beside the Burro crane, his scarlet bush shirt a splash of colour in the gathering dusk. "Yeah, you. What the hell do you think you're doing up there—watching a rodeo or somep'n?"

His voice and the way he stood there suggested authority, and I scrambled quickly down, conscious that he was watching me. "If you're not working, just keep clear of the steel-laying," he shouted. "How many times I got to tell you guys?"

He was still watching me as I reached the track, and I turned my back on him and hurried down the train. Maybe it was imagination, but I felt I had aroused his curiosity and that he'd come after me and question me, if I didn't get away from there.

Maybe he would have done, but at that moment the train hooted—a different note this time, long and summoning. A whistle blew. A voice near me called out "Chow." And then the steel-laying gang were coming down the cut, walking with the slack drag of men whose muscles are suddenly relaxed. I was swept up in the movement and went with the tide down past the rail transporters and the locomotive to the bunkhouse coaches. There were other gangs coming up from the rear of the train, all converging on the diner. I waited my turn and clambered up, relieved to feel that I was no longer alone, but one of a crowd. Besides, I was hungry. If I was going up beyond Head of Steel, then it would be better to go after dark when nobody would see me, and with a full belly.

The lights were on inside the diner, and there was warmth and the smell of food. Nobody spoke to me as I pushed my way into a vacant place at the trestle table, and I didn't speak to them but just reached out for whatever I wanted. There was soup, steak with fried egg and potatoes and cabbage, canned fruit and cream, a mountainous heap of food to be shovelled in and washed down with tea and coffee. And when I'd finished I cadged a cigarette off the little Italian next to me and sat over my mug of coffee, smoking and listening to the sudden hubbub of conversation. I felt tired and relaxed now, and I wanted to sleep instead of going out into the cold again.

There was a sudden cessation of sound from the end of the diner and through the smoke haze I saw the man in the scarlet bush shirt standing in the doorway. The boss of the steel-laying gang was with him and they were looking down the length of the table.

" Who's that?" I asked the Italian.

" The guy in the red shirt?" he asked. " You don't-a-know?" He seemed puzzled. " That's Dave Shelton. He's in charge at Head of Steel."

I glanced quickly at the doorway again. The two men were still standing there and Shelton was looking straight at me. He turned and asked the other man a question and I saw the gang foreman shake his head.

" You wanna keep clear of him," the Italian was saying. " He drive all-a time. Last week he bust a man's jaw because he tell him he drive-a the men too hard."

Shelton glanced in my direction again, and then the two of them were pushing their way down the diner, and I knew I was trapped there, for there was nothing I could do, nowhere I could go, and I sat, staring at my mug, waiting.

" You work here?" The voice was right behind me, and when I didn't answer, a hand gripped my shoulder and swung me round. " I'm talking to you." He was standing right over me, broad-shouldered and slim-hipped, with a sort of thrusting violence that I'd only once met before, in an Irish navvy. " You're the guy I saw gawping at the steel-laying gang, aren't you?"

The men round me had stopped talking so that I was at the centre of a little oasis of silence.

" Well, do you work here or don't you?"

" No," I said.

" Then what are you doing in this diner? "

" Having a meal," I said, and a ripple of laughter ran down the table. The line of his mouth hardened, for it wasn't the most helpful reply I could have made, and in an effort to appease him, I added quickly, " I'm an engineer. It was supper time when I got here, and I just followed the others——"

" Where's your card? " he demanded.

" My card? "

" Your card of employment as an engineer on the line. You haven't got one, have you? " He was smiling now, suddenly sure of himself. " What's your name? " And when I didn't answer, he said, " It's Ferguson, isn't it? "

I nodded, knowing it was no use trying to deny it.

" Thought so." And he added, " What do you think you're playing at, pretending you're an engineer? Alex Staffen's mad as hell about it."

" I am an engineer," I said.

" Okay, you're an engineer. But not on this railroad." His hand fastened on my shoulder again and he dragged me to my feet. " Come on. Let's get going, feller. I've instructions to send you back to Base just as fast as I can." He jerked his head for me to follow him and led the way towards the door.

There was nothing I could do but follow him down the diner, feeling rather like a criminal with the gang foreman close behind me. Once outside, away from all the men, I could probably get him to listen to my explanation. But I didn't see what good it would do. Staffen had set the machinery of the organisation in motion to get me returned to Base, and unless I could make this man Shelton understand the urgency of the matter, he'd stick to his instructions. He'd have to.

Half-way down the diner he stopped abruptly. " Your speeder still on the track, Joe? " he asked one of the men.

He was a big fellow with a broken nose who looked as though he'd been a heavyweight boxer. " Sorry, Mr. Shelton," he said. " I cleared it just before——"

" Well, get it back on the track right away. You're taking this guy down to Two-twenty-four."

" Okay, Mr. Shelton." The man scrambled to his feet, not bothering to finish his coffee.

" He'll have to wait till we've dumped the empty steel

wagons," the foreman said. "The train'll be backing up to clear the cut any minute now."

"Well, see if you can get your speeder on the track and parked down the line before they start. Otherwise, you won't get started for an hour or more."

"Okay, Mr. Shelton." The man headed for the door and pushed his way through the group gathered about the swill bin. Shelton stopped to have a word with one or two of the other men seated at the table, and by the time he reached the door the men were leaving the diner in a steady stream.

"Could I have a word with you in private?" I asked. "It's important."

He was pushing his way through the men, but he stopped then. "What's it about?"

"I had a reason for coming up here," I said. "If I could explain to you . . ."

"You explain to Alex Staffen. I got other things to worry about."

"It's a matter of life and death," I said urgently.

"So's this railroad. I'm laying steel and winter's coming on." He forced his way through the doorway. "People like you," he said over his shoulder, "are a Goddamned nuisance."

I didn't have another chance to make him listen to me. We were out on the platform now, and as we reached the door to the track a voice called up, "That you, Dave?" The earth of the cut was yellow in the lights of the train and there were men moving about below us, dark shapes with here and there the glow of a cigarette. "They want you on the radio," the voice added. "It's urgent."

"Hell!" Shelton said. "Who is it?"

"They didn't say. But it's Two-two-four and they're asking for the figure for track laid to-day and a schedule of shifts worked. . . ."

"Okay, I'll come."

"Sounds like the General Manager's there," the foreman said. "He was due at Two-two-four to-day, wasn't he, Dave?"

"That's right. And one of the directors, too. I guess they're going to turn the heat on again." And he added, "Christ Almighty! We're laying more than one and a half miles a day already. What more do they expect?"

"I guess two miles would sound better in their ears," the foreman muttered dryly.

"Two miles! Yeah, that'd be sweet music. But the men can't lay it that fast."

"You could try paying them a bonus."

"It's not me. It's the Company. Still, with the freeze-up due . . ." Shelton hesitated. "Yeah, well, maybe it's an idea." He turned to me. "You wait here in the diner. And you better wait with him, Pat," he told the foreman. And he jumped out and disappeared up the track.

The men were streaming out of the diner now and the gang foreman and I stood back to let them pass. I wondered whether it was worth trying to explain to him about Briffe being alive, but one glance at his wooden features told me it wouldn't be any good. He hadn't the authority to help me, anyway.

In fact, at that moment I think I had lost the will to do anything more. Now that instructions about me had been sent up from Base, there didn't seem any point. The whole organisation had probably been alerted, and in that case there was nothing I could do. And yet I would like to have talked with Darcy. Perkins had said he knew more about Labrador than anyone else on the line, and there were things I wanted to know, things that perhaps he could have told me.

"Go on back to the diner," the foreman said. "It'll be warmer in there." The stream of men had thinned and he pushed me forward. I checked to let two men come out, and as they reached the exit door, a voice from the track called up, "Take this, will you?" One of them reached down, grabbed hold of a suitcase and dropped it on the platform almost at my feet.

I don't know what made me bend down and look at it—something about its shape maybe or perhaps subconsciously I had recognised the voice. At any rate, I did, and then I just stood there, staring at it stupidly. It was my own suitcase, the one I'd left in the bunkhouse train ten miles down the line when I'd jumped Lands' speeder.

And then I heard Lands' voice, outside on the track. "Okay, but we can't do that till we've seen Dave. Anyway, I want to get a radio message through to Two-sixty-three. My guess is . . ." The rest was drowned in a prolonged hoot from the locomotive. And when it ceased abruptly I heard some-body say, " Why bring Darcy into it? " And Lands answered impatiently, " Because they're all construction men up there. They got a target on that grade. Ray's the only guy with a vehicle who's got the time. . . ."

I didn't hear any more and I guessed he'd turned away. Peering out, I could see his padded bulk moving off up the train. There was somebody with him, but I couldn't see who it was for he was in the shadows, close under the next coach.

" What are you up to? " The foreman's hand gripped my arm.

" Nothing," I said. I was wondering whether it was Laroche I'd seen in the shadow there.

" Well, come on into the diner."

I hesitated. " That was Lands," I said.

" Bill Lands? " He had let go of my arm. " Well, what if it was? You know him? "

I nodded. I was thinking that I'd nothing to lose. If I went to Lands now, of my own accord, maybe he'd listen to me. I might even convince him there was a chance Briffe was still alive. At least the responsibility would be his then. I'd have done all I could. And if Laroche were there, then perhaps Lands would see for himself that the man was half out of his mind. " I'd like a word with Lands," I said.

The foreman looked at me with a puzzled frown. He hadn't expected that and he said, " Does he know you're up here? "

" Yes," I said. And I added, " I came up on his speeder."

That seemed to impress him. " Well, you'll have to wait till Dave Shelton gets back. Ask him." And he added, " You a newspaper man? "

" No." And because I felt that it would do no harm for him to know why I was here, I said, " I came up the line on account of that plane that crashed. You remember? "

He nodded. " Sure I remember."

I had aroused his curiosity now, and I said, " Well, Briffe's still alive."

" Still alive? " He stared at me. " How the hell could he be? They searched for a week and then the pilot came out with the news that the other two were dead. I heard all about it from Darcy, when he was down here a few days back, and he said the guy was lucky to be alive."

" Well, Briffe may be alive, too," I said.

" Briffe? You crazy?"

I saw the look of absolute disbelief in his eyes and I knew it was no good. They were all convinced Briffe was dead—this man, Lands, all of them. Shelton would be the same. And Darcy. What about Darcy? He'd been with Laroche for an hour—all the way up to Two-ninety. Would Darcy think I was crazy, too? " I'd like to talk to Lands," I said again, but without much hope.

And then the locomotive hooted again, two short blasts. " You'll have to wait," the foreman said. " We're gonna back up clear of the cut now."

There was a clash of buffers and the coach jerked into motion, the yellow sides of the cut sliding past the open door. It came to me in a flash then that this was my chance. If I were going to contact Darcy, I'd have to make the attempt now. But I hesitated, wondering whether it was worth it. And then I looked down at my suitcase, resting there right at my feet. I think it was the suitcase that decided me. Unless Lands or Laroche had removed them, it contained my father's log books. At least I'd have those to show Darcy, and I felt suddenly that I was meant to go on, that that was why the suitcase was there. It was a sign.

I suppose that sounds absurd, but that was the way I felt about it.

The clatter of the wheels over the rail joints was speeding up, the sides of the cut slipping by faster, and I reached for the suitcase. " What are you doing with that?" The foreman's voice was suspicious.

" It happens to be my suitcase," I said. I saw the look of surprise on his face, and then I jumped. It was a standing jump, but I put all the spring of my leg muscles into it, and it carried me on to the side of the cut where the ground was softer. I hit it with my body slack, my shoulder down, the way I'd been taught in the Army during National Service, and though it knocked the breath out of my body and I rolled over twice, I wasn't hurt.

As I scrambled to my feet, I saw the foreman leaning out of the coach door, shouting at me. But he didn't jump. He'd left it too late. The locomotive went by me with a roar, and in the light from the cab I found my suitcase. The rail transporters followed, finally the Burro crane, and after that the track was clear and it was suddenly dark.

I stood quite still for a moment, listening. But all I could hear was the rumble of the train as it ran back out of the cut. No voices came to me out of the night, no glimmer of a cigarette showed in the darkness ahead. All that seething crowd of men seemed to have been spirited away, leaving a black, empty void through which a cold wind blew. But at least it meant I could keep to the track, and I followed it north, breaking into a run as soon as my eyes became accustomed to the darkness.

Behind me the sound of the train faded and died, and when I glanced back over my shoulder, it was stationary on the track, a dull glow of light that glinted on the rails. Torches flickered and I thought I heard shouts. But it was half a mile away at least, and I knew I was clear of them.

A few minutes later I reached the end of steel. It was just the empty grade then, no track to guide me, and I stopped running. Behind me the lights of the train had vanished, hidden by the bend of the cut, and with their disappearance the black emptiness of Labrador closed round me. The only sound now was that of the wind whispering dryly through the trees.

The night was overcast, but it didn't matter—not then. The grade rolled out ahead of me, flat like a road and just visible as a pale blur in the surrounding darkness. But it didn't last. It was like that for a mile, maybe two, and then the surface became rougher. There were ruts and soft patches, and a little later I blundered into a heap of fresh-piled gravel.

After that the going was bad. Several times I strayed from the track into the bulldozed roots of trees piled at its edge. And once the ground dropped from under me and I fell a dozen feet or more to fetch up against the half-buried shovel of a grab crane.

I was more careful after that, moving slower. And then I came to another section of completed grade and for about a mile the going was easier again. But again it didn't last.

It was not much more than twenty miles from Head of Steel to Camp 263, but to understand what the going was like, particularly at night in those conditions, I should perhaps explain the general method of grade construction employed by the contractors. It was not a continuing thrust into Labrador as was the case with the steel laying, but a series of isolated operations, spreading north and south and ultimately linking up.

In the initial stages of the project a pilot road—known as the Tote Road—had been constructed all the way from the base at Seven Islands to the iron ore deposits in the neighbourhood of Knob Lake almost 400 miles to the north. This road, which was little more than a track bulldozed out of the bush, followed the general line of the proposed grade, and though it paralleled it in many places, its course was far from straight, since it followed the line of least resistance offered by the country. It was up this road that the heavy equipment had advanced—the drag cranes, grab cranes, bulldozers, tumble-bugs, scrapers, " mule " trucks and fuel tankers.

At the same time that the Tote Road was being constructed, engineers, flown in by float-plane and operating from small tented camps, surveyed and marked out the line of the railway. Airstrips constructed at strategic intervals were then built, and from these focal points construction camps, supplied largely by air lift, were established and gangs of men deployed to build the grade, section by section.

At the time I started north from Head of Steel the overall plan was to push the steel as far as Menihek Dam, at Mile 329, before winter brought work to a virtual standstill. This dam was a shallow one constructed almost entirely from air-lifted supplies where the waters of the ninety-mile Ashuanipi Lake ran into the great Hamilton River. All it needed now was the generators to make it operational, and the whole weight of the contractors' organisation, backed by some hundreds of pieces of heavy equipment, was concentrated on this stretch of the grade.

The effect, so far as I was concerned, was bewildering. A section of completed grade, scraped smooth as a road, would suddenly end in piled heaps of gravel or drop away into the quagmire of an uncompleted fill. The half-finished cuts were full of rock from the day's blasting, and the whole line of the grade was littered with heavy machines that were a death trap in the dark.

Somewhere around midnight the wind died away and everything was preternaturally still—a stillness that had a quality of hostility about it. And then it began to snow, a gentle floating down of large flakes that were wet and clinging. The darkness around me slowly changed to a ghostly white, and once again a completed section of grade petered out and I was stumbling through ridged heaps of sand, keeping by instinct rather than sight to the open swathe that had been bulldozed through the jackpine.

It was shortly after this that the ground abruptly dropped away from me, and I slithered down into the mud of a gulley, where the corrugated metal sheets of a half-completed conduit stood like the whitened bones of a huge whale. It was muskeg here and I knew it was hopeless to try and cross it in the dark. Weary and cold, I paused for a spell, and then I retraced my steps to an opening I had seen in the white wall of the jackpine, and when I found it, I abandoned the grade, dully conscious that I was on some sort of a track.

But the track was little better than the grade. The ground became soft under my feet as I descended into the same shallow depression that had called for a conduit in the grade construction. Patches of water showed dark against the snow, and as I splashed through them, I could hear the soft crunch of the paper-thin layer of ice that had already formed on the surface. And then it was mud, thick and heavy and black, with deep ruts in it where bulldozers had wallowed through.

But the ground under the mud was frozen hard, and when I was through the worst of it and the ruts still continued, I knew I had found a section of the old Tote Road. Gradually the surface hardened as the ground rose again, the ruts disappeared and the country became more open, the trees stunted. I had difficulty in keeping to the track then and twice within a matter of minutes I found myself blundering through thick scrub, and the snow shaken from the branches of the trees soaked me to the skin. I was very tired by then, my senses dulled. The handle of my suitcase was like the cold edge of a piece of steel cutting into my stiffened fingers, and the boots that were too big for me had raised blisters that burned with the pain of frostbite.

When I lost the track again, I gave it up and made a bed of pine branches and lay down to wait for dawn. I would go on then, I told myself—when I was rested and could see. The sweat was cold on my body, but I didn't care because of the relief I felt at just lying there, making no effort.

The snow fell softly, but it didn't seem cold any more and the stillness was overwhelming. In all the world there was no sound, so that I thought I could hear the flakes falling.

I hadn't intended to sleep, but once I had relaxed I suppose there was nothing to keep me awake. The snow whispered, and I lay drifting in a white, dark world until consciousness began to slide away from my numbed brain.

Maybe I heard the car and that's what woke me. Or perhaps it was the gleam of the headlights. I opened my eyes suddenly to find myself staring up at a jackpine floodlit like a Christmas tree, and a voice said, "I guess you must be Ferguson."

I sat up then, still dazed with cold and sleep, not quite sure where I was. But then I saw the track and the trees all covered with snow and the man standing over me, black against the lights. He was short and broad, with a gnome-like body, swollen by the padding of his parka, and my first thought was that this wasn't either Lands or Laroche. This was a man I'd never seen before. His face was square and craggy, the colour of mahogany, and the snow clung white to tufted eyebrows as he leaned forward, peering down at me through rimless glasses.

"A fine dance you've led me," he growled, and he reached down and dragged me to my feet. "I bin all along the grade as far as Head of Steel searching for you. Came back by the Tote Road, just in case."

I mumbled my thanks. My limbs were so stiff with cold I could hardly stand. Numbness deadened the pain of my blistered feet. "Come on," he said, grabbing hold of my suitcase. "There's a heater in the jeep. It'll hurt like hell, but you'll soon thaw out."

It was a jeep station wagon, a battered wreck of a car with one mudguard torn off and the bodywork all plastered with mud and snow. He helped me in and a moment later we were bumping and slithering between the trees that lined the track, and the heater was roaring a hot blast that was agony to my frozen limbs. His face showed square and leathery in the reflected glare of the headlights. He wasn't a young man and the peaked khaki cap was strangely decorated with a cluster of gaudy flies. "You were searching for me, were you?" I asked. And when he nodded, I knew that Lands must have contacted him. "You're Mr. Darcy then," I said.

"Ray Darcy," he grunted, not taking his eyes off the road. He was driving fast, the car slithering on the bends that rushed towards us in a blaze of white. " Bill reckoned I'd find you around Mile Two-fifty."

" You saw him then?" I asked.

" Sure I did."

" And Laroche? Was he there?"

" Laroche?" He glanced at me quickly. " No, I didn't see Laroche."

" But he was up there, wasn't he? He was at Head of Steel?"

" So they told me." And he added, " You just relax now and get some sleep. Guess you're pretty near all in."

But this was the man I'd trekked through the night to see. Circumstances had brought us together, and I wasn't going to waste the opportunity, tired though I was. " Did Lands tell you why I was here?" I asked him. " Did he tell you about the transmission my father picked up?"

" Yeah. He told me."

" And I suppose he told you I was crazy to think Briffe might be still alive."

" No. He didn't exactly say that."

" Then what did he say?" I asked.

Again that quick sidelong glance. " He said you were James Finlay Ferguson's grandson, for one thing." He dragged the car through the mud of a long S bend. " And that to my way of thinking," he added, " is about as strange as the idea that Briffe should have been able to transmit a message."

" What's so strange about it?" I asked. Why did it always come back to the Ferguson Expedition? " It's just a coincidence." The warmth of the heater was making me drowsy.

" Damned queer coincidence." He said it almost savagely.

" It explains my father's interest in Briffe's party."

" Sure. But it doesn't explain you."

I didn't know what he meant by that, and I was too sleepy to ask. I could hardly keep my eyes open. My mind groped back to the Ferguson Expedition. If I could just find out what had happened. " Perkins said you knew more about Labrador than anybody else on the line." My voice sounded thick and blurred. " That's why I came north . . . to find you and ask . . ."

" You go to sleep," he said. " We'll talk later."

My eyes were closed, waves of tiredness engulfing me. But

then we went into a skid and I was jerked back to consciousness as he pulled the car out of it. "You do know what happened, don't you?" I said thickly. "I must know what happened to my grandfather."

"I've read it up, if that's what you mean." He turned his head and looked at me. "You mean to say you really don't know the story of that expedition?"

"No," I replied. "That's the reason I wanted to contact you—that and the fact that you brought Laroche out."

He stared at me. "Goddammit!" he said. "If that isn't the queerest thing about the whole business."

"How do you mean?"

"You not knowing." He was still staring at me and we hit the edge of the road so that snow-laden branches slashed against the cracked windscreen. He pulled the car back on to the track and said, "Now you just relax. Plenty of time to talk later."

"But what did happen?" I asked.

"I said relax. We'll talk about it later." And then he added, "I got to think." It was said to himself, not to me. And when I tried to question him further, he turned on me angrily and said, "You're not in a fit state to talk now. And nor am I. I been up all night chasing after you and I'm tired. Now go to sleep."

"But——"

"Go to sleep," he almost shouted at me. "Goddammit! How do you expect me to drive with you asking questions all the time?" And then in a gentler voice, "Take my advice and sleep whilst you can. I'll talk when I'm ready to—not before. Okay?"

I nodded, not sure what he meant. I was too tired to argue anyway. I'd come a long way and I'd found the man I thought could help me. My eyes closed of their own accord and consciousness slid away from me. I was adrift then in a sea of ruts, rocking and swaying to the steady roar of the engine. And when I opened my eyes again, dawn was breaking and we were running down into a hutted camp.

"Two-sixty-three," Darcy said, seeing that I was awake.

The place looked raw and desolate in the cold morning light, the wooden buildings standing bleak and black against the snow. It was a new camp built on a slope above the grade,

the site only recently bulldozed out of the bush. Great piles of
sawn logs stood outside every hut and all round the edge of the
camp was a slash of lopped branches and uprooted trees.

We bumped over rough ground and drew up outside a hut
that was set a little apart. " I'm usually better organised than
this," Darcy said as he scooped up an armful of logs and
pushed open the door. " But I only been here a few weeks."
He went over to the iron stove at the back and fed logs into
it.

He only had part of the hut, a small bare room with two
iron beds, some shelves full of books, several lockers and a
cupboard built of three-ply. It reminded me of an army hut
and the mud on the floor showed what the ground outside
would be like when the snow melted. A big refrigerator,
gleaming new, stood incongruously against one wall. The room
looked drab and cheerless in the dim light that filtered through
the dirty windows, but it was warm and the flames that licked
out of the top of the stove as he opened the ash door flickered
on the bare wood walls to give it an illusion of cosiness. There
were several pictures, too ; oil paintings of Labrador—a river
scene, all black and greys, a study of jackpines in the snow,
and one of a little group of men round a camp fire that looked
so lonely and desolate that it reminded me of Briffe.
" Yours?" I asked. He turned and saw I was looking at the
picture of the camp fire. " Yeah. All my own work." And he
added, " Just daubs." But I knew he didn't mean that, for he
was staring at the picture with a self-critical intenseness. He
was serious about this and he said slowly, " I guess that's the
best I ever did. Like it?"

" I don't know much about it," I murmured awkwardly. " It
looks cold and lost——"

" It's meant to." He said it almost harshly. And then he
replaced the lid of the stove with a clang. " Okay, now you
get your wet clothes off and hit the sack. You can have that
bed." He nodded to the one that wasn't made up. " Sorry I
can't give you a shot of liquor, but liquor ain't allowed up the
line. Too many alcoholics up here. Anyway, you'll be okay.
All you need is warmth and sleep."

Steam was rising from my clothes. I sat down on the bed.
I felt suddenly very tired—too tired to take off my clothes or
do anything but just sit there. " I've got to talk to you," I said
and my voice sounded blurred.

" Later," he answered.

" No, now," I said with an effort. " Laroche will be here later. Lands, too. If I don't talk to you now, it'll be too late."

" I've told you before, and now I'm telling you again—I'll talk to you when I'm ready, and not before. Okay?" And he turned abruptly away from me and went to the corner beyond the stove. " You don't have to worry about Laroche or anybody else," he said over his shoulder. " Not for several hours yet. There's no airstrip here ; they'll have to come by jeep, and they won't start till after breakfast." He came back with a pair of long rubber boots. " You just get your clothes off and turn in. You're dead beat." He reached across me to the shelf above the bed and took down a green tin box. " Go on, get some sleep, I'll be back in an hour or so."

He was moving towards the door and I jumped to my feet. " Where are you going?" I cried.

" Fishing." He had turned and was staring at me curiously.

It didn't seem possible he could be going fishing, not after being up all night. I don't know why, but I'd come so far to see him I'd somehow taken it for granted he was on my side, and now I suddenly wasn't sure. There was a radio somewhere in the camp. He could talk to Lands at Head of Steel, probably Staffen down at Base. " What instructions did they give you about me?" I asked him.

He reached out to a rack on the wall and took down a fishing-rod swaddled in a green canvas case, and then he came back across the room towards me. " See here, young fellow," he said. " If I say I'm going fishing, I'm going fishing. Understand?" His voice shook and his eyes glared at me from behind the rimless glasses. " Don't ever try doubting my word. I don't like it."

" I'm sorry," I murmured. " It was just that I thought . . ."

" You thought I was going to report to Lands, is that it?" He was still glaring at me. " Well, I'm not," he said. " I'm going fishing. Okay?"

I nodded and subsided on to the bed. " It seemed so odd," I murmured.

" Odd?" His tone was still belligerent. " What's odd about going fishing?"

" I don't know," I muttered, trying to think of something that would pacify him. " I should have thought you'd need some sleep, too."

"I'm not a kid," he snapped. "I don't need a lot of sleep. And fishing helps me to think," he added. He smiled then and the gust of anger that had shaken him seemed suddenly swept aside. "You're not a fisherman, are you?"

I shook my head.

"Then you wouldn't know. It's like painting—it helps. You need things like that up here." He stared at me for a moment. "There's a lot of things you don't know yet," he said gently. "About the way life is in a Godforsaken country like Labrador. I been two years up here." He shook his head, as though at some folly of his own. "I came up here for a month's fishing, a sort of convalescence, and I ain't been outside since—not even down to Seven Islands. That's a long time." He turned away. "Christ! It's a long time." He was staring out of the window, at the camp and the country beyond it. "It does things to you." And then, after a moment, he looked at me again, smiling. "Such as making you quick to take offence when a young fool doubts your word." And he added brusquely, "Now you get some sleep. And don't worry about what I'm up to. I'm just going down the grade as far as the river, and with any luck I'll come back with a *ouananish*, maybe some lake trout. Okay?"

I nodded. "I just wanted you to hear what I had to say before you did anything."

"Sure. I understand. But there's plenty of time." He went to the door and pulled it open. "I'll be back in a couple of hours or so." And then he was gone, the door shut behind him. But though he was no longer there, something of his personality still lingered in the bare room.

I sat there for a long time, wondering about him. But gradually weariness overcame me, and I stripped off my clothes and climbed into the bed. The blankets were rough and warm against my skin. I didn't care that they were musty with the smell of dirt. I didn't care about anything then. I was satisfied that I'd found somebody who felt about Labrador the way my father had, and though he was strange and I was a little scared of him, I knew he would help me—and I closed my eyes and went to sleep with a picture in my mind of a tough little man, knee-deep in a cold river, fishing with long, practised casts.

I woke to find him standing over me, and the sun was shining in through the window. "Do you like salmon?" he said.

I sat up. "Salmon?"

"Sure. I brought you some salmon. Land-locked salmon. The Montagnais call them *ouananish*." He pulled up a chair and set a big dish down on it and a knife and fork and a hunk of bread. "Caught two. The boys and I had one. You got most of the other. Strictly against camp rules. No fish to be cooked. Give you tape worm if they're not properly cooked. You ever had tape worm?"

"No."

"You're lucky. You feed like a horse, but it's the worm feeding, not you, so you just go on getting thinner." He was searching in a desk in the corner and he came up with a sheet of graph paper. There was the sound of voices and the scrape of boots in the other half of the hut beyond the partition. "Lucy!" he shouted. "You boys ready yet?"

"*Oui, oui.* All okay, Ray."

"I got to get the boys started on levelling up a new section of the grade," he said, turning to me. "I'll be about an hour. After that we'll go north as far as the trestle. Maybe I'll fish a bit whilst you tell me your story." The eyes glinted at me from behind their glasses. "Then we'll see. Maybe we'll go and have a word with Mackenzie."

And with that he turned and went out. The door closed and after a moment I began to eat my first *ouananish*. It was close-fleshed and pink, and there was a lot of it. And whilst I ate I was thinking about Darcy again—about his painting and his mania for fishing. Crazy Darcy that young engineer had called him. Two years without a break was certainly a long time, long enough to drive a man round the bend. I remembered something Lands had said and wondered whether Darcy was what they called "bushed."

I ate the whole of that fish, and when I had finished it energy was flowing back into my body so that I no longer felt tired. There was a basin beside Darcy's bed and a bowl of water steamed on the stove lid. I got up stiffly and had a wash, standing naked over the basin. Bushed or not, the man was closer to the country than anybody else I'd met. I had a shave and then I sat on the bed and broke the blisters on my heels and covered them with adhesive tape I found in the medical kit on the shelf above the bed. There were books there, too, and the photograph of a young Canadian soldier in a battered leather frame.

My clothes had dried out with the heat of the stove and I put them on. And then I went back to the shelf and the books, wondering whether they would tell me anything about the man. They were mostly technical, but there was Izaak Walton's *Compleat Angler,* a single leather-bound volume of Shakespeare, the collected poems of Robert Service, several books by Jack London, and then four books that took me right back to the little room where my father had had his radio. They were *Labrador,* by W. Cabot, two volumes of *Outlines of the Geography, Life and Customs of Newfoundland-Labrador* by V. Tanner and a small slim book titled *Labrador—In Search of the Truth* by Henri Dumaine.

Tanner's book I knew. I'd often looked at the pictures in those two volumes when I was a kid. And Cabot's book, too —that had been on my father's shelves. But Henri Dumaine's book was new to me and I took it down and opened it, casually leafing through the pages. It was a record of a journey into Labrador, not very well written. I glanced at the fly-leaf. It had been published by a Toronto firm in 1905, and thinking that perhaps it might have a reference to my grandfather's expedition, I started going carefully through the pages from the beginning.

I found a reference to it almost immediately, at the foot of page five. He had written: *Thus it was on June 15, 1902, that the ship brought me to Davis Inlet and the Hudson's Bay Post there. I was at the starting point of the Ferguson Expedition at last. . . .*

I stared at that sentence, hardly able to believe my eyes. Here, in this hut at Camp 263, I had stumbled on a book that could help me. My eyes were devouring the printed words now, and a few lines further on I read: *Standing there, looking at the Post, so clean and neat in the cold sunlight, the red shingle roofs of the buildings glistening with the rain that had just passed and the planked walls gleaming in their fresh coat of white paint, I was thinking of Pierre. It was to this place that the poor fellow had returned—alone. I was thinking, too, of my wife, Jacqueline, and of all the hopes she entertained of my present journey. She had been at her brother's bedside when he died and had listened to the last strange mutterings of a mind deranged by the tragedy of what had happened and by all the terrible harships suffered. I turned my back on the Post then and looked across the water to the*

*hills of Labrador. It was then that I first felt the impact of
that lonely country and I stood there in sudden awe of it, for
somewhere beyond the black line of that escarpment lay the
truth. If I could find it, then maybe I could clear his name of
the vile accusations that had so darkened his last hours and
contributed so much to his state of mind.*

I turned the pages quickly then, searching for some statement of the accusations, some hint as to what was supposed
to have happened to my grandfather. But Henri Dumaine
seemed to take it for granted that the reader would know that,
for I could find no further reference to it. Page after page
was taken up with the rather dreary account of his struggle
up the old Indian trail to the Naskopie. He had had two coast
half-breeds with him and it was clear that neither he nor they
had much idea of bushcraft. Dogged by misfortunes, which
were largely of their own making, they had reached Cabot
Lake on July 19. They had then gone south across Lake
Michikamau and had finally turned west towards the
Ashuanipi.

*Here we found a camp of Montagnais Indians waiting for
the coming of the caribou and luck was with us for two years
ago at this very spot a lone white man had passed them,
going towards the great lake of Michikamau. He had a canoe,
but his supplies must have been getting low for he had avoided
them and they had been scared to go near him for some
reason, so that they could tell me little about him except that
his clothes were ragged and his feet bound with strips of
canvas and he talked to himself as though communing to some
unseen spirit. They showed me the place where he had camped
beside the river. There were several caribou bones and close
by the place where he had built his fire was a little pile of
cartridges, the greased wrapping partly disintegrated.*

*There was no doubt in my mind then that this was one of
the places where my brother-in-law had camped on the way
back, and the cartridges so recklessly jettisoned proved that
his situation was already desperate. Clearly we were still some
distance from the place where death had overtaken Mr.
Ferguson and I asked the Indians if they knew of the Lake I
sought. I described it to them as Pierre had described it so
often in his delirium. But they did not know it, and of course
the name that Pierre had given to the Lake meant nothing to
them, and so we left them, giving them two packages of tea*

and a small bag of flour, which was all we could spare of our supplies. And after that we went south, following the Ashuanipi, and searching all the time. . . .

The door behind me burst open and I turned to find Darcy standing there. " All set?" he asked impatiently, as though I had kept him waiting. And then he saw the book in my hand. "Oh, so you found that." He came in and shut the door. " I wondered whether you would." He took it out of my hand, leafing idly through the pages. " Dull stuff," he said. " But interesting when you know the country."

" Or when you know what happened," I said.

"To Ferguson?" He looked at me quickly. " Nobody knows that."

" When you know what's supposed to have happened then," I corrected myself. " On page five . . ." I took the book from his hand and pointed to the line referring to " vile accusations." " What were the accusations?" I asked him. " They were made against the survivor, weren't they? That was Dumaine's brother-in-law. It says so there. Who accused him and what did they accuse him of?"

" Goldarnit!" he exclaimed, staring at me. " It's the damnedest thing I ever heard. You come all this way, right up here to this camp, where you're not more than fifty miles or so from where your grandfather died, and you say you don't know the story."

" Well, I don't," I said. " I came up here because of Briffe."

" Because of Briffe, or because Laroche crashed his plane in the same area?"

" Because of Briffe," I said. I was watching his face, wondering whether he, too, had guessed where the plane had crashed. I glanced down at the book again. I had only got about two-thirds through it. " Did Dumaine reach Lake of the Lion?" I asked.

" Ah, so you know about Lake of the Lion, do you?"

" Yes, but I don't know what happened there."

" Well, it's like I told you," he said. " Nobody knows for sure. Dumaine never got farther than the Ashuanipi." He reached over and took the book from me again. " Some Indians showed him a lone white man's camp on the banks of the river, and after that he found two more. But that was all." His grizzled head was bent over the book, his stubby, wind-cracked fingers leafing through the earlier pages. " The

poor devil spent more than a month searching for that lake,"
he murmured. " And all the time he should have been getting
the hell out of the country." He seemed to be trying to check
on something in the first few chapters of the book. At length
he said, " The big freeze-up was on them long before they'd
reached Davis Inlet. If it hadn't been for the half-breeds, he'd
never have got out alive." He snapped the book shut and replaced it on the shelf beside the photograph. " The irony of it
was," he added, looking at me curiously, " there was a woman
came to Davis Inlet that year and strolled across half Labrador
as though it were no worse than her own Scots moors. She had
three trappers with her who knew the country and she covered
the same area that Dumaine covered, and she went out by way
of the Hamilton and the North-West River Post as fit as when
she started."

But I didn't intend to be side-tracked. " This man who
accompanied my grandfather," I said. " Dumaine talks of him
as though he were mad. *A mind deranged by the tragedy of
what happened*, he says. What sent him mad?" I asked.

He gave a quick shrug and turned away towards the stove.

" Can't you give me some idea of what happened?" I persisted. And when he didn't answer, I added, " At least you must
know what the accusations were. What was he accused of?"

He was leaning down, staring at the red-hot stove, but he
turned to me then and said, " He was accused of murdering
your grandfather." And he added quickly, " Nothing was
proved. Nobody knows what happened. It was just a wild
accusation made out of——"

" Who made it?" I asked.

He hesitated, and then said, " The woman I was talking
about—Ferguson's young wife, Alexandra." He was staring at
me with a puzzled frown. " You must know that part of it at
least. Hell, boy, she was your own grandmother." And then,
when he realised it was new to me, he shook his head and
turned back to the stove. " The newspapers got hold of her
and printed some pretty wild things. Not that there was anything new in it. There'd been a lot of talk when the poor
devil had come out alone raving of gold and a lake with the
figure of a lion in rock. He was half out of his mind then, by
all accounts."

" So it was gold my grandfather was after, was it?" I was
remembering what my mother had said about him.

"Sure. You don't imagine a seasoned prospector like Ferguson went into Labrador for the good of his soul, do you?" He fell silent then, but after a while he said, "She must have been a remarkable woman, your grandmother. Didn't you know her at all?"

I explained how we'd stopped going to the house in Scotland after my mother had found her talking to me in my room that night, and he nodded. "Maybe your mother was right. And yet in spite of that you're here. Queer, isn't it?" And then he went back to my grandmother. "It would be remarkable even to-day. You wouldn't understand, of course —not yet. All you've seen of the Labrador is a railway under construction. But you get away from the camps and the grade, the country's different then—a land to be reckoned with."

"In fact, the land God gave to Cain." I said it without thinking, repeating Farrow's words.

He looked at me, a little surprised. "Yeah, that's right. The land God gave to Cain." And the way he said it gave a significance to the words that chilled me.

"Did my grandmother reach Lake of the Lion?" I asked then.

"God knows," he said. "But if she did, she kept damn quiet about it, for there's no mention of it in the newspaper reports. But she back-tracked their route in and got farther than Dumaine did, or else she got there first, for she came out with a rusted pistol, a sextant and an old map case, all things that had belonged to her husband. She had those photographed, but she never published her diary, though she admitted she'd kept one. I guess she'd have published that all right if she'd found her husband's last camp. Is the diary still in existence, do you know?" he asked me.

"I don't know," I replied. "I've seen the pistol and the sextant and the map case. My father had them hanging on the wall of his room. There was part of a paddle, too, and an old fur cap. But I never knew there was a diary."

"Too bad," he murmured. "It would have been interesting to know the basis of her accusations. She was three months up here in the wild and all the time following the route her husband took. I guess those three lonely months gave the iron plenty of time to enter into her soul." He went over to the stove and held his hands close to the iron casing, warming them. "The strange thing is," he said, "that Dumaine never mentions her once in that book. And yet the two parties started out from Davis Inlet within a few days of each other, and they were covering the same ground. I wonder whether they ever met?" he murmured. "Even if Dumaine never met her face-to-face, he must have come across traces of her party. And yet he never mentions her. There's not one reference to Mrs. Ferguson in the whole of the book."

"That's hardly surprising," I said, "considering she'd accused his wife's brother of murder."

"Well, maybe not. But she didn't put it as bluntly as that, you understand. And there'd been all that talk . . ." He was staring down at the stove again. "It's a queer thing," he murmured, half to himself. "Those two men—I would have thought it would have been the other way about."

"How do you mean?" I asked.

He shrugged his shoulders. "I dunno. A question of character, I guess. I've thought a lot about it since I been up here. Take Ferguson." He was staring down at the stove. "Came over as a kid in an immigrant ship and went out west, apprenticed to one of the Hudson's Bay posts. A few years later he was in the Cariboo. I guess that's where the gold bug got him, for he was all through the Cariboo and then up to Dawson City in the Klondike rush of the middle nineties." He shook his head. "He must have been real tough."

"And the other man?" I asked.

"Pierre?" he said quickly. "Pierre was different—a man of the wilderness, a trapper. That's what makes it so odd."

He didn't say anything more and I asked him then how he knew all this. "It's all in Dumaine's book, is it?"

"No, of course not. Dumaine was storekeeper in a small town in Ontario. He didn't understand the wild, so he never bothered to assess the nature of the two men's personalities. His book is a dull inventory of the day-to-day tribulations of a man whose wife had talked him into a journey that was beyond his capabilities."

"Then how do you know about my grandfather?" I asked.

He looked up at me. "Newspaper cuttings chiefly. I had somebody look them up and type them all out for me. There was a lot about it in the Montreal papers, as you can imagine. I'd show them to you, only they're in my trunk, and that's up at Two-ninety still."

"But what made you so interested?" I asked him.

" Interested?" He looked at me in surprise. " How the hell could I fail to be interested?" His craggy face was suddenly smiling. " You don't seem to understand. I'm not up here because I like engineering. I don't even need the dough. I'm fifty-six and I made enough money to keep me the rest of my life." He turned and reached for his gloves. " No," he added. " I'm up here because I got bitten by the Labrador." He laughed softly to himself as he pulled on the gloves. " Yeah, I guess I'm the only man along the whole stretch of line that's here because he loves it." He was talking to himself again and I had a sudden feeling that he often talked to himself. But then he looked across at me. " Know anything at all about the Labrador?" he asked me.

" My father had a lot of books," I said. " I've read some of them."

He nodded. " Then you'll know that all this is virgin country, unmapped and untrodden by white men till the Hollinger outfit got interested in the iron ore deposits up at Burnt Creek. Hell!" he added. " It's only four thousand years ago that the last Ice Age began to recede. It was all glaciers then. And until floatplanes came into general use for prospecting, only a handful of white men had penetrated into the interior. A few rough maps of the rivers and all the rest blank, a few books like Dumaine's on journeys made by canoe and on foot—that was all anybody knew about the Labrador. It wasn't until 1947 that the Government began an aerial survey. And you ask me why I'm interested in the story of the Ferguson Expedition. How the hell could I help being interested, feeling the way I do about the country?" And then he added, almost angrily, " You don't understand. I guess you never will. Nobody I ever met up here feels the way I do— the lonely, cruel, withdrawn beauty of it. Like the sea or the mountains, the emptiness of it is a challenge that cuts a man down to size. See what I mean?" He stared at me belligerently, as though challenging me to laugh at him. " The aircraft and the railway, they don't touch the country, never will, I guess. It's wild here—as wild and lonely as any place on earth. Do you believe in God?"

The abruptness of the question startled me.

" Well, do you?"

" I haven't thought much about it," I murmured.

" No. Men don't till they suddenly discover how big Nature

is. You wait till you're out there in the silence of the trees, and the bitter cold is freezing all the guts out of you. You'll think about Him then all right, when there's nothing but the emptiness and the loneliness and the great stillness that remains a stillness in your soul even when the wind is blowing to beat hell." He laughed a little self-consciously. " Okay," he said abruptly. " Let's go." He strode across to the door and pulled it open. " Mackenzie's camped up by the trestle. If we're going to talk to him, we'd better get moving." His voice was suddenly impatient.

I followed him out of the hut and climbed into the jeep. " Who's Mackenzie?" I asked as we drove off.

" Mackenzie, he's an Indian—a Montagnais. One of the best of them." He swung the car on to the camp road. " He acts as guide for the geologists," he added. " But right now he's hunting. He may be willing to help you, he may not."

" Help me—how?" I asked.

" Mackenzie's never seen a lion," he said. " The word means nothing to him. But he's seen that lake." His eyes were suddenly fixed on mine, an ophidian blue that held me rigid. " I take it," he said, " that you haven't come all this way to sit on your fanny in a construction camp or to wait around until you're sent back to Base?" And then his gaze was back on the road again. " Anyway, that's what I decided whilst I was fishing this morning—that I'd take you to see Mackenzie. I've sent him word by one of the Indians that hang around here to wait for us at his camp."

IV

WHAT EXACTLY I'd expected from Darcy I don't know, but it came as a shock to me to find him taking it for granted that I'd want to pursue my objective to its logical conclusion. And as we bumped across the iron-hard ruts, up out of the camp on to the Tote Road, I began to consider the problems it raised, for I couldn't just walk off into the bush with this Indian. I'd need stores, equipment, things that only the construction camp could provide. I started to explain this to Darcy, but all he said was, " We'll discuss that when we've seen Mackenzie. He may not want to leave the hunting. Winter's coming on and the hunting's important."

We were headed north and after a while he said, " I suppose you realise you've caused near-panic down at the Base. They've never had anybody gate-crash the line before and one of the directors is on a tour of inspection. There've been messages flying back and forth about you all night. If I weren't something of a rebel in this outfit," he added with a quick grin, " I'd have had nothing to do with you."

I didn't say anything and he went on, " But since I've got myself involved, I guess it's time I had all the facts. Bill gave me the gist of them, but now I'd like to have the whole story from you."

Once again I found myself explaining about my father's death and that last radio message. But this time it was different. This time I was explaining it to someone who could understand how my father had felt. He listened without saying a word, driving all the time with a furious concentration, his foot hard down on the accelerator. It was beginning to thaw, the snow falling in great clods from the jackpine branches and the track turning to slush, so that the jeep slithered wildly on the bends, spraying the mud up in black sheets from the wheels.

I was still talking when the trees thinned and we came out on to the banks of a river, and there was the trestle, a girder-like structure built of great pine baulks, striding across the grey stone flats of the river to the thump of a pile-driver. He stopped by a little group of huts that huddled close under the towering network of the trestle and cut the engine, sitting listening to me, his gloved hands still gripping the wheel.

And when I had finished, he didn't say anything or ask any questions, but just sat there, quite silent, staring out across the river. At length he nodded his head as though he had made up his mind about something. "Okay," he said, opening his side door and getting out. "Let's go scrounge some coffee." And he took me across to the farthest hut where a wisp of smoke trailed from an iron chimney. "The last time I was here," he said, "was when I brought Laroche out." He kicked open the wooden door and went in. "Come in and shut the door. The bull-cook here's a touchy bastard, but he makes darn good blueberry pie." This in a loud, bantering voice.

The hut was warm, the benches and table scrubbed white, and there was a homely smell of baking. A sour-looking man with a pot-belly came out of the cookhouse. "Saw you drive up," he whispered hoarsely, dumping two mugs of steaming black coffee on the table. "Help yourselves." He pushed the canned milk and a bowl of sugar towards us.

"Where's the pie, Sid?" Darcy asked.

"You want pie as well?"

"Sure we want pie."

The cook wiped his hands down his aproned thighs, a gesture that somehow expressed pleasure. And when he had gone back into the cookhouse, Darcy said, "Sid's quite a character. Been in Labrador almost as long as I have—and for the same reason."

"What's that?" I asked.

But he shook his head, his eyes smiling at me over the top of his mug as he gulped noisily at his coffee. And then I asked him about Laroche. "You say you stopped here on your way up to Two-ninety?"

"Yeah, that's right. I thought he could do with some hot coffee. And I wanted blankets, too. His clothes were soaked." The cook came back with the blueberry pie and Darcy said, "Remember the last time I was through here, Sid?"

"Sure do." The cook's eyes were suddenly alive. "You had that pilot with you, and he sat right there where you're sitting now with that look in his eyes and muttering to himself all the time. And then he went off to sleep, just like that."

"He was in a bad way."

" Sure was. More like a corpse than anything else."

" It was the warmth sent him to sleep," Darcy said. " He hadn't been warm since he'd crashed."

" Yeah, I guess that's what it was. But I reckoned you'd have a corpse on your hands by the time you got him to the aircraft." The cook hesitated. " I ain't seen you since then."

" No, I been busy." Darcy stared at the cook a moment and then said, " What's on your mind, Sid?"

" Nothing. I been thinking, that's all." And he looked at Darcy with a puzzled frown. " It was his eyes. Remember how they kept darting all round the place, never focusing on anything, as though he were scared out of his wits. And every now and then he'd mutter something. Do you reckon he was bushed?" And when Darcy didn't say anything, the cook added, " I only seen a man bushed once. That was in the early days down at One-thirty-four."

" Mario?" Darcy said.

" Yeah, Mario—that Italian cook. He moved his eyes the same way Laroche did, and he had that same scared look as though he expected to be murdered in his bunk. Queer guy, Mario." He shook his head. " Always muttering to himself. Remember? You were there." Darcy nodded. " And then running out naked into the bush that night; and all those crazy things he wrote in the snow—like ' I want to die ' and ' Don't follow me. Leave me alone.' As though he was being persecuted."

" Well, he was." Darcy cut the blueberry pie and passed a thick wedge of it across to me. " Those Germans," he added with his mouth full. " They played hell with the poor bastard. Good cook, too."

" Sure he was. And then they got another wop for cook and they tried playing hell with him. Remember how he fixed them?" The cook was suddenly laughing. " So you make-a the fool of me, he told them. You wanna have fun at my expense. How you like-a the soup to-day, eh? Is okay? Well, I urinate in that soup, and every time you make-a the fool of me, I urinate in the soup. That's what he told them, wasn't it? And never another peep out of them." His laughter died away and he fell suddenly silent. And then he came back to the subject of Laroche. " You'd think when a guy's left two men dead in the bush he'd want to tell somebody about it soon as he was picked up. But he wouldn't talk about it, would he?"

"He was pretty badly injured," Darcy said.

"Sure he was. But even so—you'd think he'd want to get it off his mind, wouldn't you? I know I would. I'd have been worried sick about it all the time I was trekking out." He nodded his head as though to emphasise the point. "But you had to try and dig it out of him. What happened, you asked him. What about Briffe and the other guy? But all he said was Dead. Just like that. Dead—both of them. And when you asked him how it happened, he just shook his head, his eyes darting all round the room. Wouldn't say another word."

So Laroche hadn't been normal even then. "You think he was bushed, do you?" I asked. "Or was it because of his injury?"

The cook's beady eyes were suddenly suspicious. "You're a newcomer, aren't you?" I think he'd forgotten I was there. "An engineer?" he asked Darcy.

But instead of saying Yes and leaving it at that, Darcy said, "Ferguson's up here because he believes Briffe may still be alive."

"Is that so?" The cook regarded me with new interest. "You think maybe Laroche made a mistake, saying they were both dead?"

And then, to my surprise, Darcy began explaining to the man the circumstances that had brought me out from England.

"Hadn't we better get moving?" I interrupted him. I was annoyed. It hadn't occurred to me that he'd repeat what I'd told him.

"What's the hurry?" he said. "Nobody will look for you here." And the cook, sensing the tension between us, said, "You like some more cawfee?"

"Sure we'll have some more coffee," Darcy said. And when the man had gone out, he turned to me. "If you think you can keep the reason you're up here a secret, you're dam' mistaken. Anyway, what's the point?"

"But he'll gossip," I said.

"Sure he'll gossip. Cooks are like that—same as barbers. And there's a bush telegraph operates along the grade here faster than you can get from one camp to the next. It'll go all

up the line from here to Menihek and beyond, and right the
way down to Base, until there isn't a soul doesn't know you've
come all the way from the Old Country because you believe
Briffe's alive. That's why I brought you in here." And then
he got up and thrust his round head forward, his eyes staring
at me from behind the glasses. " What are you afraid of?
That's the truth you told me, isn't it?"

" Of course it's the truth."

" Well, then, what have you got to lose? The more people
know your story, the more chance you've got of getting something done. Okay?"

The cook came back with the coffee pot this time. " Help
yourselves," he said. And then he asked, " What happens
now? Do they resume the search?"

" No," I said. " They won't do a thing."

" But suppose you're right and they're alive. . . . They
going to be left to die, is that it?"

Darcy was looking at me and I knew what he was thinking.
I'd come all this way. . . . " No," I heard myself say. " No,
I'll go in myself if necessary." But even as I said it, I was
thinking it was a forlorn hope. So much time had elapsed
since Briffe had made that transmission.

And then I saw Darcy nod his head, as though that was
what he had expected me to say. He gulped down the rest of
his coffee and said, " We got to be going now, Sid." He set his
mug down on the table. " Mackenzie still camped in the same
place?"

" Yeah, same place—up beyond the trestle."

" Well, thanks for the coffee." Darcy gripped my arm and
as we moved to the door, the cook said, " I wish you luck,
Mr. Ferguson."

It made me feel good to have somebody wish me luck. But
then we were outside, and I became conscious again of the
desolate emptiness of the country crouched along the steel-
grey river. I thought I'd probably need some luck then. " You
were the first person to question Laroche, weren't you?" I
asked Darcy.

We had reached the trestle and he paused at the foot of a
wooden ladder. " Well?"

" If you thought his behaviour odd, why didn't you report
it at the time?"

" A man's entitled to a certain oddness of behaviour when

he's been through as much as Laroche had," he said slowly.
" He was skin and bone when we stripped his clothes off him
and carried him out to the car again. A human skeleton, like
something out of a death cell, and covered with sores. There
was that head wound, too. How was I to know his brain
wasn't injured?"

" All right," I said. " But you and the cook, you both had
the same reaction, didn't you?"

He seemed to consider that. " I'll give you this much," he
said finally. " I went in there this morning to find out whether
Sid's reaction had been the same as mine. Needless to say, we
didn't talk about it at the time—we were too busy trying to
stop Laroche dying on us." And he started up the ladder.

When I joined him at the top, he added, " You don't have
to be half-crazy to be bushed, you know. I'm bushed. And
there's a lot of other guys who are what the docs would call
bushed. It simply means that you've been withdrawn from the
outside world for so long that you don't want to be bothered
with it. You just want to be left alone to the freedom of your
own little world and let the rest go hang. I guess that's the
real reason I didn't do anything about Laroche. That's why
I went fishing this morning, to get things straight in my own
mind. You were the outside world breaking into my comfortable solitude and I can't say I was pleased to see you." He
gave me a wry little smile and then started out across the
timbered top of the trestle. " You're an engineer," he said,
suddenly changing the subject. " This should interest you." He
indicated the girder-like structure with a movement of his
hand. " Down in the Rockies the Canadian Pacific are filling
in their trestle bridges. The timber lasts about twenty years
and now it's too costly to rebuild them. But it's still the quick-
est way of pushing a railway through virgin territory."

We reached the other end of the trestle and he paused, looking back. The long curve of the timber stood black and
gaunt above the river. " This far north it could last for years,"
he said. " Timber don't rot in this country. There's no ter-
mites and no fungi. Queer, isn't it? Up at Burnt Creek they're
building houses of raw, unpainted plywood." As he stood
there, his squat, heavily clothed body outlined against the
stark light of the Labrador sky, he was looking at the trestle
with the appreciation of a man who understood the technical
achievement it represented, and at the same time his eyes were

drinking in the beauty of it in that setting—and it had a strange, arrogant, man-made beauty. He was a queer mixture, part engineer, part artist, and I wasn't certain that he hadn't a touch of the mystic in him as well.

"Maybe I'll try and paint that sometime," he murmured. And then abruptly he tore himself away from the scene. "Okay, let's go find Mackenzie." And he jumped down on to the gravel fill that would carry the steel on to the trestle, and as we scrambled down to the river's edge, the noise of the water came up to meet us, drowning the thump of the pile-driver.

I caught up with him on a grey pebble bank, where the waves set up by the current broke with little slaps, and I asked him how long he'd known that the Indian had found the lake. I had to shout to make myself heard above the sound of the water.

"Couple of weeks, that's all," he answered. "It was just after Laroche came out. I was talking to Mackenzie about it, telling him the story of the old expedition—and when I mentioned Lake of the Lion, he asked what a lion was. He'd never seen one, of course, so I drew him a picture of a lion's head. He recognised it at once and said he knew the lake. He called it Lake of the Rock With a Strange Face." Darcy had stopped and was looking intently at the river so that I thought he was considering the fishing on that stretch. But then he said, "I was thinking of going in myself. Next spring with a geologist friend. I'm due some time off. Thought maybe I'd find Ferguson's gold and make my fortune." He gave a quick laugh and went on across the pebble bank, up into the thick scrub that edged the river.

There was no track here and the going was rough, the undergrowth interspersed with patches of reed. And then the scrub opened out into a small clearing and there was a weather-beaten tent and a canoe and two Indian boys chopping firewood. I stopped then, conscious of an intense awareness. This was the logical outcome of my journey and I knew there was no turning back from it. The stupidity of it! The probable futility of it! I was suddenly appalled. It was as though Labrador were waiting for me.

And then I remembered what Darcy had said. A challenge he had called it. Perhaps that was the way I felt about it, too, for I knew I should go on, even if it killed me. I rediscovered in that moment the fascination in a lost cause that was something deep-buried, a part of my Scots heritage, and realised dimly that I had within me the instincts and the courage that had carried my race through countless generations to the distant corners of the globe. I felt I wasn't alone any more and I walked slowly into the clearing towards the tent where Darcy was already talking to Mackenzie.

"He thinks he could guide you to the lake all right," Darcy said as I came up. "But he doesn't want to leave now. It's like I said—he's hunting, and he needs the meat for the winter. Also, it's a bad time of the year for travelling."

"Yeah, bad time." The Indian nodded. "Very bad." He was a small, square man dressed in a deer hide jacket and blue jeans, his feet encased in moccasins. His face was broad and flat and weather-beaten, and yet strangely smooth, as though the winds had not touched it. And because he was beardless he might have been any age.

"How many days do you reckon?" Darcy asked him.

The man shrugged his shoulders. "Very bad land. Water and muskeg. Better you wait for freeze-up," he added, looking at me. His eyes, no more than slits in the lashless flesh, were dark and remote, with a touch of the Mongol about them.

"Laroche took five days coming out," Darcy said.

Again a shrug of the shoulders. "Then maybe five days." His face was impassive, his manner obstinate. "Bad time to go."

"He's right, of course," Darcy said, turning to me. "Any moment now you can expect the freeze-up. It's the wrong time."

"Yeah, wrong time." The Indian nodded. "You wait for winter, eh? Then you go on snowshoe and water all frozen. Two-three day then."

I should have been thankful for the chance to back out of it, but instead I said, "Suppose we left to-morrow? It would only be five days." And I turned to Darcy. "If my father's right, then there's a radio there. We could radio for a plane. Surely the freeze-up won't come in five days?"

"I can't answer that," he said. "Nor can Mackenzie. It might be early, it might be late."

"I'll have to chance that," I said.

He stared at me hard for a moment, and then he nodded.

"Okay," he said. "Leave it to me. It's the hunting he's worried about. The winter's a long one up here. You take a walk and I'll see what I can do."

A little reluctantly I strolled off along the bank. The sun had come out, the sky fluffy with cold streamers of wind-blown cloud, and the river ran swift and breaking over the shallows. Occasionally a fish jumped, and down by the solitary tent I could see Darcy and the Indian standing on the dark glacier silt where the canoe lay. They stood close together and sometimes Darcy's hands would move in a gesture of insistence or explanation.

And then at last he turned away and came towards me. "Well?" I asked. "Will he take me?"

"I don't know," he answered, and his manner was strangely preoccupied. "Maybe he will. But he doesn't like it."

"Surely the weather can't change as suddenly as all that?" It was quite warm standing there in the sunshine of the clearing.

"I don't think it's the weather that's bothering him," he said thoughtfully.

"What is it then?" I was impatient to get the thing settled.

"It's the place he doesn't like. That's what it boiled down to in the end. Bad place he called it and kept on talking about spirits."

"Spirits!" I stared at him. "What sort of spirits?"

He shrugged his shoulders. "He wouldn't say."

But it was obvious what it was. He'd told him about my grandfather. "If you hadn't told him about the Ferguson Expedition . . ." I said.

"Then I wouldn't have known he'd found the lake." He hesitated and then added, "But all I told him was that another expedition had come to grief in that area a long time ago. I told him the leader had died and I described the lake. But that was all."

"You didn't tell him my grandfather was supposed to have been killed there?"

"No."

It was odd that he should have reacted like that. "When did he find the lake?" I asked. "Was it recently?"

"No. It was on a hunting trip two winters back, he said."

I wished then that I knew more about the Montagnais. "Are they superstitious?"

"Who—the Indians?" He shook his head. "Not particularly. And I certainly wouldn't have thought Mackenzie superstitious. I can't understand it," he added, and his voice sounded puzzled. "Maybe it was just an excuse. They're like that—they don't like to give a direct refusal. Oh, well." He shrugged his shoulders. "I got work to do, I guess." And he started back along the river bank. "You're to come and see him to-morrow. He'll talk to his wife and his sons and he'll give you his decision then."

"That's too late," I said. Now that we had started back I was remembering that instructions had been issued for me to be sent down to Base.

But he looked back at me and said, "The Company doesn't own Labrador, you know. It's only got concessions here. And once you're clear of the line of the grade . . ." There was a suggestion of a smile in his eyes. "What I'm saying is that nobody can stop you—if you've really made up your mind to go."

We returned to the car and all the way back down the Tote Road Darcy talked, giving me the benefit of his experience, all he'd learned of bushcraft in the two years he'd been up in Labrador. I can't remember now a quarter of what he told me; how to get a fire going from reindeer moss when everything was sodden, how to live off the land—the things you could eat, the fish you could catch—and the way the country had been fashioned by the thrust of glacier ice so that I'd never get lost, even with no compass and the sun hidden by leaden skies. I doubt whether I took it all in at the time, for even then I hadn't quite convinced myself that it was real and that the next day I might be out there in the wild with nobody but the Indian for company.

He set me down where the track to the camp led off the Tote Road. "I'll be back in about an hour," he said. "Then we'll see about kit and decide what's to be done. Somebody ought to go in with you." He drove off then to have a look at his survey team and I went down towards the camp, wondering whether in the end I'd be able to persuade him to come with me.

A bulldozer climbing the muddied slope out of the camp checked as it drew level with me, and a face like mahogany under a shapeless hat leaned down. "That Ray Darcy just dropped you off?" And when I nodded, he said, "Guess you must be Ferguson then." The big diesel throbbed against the stillness of the trees. " Somebody's asking for you down at the camp. . . . Waiting for you at Ray's hut." The gears crashed and the monstrous piece of machinery lurched forward, ploughing two deep tracks in the mud.

It could only be Lands—Laroche, too, probably. I stood and watched the water seeping into the tracks left by the bulldozer, wondering what I should do. But I'd have to face them sooner or later, and in the end I started slowly down towards the camp, wishing that Darcy were still with me. I wasn't altogether convinced that Lands couldn't stop me if he wanted to. The Company might not own Labrador, but right now they were in possession of it.

I hesitated a moment at the door of Darcy's hut, remembering how Lands had been the last time I'd seen him. But he'd had time now to get used to the idea of my being up here, and with a sudden desire to get it over and done with, I lifted the latch and pushed the door open.

My first thought was that the room was empty. There was nobody standing there, waiting for me, and when I went inside everything was just as I'd left it—the stove roaring, the wash bowl still with dirty water in it and my empty plate beside it, and the cupboard door half-open with Darcy's clothes hanging there.

And then I saw the rucksack and the heavy boots and the figure lying in Darcy's bed, the blankets pulled up round the shoulders and the face turned to the wall so that only the black hair showed. I was so convinced it was Laroche that I was on the point of slipping out again. But at that moment the sleeper stirred and turned over. The eyes blinked at me uncertainly from behind their dark lashes.

It wasn't Laroche. It was Briffe's daughter. And when she saw me standing there, she threw off the blankets and swung her legs out of bed. " I thought perhaps you are gone for the day, so I went to sleep. She pushed her hand up through her close-cropped hair in a gesture that reminded me of Laroche.

I was too surprised to say anything for the moment, but just stood there, staring at her. She was dressed in faded green corduroys and a thick bush shirt with a red check, and her face was still flushed with sleep.

"How did you get here?" I asked, suddenly finding my voice.

"By plane—last night," she answered. "I stopped off at Two-ninety, and from there I hitch a ride in a truck coming south."

"South?" I had forgotten for the moment that there were other camps to the north, a whole string of isolated outposts linked by the thread of the air lift.

"I am here just after you leave with Ray," she added.

Her feet were encased in thick woollen socks. The socks and the heavy boots under the bed had a purposeful look. My gaze shifted to the rucksack. It was the sort of pack a man would take for a week's hike through mountains. A fishing-rod lay beside it and a rawhide belt with hunting-knife and axe, and flung down on top of it was a thick polo-necked sweater and a leather jacket like the one I'd seen her wearing down at Seven Islands, but older. "What made you come here?" I asked, my mind still on that pile of gear.

"What else am I to do?" Her tone was impatient. "Do you expect me to stay down in Seven Islands when you have gone north up the line?"

"Then you came here to see me?"

"But of course."

And she had come straight here. "How did you know where to find me?"

She was staring at me and there was a hardness in her brown eyes that I had never before associated with that colour. "If you don't believe Albert's story," she said, "then you must come here. It is the nearest camp to where he came out of the bush. Also Ray Darcy is the man who brought him in to the aircraft." Her eyes hadn't moved from my face. They stared at me, wide and unblinking, and I had a sudden uneasy feeling that she could read my thoughts. But it wasn't only her eyes that unnerved me. There was something about her, a peculiar quality of stillness and tension, as though all of her were coiled up inside her body like a spring. She was half-Indian. I don't know how I knew it, but I did, and it scared me because I knew nothing about them.

She got to her feet in one swift, almost cat-like movement. "You still think my father is alive, don't you?" Her voice had a peculiar flatness, so that I knew she had accepted the fact of my belief. And yet, the way she said it, it was an accusation, as though I were guilty of a terrible heresy.

I knew then that she hated me. She hated me for the choice I was forcing on her, and I couldn't blame her. She was torn between love of Laroche and love of her father, and it was my presence that had forced those two loyalties into conflict. I had known what it must do to her ever since that meeting with her down at Seven Islands. But it had never occurred to me that she would follow me up the line.

" You don't answer," she said, frowning.

" How can I?" I said. " I don't know." I couldn't possibly be certain he was still alive.

She got my meaning at once. " Of course not. But he was alive when—when Albert left him. You're certain of that, aren't you? That is why you came north, instead of going back to England."

Half-Indian or not, her mind was logical enough. She had thought it out and reached the inevitable conclusion. What it had cost her to do that I didn't dare to think, but the strain was there in her small, tense face. I didn't say anything, just nodded my head. " And now?" she asked. " What are you going to do now?"

I hesitated. But if I were going to do anything more about it, she'd a right to know. " There's a chance we may be able to locate the lake where they crashed," I said.

" Lake of the Lion?"

" Yes, I'm hoping to start to-morrow."

" You!" Her voice was suddenly incredulous. " But you cannot possibly go in by yourself. Besides, Albert has flown in twice by helicopter and each time he has failed to find it."

I realised then that she hadn't considered the possibility that he might not want to find it, or if she had, her mind had rejected it. " I'm not going in alone," I said. And I told her about the Indian and how he'd recognised the lake from Darcy's drawing of a lion. " But I don't know yet whether he'll go. He's worried about the hunting, and he's scared of the place. He's going to talk it over with his family and let me know to-morrow."

" What is the Indian's name?" she asked. " I know some of them who hunt up here." And when I told her, she seized on it eagerly. " Mackenzie! Which Mackenzie? There are so many—a whole tribe."

"I don't know," I replied. "But Darcy said he acted as guide to the geologists."

"Then I know him," she cried. "I was hoping perhaps it is the same one. He was guide to my father three years back." She sat down on the bed and reached for her boots. "Where is he camped?" she demanded as she hurriedly put them on.

I told her. "But he doesn't know anything," I said. "It's two years ago that he found the lake. And even if he does agree to act as a guide for me," I added, "there's no certainty that he'll be able to find it again."

"If he has been there once," she said firmly, "then he will be able to find it again." And then she was staring up at me, frowning. "You were really planning to go in with him alone?" she asked.

"Yes," I said. And because she looked so incredulous, I added, "It's bad country, I know. But at the worst it'll only take five days and there'll be the radio there——"

"How can you be so stupid?" she cried angrily. "I tell you before it is not possible. Do you think you can walk into Labrador as though you are strolling down a country lane in England? The Montagnais pace would kill you. And it is necessary we move fast," she added.

She had said "we," and I knew then what that pile of gear meant. She intended to come in with us, and my heart sank. It was bad enough to have her up here in this camp, but the thought of her trekking in with us to Lake of the Lion appalled me, for if, when we got there, my fears were confirmed, then its effect on her didn't bear thinking about.

I suppose she misunderstood my reaction for she jumped up off the bed and, with a quick change of mood, came and put her hand on my arm. "I am sorry," she said. "That was not very kind of me and maybe I owe you a great deal. I am still half-asleep, I think. I don't get any sleep last night. But it is true what I said," she added. "I was brought up to this country. I know what it is like."

"Well, anyhow, he probably won't agree to go," I said. And I realised that it was what I was beginning to hope.

"He'll go if I ask him," she said. "But I'll have to hurry." She knelt down and began to lace up her boots.

I watched her then as she pulled on her outer clothes, moving quickly with a sense of urgency. "You're going to see him now, are you?" I asked. And when she nodded, I said, " I'll come with you."

" No. It is better I go alone. Because I am a woman, he will be shamed, and he will do what I ask."

" Well, you'd better wait for Darcy," I told her. " At least he'll drive you as far as the trestle."

But she shook her head. " Ray has his work to do. By the time he returns it may be too late." She looked like a boy as she stood there facing me in all the bulk of her clothes, except that her face was too small and the large brown eyes burned with a feverish intensity. " You see," she explained, " Mackenzie will not like to say No to a white man. If he does not like the place and decides not to go, then he will simply move his camp and it will be days before we can find him again."

" I wish you'd wait till Darcy gets back," I said. Darcy would know whether it was right for her to go up to Mackenzie's camp on her own. But probably it was. Bill Lands said she'd been raised in her father's survey camps.

A car drew up outside and there was the slam of a door. " Here's Darcy now," I said, feeling relieved.

But it wasn't Darcy. The latch clicked, the door was flung back, and Laroche stood there, facing me. He didn't see the girl at first. I think she had stepped back so that I was between her and the door. " I was told I should find you here," he said, and the dark eyes seemed unnaturally bright. " I have something to tell you—something I felt I should tell you myself. We've decided——" He saw her then and he stopped, his face frozen with the shock of seeing her. " Paule!" He was standing quite still, framed in the rectangle of the door with the muddied clearing of the camp sharp-etched in sunlight behind him, and the surprise on his face turned to an expression that I can only describe as one of horror. It was there on his face for an instant, and then he turned and slammed the door to. The crash of it seemed to release the sense of shock in him, and he strode across the room towards her, suddenly talking in a furious spate of words.

I didn't understand what he said, for he was speaking in French, but I could see the anger blazing in his eyes. And then he was gesturing at me with his hand and Paule Briffe was answering him, standing very still and tense, staring up into his face. The anger in him seemed suddenly to flicker out.

"*Mon Dieu!*" he breathed. "It only needed this." And he turned to me and said, "What have you been telling her?"

I hesitated. They were both looking at me, and I could feel their hostility. I was an intruder and because of that they were drawn together again, both of them hating me for coming between them with facts that couldn't be answered. "Well?" His voice trembled.

"There's an Indian," I said nervously, "camped up beyond the trestle. He says——"

"Mackenzie. Yes, I know about him. We met Darcy down the Tote Road and he told us." He loosened the scarf about his neck. It was a slow, deliberate movement to give himself time. "You were thinking of going in with him, weren't you? That's what Darcy told us. You were going in with Mackenzie to try and find Lake of the Lion."

I nodded, wondering what was coming.

He was staring at me and the anger seemed to have drained out of him. "Well, I guess there's nothing else for it." His breath came out of his mouth in a little sigh as though he were suddenly resigned. "I don't understand you," he murmured, "why you are so determined." He sounded puzzled and pushed his hand up over his scalp as though the wound still worried him. "But it doesn't matter now," he added. "I'm going in with you. That's what I came to tell you."

"You're going in with me?" I couldn't believe it for a moment.

"That's right." He nodded.

I stared at him, feeling no elation, only a sudden, inexplicable sense of fear. "But why?" I murmured. What had made him change his mind?

"You've given me no alternative, have you?" It was said quietly, and I was conscious of a change in him. He was different, more relaxed, as though he had come to terms with something inside himself. "I talked it over with Bill Lands driving up this morning," he went on. "We agreed that I should make one more attempt—try and back-track my route out. And then we met Darcy and heard about this Indian."

"Then you're not going to try and stop me?" I was still bewildered by his change of attitude.

"Why should I?" He smiled, a touch of the boyish charm that I'd noticed down at Seven Islands. Somehow I found that more deadly than his anger, and suddenly I knew I didn't want to go into the bush with him. It was a strange thing, but now that the opposition I had been fighting against ever since my arrival in Canada had crumbled, all I wanted to do was to get out of this desolate country and go home and forget about the whole thing. But I couldn't do that—not now; and I heard myself say, " When did you think of starting? "

" First light to-morrow. That is, if Mackenzie agrees to guide us." And then he had turned to Paule Briffe again and was talking to her in French. I think he was trying to dissuade her from coming, for I saw an obstinate look come into her face. " Excuse us a minute," Laroche said. " I have to talk to Paule alone." And they went outside, closing the door behind them.

I could just hear their voices then. They were arguing in French and gradually the tone of his voice changed. He was pleading with her. And then suddenly there was silence.

I went to the window and saw them standing close together by the car, not talking. He was staring out across the camp and she was standing, looking at him, her small figure stiff and somehow very determined. And then he gave a shrug and said something to her, and they climbed into the car and drove off.

I was alone again then, and the sense of fear was still with me, so that my whole body felt chilled, and I went over to the stove and piled more wood on and stood there, warming myself. But the heat of it couldn't drive out a coldness that came from nerves. It sounds absurd, writing about it now in cold-blood, but I had what I can only describe as a premonition—a premonition of disaster.

It's not a nice feeling to be scared, particularly when there's nothing positive to be scared of, and I tried to reason myself out of it. I hadn't been scared at the thought of going into the bush with the Indian—nervous, yes, but not scared. Why should I be scared now? But the answer was there in the memory of Laroche and Paule Briffe staring at me. To go in with Mackenzie was one thing, but it was quite another to go in with those two for company. And the fact that they were foreign to me, both in temperament and race, only added to my sense of uneasiness.

There was something else, too, something that I think had been at the back of my mind ever since that meeting with him at Camp 134, and it sent me hurrying over to the bookshelf to take down Henri Dumaine's book again and search the pages anxiously for any mention of the surname of the man who had accompanied my grandfather. But the only name he gave him was Pierre, and as I searched the pages I was gradually absorbed into the story of his journey. As Darcy had said, it was a trivial day-to-day account of the hardships and appalling travelling conditions he had experienced, but now that I was on the brink of a similar journey it had a significance that held me fascinated. Outside, the sunlight vanished, and as I read on, the light faded and it began to snow, and I felt again that Briffe couldn't be alive.

It was shortly after this that Darcy returned, and he had Bill Lands with him. They came in stamping the snow off their boots, and when Lands saw me, he said. " Well, I guess Bert told you. We're gonna have one last try at locating them." It was in my mind to tell him that he'd left it too late, that they'd be dead by now, but his next words silenced me. " You may be right," he said in a surprisingly gentle voice. " Or you may be wrong. I guess it doesn't much matter either way. You're here and by to-night there won't be a man up and down the line who doesn't know why you're here. There's talk already. God knows where it started—that fool Pat Milligan down at Head of Steel, I guess." He came across to me, his eyes fixed on my face. " If it's any satisfaction to you, your damnfool obstinacy has left me no alternative." He stood there, glaring at me. And then abruptly he said, " Where's Paule? We just been talking to the Camp Superintendent. He said she got in from Two-ninety this morning. Have you seen her?" And when I told him I'd found her asleep in the hut, he asked me how she was dressed. " Did she have cold weather clothing and a lot of gear with her?"

I nodded.

" Goddammit!" he cried, and he swung round on Darcy. " I told you, Ray. Soon as I knew she was here. Where is she now?" he asked me.

" I think she's gone up to the trestle," I said. " She was going to talk to Mackenzie."

He nodded angrily. " Yeah, I remember now. He was guide to her father one season. And Bert? Where's Bert?"

" He was here," I said. " They drove off together."

" So he's with her?"

I nodded.

"Well, I suppose that was inevitable." He unzipped his parka.

"You think she intends to go with them?" Darcy asked.

"Of course."

"But surely you can stop her?"

"How? She's as obstinate as the devil. And I don't know that I'd care to try now," he added. "Her hopes have been raised and she's entitled to see it out to the bitter end, I guess." He swung round on me. "Christ Almighty!" he said. "You'd better be right about this or . . ." He scowled at me, pulled up a chair and sat down on it heavily. "Well, it can't be helped." His voice was suddenly resigned. "But I don't like it, Ray. It's too late in the season."

"Maybe you could get the use of the helicopter again," Darcy suggested.

But Lands shook his head. "They need it on the grade right now. Besides," he added, "the Indian would never find the lake from the air. It's got to be a ground party." He looked across at Darcy. "Will you do something for me, Ray? Will you go in with them? I'd go in myself, but things are piling up and I got to get that new ballast pit going."

"I don't know how Staffen would take it," Darcy said.

"I think I can square Alex for you. If I can . . ." He hesitated, shaking his head. "Bert's no fool in the bush. But he's been injured and I'm not certain—how he'll stand up to it. I don't want anything to go wrong, Ray. I know it's asking a lot of you. . . ."

"Okay," Darcy said, his tone flat and matter-of-fact. "So long as you square Staffen."

"Thanks. Thanks a lot, Ray." His tone was relieved. And after a moment he got to his feet. "I'll go down to the radio shack and contact Alex. You'd better start getting organised. You'll need stores for five of you, including the Indian."

"You think he'll agree to act as guide?" Darcy asked.

"Sure he will. Paule will see to that. You'd better leave it to him to decide whether it's worth lumping a canoe along and portageing. Depends how much water you're going to strike between here and the lake. And take one of those lightweight tents and those down sleeping-bags we issue to the smaller survey parties. If they haven't any in store here, get them sent down from Two-ninety. And see that Bert and Ferguson are properly kitted out." He turned to me. "You'll go in with them. Do you good," he added savagely, "to see what it's like, since you're responsible for the whole thing." And he turned and strode out of the hut.

"He's hoping it'll kill me," I said.

"Oh, don't let Bill worry you," Darcy said, with a smile. "He's upset on account of the girl."

"Anybody'd think he was in love with her." I said it only because I was annoyed at his attitude, but Darcy took it seriously. "Maybe you got something there. Maybe he is— in a fatherly sort of way." And then he came over and looked down at the book I had dropped on the bed. "Did you find anything?"

He seemed afraid that I might have discovered something vital in it, and I remembered how he had searched through the pages when he had found me reading it that first time. "No," I said. "Nothing new." And the relief on his face convinced me I was right, and I saw again the name LAROCHE written in capitals in my father's log book.

He nodded. "Well, let's go up to the store and see what we can dig up in the way of clothing. And then we'd better go and talk to the cook about stores." He seemed to take the whole thing very calmly, as though a five-day trek into the bush were all part of the day's work.

I felt very different about it myself, and as we walked down through the camp, I had the impression that the country was lying in wait for me. It is difficult to convey my feeling, because nobody who hasn't been there can fully appreciate the latent menace of Labrador. I am told there is no country quite like it anywhere in the world. Maybe it's something to do with the fact that it has so recently—geologically speaking —emerged from the grip of the Ice Age. Whatever the reason, the raw emptiness of it took hold of me that morning in a way it hadn't done before. The camp was deserted, of course— and that made a difference. All the men were at work on the grade, and though I could hear the distant rumble of their machines, it was an isolated sound, tenuous and insubstantial in the virgin vastness of the surrounding country—a vastness that seemed to dominate—and the huts, black against the snow, looked solitary outposts without any sense of permanence.

Unconsciously my mind conjured up the picture of Briffe crouched alone by that radio set—the only hope he had of contacting the outside world. "Can you handle a transmitter?" I asked Darcy, for I had a sudden feeling that in the end our own safety, too, might depend on it.

"No. I don't know a dam' thing about radio. Do you?"

"Not enough to transmit."

"Well, Bert Laroche will know."

But I didn't want to be dependent on Laroche. "He might not . . ." I hesitated. "He might get sick," I said.

"You're thinking of the survey party's radio?" His tone was preoccupied. "Well, yes, I guess it'd help if somebody besides Bert knew about it. We'll have a word with the operator here some time this evening."

We were at the store then, and for the next hour we were busy kitting-up. I came out of the hut completely reclothed right down to string vest, long pants and bush shirt, and in one corner we left what seemed to me a mountainous pile of things that included axes and cooking utensils. By then it was time for lunch and the camp had filled up again, men streaming in from the grade on foot and in trucks. The big dining hut was full of the smell of food and the roar of men eating.

"All set?" Lands asked us as we seated ourselves at his table.

"It's coming along," Darcy answered. And Lands nodded and resumed his discussion with a group of contractors' foremen. For him this was just one more project for which he was responsible.

We were half-way through our meal when Laroche and Paule came in, and the set, bleak look on her face as she sat down told me that something had gone wrong. Lands saw it too. "Did you see Mackenzie?" he asked her.

She nodded. But she didn't say anything—as though she couldn't trust herself to speak. It was Laroche who answered. "Mackenzie wouldn't come."

"Why the hell not?"

"The caribou. He'd got word of a herd on the move to the north."

"Dam' sudden, wasn't it?" Lands was frowning as he stared down the table at Laroche. And Darcy said, "It's just his way of saying he doesn't want to go."

Paule nodded. "Except for his tent, he was all packed up when we got there. He had one canoe already loaded. In another half-hour we would have missed him."

"And you couldn't get him to change his mind?" Lands asked.

She shook her head. "I did everything I could to persuade him. I offered him money, stores for the winter . . . but, no, he must have caribou. Always it was the caribou. They must come first. And when I said men's lives came first, and that it was my father whom he knew and loved as a brother, he told me it was no good—my father would be dead by now." She was near to tears. "And then he was talking about the caribou again. I don't believe there were any caribou," she cried. "It was just an excuse."

"He said there were caribou," Laroche murmured. "A big herd three days to the north."

"It was just an excuse," she repeated. "I know it was." And she looked at Darcy. "Why didn't he wish to come? What is he afraid of?"

"Spirits—that's what he told me."

"Spirits! But he is not superstitious. And he was afraid of something—something positive. He would not look at me, not all the time I was talking to him." And then she turned to Laroche. "But he was looking at you. Every now and then he looked at you. I think if you had not been there . . ." Her voice trailed away and then she gave a hopeless little shrug of her shoulders.

"I only wanted to help." His voice sounded tired as though they had been through all this before. And he added, "Anyway, you went off into his tent and talked to him alone, but you still didn't get him to change his mind."

"No."

"So we're back where we were before." Laroche glanced uncertainly round the table. "I suggest a small party—just one other guy and myself. That's what we agreed this morning, Bill." He was looking at Lands now. "A small party, moving fast, and I'll see if I can trace my route out."

"No." Paule's voice was clear and determined. "Whatever is decided, I go with you. You understand? I go, too." Her insistence might have been due solely to a determination to be present when her father was found, but I couldn't help wondering whether it wasn't something more, a feeling of distrust. And then she said, "Anyway, you have to take me. I have something here. . . ." She put her hand to the breast pocket of her jacket. "A map of how to get there."

"A map?" Laroche's tone was sharp with surprise. And Lands said, "Let's see it, Paule. If it's clear enough——" He held out his hand for it.

She hesitated. "It's very rough," she said. "I got Mackenzie to draw it for me in the tent." She pulled a sheet of paper out and passed it across to Lands. "It is not very good, but I think perhaps we can follow it." She watched nervously as Lands spread it out on the table. "At least it gives the lakes," he said. "Did he put them all in?"

"No. I think just those that have a shape or something by which we can distinguish them. Also he has marked in some hills and some muskegs and a section of trail that is blazed. It is very rough, but I think it is possible for a party on the ground to follow it."

"I was thinking of an air reconnaissance. Bert, you come and look at it. See what you think." Laroche got up and peered at it over Lands' shoulder. "Do you reckon you could follow it?"

Laroche hesitated. "Be difficult," he said. "His choice of landmarks is based on ground observation. You'd have to come right down on to the deck to get the same perspective. Even then——"

"Suppose you had the helicopter?"

"I don't know." He glanced quickly at Paule and then down at the map again, licking his tongue across his lips. "Worth trying."

"That's what I think." Lands got to his feet. "I'll get on to Two-ninety right away."

"I'll come with you," Laroche said.

Lands nodded, glancing at his watch. "If Len Holt got it down here by two-thirty, that'd give you four and a half hours. Okay?"

"For a reconnaissance—yes, I guess so. But the weather's not too good."

"No, but it's going to get worse. The forecast's bad."

They went out and Paule Briffe watched them go with a tenseness she didn't bother to hide. "Do you think Bill can get them to send the helicopter down here?" she asked Darcy.

"Depends on the Grade Superintendent. It's his machine. But he's a reasonable guy, and Bill's got a way with him when he's made up his mind to something."

She nodded and got on with her food. She ate like the men,

fast and with concentration, and watching her, covertly, I was amazed that so much vitality and determination could be packed into such a small person, for she did look very small, seated there in that huge dining hall, surrounded by construction men. And yet she seemed quite at home amongst them, entirely oblivious of the fact that she was the only woman there. And the men themselves seemed to accept her as though she were one of themselves. Glancing round the hut, I saw that, though they were all conscious of her presence and glanced at her curiously once in a while, they were careful not to make their interest obvious. They had been up there, some of them for months, and in all that time this was probably the first woman they'd seen, and yet even the roughest of them was possessed of innate good manners in this respect. It was a part of their code, and I realised that this was the same code that must have operated in every frontier town since the North American continent began to be opened up.

" Cigarette?"

She was holding out the pack to me in a slim brown hand, and as I took one, I was conscious again that there must be Indian blood in her somewhere, the wrist was so thin, the fingers so wiry looking. If Briffe was really descended from the *voyageurs*, there'd almost certainly be Indian blood. I lit her cigarette and her dark eyes watched me through the smoke. " Don't you find it strange that we should be going to this Lake of the Lion?" she said.

" How do you mean?" I asked.

" You will maybe find out the truth about your grandfather and what happened there."

" You know the story then?"

She nodded, and I remembered then that she'd said her father had always been talking about the lake. " It's not all that important to me," I said.

" But your grandfather is supposed to have been murdered there."

" Yes, I know. But it's past history now."

And then Darcy said, " He'd never heard of the expedition until he came to Canada. All he knows about it is what I've told him." He was leaning towards her and a quick glance passed between them. It was almost as though he were trying to warn her of something.

" So." She stared at the smoke curling up from her cigar-

ette. " That's very strange." And then, before I had time to
explain, her eyes suddenly looked at me with disconcerting
directness and she said, " And you are quite certain that it is
Lake of the Lion that my father transmitted from?"

" Yes." And I gave her the details of the message, though I
was perfectly well aware that she already knew them. " What
I can't understand," I added, " is why your fiancé didn't admit
that it was Lake of the Lion in the first place."

" Perhaps he is not sure." Her eyes were suddenly clouded
and on the defensive.

" He seems to have accepted the fact now."

" I can understand," she said. And then she stubbed out her
cigarette with quick jabs and got to her feet. " I am going to
rest now. I think you should get some sleep, too." I started to
follow her, but Darcy stopped me. " Sit down a minute." He
was watching her as she crossed the big room, a small, lonely
figure threading her way between the crowded tables. " Don't
ask her that question again," he said.

" What question? About Laroche not admitting it was Lake
of the Lion?" He nodded. " But why ever not?"

" Just don't ask her, that's all," he said gruffly. And then he,
too, got to his feet and I went with him. Outside we found
Lands and Laroche standing by a jeep. " Well, I managed to
fix it," Lands was saying to him. " They didn't like it, but
they'll let you have it for the afternoon. It'll be here in half an
hour." He looked up at the sky. A ridge of cloud lay motion-
less to the west, its darkness emphasised by the fitful gleam
of sunlight that flitted across the camp. " More snow by the
look of it." He shrugged his shoulders. " Well, it's your only
hope of an easy passage, so you'd better make the best of it,"
he said to Laroche. " Take him with you." He jerked his hand
in my direction. " Give him some idea what the country's
like."

" What about Paule?" Laroche said.

" I'll tell her women aren't allowed in the helicopter. It'll
make her mad and she'll chew my head off, but I'm not having
her risk her neck in that thing."

" It's safe enough," Laroche said.

" Maybe. Well, good luck, Bert. I hope you find the place."
And he got into the jeep and drove off up the camp road.

We went down to the grade then and waited for the helicopter. It came from the north with an ugly buzz-saw of sound,

looking like some huge gad-fly, silver against the dark cloud. All along the grade heads lifted and turned to watch it, fascinated; it had an eerie quality about it, like a visitant from another planet, but I suppose the men saw in it tangible evidence that other parts of this wilderness were occupied. It plumped down on a flat section of the grade not far from us and the rotors slowed and stopped.

It was my first flight in a helicopter, and as I climbed in, I thought it was an odd place to make it. It was a small machine, so finely balanced that the pilot had to transfer the battery aft to its fuselage seating in order to compensate for my additional weight. It had one of those Perspex curved fronts so that there was nothing to obstruct the view. I was squeezed in between Laroche and the door, and as we rose vertically into the air, it was like being borne aloft in an arm-chair. The pilot shifted his grip on the juddering control column and we slid off sideways along the grade, gaining height all the time until even the big yellow tumble-bugs looked like toys and the grade, running away to the north, was just a slender, broken ribbon of yellow, a frail line scored by ants across the fir-black face of Labrador.

We followed the grade almost as far as the trestle, and then we turned east and went riding high over country that was nothing but jackpine and lake. The sun had gone and the land was a black plateau shot with lakes, dozens of little lakes that all ran north-west south-east, the way the glaciers had scoured the rock base, and the water was steel-grey.

Laroche had the map Mackenzie had drawn for Paule open on his knee and after about ten minutes he signalled the pilot down. The noise of the rotors made it quite impossible to talk. We hovered at almost tree-top height, and after peering closely at a lake a little ahead of us, Laroche nodded his head and we went on.

Just beyond the lake was a clearing. The pilot shouted something and then the machine was hovering over it and we began to descend. We touched down light as a feather amongst the jackpine and the pilot got out, ducking beneath the gently turning rotor blades. " What have we stopped for?" I asked.

Laroche smiled at me. " I think Len has been drinking some beer," he said, and the smile smoothed the lines out of his face so that he looked almost boyish.

It was the first time it ever occurred to me that you could put a plane down in the middle of nowhere just to relieve yourself. It was so sublimely- ridiculous that I found myself laughing. Laroche was laughing, too, and in the moment of sharing the joke, the tension between us was temporarily eased.

After that we stayed close above the trees, for the map showed a trail running north and south. It was an old trail and difficult to distinguish. But Laroche seemed to have an instinct for the country, so that I began to think that perhaps we would find the lake that afternoon. He sat hunched forward, his eyes peering down at the ground, and every now and then he'd signal with his hand and the stunted tops of the trees would slide away beneath us.

We reached the end of the trail and there was the next lake marked on the map, a long, narrow sheet of water trailing away to muskeg at the farther end. Laroche pointed to the map and nodded, and he shouted something in the pilot's ear and made a quick urgent movement of his hand. I had a feeling then that he was in a hurry, as though he wanted to get it over. The map showed only three more lakes, but no distance was given. "How much farther?" I shouted to him.

He shrugged his shoulders and I sat back, staring at the bleak loneliness of the strip of water that was coming towards us, praying to God that we'd find Lake of the Lion and not have to do all this again on foot. All the brightness seemed to have gone out of the sky and the land had a stark look, as though suddenly deadened by the fear of winter. The joke shared in the clearing seemed a long way back, and as we skimmed the surface of the lake, little cat's-paws of wind ran away from us on either side.

Laroche turned his head, craning his neck to peer up at the sky behind us. The pilot glanced back, too, and when I looked back out of my side-window, the lake behind me had almost disappeared and the country beyond was blurred and indistinct, the sky above it frozen to a grey darkness. And then the storm caught up with us and everything was blotted out by driving sleet that rattled on the Perspex with a hissing sound that could be heard even above the noise of the engine. All we could see was the ground immediately below us, the trees whipped by the wind and slowly greying as the sleet turned to snow and coated them.

I glanced at the pilot. His lips were tight-pressed under the beaky nose, and his hands gripped the control column so tight that the knuckles showed white. He didn't say anything, and nor did Laroche. They were both leaning slightly forward, their eyes straining to pierce the murk, and their tenseness was instantly communicated to me.

I had seen it snow the night before, but not like this, not with this cold, malignant fury. And though I had been alone then, I had still been close to the grade so that I had felt no sense of danger. But now it was different. The grade was miles behind and we were being tossed about in a land devoid of humans. This, I knew, was the real Labrador and, shivering, I thought of that lonely voice calling to my father out of the ether.

The trees vanished and there was another stretch of water below us. Little white caps danced on the ridged surface. And then it was gone. And after that there were more lakes, small grey patches of water that came up one after another and vanished abruptly, and then a big sheet of water and a pebble bank—the third lake marked on the map. The helicopter dropped like a stone, plummeting down on to the grey back of the pebble island, and as the skids touched, the pilot and Laroche jumped out, holding the fuselage down until the rotor stopped and then piling stones on to the skids.

We sat in the helicopter and time dragged by whilst a rime of white gradually covered the bank and the spray froze on the shelving pebble beach. And then the storm passed and the wind subsided. But the cold remained, striking through the Perspex as though we were all locked in a deep-freeze. Laroche looked at his watch and then at the pilot, who climbed out and stood looking up at the sky. "Well?" Laroche asked.

The pilot shook his head doubtfully. "Looks bad," he said.

Laroche got out then and the two of them stood together, staring up-wind and talking quietly. The pilot looked worried and he, too, glanced at his watch, and then he said something to Laroche, who nodded and gave a little shrug of the shoulders. It was a gesture of acquiescence and I watched him deliberately fold the map and put it away in his pocket. They removed the stones from the skids then and the pilot climbed back in. "We're going back," he said.

I couldn't believe it. The storm had passed and we were half-way there. "Surely having come this far——" My words were drowned in the roar of the motor as Laroche swung the rotor blade.

"Sorry," the pilot shouted in my ear. "But my orders are not to risk the machine. It's about the most vital piece of equipment we've got."

"Men's lives are more important than a helicopter," I said.

"Sure." He nodded sourly. "But if you want to get caught out here in a blizzard, I don't. Anyway, Bert agrees with me, and he knows more about this country than I do."

So it was Laroche who had finally decided the matter. "Surely it's worth taking a chance on it?" I said as he squeezed in beside me and slammed the door.

"You want to go on?" He looked at me quickly, a nervous, unhappy glance. And then he leaned across to the pilot. "It's up to you, Len—you understand that?"

"Sure. And I'm going back just as fast as I can." He was revving the engine. "We'll be lucky if we make it back to the grade before the snow starts again," he shouted as he lifted the machine off the ground, slipping sideways across the leaden surface of the lake. "As for those two guys, they'll be dead anyway by now. If they were ever alive," he added.

"But I told you——"

"It's for Len to decide," Laroche said sharply. "He's the pilot, and he says we're going back—okay?"

I left it at that. I couldn't argue with them. And anyway, now that we were headed into the wind I wasn't too happy about the position myself. We were crossing the little lakes again and all ahead of us the sky was dark and louring, black with cold. Visibility was steadily decreasing and a few minutes later we flew into more snow. At least we'd reconnoitred the route as far as the third lake marked on the map and had got about half-way to our objective. We'd proved that the map could be followed, and that was something.

We struck the grade only a few miles north of the camp, and if it hadn't been for the blaze of a fire fed by a work gang, I think we'd have overshot it, for the snow was like a solid grey wall and the white carpet of it on the ground almost obliterated the line of the grade itself.

We landed at the same spot, and as we got out I saw Paule Briffe get up from a pile of gravel where she had been keeping a lonely vigil. She watched us for a moment, and then she turned abruptly away and began walking slowly back towards the camp. Laroche had seen her, too, and the lines of strain were back on his face and his eyes had a haggard look as he watched her go.

The helicopter took off again immediately, heading north and hugging the grade, and as it disappeared into the snow, a mood of extreme depression took hold of me. I knew we shouldn't get the use of it again and that our last chance of flying in had been lost on account of the weather.

This was confirmed by Lands that evening. He called us into Darcy's hut immediately after the supper meal and told us bluntly that if we still intended to try to reach the lake, we'd have to make it on the ground. "I had the General Manager and one of the directors through here to-day," he said. "And they made it plain to me that the helicopter was not to be used for anything but supervising the construction of the grade. Well, that's that, I guess." He gave a little shrug. He was looking at Paule.

"But surely," I said, "if it were explained to them——"

"If what were explained to them?" he demanded harshly. "They know all there is to know." He hesitated, and then said awkwardly, "They don't believe Paule's father is alive. Anyway," he added quickly, "they have a lot on their plate. There's more than a thousand men working on the grade north of here, and a hell of a lot of machinery, and that helicopter is the only means the Superintendent has of keeping them driving." And then he was staring at me. "Well, you've seen a bit of the country, you know what it's like now. Do you still say that your father was sane and that message a genuine transmission?"

They were all staring at me, and I suddenly realised that this was the moment of decision. I had only to say I wasn't sure and Lands would veto any further attempt. His eyes were fixed on me and I could almost feel him willing me to say it. Laroche was watching me intently, too, his long fingers nervously running the zipper of his parka up and down. Darcy's expression was one of curiosity, an artist watching human behaviour. And Paule, she was staring at me, too. But I couldn't see what she was thinking. Her face was a sallow mask, the features fine-drawn, the mouth a tight line. And then I heard myself saying in a flat, colourless voice, " I'm quite satisfied my father was sane and I'm perfectly certain he received that transmission."

What else could I say? If there'd been a way out, then I think I'd have taken it. But there wasn't. I'd gone too far to turn back now.

In the sudden silence I heard the girl's breath expelled in a little hiss of sound, and then Laroche said, " How can you be certain?" The words seemed dragged out of him."

" Because my father had been a radio operator all his life," I told him. " A man doesn't make a mistake like that when his whole life has been given to one thing." I hadn't meant to emphasise the word " mistake," but as I said it, it seemed to hang in the air, and I felt Laroche withdraw into himself.

" Okay," Lands said. " That settles it, I guess." But he sounded uneasy about it. " It's up to you now, Ray," he added, turning to Darcy. " You willing to go in?"

" I guess so." Darcy's voice was flat, matter-of-fact.

" And you, Bert?"

Laroche glanced at Paule Briffe. " If that's what you want?" And when she nodded, he said, " Okay then." But, like Lands, he didn't look happy about it. And the girl, aware of his reluctance, said impatiently, " What else is there to do—if we cannot have the helicopter again?" She looked across at Lands and he shook his head. " There's no question of that, I'm afraid."

" Then it is agreed?" She was looking round at the rest of us. " We will start at dawn, yes?"

And so it was settled. We came down to the details, then and there was a long discussion as to whether or not we should take a canoe with us. In the end it was decided we should. From what we had seen of the country from the air, there was as much water as land ahead of us, and though the portageing of a canoe would slow us up on the land stretches, it was felt that we should more than make up for it by avoiding the long detours necessary in skirting lakes and muskeg. It could always be abandoned if it didn't work out as we hoped.

The task of getting together all the things we needed for a bare existence in the bush took us about an hour and a half. We collected them in Darcy's hut—food, cooking utensils, clothing, packs, a gun, axes, fishing gear; a great pile of equipment that had to be sorted and divided into loads for portageing. We finished shortly after nine and then I asked Darcy to take me down to the radio shack.

I had already raised with them the question of the transmitter Briffe had used. It seemed essential that we should be able to make use of it if necessary and I thought Laroche would say he could operate it. But all he said was, " The transmitter went down with the plane. I told you that already." He said it flatly, with an insistence that carried conviction, and though it made nonsense of the whole basis of our expedition, I could see that the others believed him.

Trudging down through the frozen camp, I wondered if I could persuade the operator to keep a regular watch for us on Briffe's frequency. " I suppose the radio operators here are kept pretty busy?" I said to Darcy.

" Oh, I wouldn't say that," he answered. " There's not all that traffic. Mostly they're brewing coffee or reading paperbacks."

The dark shape of a hut loomed up behind the blazing eyes of its windows. Darcy went to the far end of it and pushed open the door. The heater was going full blast, the small room oven-hot, and a man in a T-shirt raised his eyes reluctantly from the magazine he was reading. His face looked pale behind a straggling beard and his body lay slack against the tilted chair. Even when I explained what I wanted, and why, his tired eyes showed no flicker of interest. Yes, he knew how a 48 set worked, and when I insisted that he explain it to me in detail, he grudgingly drew it out for me on his pad.

I couldn't help comparing him with Ledder. Simon Ledder had been like my father, an enthusiast. This man was just an employee doing a routine job. As soon as he had finished explaining the workings of the set to us, he tilted his chair back again and picked up the magazine.

I hesitated then, unwilling to commit ourselves to him. Our lives might depend on radio contact, and I thought of Ledder again. " Could you contact a ham radio operator at Goose Bay for me?" I asked. " The call sign is VO6AZ."

He shook his head. " I got to stay tuned to our own frequency."

" You expecting news of world-shaking proportions?" Darcy asked. I think he realised what was in my mind.

The operator stared at him with a puzzled look, not understanding the sarcasm. " My orders are——"

" To hell with your orders!" Darcy exploded. " You're here

to operate a radio service. Now get your fat arse off that seat and see if you can raise this ham. And hurry—it's urgent."

"Okay, Mr. Darcy. If you say so." He hitched his chair forward. "What's the frequency?" he asked me.

I told him and we stood and watched him as he fiddled with the dial settings. He tried Voice first and then Key, and as the minutes slipped by on the clock above the transmitter I knew it was no good. I'd either have to trust him to get a message through or . . . "Could you get Perkins down at One-three-four?" I asked him, wondering why I hadn't thought of it before.

He lifted one of the earphones. "What was that?"

"Perkins at Camp One-three-four. Could you get him?"

"Sure. If he's on duty." He shifted the dials and began to call: "CQ—CQ—CQ. Two-six-three calling One-three-four. Come in One-three-four. Over." And then Bob Perkins' voice was there in the room, the solid North Country accent sounding homely and reliable. The phone was put in my hand and when I told him who I was, he cut in immediately with the information that a cable had come in for me from Farrow. "Arrived shortly after midday, but I decided to sit on it. There's been a proper flap on about you and I was afraid if I started radio-ing messages to you at Two-six-three, it'd give the game away like. You're at Two-six-three now, are you? Over."

"Yes," I said, and flicked the switch back to receiving.

"Aye, I thought you'd make it all right. But I suppose they've caught up with you now. Are they sending you back to Base, or what? Over."

"No," I said. "We're to make one more attempt to locate Briffe. I'm leaving in the morning with Laroche and Darcy." And I explained then that I hoped to find Briffe's old transmitter still serviceable. "Will you do me a favour and keep a radio watch for us on Briffe's old frequency. Any time you like, but I must know that I can rely on somebody to pick up any message. Over."

"So you're going in with Laroche, eh?" Even the loudspeaker couldn't conceal the surprise in his voice. And then, after a pause, he said, "Maybe you'd better take down Farrow's cable and then have a right good think about it. I'll read it to you slowly." The radio operator pushed his message pad towards me and reached for the pencil behind his ear. And then Perkins' voice was saying: " It's a night letter cable signed Farrow. Message reads—' Mother desperate your departure Labrador in ignorance Alexandra Ferguson's diary stop Diary shows grandfather killed by partner Lion Lake stop Partner's name Pierre Laroche stop Fears may be some connection. . . .' "

Laroche! So I had been right. There was a connection. It was as though my father had suddenly called a warning across the ether in Perkins' tin-box voice. No wonder he had written the name in capitals. And that scribbled line that had so puzzled me. . . . *L-L-L-it can't be.* It was all clear to me in a blinding flash and I turned on Darcy. " They're related, aren't they?" I cried. " You knew they were related." I didn't need his nod to confirm it; he'd been so careful not to mention the surname of the man who'd come out raving. " My God!" I breathed. " No wonder my father was so absorbed in Briffe's expedition." And I added, " Does Lands know about this?"

He nodded.

" And Paule Briffe?"

" I don't know. But I guess so."

Everybody but myself! They had all known. " What's the relationship?" I asked. " What's this Laroche to the one that murdered my grandfather?"

" Same as yours to Ferguson," he answered. " He's Pierre Laroche's grandson."

So it was as direct as that. The third generation. No wonder I'd been scared at the thought of his coming with us. And then I became aware again of Perkins' voice. " Have you got it?" His tone was impatient. " I repeat, have you got it? Come in, please. Over."

I pressed the sending switch. " Yes," I said, and I turned again to Darcy, wondering whether he was feeling about it the way I was—the way I knew my father had . . . feeling that history was repeating itself. " Do you think . . ." But I stopped there, unwilling to put it into words.

" It's just a coincidence," he said harshly.

A coincidence—yes, but a damned strange one . . . the two of us up here in Labrador and leaving together in the morning for the scene of that old tragedy.

I was so dazed by it that I had to ask Perkins to repeat the message. Apparently my mother, faced with the fact that I was actually in Labrador, was determined now that I must see the diary before I took any further action. It was being flown out to Montreal on the next flight and from there it would be posted direct to Perkins.

But it was too late, and, anyway, it didn't seem to matter. The one vital fact was in my possession. " We leave first thing in the morning," I told Perkins, and then went on to arrange with him that he should keep watch between seven and half-past, morning and evening. He said he would contact Ledder and arrange for him to keep watch, too.

It was the best I could do. Between the two of them they ought to pick us up if we were able to transmit. His last words were, " Well, good luck, and I hope it keeps fine for you." Banal words, and only a voice out of the ether, but it was good to know that somebody would be listening for us the way my father had for Briffe.

And then we were outside the radio shack and it was snowing ; not soft, gentle flakes like the night before, but hard little crystals of ice driving almost parallel to the ground and dusting the edges of the ruts like a white powder. Darcy took my arm, his gloved fingers pressing hard against the bone. " It's a co-incidence," he repeated. " Just remember that." And when I didn't say anything, he added, " Best forget all about it. This isn't going to be any picnic."

I didn't need him to tell me that! But it was manifestly absurd for him to suggest that I should forget that Laroche was the grandson of a homicidal maniac. Once a thing like that is put into your mind, it stays, and all the time we were discussing the final arrangements for our departure in the morning, I found myself covertly watching Laroche's face, searching for some definite indication of the mental instability that I was certain he'd inherited ; appalled at the thought of what the next few days would bring. And later, after we'd turned in, I couldn't get the past out of my mind, and lay awake for a long time, watching the red-hot casing of the stove gradually dull and listening to the howl of the wind against the thin wood walls of the hut.

PART THREE

LAKE OF THE LION

I

I WOKE to the shrill of the alarm clock in that dead hour before the dawn and knew that this was the day and that there was no turning back. The light snapped on and I opened my eyes to see Darcy bent over the stove in his long woollen underpants. " Is it still snowing? " I asked him, reluctant to leave the warmth of the blankets.

" I guess so." He struck a match and flames licked out of the top of the stove. " You'd best get moving. Breakfast's in quarter of an hour."

We washed and shaved and then went down through the white desert of the camp. Paule Briffe was already in the diner and the lights blazing on the empty tables made the place look vast. Laroche came in shortly afterwards. " Even if they'd let us have the helicopter,". he said, " Len couldn't have flown in this weather." It was still blowing hard and the snow was the same mist of drifting, powdery crystals.

We ate in silence, joined by the driver of the truck we'd been allocated, each of us wrapped in our private thoughts. And then we loaded the truck and left, and the wretched little oasis of the camp was swallowed up by the blizzard before we'd even reached the Tote Road.

The truck bringing the canoe down from Camp 290 was due at the rendezvous at 0700 hours. But when we finally got there, more than two hours late because of the drifts, there was no sign of it. There were no tyre tracks either, and when we reached the trestle, five miles farther on, and there was still no sign of it, we knew it had failed to get through.

There was nothing for it then but to sit in the cookhouse hut, drinking Sid's coffee and waiting. We didn't talk much and there was an atmosphere of strain, for Paule and Laroche were like two strangers, united only in their hostility to me, which they scarcely bothered to conceal. This, I realised, was something I should have to learn to live with.

" I don't think we should wait any more," Paule said finally. " The lakes will be freezing over and in this cold per'aps it is better without the canoe." Her small, peaked face was pale and the edge to her voice revealed her impatience.

"There's the tent," Darcy reminded her. "The sleeping-bags, too. We can't leave without those."

She nodded and went back to plucking at the frayed edges of her parka. And then she slipped her hunting-knife out of its sheath and began trimming the threads. It was an Indian knife with a carved handle and a long, slender blade worn thin by constant whetting. It wasn't the sort of blade you'd expect a girl to have, and to see it in her small, capable hands sent a cold shiver through me, for its thinness was the thinness of constant use, a reminder that the North was her element. She finished trimming the edges, and after that she sat staring dully at nothing, the knife still in her hands, her fingers toying with the bright steel of the blade, and I couldn't help thinking that I was now in a land where there was no law as I understood it, where justice was something to be meted out on the spot, and I looked across at Laroche and saw that he, too, was watching her play with that knife.

It was shortly after eleven that the truck finally rolled in. We transferred the canoe and the tightly rolled bundle of tent and sleeping-bags to our own vehicle and went back down the Tote Road, to the point where Laroche had crossed it on his trek out. And then we started into the bush, carrying the big canoe as well as our loads.

For a few paces the sound of the truck's engine stayed with us, but then it was lost in the noise of the wind, and when I looked back, the Tote Road had disappeared and there was nothing but the jackpines drooping under their load of snow. We were alone then, just the four of us, with all Labrador stretched out ahead, and not a living soul between us and the coast, almost three hundred miles away.

We camped that night on the pebble shores of a lake no bigger than a mountain tarn. The blizzard had blown itself out and in the dusk, under the frosty stars, the trees had a Yuletide stillness, their whitened branches mirrored in the steel-grey water, and all round the edge of the lake was a crusting of new-formed ice that became a pale, almost luminous ring as darkness fell.

It had been a bad day—the late start and then heavy going through deep snow with several bad patches of muskeg. We had only been able to use the canoe twice, and that on short stretches of water. The rest of the time we had carried it. We were wet and dirty and tired, and we hadn't even reached the first lake marked on Mackenzie's map. We were now amongst the dozens of little lakes that Laroche and I had flown over so easily and so quickly in the helicopter the previous afternoon.

Darcy fished till the fire was blazing and the coffee made, and he came back empty-handed. " Too cold for them, I guess." He flung his rod down and held his hands to the blaze, his wet feet amongst the embers. " Goldarnit! I could have done with a nice salmon." He grinned at us ruefully and I found my mouth watering at the memory of the pink-fleshed *ouananish* I had eaten the previous day. Instead, we had to be content with a mixture of dehydrated soup and potatoes mixed with bacon and beans. After that there was more coffee, black and strong and sweet, and we sat, smoking, the mugs cupped in our hands.

" Feel better?" Darcy's hand dropped on to my knee, gripping it in a friendly gesture.

I nodded. My shoulders still ached and the rawness remained where the straps of the pack had rubbed; the blisters on my heels were throbbing, too. But the bone-weary feeling of exhaustion had gone and my body was relaxed. " I'm fine," I said.

" Feel you got the Labrador licked, eh?" He stared at me hard, smiling, but not with his eyes. " My guess is we've done no more'n five miles as the crow flies—one-tenth of the least possible distance. One-twentieth if you count the trek out as well."

" Is that meant to boost our morale?" Laroche said.

Darcy turned his head and looked across the firelight at him. " I just figured he'd better know the score, that's all." And then he added with a grim little smile, " There's one consolation. As we eat into our supplies, the packs'll get lighter."

It was a warning. We were starting very late in the year and whilst he'd fished, he'd been considering our chances. They were all three of them thinking about it, and because I knew what was in their minds, I found it necessary to justify myself. " If it's tough for us," I blurted out, " It's a lot tougher for Paule's father."

They stared at me, frozen into silence by my words. And then, with a quick movement, Paule picked up the cooking pot and went down to the lake to wash it. Darcy got to his feet, too. "Okay," he said gruffly. "Just so long as you're sure." And he picked up his axe and went into the timber to cut more wood.

Laroche hadn't stirred. He was staring into the fire and the flames, flickering on his high cheekbones, gave to the skin a ruddy, coppery glow that made him look half Indian. His head was bare and the wound was a black shadow across his skull. "You shouldn't have said that." He spoke in a tone of mild reproach.

"About her father? Why not?" I said. "She knows perfectly well——"

"Just don't talk about it, that's all I'm asking." He stared at me across the glowing circle of the embers. "It only raises her hopes if you talk like that." His eyes dropped to the fire again, and after a moment he murmured, "You see, for her there isn't any hope—either way." He said it quietly, almost sadly. And then, as though speaking to himself, he added, "He'll be dead anyway by now." And the way he said it, I knew it was what he was hoping.

"But he wasn't when you left him, was he?" The words were out before I could stop myself.

But he didn't seem to notice, or else he didn't care whether I knew or not. He sat, staring down at the embers, lost in thought, and I wished I could see into his mind. What had happened after the crash? What in God's name had induced him to say Briffe was dead when he wasn't? And then I was thinking of his grandfather and what had happened at that lake before, and my gaze fastened on that ugly gash. His head was bent slightly forward and the wound looked livid in the firelight. He would be marked by it for life. Like Cain, I thought suddenly.

As though conscious of that thought in my mind, he suddenly raised his head and looked at me. For a moment I had the impression he was about to tell me something. But he hesitated, and finally his lips tightened into a thin line and he got abruptly to his feet and walked away.

I was alone by the fire then. Yet my mind still retained a picture of him sitting there with his head bent to the blaze, and the certainty that he wasn't any saner than his grandfather had been took hold of me again. It was a terrifying thought and I tried to put it out of my mind. But once there it seemed to take root. And later, when the four of us huddled together for warmth inside the tent, I became convinced of it, for what other possible explanation could there be?

I remember telling myself that it wasn't his fault. He had been badly injured. But insanity is something of which we all have a primitive dread, and though I could pity him, I was still appalled at his presence among us, sleeping peacefully on the far side of the tent. It seemed so much worse out there in the bush, for we were shut in on ourselves, entirely dependent on each other. No doubt I was affected by the unnatural quiet that surrounded us. There wasn't a sound except for Darcy snoring gently beside me, and the cold that came up from the hard ground and seeped in through the thin walls of the tent prevented me from sleeping.

It seemed different in the morning. We were up at first light, busy rebuilding the fire and cooking breakfast. It was a raw morning, a thick mist lying over the water, which was lightly filmed with ice. Seeing the methodical way Laroche went about the job of striking and folding the tent, it was difficult to believe that he wasn't normal. And yet the very normality of his behaviour only served to increase my uneasiness, and the frightening thing was that there was nothing I could do about it. I could only watch him and hope that the strain, as we neared our objective, wouldn't drive him beyond the edge of sanity again.

"What are you thinking?"

I turned to find Paule standing behind me. "Nothing," I said quickly. She was the last person with whom I could share my fears. Darcy, yes—I would have to talk to him about it some time when we were alone. But not Paule—not yet.

She frowned. "Then perhaps you will help me load the canoe."

The canoe proved its worth that day. We crossed three lakes in it during the early morning, with only short portages between, and just after ten we reached the long, narrow stretch of water that we'd identified from the helicopter as the first of the lakes marked on the map.

We crossed it diagonally, picked up the old Indian trail and in no time at all, it seemed, we had reached the second of Mackenzie's lakes. But after that the country changed and became featureless. There were no longer rock outcrops, and

the lakes weren't buried in deep-scored clefts, but lay in flat
alluvial country, so that water and land were intermingled with
little change of level. We kept due east as far as possible, but
there was nothing to guide us, and the fact that we'd flown
over it didn't help, for it was here that the snowstorm had
overtaken us.

The going was good, however, the portages short and mostly
easy. As a result I was never alone with Darcy all that morning. In or out of the canoe, we were all together in a tight little
bunch. And the only rest we had was when we were paddling.
We ate our lunch of chocolate, biscuits and cheese on the
march, not stopping, and the extraordinary thing was that it
was the girl who set the pace.

Darcy, of course, was much older than the rest of us, and as
the day progressed and the portages became longer and more
difficult, the pace began to tell on him. It told on Laroche,
too ; the skin of his face became tight-drawn and all the spring
went out of his stride. More and more often he stopped to
look at the map, but whenever Paule asked him whether he
recognised anything, he only shook his head. And when the
next lake—the one with the pebble bank failed to materialise
after ten miles of good going, she began to get worried.

I was up in front with her now, for my body had adjusted
itself to the conditions of travel and though the blisters on my
heels still troubled me, I had begun to get into my stride. We
didn't talk much, for she was preoccupied with our direction
and I was looking about me at the country, even enjoying it,
for it had an austere beauty of its own.

And then we came to a small lake and had to wait for Darcy
and Laroche, who were bringing up the canoe. " How much
farther to the lake where you landed the helicopter?" She
stood there, staring at the flat surface of the water with a
worried frown, and when I said I didn't know, she dropped
her load and stretched herself out on the coarse silt of the
beach. " Well, anyway, it's nice here." She closed her eyes in
an attempt to relax. The sun had come out, and though it was
alreay low over the trees behind us, there was no wind and it
was almost warm. " If only there were a hill," she murmured.
" We could get a view of the country if there were a hill. As it
is we shall have to waste time scouting for this lake." After
that she was silent for so long that I thought she had fallen

asleep. But then she suddenly sat up. " You're sure it is Lake of the Lion where they crashed?" she demanded.

The suddenness of the question took me by surprise. " Yes," I said. " It's quite clear from the message——"

" I know," She made an impatient gesture with her hand. " But Albert has never admitted it is Lake of the Lion. He never saw any resemblance to a lion in the rock he hit. And now he says Mackenzie's map is taking us too far south. He wants us to go farther north."

I knew then that Laroche was going to try and turn us away from the Lake, and I asked, " How does he know we're too far south?"

" Because he has recognised nothing. If it is Lake of the Lion and the map is correct, then all day we must have been passing through the same country he came through on his trek out, but he does not recognise it. The other night, after you have made the attempt in the helicopter, he warned me he thought the direction wrong. Now he is convinced of it." She frowned down at the pebble she had picked up and then tossed it into the water. " I don't know what is best to do—to follow the map or turn north until we find something that he recognises."

There was a movement in the jackpine behind us and Laroche and Darcy emerged, bent under the cumbersome load of the canoe. " We must stick to the map," I told her urgently. And because she still looked doubtful, I repeated it. " If we abandon the map now and turn north . . ." I had been going to say that we'd never find her father then, but that meant trying to explain to her why Laroche should want to turn us away from Lake of the Lion, and I let it go at that.

She had got to her feet. " Did you see anything you recognised on that portage, Albert?" Her voice was devoid of any hope, and when he shook his head, she said, " Not even that big rock outcrop?"

" I told you before, my route was north of the one Mackenzie drew you." He was tired and his voice sounded petulant. " And now we're even south of that."

" How do you know?"

" We've come a long way from the Indian trail and that last lake we identified. We should have reached the next one by now, the one where we landed yesterday."

"But you said it was snowing and the visibility was bad. How can you possibly be certain that we're south of our course?"

"Because we're getting pushed south all the time." He said it wearily, and then he turned to Darcy. "What do you think, Ray?" And Darcy nodded. "It's like Bert says," he told Paule. "It's the way the darned country's built. It's edging us south all the time, particularly on the portages."

She hesitated, glancing from one to the other of them. "Then we'd better head north-east for the rest of the day," she said at length. "And if we don't find that lake by nightfall, then we must begin scouting for it."

"Why bother about the lake?" Laroche said. "My view is we should keep going north-east till I pick up my route out."

She was looking at him uncertainly and at length she said, quietly, "But how can you be sure you will recognise it? So far you have recognised nothing—not even when we started in from the Tote Road."

And Darcy said quickly, "Well, anyway, we head north-east till nightfall. We can discuss this later." And so it was decided. Nobody asked me what I thought, and, anyway, I couldn't have argued with them. It was perfectly true that the country was forcing us south. But I didn't like the thought of turning north, even for the remainder of the day. It was the way Laroche wanted us to go, and north lay the Arctic.

We crossed that lake and two more on the new compass course, and in the early evening we reached a broad sheet of water with a pebble bank in the middle of it, and for a moment my mind was thrown into confusion, for I thought Laroche had brought us to the third lake marked on the map, the one where we'd landed the helicopter in the storm. But then I saw that the shape of it was different and the pebble bank had a stunted growth of trees.

But Paule was instantly convinced that this was the lake we were looking for. So was Darcy. Laroche said nothing, and when I tried to tell them that it wasn't the place where we'd landed in the helicopter, she said, "But how can you be sure? There was a snowstorm and the visibility was bad."

"But we landed on the pebble bank," I said. "We'd have seen the trees if there'd been any."

She asked Laroche to produce the map, and leaning over his shoulder as he squatted on the ground holding it for her,

she cried, " There, you see! He has marked that bank. I remember he told me it only just showed above the water, an
island of pebble he called it. I'm sure this is the lake he meant.
Even the shape of it is the same."

Laroche still said nothing and I turned to Darcy. " How far
have we come to-day?"

He considered for a moment. " All of twenty miles, I guess.
Maybe more."

" Then we're about half-way."

" If it's fifty miles altogether, yes."

And we were in the same sort of country, flat, with the
alluvial debris of the Ice Age. I glanced at Laroche, for it had
occurred to me that perhaps this was really the lake Mackenzie
had meant and not the one where we'd landed. He must have
guessed what was in my mind, for he said, " There isn't much
to choose between this and the lake where we landed yesterday." He began to fold the map. " Either of them would fit
a map like this."

Paule frowned. " Let me have another look at it. Mackenzie is usually very accurate."

But he had already risen to his feet. " However much you
look at it," he said, " you'll never be certain whether it's this
lake or the other." And he put the map back in the breast
pocket of his parka.

She stood up and faced him then. " But I want to look at it
again," she said obstinately.

" You can look at it later," he answered, moving away from
her, down towards the canoe. " If we're going to cross before
dark, we'd better get moving."

Whether she had suddenly become suspicious, I don't know.
It was a fact—and I had been conscious of it for some time—
that Laroche had never once let the map out of his hands
since we started. Maybe it was just that she was tired and in a
petulant mood. At any rate, she ran after him and caught
hold of his arm. " Albert. Give it to me. It's my map." And
when he told her it was quite safe in his pocket, she repeated,
" It's my map. I want it." Her voice was suddenly quite
shrill.

" For heaven's sake, Paule." He shrugged her hand off.
" Just because you're not certain this is the right lake——"

" I am certain."

" Then what do you want the map for?"

" Because it's mine." She grabbed hold of his parka. " Give it to me. Please." She was almost sobbing.

It would have been childish, except that it suddenly brought the tension between them out into the open. I remember the shocked expression on Darcy's face. He knew it was serious and he moved in quickly. " Steady, Paule." He caught hold of her arm none too gently and pulled her away. " The map's okay and we've got to get across. A lake of the size of this could hold us up for days if it came on to blow."

She hesitated, staring at Laroche as though she wanted to tear the map out of his pocket. And then abruptly the violence of her mood vanished. " Yes, of course," she said. " You are right ; we must hurry." And she gave Darcy a quick smile and went quietly down to the canoe.

The temperature had fallen quite sharply and it was cold out on the water. We paddled in silence and the only sound was the dip-dip of the paddle blades and the whisper of water along the skin of the canoe. All the world seemed hushed with the gathering dusk and so still that the endless blacks and greys had the static quality of a photographic print.

And then, from beyond the pebble bank, came the call of a goose, so clear and perfect in the stillness that it took my breath away. We saw them as we glided round the end of the bank, four birds like white galleons swimming in line astern, and Darcy reached for his gun. He fired as they spread their wings ; three birds thrashed the water and became airborne, the fourth keeled over and lay on its side. And when we'd pulled it into the canoe, the quiet returned, so that it was difficult to believe it had ever been disturbed by the shot and the frenzied beat of wings.

Darkness was falling when we reached the farther shore and we went straight into camp on a little promontory of stunted trees. Whilst Paule plucked and cleaned the goose, we got a roaring fire going, and in no time at all the bird, neatly skewered with slivers of wood, was hanging from a cross-pole supported by two forked stakes and turning slowly before the blaze, the frying-pan set below it to catch the fat. The sight and smell of that roasting bird was something out of this world in that remote wilderness. We sat round the fire, drinking coffee and talking, and eyeing it with the eager anticipation of children at a feast. The affair of the map seemed to have been entirely forgotten.

It takes a long time to roast a goose in front of a fire, but at last the juices ran at the prick of a knife and we cut it down and fell on it ravenously, burning our fingers with the hot fat. Paule used the same little thin-bladed Indian knife that she must have used at countless camp fires, and the sight of the worn steel winking red in the firelight reminded me that it was her father who had done the hunting then. But I was too absorbed in the flavour of that goose to worry about what she might be feeling. It was only afterwards, when my stomach was full, that I noticed the tense, withdrawn look on her face and became conscious of Laroche's moody silence.

After such a meal they should have been relaxed, like Darcy. But they sat so still and tense that it was impossible not to be aware of the atmosphere of tension between them. And if this were really the lake Mackenzie had meant, then to-morrow or the next day we'd be at the Lake of the Lion. Time was running out, and when Darcy got up and strolled off into the darkness of the timber, I followed him. " I've got to talk to you," I said when we were out of earshot of the camp.

He stopped and waited for me to say what I had to say, standing quite still, his bulky figure in silhouette against the glimmer of the water. " It's about Laroche," I said. But it was difficult to put my fear into words, and when I tried, he stopped me almost immediately. " Now, listen, Ian. You got to forget he's the grandson of Pierre Laroche. I told you that before. What happened at that lake between your grandfather and his is nothing whatever to do with the present."

" I think it is," I said. And then, in a rush, I poured out all my fears, not giving him time to interrupt me. And when at last I had finished, he stood there, staring at me in silence with the starlight gleaming frostily on his glasses. " You realise what you're saying?"

" Yes."

" And you believe that? You think he tried to kill them?" His breath hung like steam in the night air. " Good God!" he breathed, and after that he was silent a long time, thinking it out. " He seems sane enough," he murmured half to himself. " It was Paule I was beginning to worry about." And he shook his head as though he still couldn't believe it. And then his hand gripped hold of my arm and he said, " Why have

you told me this? What do you expect me to do about it?"
His voice sounded angry and bewildered.

"Nothing," I replied. "There's nothing either of us can do
about it, except watch him."

"Hell! There must be some other explanation."

"What other explanation can there be?" I demanded impatiently. "It's the only possible explanation—the only one
that fits all the facts."

He let go my arm then. "It's bad enough having you along
with us, believing a thing like that. But if it's true . . ." His
voice was suddenly an old man's voice, tired and angry.

"If it isn't true," I said, "why do you think he's always
trying to get us to turn north? He daren't let us reach Lake
of the Lion. He daren't even face the sight of it himself. Anyway," I added, "I've warned you."

"Yeah." He stood for a moment longer with the sky behind
him full of stars and the northern lights weaving a luminous
pattern in the night. "Okay," he said wearily. "Let's go back
now. It's cold out here." And he started towards the fire which
showed a red glow through the sticks of the trees. "You
haven't said anything to Paule about this, I hope?"

"No."

"Well, don't," he said.

But back at the fire I wondered whether she hadn't guessed
it already, for they were sitting there just as we'd left them,
sitting quite still and not talking, and I could feel the tension
between them. Darcy noticed it, too. "It's late," he said
gruffly, and as though glad to be released by the sound of his
voice, they got up at once and followed him to the tent.

I threw some branches on to the embers of the fire and
watched the crackling flare as the needles caught. It was so
peaceful, so unbelievably peaceful. And beyond the leap of
the flames lay the immensity of Labrador, all still and frozen
in the night. I sat down, cross-legged in front of the fire, and
lit a cigarette, and let the stillness seep into me. It gave me a
strange sense of peace, for it was the stillness of space and
great solitude, a stillness that matched the stars and the northern lights. This, I thought, was the beginning of Creation, this
utter, frozen stillness, and the fire felt to me then the way it
must have felt to the first man who'd experienced it—the
warmth of something accomplished in a cold, primitive
land.

There was a movement behind me, the snap of a twig, and I turned my head to find Paule there. " You should come to bed," she said. " If you sit here, you will be tired in the morning."

I nodded, " It was the night," I said. " It's so still."

" And there is so much sky—all the stars. I know." She seemed to understand my mood, for she came and sat beside me. " You have never been in country like this before?"

" No."

" Does it worry you?"

" A little," I admitted.

" I understand." She touched my arm, a quick gesture of companionship that surprised me. " It is so empty, eh?" And she withdrew her hand and held it to the blaze. " My father always said it is the land of the Old Testament."

" The Old Testament!" It seemed odd to compare this frozen country, so full of water, with a land of heat and desert sand, and yet I could see his point, for I suppose he'd never known anything but the North. " What was your father like?" I asked.

She didn't answer for a moment and I was afraid perhaps that I shouldn't have asked her that. But then she said, " When you are very near to a person, then I think per'aps it is difficult to tell what they are really like. Some men thought him hard. He drove them." And she added with a little smile, " He drove me, too. But I didn't mind."

She was silent for a moment, staring into the flames as though she could see him there. " You would like him, I think," she murmured at length. " And you would get on to-gether. You have guts, and that always appealed to him." She sighed and shook her head sadly. " But I don't think you meet him now; I don't think he can still be alive." She leaned forward and pushed a branch into the fire, watching it flare up. " It is a little sad if it is the Lake of the Lion where they crash. There is supposed to be gold there and that was his dream—to strike it rich and have a big mine named after him. It wasn't the money so much, though we never had any and my mother died when I was a little girl because he could not afford a sanatorium; it was more the need to justify him-self. He was a prospector," she added. " It was in his blood, and, like a gambler, he must always try his luck again—one

more expedition, one more attempt to find what he is searching for."

I nodded. " Like my grandfather. Ray says he was like
that."

She turned her head and stared at me, her eyes very wide
in the firelight. " That was a terrible story," she said at last,
her voice little more than a whisper, and I knew it wasn't my
grandfather she was thinking of, but Pierre Laroche. " But it
has nothing to do with my father," she declared, her voice
trembling with the effort needed to carry conviction. " Nothing
at all."

I would have left it at that, but the train of thought had
made me curious on one point. " You told me your father
often talked about Lake of the Lion," I said.

She nodded. " That and a hidden valley up in the Nahanni
River Country and another lake somewhere on the edge of the
Barren Lands ; places he'd heard about from the old-timers."
And she added, " I tell you, he was a prospector. That was his
life, and nothing else mattered." She was staring into the fire
again. " But he was a wonderful man. To see him handling a
canoe in the rapids or with a gun, and always round the fire
he would be telling stories—strange, unbelievable stories of
the Canadian wild. . . ." She stopped there and I saw she was
crying, the tears welling gently from her eyes. And then
abruptly she got to her feet, in one quick, graceful movement,
and left me without a word.

I watched her crawl into the tent, and after that I sat alone
beside the fire for a long time, staring at the star-filled night
and thinking about my grandfather, who had died in this
country, and about that indomitable woman, my grandmother,
who had followed his trail with vengeance in her heart. *The
land of the Old Testament* ; that phrase stuck in my mind, and
the frozen stillness that surrounded me seemed suddenly cruel
and menacing. And for the first time in my life I thought
about death.

I'd no religion to retreat into in the face of that ultimate
enemy, no God to support me, nothing. Science had done that
for me. Like all the rest of my generation, I hadn't dared to
think too deeply, and as a young engineer my days had been
full. I had been content to leave it at that. But here it was
different. Here, it seemed, I was faced with the world as
it had been in the beginning, when the mind of man first began

to grope after a meaning for infinity; and, as Darcy had predicted, I began to think about God.

But in the end the cold drove me to the tent, and I crawled in and lay down in my place beside Darcy. We were on spruce boughs that night and the soft, aromatic smell of them sent me to sleep almost immediately.

When I woke, the stillness was gone, shattered by the crash of waves on the lake shore and the roar of wind in the trees. It was a grey day with a savage wind blowing out of the north-west, and as we started on the portage to the next lake, it began to rain. At first it was no more than a drizzle, a thick curtain of mist driving across the country. But gradually the sky darkened, and soon the rain was sheeting down, slatting against our bodies with a fury that was almost personal.

That portage was the worst we had experienced, the ground strewn with boulders, slippery and unstable. Darcy and I were carrying the canoe, and all the time the wind threatened to take charge of it and tear it out of our hands. We were wet to the skin long before we reached the next stretch of water, and when we stood on its shores, our backs to the rain and our clothes streaming, we were a sorry sight.

It was a small lake expansion, not more than two hundred yards across, yet the surface of it boiled under the lash of the storm and the waves were two feet high and breaking. " Will the canoe make it?" I asked Darcy, and in turning to speak to him, the wind drove solid water into my mouth.

It was Paule who answered me. " Of course it will," she said. But I could see Darcy didn't like it. He stood there, wiping his glasses on a sodden handkerchief, staring at the lake and muttering to himself.

We shipped so much water on the crossing that the canoe was half full by the time we reached the other side. And as we stumbled on over the next portage, the country changed again; the timber became thicker, and between the boulder ridges we began to encounter muskeg. At first they were only small patches, which we were able to skirt. But then we came to a big swamp, and though we scouted north and south along its edge, we could see no end to it. There was no alternative then but to cross it, which we succeeded in doing after a long, heart-breaking struggle, in the course of which we were often up to our waists in water.

We came out of it wet and filthy and utterly exhausted, only to be met by more muskeg beyond the next ridge. "Did you meet much of this on your way out?" Darcy asked Laroche as we stood looking at it.

"You saw the condition I was in."

"Yeah." Darcy nodded. "But how much of it is there, that's what I'd like to know?"

Laroche hesitated, glancing nervously from one to the other of us as we stood staring at him. "We'll get into better country soon, I guess."

"How soon?" Paule asked.

"When we're near the lake. We'll be on rock then."

"Well, how near have we got to get before we're out of this damned muskeg country?" Darcy demanded. "Two miles from the lake, five, ten?"

"I don't know." Laroche licked the water from his lips. "About five, I guess."

"And all the rest is muskeg, is that it? Fifteen miles of it at least."

Laroche shook his head. "I can't seem to remember very clearly. There was muskeg, I know. But not fifteen miles of it. I'm sure it wasn't as much as that." And then he added, "It just bears out what I've been saying—we're still too far south. We should turn north until we strike the route I took coming out."

"No, we'll stick to the map," Paule said.

"But you can't be certain that lake we crossed last night——"

"I am certain." Her voice was suddenly shrill again. "And you admit yourself that you don't remember your route very clearly."

Darcy moved towards the canoe. "No good standing here arguing," he said. "We'll only get cold."

Paule and Laroche stood facing each other a moment longer, and then they shouldered their packs and we started down into the muskeg. It stretched ahead of us as far as our eyes could see through the curtain of the rain and we waded on and on through country in which sodden tussocks of cotton grass were the nearest approach to dry land, and never a stretch of open water in which we could use the canoe.

We went into camp early that day on a little stretch of gravel where a few morose-looking jackpine grew. It looked no more than an island in that sea of muskeg, but it was a relief just to stand on something firm, and we were too wet and exhausted to care that we'd only covered a few miles. We managed to get a fire going, but though it enabled us to cook some sort of a meal, there was no real heat to it and the smoke blackened our faces and made our eyes sore. The rain was still teeming down when we crawled into the tent and lay there steaming in our sodden clothing.

All night the wind beat at the tent. Twice we had to go out and weight the walls down with stones, and in the morning it was still blowing. But the rain had stopped and we saw then that our island was, in fact, a long spit of gravel running out from the shores of a lake that was bigger than any we had so far encountered. It was fortunate that the rain had stopped, for we were on the lee shore and in poor visibility we might have attempted the crossing, which would have been disastrous. There was a big sea running out in the centre, and there was nothing for it but to camp there on the shore and wait for the wind to drop.

It was here that we lost the map. Laroche had placed the damp sheet of paper on a rock to dry in the wind, and he'd weighted it down with a stone. At least, that was what he said, and certainly the stone was still there. But the map was gone, and though we searched all along the gravel beach, we couldn't find it. " I guess it must have blown into the water," Darcy said, and Laroche nodded. " I didn't realise the wind was so strong here," he murmured, not looking at any of us.

Paule stared at him for a moment, and then she turned quickly away, got a notebook out of her pack and set to work to redraw the map from memory. But though we all checked it with her on the basis of what each of us remembered of the original, we knew we could never place the same reliance on it. Our only hope was that we should recognise the river when we came to it. The river had been the last thing marked by Mackenzie on the map, with the falls a guiding mark only a few miles from Lake of the Lion. But, as Darcy pointed out, rivers in Labrador are apt to be lost in lake expansions, and often the current is so slight as to make the lake unidentifiable as part of a river system.

We were pinned there on the shore of that lake until dusk, when the wind suddenly dropped and the temperature with it. We crossed at once on a compass bearing in almost complete darkness. It was the worst crossing we'd had, for though the waves were no longer breaking, they were still big, and the movement was so violent that we were in imminent danger of capsizing, and the water rolled green over the sides of the canoe, so that we had to bale continuously. And when we reached the other side, it took us a long time to get a fire going.

We were all of us at a low ebb that night, and as we sat in the smoke of the fire, cooking our meal, the tension that had been building up all day between Paule and Laroche suddenly exploded. We had been arguing about the lake we had just crossed. It was too big for the Indian to have ignored it when drawing the map, and we were all of us quite sure that this wasn't the next lake he'd marked, the one he'd called Burnt Tree Lake. There were no burnt trees here. " Maybe I was wrong," Paule murmured unhappily. " Maybe we should have searched for the lake where you land in the helicopter." She looked across at Darcy. " I guess I was tired."

" We were all tired," he said.

She turned to Laroche then. " Are you sure you don't remember this lake when you are trekking out? It is so big——"

" Exactly," he said. " It's so big it would have meant a detour of several miles."

" But you may have forgotten it. You were injured and——"

" *Mon Dieu!* I'd no canoe. Do you think I'd have forgotten about a lake the size of this?"

" No. No, I suppose not. But then you have recognised nothing—nothing at all." There was a note of exasperation in her voice.

" I've told you before," he said irritably, " I was much farther north."

" But not when we started. We started from the same point where Ray picked you up. Yet you recognised nothing."

" Why should I?" he cried angrily. " I was at the end of five days with no shelter and little food. I was in no state to remember the country."

" But you remembered the muskeg."

" Sure. But I was fresher then, and it doesn't mean it was the same muskeg."

" Muskeg's much the same any part of this country," Darcy said soothingly.

But she was looking at Laroche. " If only you hadn't lost the map," she said furiously. " Now we can never be certain . . ."

" Well, I lost it, and that's that. I'm sorry." He waved the smoke away from his face. " But I don't see what difference it makes. We couldn't identify the last lake for certain and we can't identify this one. The map was only a rough one, far too rough to follow in this sort of country." And he added, " I still say we should turn north and try and pick up my route out."

His insistence annoyed me, but as I opened my mouth to make some comment, I caught Darcy's eye and he shook his head urgently. I hesitated, afraid that by constant repetition he'd convince her. But when she didn't say anything, I returned to the condition of my feet. I had taken off my boots and was attending to my blisters, which had become a suppurating mess under my wet socks. But then she said, " Why are you so insistent that we go north, Albert?" Something in the quietness of her voice made me look up, and after that I forgot about my blisters, for she was staring at him through the smoke and there was a frightened look in her eyes. " You never wanted us to follow the map, did you?"

" I was never convinced we'd crashed at Lake of the Lion," he answered her.

" Then why did you lose the map?" It was such a sudden direct accusation that I stared at her aghast.

" It was an accident, I tell you." His eyes darted from her to Darcy. And then he was staring at me and his face had the wild, trapped look that I'd seen that night at Camp 134 ; I thought then that if she persisted in her questions, she'd drive him over the edge, and I began to put on my boots.

" Very well. It was an accident." Her voice trembled. " But why did you refuse to let me have it? It was my map. Why did you insist on keeping it yourself?" And then, before I could stop her, she cried out, " What are you afraid of, Albert? You don't want us to get to Lake of the Lion. No, don't deny it, please. I have been feeling this for some time. You are afraid of something. What is it?"

I had got my boots on then and all my muscles were tense, for I didn't know what he'd do. But all he said was, " You must think what you like, Paule." And he got up wearily and went off into the trees. Darcy glanced quickly at me, and then he got up and went after him.

I was alone with Paule then. She was sitting quite still as though her body were frozen rigid. But at length she turned to me and said, " What happened there, Ian? Please. Tell me what happened." Her face looked ghastly in the firelight and there were tears in her eyes. And when I didn't say anything, she caught hold of my arm. " I must know what happened," she insisted. " Please." And then with sudden violence: " Don't you understand—I love him. I love him, and I can't help him if I don't know."

" I don't know what happened," I said awkwardly. What else could I say? I couldn't tell her my fears.

" But something happened. Something terrible happened out there after they crashed. I can feel it." Her voice was distraught and she was trembling.

Darcy came back then and she let go of my arm. " I guess we're all pretty tired," he said heavily. " Time we turned in." Laroche came back, too, and asked for more coffee, and Paule gave it to him. The moment of crisis was over. But later, as we were going into the tent, Darcy stopped me. " I think," he whispered in my ear, " that we should see to it those two aren't left alone again."

I nodded. " It's only twenty miles now," I said. " To-morrow or the day after we should know the truth—if the going's good."

" I hope you're right." He had turned his head towards me and his craggy, weather-beaten face was set in deep lines. " I sure hope you're right," he reiterated. " Because my guess is that right now we're lost." And then he added, " If we have to go casting about in search of this lake, then our bellies are going to feel the pinch. The last two days we've got no fish. The only game we've had is that one goose. Just re-member that when it comes to a decision whether to go on or turn back."

It was cold that night, so cold that I lay shivering on the edge of sleep, and when Laroche stirred and sat up, my eyes were instantly open. There must have been a moon, for the inside of the tent was quite light and I could see him staring at me. And then he crawled quietly out through the flap. I was on the point of following him, but then I realised it was only nature that had called him because of the cold, and a moment later he was back and had lain down in his place on the other side of the tent.

I suppose I slept after that, for the next thing I knew it was morning and Darcy was coaxing the fire into a blaze, and when I crawled out, it was to find the world frozen into stillness and all the lake-shore rimmed with new ice. " And how are you to-day?" Darcy said.

" Fine," I replied, and it was true; I did feel fine. The air was so clean and fresh it seemed to sparkle.

" A dandy morning like this, we should make good progress." He put the coffee on, humming tunelessly to himself. And when the others emerged, they, too, seemed affected by the frozen stillness that surrounded our camp. After being battered by the wind for two days, it had a quality of peace about it that was balm to our frayed nerves, and all the tension of the previous night seemed to have vanished away.

The sky turned to palest blue, and as we started out, the sun rose. And it wasn't only the weather that had improved; it was the country, too. We seemed to have left the muskeg behind. Ahead of us, it was all gravel, flat as a pan and full of water; small featureless lakes that ran into one another or were separated only by short portages.

By midday we had covered well over ten miles and all along the horizon there was a black, jagged line of hills. They were only small hills, little more than rock outcrops, but they marked the rim of the gravel pan; and when Darcy asked Laroche whether he remembered this stretch of country, he nodded. But though he stood for a long time looking at the line of little hills, he didn't seem able to recall any particular feature. " All I remember is that I came out of the rock into this flat country and the going was easier for a time." His voice sounded flat and tired in the windless cold.

" But can't you see something you recognise?" Paule asked. He shook his head.

" I don't understand," she cried, and the note of exasperation was back in her voice. " Surely you must have marked the spot where you came out into the flat country here."

" You seem to forget I was injured," he said sharply. " Just to keep going was about all I could manage."

" But you knew you would have to go back and look for my father. You knew it was important to have some landmark to guide you."

" I tell you I was too ill and exhausted to care."

She was about to make some comment, but Darcy stopped her. " It doesn't matter," he said. " Bert's already told us we'll be within about five miles of the lake when we get back into rock country. And if Mackenzie's map was accurate, then the river runs right across our line of march. When we reach it, we've only got to scout along it till we find the falls, and then we're almost there. That shouldn't be difficult." And he picked up his end of the canoe again and we started forward.

Two hours later we reached the hills. They were covered with a dense growth of conifer, and as we started in, we lost the wide Labrador skies, and the going became rough and difficult. It was all rock outcrops, most of them so steep that there was no question of keeping to a compass course, and we went into camp early at the first lake we came upon.

It was a sombre little stretch of water, and though Darcy and Paule both fished it all the time Laroche and I were making camp, they had no luck, and we went to bed very conscious that if we didn't find Lake of the Lion within the next two days we should be forced to turn back for lack of supplies. There was some talk of abandoning the canoe at this stage, but I don't remember what was decided because I fell asleep in the middle of the discussion.

I had meant to stay awake, for now that we were so close to our objective, I was afraid Laroche might make some desperate attempt to stop us. But though I was too tired to fend off sleep, my senses must have remained alert, for I woke suddenly in the early hours to the certainty that something was wrong and saw that Laroche was no longer in his place beside Paule. I could hear him moving about outside, and for a moment I thought the cold had driven him out as it had the previous night. But his movements were different, and when he didn't immediately return, I leaned forward and peered out through the flap of the tent.

I could see him quite clearly in the moonlight. He was standing over the embers of the fire, shouldering his way into his pack. I opened my mouth to ask him what he was doing, but my voice seemed suddenly to have deserted me. I watched him pick up his axe and fit it into his belt, and then he was gone from my line of vision and I heard his boots on the rocks of the lake shore. The sound gradually faded. I scrambled out of the tent then to see his tall figure moving like a ghost in the moonlight down the far end of the lake.

He was heading south—south, not north—and without stopping to think, I laced up my boots and went after him, moving quickly through the timber. I emerged at the far end of the lake, and from the shelter of the trees watched him climb to the top of a bare outcrop of rock that stood at its southern end. He stood a moment on the very summit of the outcrop, a lone, black, figure against the moon's light, gazing back at our camp and then all round him, as though to get his bearings. Finally he turned and disappeared from sight.

I found my voice then and called to him as I scrambled after him up the steep rock slope of the outcrop. I shouted his name all the time I was climbing, and when I reached the top I hesitated. Clouds were beginning to cover the moon. But I could hear him ploughing his way down through the timber on the far side, and a streak of grey light in the east told me that it would soon be dawn. Without thinking what the clouds might mean in that country, I plunged after him, suddenly determined that he shouldn't escape us, that I'd catch up with him and confront him with the truth, whatever the risk.

It was a stupid thing to do, for I'd no compass, no food, no equipment, nothing but what I was wearing, and the conifer growth was so thick that I could only follow him by ear. This meant pausing every so often to listen and, as a result, he gradually drew away from me, until I lost the sound of his movement entirely. I didn't know what to do then, and I stopped, undecided, in a small clearing. It was almost daylight, the sky was heavy and overcast and a light sprinkle of snow falling, and suddenly I realised that I didn't know my way back. Travelling by sound only I had lost all sense of direction.

I had a moment of sheer panic then and stood screaming Laroche's name at the top of my voice. And then, because there was nothing else I could do, I plunged forward again in the desperate hope of catching up with him. Luck was with me, for not more than a hundred yards farther on I came suddenly out of the timber on to the shores of a small lake, and there was Laroche, skirting the far end of it. I could only just see him, for it was snowing heavily now. "Laroche!" I yelled. "Laroche!"

He stopped abruptly and turned, and then he stood staring

back at me in silence. "Laroche! Wait!" I called. He was on the very edge of visibility and I knew, as I started towards him, that he'd only to turn and dive into the bush and I should have lost him for ever.

But instead of trying to escape, he stood quite still, waiting for me. It was only when I was a few yards from him that I saw the dull blade-gleam of the axe gripped in his hand, and I halted with my heart in my mouth, for I'd no weapon with which to defend myself.

II

THAT BLEAK little lake with the snow falling softly—it might have been the lake where he'd tried to kill the others. My knees were trembling as I stood there, facing him; there was only a few yards between us and I thought that this was how it had been before, when he'd had the brainstorm, with him standing so still and the axe gripped in his hand, and all my body was tense, waiting for the attack.

But instead, his gaze went past me, down along the edge of the lake. "Where are the others?" he asked. "Are they following, too?"

I shook my head, not trusting myself to speak.

His dark eyes came back to me. "Just you—alone?" And when I nodded, he seemed to relax. "I guess you saw me leave the camp, eh?" He swore softly to himself, using the Canuk word "Tabernac!" "I thought I'd slipped away without any of you seeing." And then he added, "Well, you'd better go back to them now."

It was my chance to escape. I started to edge away from him, and then I stopped. "But I don't know . . ." The words died in my throat, for I didn't dare admit that I was lost. Once he knew that . . . My body was suddenly still with fear, a fear that was greater than any fear of him.

"Try and persuade Paule and Ray to wait there for me," he went on, his voice still reasonable, his gaze fixed now on the far end of the lake. "I'll be about two days," he added.

I stared at him, puzzled by his manner. He seemed so sane. And yet . . . "Where are you going?" I demanded.

"That's my business," he answered sharply.

And then, suddenly reckless, because anything was better than being left to die of cold and starvation: "You ran out on him when he was still alive, scared at what had happened. Isn't that the truth?"

He was staring at me, his dark eyes wide in their shadowed sockets. And then suddenly his gaze shifted to the ground. "You're so damned logical, aren't you?" It was said without any trace of hostility. And then he murmured, "Well, it's true —in a way. I was scared. I was certain Baird was dead, and there seemed nothing else . . ." His voice trailed away as though at some ghastly recollection. And after a moment, he lifted his head and looked straight at me again. " If I told you history had repeated itself there at that lake, then you'd think I'd gone mad, wouldn't you?"

" How do you mean?" My throat was suddenly dry.

He stared at me a moment longer and then he shook his head. " No, it's no good," he murmured. " I guess you can only see it the one way. I knew what you were thinking that first day at Seven Islands. *Mon Dieu!*" His voice was no more than a whisper. " Why did it have to be you? Queer, isn't it?" He gave a little, nervous laugh. " If I told you . . ." But he stopped there and shook his head again. " No, you'd twist it round in your mind. But I'll tell you this much—that Indian was right. It's a bad place."

" Then it *was* Lake of the Lion?"

" Sure it was Lake of the Lion." He was still looking at me and his lips were drawn back from the even line of his teeth in that same wry little smile. " Yeah," he said. " The place where my grandfather killed yours." And he added, " The body's still there. A heap of bones—that's all that's left of James Finlay Ferguson, and there's a hole drilled in the skull where the bullet struck him. In the back of the skull. Pierre Laroche must have come up behind him and shot him in cold blood. The forehead's all splintered." His eyes stared at me unblinkingly a moment, and then: " It's not a pretty thing," he muttered, " to discover that your grandfather is a murderer." His tone was suddenly bitter.

The fascination that old tragedy had for him, his bitterness —if I had needed to be convinced, this would have convinced me. It was the sight of my grandfather's remains, the evidence of his own grandfather's guilt that had unhinged his mind. " And what happened—afterwards?" I heard myself ask, and my voice shook slightly. " What happened then between you and Briffe?"

But he shook his head. " Oh, no," he said. " I'm not telling you that. Or what happened to Baird." He hesitated, and then he added, " But you can come and see it for yourself, if you want to."

" You mean now?"

He nodded.

" You're going to Lake of the Lion?"

" But of course." He said it impatiently. " Where else did you think I was going?"

And I stared at him, the skin crawling on my scalp. It was incredible—quite horrible. He was going back to the scene of the tragedy. Why? To gloat? Or was it the murderer's sub-conscious fascination for his crime? Whatever it was, I knew now he was mad and my voice trembled as I said, " But you're going south." Fact—anything to keep him to facts.

" South—yes." He nodded. " I have to pick up my route out."

" But you told us that was to the north."

He shrugged his shoulders. " What does it matter what I told you?" And then he added, " If you come with me, you can see for yourself what happened to Baird. Then maybe you'll believe me."

But I knew I could never believe anything he said, now or in the future, for his mind seemed so confused. Perhaps, to him there was no truth any more. " You said Baird was in-jured in the crash," I whispered. " You told me they were both injured in the crash."

But he shook his head. " No," he said. " Nobody was in-jured in the crash." And then he suddenly smiled with that touch of boyish charm that I had found so frightening before. " You mustn't think, because I told you they were injured in the crash, that it was so. I had to tell you that, because I didn't want you to pursue your inquiries." It was said with such an appalling candour that I felt almost sick. And then he said, " Well, are you going to come on with me or are you going back to join the others?"

I hesitated—not because I'd any choice, but because I was so horrified at the thought of going on alone with him. My only hope was that Darcy and Paule, by following the Indian's in-structions, would reach Lake of the Lion before us. If I were to be the only witness to what had really happened there . . . " Are you sure you can find the lake?" I asked.

" Oh, yes," he replied. " In the early stages I was very care-ful to memorise my route and even blazed some of the trees."

" But if you're prepared to let me come with you, why not the others—why didn't you tell them you could guide us in?

Damn it!" I cried. "You flew in with the helicopter twice. If you'd memorised your route out, why in God's name couldn't you find the lake then?"

He shook his head and the smile on his lips had become oddly secretive. " I could have found it," he said. " But I didn't want to. I didn't want anybody to know."

" But Paule——"

"Least of all Paule," he said harshly, the smile suddenly wiped from his face. And he added, still in the same harsh voice, "I guess you'd better come with me anyway. If you go back you'll talk, and the one person who must never know what happened there is Paule."

It surprised me that in his state of mind he should still care what Paule thought, and I took the opportunity to point out that she'd be worried about him. " They'll wonder what's happened to us," I said.

But he shook his head. " I left a note. They'll guess you're with me." And he added, " I hope to God she does what I asked and stays at that camp." He made a gesture with the axe. " Okay, let's get going. You lead the way." And he stood back to let me pass.

I barely hesitated, for if he once knew that I was lost, then it would be so much simpler for him to abandon me here. Nevertheless, as I went past him the muscles of my shoulders contracted in anticipation of a blow, even though my intelligence told me that he was now determined to take me to Lake of the Lion and that anyway, if he intended to kill me before we got there, he would have plenty of opportunity. From now on we would live as close as it is possible for two human beings to live, for we'd no tent, nothing but our own warmth to protect us from the cold.

We left the lake behind and the timber closed round us again, and after that I was conscious all the time of the sound of the axe close behind me as he blazed the trail for the return journey—but whether for his return or for mine I didn't then know, and because of that the chip and bite of the axe on wood had a hollow, mocking sound in the silence of the falling snow.

And then suddenly the timber fell away before us and I stood looking out over the same flat country that we'd come through the previous day. But now it was all white with the vastness of the sky a dirty curtain of lazily drifting snow. My first thought was that I had been right after all in thinking he was running out on us. " You're going back," I said. " You're not going to try and reach the lake."

But he shook his head. " *Pas du tout*." He smiled at me, almost cheerfully. " I've come back here to pick up my landmark."

However, it was impossible to pick out anything, for it was snowing harder than ever, and we remained in the shelter of the trees and lit a fire to keep ourselves warm. Later, when the snow eased up, we went out along a ridge of sand as far as the first lake, and from there Laroche was able to identify his mark, a lone rock outcrop topped by three ragged-looking firs.

Then began a nightmare journey that lasted two whole days. No sooner had we started back into the rock country than it came on to snow again. And even when it finally ceased some time in the late afternoon, the going remained heavy and tiring, an unending struggle through deep, wet snow with every branch unloading its sodden burden on us. The temperature fell steadily, and with the disappearance of the clouds, it dropped below freezing, so that the snow formed a crust through which we broke at every step. And all the time our progress was further slowed by the need for Laroche to search back and forth for the trail he had blazed. In the conditions in which he had marked it, there would have been no difficulty in following it, but now with the trees all blotched and weighted down with snow, it was a wonder we were able to keep to it at all.

We went into camp at dusk in a little clearing full of snow-covered rocks, and I swear if we'd had a tent, we'd have been too tired to put it up. It was as much as we could do to cut wood for a fire, and when it was lit in an angle of the rocks that would reflect the heat, we lay down in the wet snow and fell into a stupor as we shared a little of the food Laroche had brought with him.

I shall not easily forget that night. The cold was intense. At first the fire kept it at bay. But it melted the snow, so that we lay in a pool of water with the sharp edges of rocks sticking into our flesh. And later, as the fire died down, the cold crept in, numbing our bodies and turning the water to solid ice.

In these conditions it was impossible to sleep ; I simply lay in a dazed half-world of consciousness, chilled to the bone and tired beyond belief, with no vestige of hope in my heart.

Denied the blessed balm of sleep, there was no escape from the fact that the only warmth I had was to lie close against the body of a man I knew to be a murderer. This, and the circumstances of our journey—not to mention the conditions —would, I truly believe, have driven me to a state bordering on madness if it hadn't been for the fact that in that pitiless country I discovered, or perhaps I should say rediscovered, something deep-buried within me that was akin to belief in the Almighty. I do not intend to dwell on this. The conversion of the unbelieving and the unthinking into an acceptance of God is of great moment only to those who have experienced it, and that I should have done so is not much to my credit, being due more to my wretched circumstances than to any innate piety, for by then I was convinced I was going to die—if not by the hand of Laroche, then by the country. Only one of us could leave Lake of the Lion alive, and if it was to be me, then I did not know the way back to the others and I had no hope of getting out of the country on my own.

Accepting, therefore, the certainty of death, my mind dwelt again on what that step meant, and in the frozen quiet of that night I came to terms with it and made my peace with God, so that before the first dawn-light made grey ghosts of the trees, I had reached a strange state of calm that was somehow in tune with the country.

Our breakfast that morning was one biscuit apiece and a small square of chocolate. That Laroche had taken so little from the general store of our supplies was in itself somewhat surprising, but I don't think I considered it at the time—nor the fact that he was willing to share it with me. In country as bleak and inhuman as Labrador you take it for granted that the essentials of life, things like food and warmth, are shared between you, regardless of the future ; and because of that, even if I had been in a condition to think about it, I do not believe I should have reached any other conclusion than the one I had.

As it was, the pitiful inadequacy of our breakfast did little to comfort us after the wretchedness of the night, and though we built up the fire and got some warmth back into our bones, we were both of us in a wretched state as we started out that morning. Laroche, in particular ; he seemed suddenly to have come to the end of his strength. His face was flushed and his eyes unnaturally bright, and there was a slackness in his muscles that made his movements clumsy, so that he was inclined to stumble. But when I asked him whether he was all right, he pulled his stooped body instantly erect and assured me he was. " I'm stiff, that's all," he said. " It's the cold." And after that I didn't comment again on his condition, for I knew by his manner and the tone of his voice that he'd resented it, and I was afraid, as I had been from the time I had caught up with him, of precipitating a showdown.

The cold that morning was very severe. The sky, when we glimpsed it through the trees, was grey with it like a canopy of frozen lead, and the land itself was held immobile in an iron grip. Because of this, the snow was hard and the going easier.

We skirted two frost-rimmed lakes, following all the time the trail Laroche had blazed on the way out, and shortly after ten we came to a big expanse of water, curved like a bow, with the ends lost in the trees that stood thick along its banks. That was when I suggested turning back. It was going to take us a long time to skirt that lake and I felt that if we didn't turn back now, neither of us would get out alive. " It's the only sensible thing to do," I urged. " Turn back now, before it's too late."

" Listen! " He was staring northwards, his head cocked on one side. " Do you hear?"

But all I could hear was the whisper of a chill wind in the trees.

" Sounds like the falls," he said. " The water here is a lake expansion of the river Mackenzie marked on his map." He sank down on to his hands and knees and bent his ear close to the water. " Yeah, it's falls all right." And he got to his feet, and stood staring along the shore. " I guess there's more water now than when I crossed here before." It seemed to worry him. " I didn't hear the falls then."

" What's it matter?" I asked. " We certainly can't cross a river where there are falls." And then, because I was too exhausted to care any more, I said, " I'm turning back now."

I thought that would precipitate a showdown, but all he said was, " You do as you like. It's only two miles from here, and I got to hurry in case . . ." But I didn't hear the rest, for he was already wading into the water.

I couldn't believe it for a moment. He didn't seem to care whether I stayed with him or not. The water was already over his knees. He called to me over his shoulder then. " If you're

coming with me, better hurry. I shan't wait for you." And he
waded straight on into the lake.

I had moved automatically to the water's edge and there I
hesitated. I could so easily leave him now and go up to those
falls and wait for Paule and Darcy; I was sure that Paule, at
any rate, would push on as far as the river. But it took more
nerve than I possessed to deliberately abandon the company
of another human and blaze a lone trail through that sort
of country. Moreover, now that I was so near to my objective,
I found it exercising an increasing fascination, so that though
I had been offered a means of escape, I couldn't bring myself
to take it.

I stepped into the water then and the cold shock of it made
me catch my breath at the same moment that Laroche shouted
something, so that I didn't hear what he said. I thought for a
moment he was in difficulties for he was now waist deep in the
water. But he hadn't been pulled off his feet by the current. In fact, he was standing stock still, staring at the
farther bank. He cupped his hands and shouted again.
"Paule! Paule!" The name wandered down along the
jackpine fringe, a dwindling ghost of a sound swallowed by
the empty vastness of sky and water. "Paule!" And then he
went plunging forward, driving his body through the water
with a sudden, desperate energy.

I didn't hesitate then, but followed him, not caring any
longer how cold the water was or how deep. Paule was here,
and Darcy would be with her. I shouldn't be alone with him
any more.

Fortunately there was a gravel bottom to the lake expansion, for long before I reached the middle I was feeling the tug
of the current, and all the time the water got deeper until it
covered my genitals and was reaching up to my stomach,
freezing all the guts out of me. At the deepest it reached to
my lower ribs and my boots were just touching bottom. I
saw Laroche scramble out and climb the rocks that fringed the
shore. But there was no sign of the others and he didn't call
again. And when I came up out of the water I found him
alone, standing over the burned embers of a fire, staring at the
thin wisp of blue smoke that curled up from it. "You saw
them," I gasped. "Where are they?"

He shook his head and his face was deathly pale. "No, I
didn't see them."

" But you called out to Paule."

" I saw the smoke. I thought maybe . . ." He shook his head wearily. " They're ahead of us." His teeth were chattering and the bitter frustration he seemed to feel made his voice sound hollow. He pushed back the hood of his parka and ran a trembling hand up over his head. " I didn't think they could possibly get here ahead of us." He was almost crying. At any rate, there were tears in his eyes and his whole body shook as though with ague.

" But how do you know?" I cried. " If you didn't see them . . ."

" The fire," he said.

I stared down at it then, seeing it suddenly as the footprint in the sand, the proof that there were other humans besides ourselves in this desolate wilderness. And I knew that he must be right, because there was nobody within five days' march of us, except Paule and Darcy.

By then my own teeth were chattering and I could feel my clothes stiffening as they froze. A numbness was creeping through my body. But I didn't care. That wisp of smoke meant that Paule and Darcy had stood here on this lake shore and dried themselves at this fire less than an hour ago. The knowledge that they were so close comforted me. " I'll get the fire going again," I said. " Give me the axe."

But he shook his head. " No. No, I got to get on. I got to catch up with them before they reach the lake."

He was looking now at the trees ahead of him, searching for the marks he'd made. " But we must have a fire," I said. " We've got to dry our clothes."

He shook his head again, impatiently, as he moved in amongst the trees, his body still shaking with the cold. And then he found what he was looking for, and he started forward.

" Laroche! Come back!" I almost screamed his name. " You damned crazy fool!" I shouted after him. " You'll die of cold if you don't get dry."

He didn't stop, but went straight on, half-running, and though I shouted at him again and again, he took no notice. There was nothing for it then, but to follow him. I knew it was crazy. We were soaked to the waist and the temperature was way below freezing. But I'd no alternative.

I thought I'd catch him up in a moment, for he was in a

far worse state than I was. I thought that as soon as he'd got over the first shock of his surprise and began to weaken, I could persuade him to stop and get a fire lit. But in fact I was only just able to keep him in sight. He seemed suddenly possessed of a demoniacal energy. The timber was sparse here and he was running, not caring that the ground was rocky and treacherously strewn with moss-covered boulders. Twice I saw him fall, but each time he scrambled to his feet and plunged on at the same frantic pace.

We went on like that for a long time, until I, too, was so exhausted I could barely stagger, and then suddenly the ground fell away and through the bare poles of the trees I caught a glimpse of water. A moment later I stumbled out of the timber on to an outcrop, and there was the rock, crouched like a lion in the middle of the lake.

I stopped then and stared at it, hardly able to believe my eyes. I had reached Lake of the Lion, and the sight of it gave me a sudden chill feeling of despair, for it was a black, sombre place. The lake itself had a white rime of ice round its edge, and all the length of the long, narrow cleft, its surface had the dull, leaden look of water beginning to freeze over. The Lion Rock stood in the very centre of it, the blackness of it emphasised by the ice that ringed it round.

"Paule!" Laroche's despairing cry came up to me through the trees, and it had the lost quality of the damned in it. "Paule! Wait! Please, Paule!"

He was running down the steep-timbered slope towards the lake, and beyond his bobbing figure I caught the glint of metal. It was the Beaver floatplane, and it wasn't sunk after all. It lay with its wings sprawled along the ice at the water's edge. And to the right of it, two figures stood against the black bulk of some up-ended rocks that formed a platform overlooking the lake, a repetition at a lower level of the outcrop on which I stood. They were standing quite still, and like me they were staring down at the plane.

"Paule!" That cry, so full of fear and despair, rose crazily up to me again, and as though the cry had galvanised the two figures into action, one of them detached itself from the other and went scrambling down towards the lake and the half-sunken aircraft. It was Paule. And then Darcy started after her, and he was calling to her, a cry of warning.

No doubt he thought Laroche, in his demented state, might

be dangerous. It was my own immediate thought, for the Beaver floatplane was evidence that he'd lied, and I left the outcrop and went racing down the slope, shouting to her to stay with Darcy.

It's a wonder I didn't break my neck on that hillside, for it was a tangle of roots and I went down it regardless of the fact that I was dead weary and all my muscles uncontrollable through weakness. But I was unencumbered by any pack and I reached the lake shore only a little behind Darcy, who had stopped and was standing with a shocked look on his face. And beyond him, Paule had stopped, too, and so had Laroche —the three of them quite still like a tableau.

They were all of them staring at something down along the lake shore, and as I passed Darcy, I saw it, too; a body lying crumpled in the snow, with the torn canvas of a tent forlornly draped from its slanting pole. I checked then, and I, too, stood momentarily frozen into immobility, for beside the body were two rusted steel containers, and from one of them the thin line of an aerial swept up to the trees that fringed the lake.

So my father had been right. That was my first thought, and I went slowly forward, past Laroche, past Paule—until I stood looking down at the pitiful remains of the man I'd come so far to find. He lay on his side, a stiff-frozen bundle of ragged clothing, and his thin, starved face was turned upwards, staring with sightless eyes at the Labrador skies. One hand still clutched the phone mike of the transmitter; the other, wrapped in a filthy, bloodstained bandage, lay by the handle of the generator. My only thought then was that he had never given up; right to the very end he had been trying to get through, and he had died without knowing he had succeeded. Across all those thousands of miles he had made contact with my father, a disembodied voice on the ether crying for help. And my father had met that call with a superhuman effort that had been his death. And now I had failed him.

Behind me I heard Paule echo my thoughts in a whisper so hoarse that I barely recognised her voice. " *Mon Dieu!* " she breathed. " We are too late."

"Yes," I murmured. "We're too late." And then I looked up at the Lion Rock standing there in the middle of the lake. At least I had reached Lake of the Lion. I had done what my grandmother had tried to do—what my father would doubtless have done in the end, if he hadn't been so badly injured in the war. I had reached James Finlay Ferguson's last camp. That at least was something.

I looked down at Briffe's body again and my eyes, blurred with exhaustion, seemed to see it as that other body that had lain here beside this lake for more than fifty years, and I remembered what Laroche had said: *a heap of bones—and a hole drilled in the skull*. At least Briffe hadn't died like that, but still a shudder ran through me, for the drawn and sunken features told of a slower death, and close behind me Paule whispered, " He killed him, didn't he?"

I turned then and saw her standing, staring down at her father with a blank look of misery and despair on her face. I didn't say anything, for she knew the truth now; the body and the transmitter were evidence enough. And then slowly, almost woodenly—like a puppet on a string—she turned and faced Laroche. " You killed him!" The whisper of her words carried down the lake's edge, so clear in the frozen stillness that she might have shouted the accusation aloud, and her face as she said it was contorted with horror. " You left him here to die —alone."

Alone! That one word conjured a vision of what Briffe's end had been. I think Laroche saw it, too, for his face was quite white, and though he tried to speak, he couldn't get the words out. And then Paule repeated her accusation in a rising crescendo of sound that bubbled out of her throat as a scream of loathing and horror. " You killed him! You left him here to die. . . ." Her throat closed on the words and she turned away from him and went stumbling blindly up through the trees like an animal searching for some dark corner in which to hide.

If Laroche had let her go, it might have been all right; but he couldn't. " Paule—for God's sake!" he cried. And before Darcy or I could do anything to stop him, he had started after her. And he was up with her in a second, for she was sobbing so wildly, so hysterically that she tottered rather than ran up the slope. He reached out and caught hold of her arm. " Paule —you've got to listen to me." He jerked her round, and then his hand fell from her elbow and he stepped back as though at a blow for her eyes blazed with hatred and her white face had a trapped look, full of bewilderment and fear.

" Paule!" He held out his hand to her in a pleading gesture.

But in the same instant, she cried, " Don't touch me. If you
touch me, I'll——"

" Paule, you've got to listen to me."

I heard her cry, " No. Keep away from me." It was said as
he reached out and gripped hold of her again, and in the same
instant she made a quick movement of her arm, there was the
glitter of steel, and then she was stabbing at him with that
thin-bladed Indian knife, stabbing at him again and again,
screaming something at him in French, or it may have been
Indian, until finally his knees sagged under him and he sank
groaning to the ground at her feet. He looked up at her then,
and for a moment they stared at each other, and then he suddenly collapsed and lay still, and she was left standing, staring
with a dazed expression at the knife in her hand. She stared
at the reddened blade and a drop of blood gathered on the
point and fell like a piece of red confetti on to the trampled
snow.

Suddenly she flung the knife from her and with a sobbing
intake of breath, fell on to the snow beside him. " Darling!"
She had seized hold of his head and was staring down into his
face, which was paper-white and blooodless under the stubble.
" *Mon Dieu!*" She looked up then and searched about her
blindly as though for aid, and finally her eyes lighted on
Darcy and myself, still standing there, helpless spectators of
the tragedy. " I think I've killed him," she said in a toneless
voice. " Would one of you see, please." And as Darcy went
and knelt beside Laroche's body, she laid the head down and
stood up, suddenly quite composed. " I am going to—see to
my father now," she said, and she went slowly down through
the trees towards the half-sunken aircraft and the sandy beach
below the rocks that had been Briffe's last camping place,
moving slowly like a girl walking in her sleep.

I went over to Darcy then, my knees trembling and weak
with the shock of what had happened. " Is he—dead?"

Darcy didn't reply. He had laid Laroche's body out on the
snow and was unzipping his parka.

" It all happened so quickly," I murmured.

He nodded. " Things like that always do."

" I was thinking about Briffe and what had happened here."

He had undone Laroche's parka and the sweater underneath
was all soaked in blood, sodden patches that ran into one

another, dark red against the dirty white of the wool. He cut it away with his knife, deftly exposing the white flesh beneath the bush shirt and the sweat-grimed vest, as though he were skinning an animal. And when he had the whole chest exposed, with the half-dozen knife wounds gaping red and slowly welling blood, he put his head down and listened to the heart. And then he nodded slowly like a doctor whose diagnosis has been proved correct. " Where's that girl gone?" he demanded, looking up at me.

" She's gone to see to her father."

" Well, she can't do anything for him. Fetch her back here. I want a big fire built, and hot water and bandages."

" He's alive then?"

" Yeah—just. I guess the thickness of the parka saved him." He looked quickly about him. " Build the fire over there in the shelter of those rocks where Briffe had his camp. And tell Paule to find something clean for bandages." Darcy slipped his axe from his belt. " Here, take this. I want a big fire, and I want it kept going. Now get moving." And as I left him, I heard him say, " This is a hell of a thing to have happened." And I knew he was wondering how we were to get out with a wounded man.

I went back through the trees and down over the rocks to the little beach where Paule knelt on the gravel beside the frozen body of her father. I remember I was surprised to see how small a man he was, and though death had smoothed some of the wrinkles from the weather-beaten skin, the face was the face of an old and bitter man. Starvation had shrunk the flesh of the cheeks and stretched the skin tight across the bones, so that the features looked shrivelled and only the grizzled beard had any virility left in it. His body, with the lower half still encased in his sleeping-bag, was sprinkled with a light dusting of snow. There was snow on the radio set, too, and all the simple necessities with which he had endeavoured to support life lay scattered around him, half-buried in a white, frozen crust.

I told Paule what she had to do, but she didn't seem to take it in. " He's dead," she murmured. " My father's dead."

" I know," I said. " I'm sorry. But there's nothing you can do for him now."

" We were too late." She said it in the same dull, flat voice, and though she wasn't crying, she seemed utterly dazed. " If only I had done something about it when that first report of a transmission came through. Look! He was trying to get through to me. And I agreed with them," she murmured brokenly. " I agreed that the search should be called off."

" It wasn't your fault," I said.

" It was my fault. I should have known." She gazed dully round her at the snow-covered camp site. " There's no sign of a fire," she said. " He hadn't even a fire to keep him warm. Oh, God!" she breathed. And then she was staring up at me, her eyes wide in the pallor of her face. " Why did Albert do it?" she cried. " Why did he leave him here? And then to say he was dead!" Speaking of Laroche seemed to remind her of what she'd done. " Have I killed him?" she asked.

" No," I said. " He's still alive. But we've got to get a fire going and some bandages." And then, because she was looking down at the corpse of her father again, lost to everything but her own misery, I caught hold of her arm and dragged her roughly to her feet. " Pull yourself together, Paule," I said. " There's nothing you can do here."

" No—nothing." And she seemed suddenly to collapse inside. " It's all so terrible," she cried, and she began to sob, wildly and uncontrollably.

I shook her violently, but she didn't stop, and because I didn't know what else to do, I left her there and went up into the trees and began to hack down branches, building them into a great pile in the shelter of the rocks. And after a while Darcy came and helped me. " I've patched him up as best I can," he said.

" Will he live?" I asked.

" How the hell do I know?" he growled. " Will any of us live, if it comes to that?" And he set a match to some dry twigs he'd gathered and nursed the little flicker of flame to life, kneeling in the snow and blowing on it gently till the branches of the jackpine steamed and finally smouldered into a crackling flame.

It was only then that I looked round to see what had happened to Paule. She had left her father and was kneeling beside Laroche in nothing but her bush shirt. She had used her parka and her sweater to cover him and keep him warm, and the sight of her there reminded me of what she had said to me when we were alone beside that camp fire. She had half-killed

the man, yet she still loved him. Whatever he had done, she
still loved him, and the knowledge brought a lump to my
throat, for it was such a terrible twist of fate.

As soon as the fire was blazing, we carried Laroche down
to it and laid him on a bed of pine branches and dried moss
close against the rocks so that the heat of the fire would be
reflected to form a pocket of warmth. At least he wouldn't die
of shock through exposure to cold. But when I said this to
Darcy, he gave me a hard, calculating look. " That's a matter
we've got to decide to-night," he said in an odd voice.

" How do you mean?"

He glanced round quickly to see that Paule wasn't listening.
" We can't carry him back and we've food for only one day.
That's all Paule and I brought with us. If we stay here with
him, we all die."

" There's the radio," I said.

" Yeah?" He gave a sceptical grunt. " It'd need a skilled
operator to get that thing working. It's been out in the open
for days. Even when it was under cover, Briffe only managed
to get that one message through." And he added, " The
chances of being able to raise anyone on that set are about as
remote as the chances of a plane happening to fly over and see
us here. Still . . ." He hesitated. " It's a pity Paule didn't do
the job properly whilst she was about it." And with that he
turned abruptly away and went over to where Paule was
searching in the snow beside her father's body.

She straightened up just as he reached her, and she had a
rusted tin box in her hand. " I found it," she said. " I knew it
must be here, because of that bandage round my father's
hand."

It was the first-aid box she'd found, and though all the
bandages had gone from it and the morphia had been used,
there was still some lint and gauze left and a bottle of anti-
septic. With these, and strips torn from a clean vest, she
bandaged Laroche's wounds, whilst Darcy and I brought the
radio set up close to the fire. I cranked the handle of the
generator, whilst he kept his fingers on the leads, but there was
no sign of life. " It's the damp," I said.

" Sure it's the damp."

" It'll be all right when it's had time to dry out."

" Think so?" He stared at me. " It'll dry outside. But it's
the inside we got to dry. Shut up in that tin box the works will

just steam like they were in the tropics. Course, if you happen to have a screwdriver on you so that we can open it up——?"

"No, I haven't got a screwdriver," I said.

He laughed. "I didn't think you had." He peered morosely at the generator. "Looks to me like it needs a whole work bench full of tools the condition it's got into; certainly we'd need a spanner for those nuts."

"Isn't that water ready yet?" Paule asked.

Darcy lifted the lid of the smoke-blackened kettle he'd filled with snow and hung over the fire. "Just coming up," he said.

"If we could find an old tin or something—I want to get him warm." She had got Laroche's boots off and was pulling her own down sleeping-bag up over his legs.

Darcy got to his feet. "I'll see what I can find. There'll be something around here that we can use."

I was on the point of following him, but Paule stopped me. "Help me lift him, please."

Between us we got Laroche into the sleeping-bag, and when it was done, she sat back on her haunches and stared at the white, bloodless face. "Ian—what are we to do?" She was suddenly looking at me, her small face set in a tragic mask. "I couldn't help myself," she murmured. "I didn't know what I was doing."

There was nothing I could say that would help her and I turned away and stared into the hot heart of the fire. We had warmth at least—so long as we had the energy to cut wood and keep the fire going. But it wouldn't last. She knew that. Gradually we'd weaken through lack of food the way her father had and then the end would come in a blizzard of snow or in the cold of the night. I thought of Dumaine then and what he'd gone through. But he'd got out in the end and so had Pierre Laroche. There wasn't much chance for us. "Maybe we'll get the radio working," I said.

But she didn't believe that either and she squatted there, quite still, watching Darcy picking over the pitiful remains of her father's last camp like a tramp going over a refuse heap. "I shall stay here," she said at last in a small, tight voice. "Whatever happens I shall stay with him."

"Even though he left your father to die?" I didn't look at her as I said that.

"Yes—even though he killed him," she breathed. "There is

nothing else for me now." And after a moment she asked, " Do you think you and Ray could get back to the Tote Road—just the two of you?"

" We could try." And I knew as I said it that I'd accepted the fact that she wouldn't be coming with us.

" If you started at dawn to-morrow . . . Per'aps, if the weather is good, you will make it in less time." But she said it without conviction. She was thinking of the muskeg and the weight of the canoe which we should have to carry if we were to cross those open stretches of water. " You must help him as much as you can." Her hand touched mine. " Ray is very tired, though he tries to hide it. He is not a young man like you, Ian." And she added, " I am not thinking of myself, or of Albert. For us, this is the end. But I would like to be sure that you two will get out alive. The knowledge that you will both be safe will make it—easier for me."

" I'll do my best," I said.

She gave my hand a little squeeze. " I wish my father had known you." She smiled, a barely perceptible movement of the lips that left her eyes still empty. She let go my hand then and went to her pack and took out a small tin of Bovril and a metal flask.

She was mixing the hot drink in her own tin mug when Darcy returned. " This do you?" he said, and placed a rusted oil can beside her. She nodded and then she was bending over Laroche, lifting his head and trying to force a little of the hot liquid between his teeth.

Darcy dropped wearily on to the ground beside me. " He buried Baird a little way back amongst the rocks," he said quietly, leaning his head close to mine. " I just seen the grave."

" Where?" I asked.

" Over there." He nodded towards the edge of the beach where boulders were piled against the rock of the shore. " I guess he was too weak to dig a hole, or else the ground was frozen. He just heaped some rocks over the body and tied two sticks together to form a cross." He hesitated, and then he opened his hand to show a piece of stone the size of a pigeon's egg lying in the palm. It was grey with grit, but where he'd rubbed it clean there was a dull gold gleam to it. " Know what that is?"

I opened my mouth to answer him, but the word seemed to

stick in my throat, for this surely was evidence of the cause of that old tragedy. And then I was suddenly remembering that first meeting with Laroche, when McGovern had been so taken aback by my certainty that the plane had crashed at Lake of the Lion. "I found that oil can on top of the grave. It had been filled with these—like some pagan offering to the dead." Darcy's voice trembled slightly, but whether it was anger or fear I wasn't certain. "Feel the weight of it," he said, and dropped it into my hand.

The cold touch of that fragment made me shiver, and I turned without thinking to stare out across the dark surface of the lake to the towering mass of the Lion Rock. In my mind I saw the rusted can on the grave more vividly than if I had discovered it there for myself, and I knew then that the Indian had been right. I hated this place and should always hate it.

"I can't get him to swallow any of it," Paule said. She had laid Laroche's head back on the pillow of her sweater and was squatting there, disconsolate, with the steaming mug in her hand.

"Then drink it yourself," Darcy said harshly. And he added under his breath: "The bastard deserves to die anyway."

She heard him and the shock of his words seemed to stun her.

He took the fragment from my hand and passed it to her. "After all the years you've spent prospecting, I guess you know more about minerals than I do," he said. "Tell me what that is."

She stared at the fragment as it lay in her hand, and then a look came into her eyes that I knew was fear. She was re-acting to it the way I had. "It's gold," she said in a small, tight voice.

"Yeah, that's what I thought it was." And he told her how he had found it.

She turned her head slowly and stared towards the boulder-strewn edge of the lake. "Oh, no," she whispered. And then she was staring at us, and the fear that had suddenly taken hold of her was there in her eyes and in the trembling of the hand that held the nugget. "Oh, no," she said again, and she got slowly to her feet and went down to the water's edge, her body stooped as she searched along the frozen margin.

In a few moments she came back with four small nuggets,

which she dropped into my lap. " It's true then," she whispered. " This place is a . . ." Her voice died away and she suddenly burst into tears.

" What's true?" Darcy scrambled to his feet. " What's the matter, Paule? What's got into you?" He had his arm round her shoulders, trying to comfort her. " What is it?"

" I don't know," she sobbed. " I'm frightened."

" We're all frightened," he said soothingly. And because she was sobbing uncontrollably, he shook her quite roughly. " Pull yourself together, girl," he said gruffly. " We're in enough trouble as it is without you going crazy just because we've discovered gold." He pulled her hands away from her eyes. " Is that what's upset you—that your father found what he'd been looking for all his life, and when he'd found it, it wasn't any good to him?"

" It's not the gold," she cried desperately.

" Then what is it?"

" Nothing. Nothing." Her voice was quite wild, and she broke away from him suddenly and went stumbling blindly down towards her father's body.

" What the devil's got into her?" Darcy was staring after her.

I shook my head, for a sudden, terrible thought had crossed my mind, and I didn't dare put it into words. " I don't know," I muttered, and I watched her as she stood staring down at her father. She was there a long time, and then she came slowly back and sat down beside Laroche, gazing down at his ashen face, and though she didn't say a word, I could feel the turmoil of doubt in her mind.

" You all right, Paule?" Darcy was watching her anxiously. She nodded dumbly, her face wet with tears. " If only he were conscious," she murmured at length, and her hand went up to Laroche's head, touching the place where the hair was growing up over the wound. " If he could just speak."

" It's better perhaps that he can't."

She turned and looked at him then. " You don't understand," she whispered.

" Don't I?" Darcy's voice was thick with the anger he was trying to hide. " This place is a gold mine, and that's explanation enough for me. Ian was right."

" Ian?"

" Yeah. He said all along Bert had gone crazy."

Her gaze went back to Laroche, and then she said to me in a voice so quiet that I barely heard her, " Do you still believe that?" And I knew she was remembering what she had said to me that night beside the camp fire when it had been so still.

"Just try to forget about it," Darcy told her gently. "He did what his grandfather did—and for the same reason. You've just got to accept it, that's all there is to it."

But she shook her head. " You don't understand," she said again. And then she turned her stricken gaze on me. " Tell me the truth, Ian," she pleaded. " Tell me what happened." And when I didn't say anything, couldn't even meet the desperate pleading of her eyes, she cried, " For God's sake, I must know the truth." Her voice had risen to a note of hysteria and Darcy gripped hold of my arm. " Better leave her alone for a while," he whispered in my ear. " She's tired and she's overwrought."

I wasn't certain whether to leave her alone or not, but she was staring down at Laroche again and in the end I went with Darcy, for I knew there was nothing I could do to help her. " Where did he bury Baird?" I asked him.

" Over there." He nodded to a group of rocks half-way between the camp site and the sunken aircraft. And when I started towards it, he called to me to wait. " Give me a hand and we'll take Briffe's body up there and bury it beside him."

But I was already moving down along the lake shore. " Later," I said. I had to see that grave. I had to be certain what had happened now. But when I reached the place it told me nothing. The grave was just a mound of rocks the length of a man, covered over with grey silt. Two jackpine branches tied with wire served as a cross. " I wonder when he died," I said as Darcy joined me.

" Does it matter?"

" I don't know," I murmured. " But Laroche was convinced he was dead when he left him. I'm quite certain of that."

" Well, he was probably killed in the crash."

But I shook my head. ' No. Nobody was even injured when the plane crashed. Laroche admitted that to me." I was thinking of that oil can full of nuggets. It was Briffe who had placed that there. " I—I think we ought to have a look at the body," I said.

" Good God! Why?"

"I don't know," I murmured uncertainly. "It might tell us something." I didn't dare tell him what I expected to find, but much as I disliked the thought of disturbing the grave I knew suddenly that I had to see for myself how Baird had died, and I went down on my knees and began pulling the silt and boulders away with my hands.

"Goddammit!" Darcy's hand seized hold of my shoulder. "What's got into you? Can't you let the man rest in peace?"

"Uncovering him won't do him any harm now," I said, tearing myself free of his hand. "He's dead, isn't he?" I added almost savagely to cover my own nervousness, for I didn't like it any more than he did. But there was no other way I could discover what had happened, and for Paule's sake I had to discover that.

My urgency must have communicated itself to Darcy, for he didn't try to stop me after that, and in the end he got down beside me and helped to shift the pile of stones. And when we had finally uncovered the upper part of the body, we stayed for a long time on our knees without moving or saying anything, for the whole side of the man's face had been laid bare.

"An axe did that," Darcy said at length, and I nodded. But though it was what I'd feared, I hadn't been prepared for such a ghastly wound. The right ear was gone completely and the cheek had been laid open to the bone, so that the teeth showed white through the curled and vitiated flesh. And yet it hadn't killed him outright, for pieces of gauze still adhered to the wound, where it had been bandaged, and the face, like Briffe's, was hollowed out by privation and suffering. The beard was still black, almost luxuriant in growth, so that he looked like the wax image of some crucified apostle.

"That settles it," Darcy said thickly. "I've made up my mind. We start back to-morrow, and we leave him here." He meant Laroche, of course, but he couldn't bring himself to mention his name, and I wondered whether to tell him what was in my mind. "Well, say something, can't you?" he cried angrily. "Do you think I'm wrong to leave a man to die—a man who could do a thing like this?"

I had uncovered Baird's right hand then, the wrist all shattered and a gritty bandage covering the wound where some fingers were missing. And below the hand was the top of a canvas bag. "Paule won't go," I said, and I wrenched the bag out from under the stones that covered it. It was an ordinary canvas tool bag and it was full of those dull-grey pebbles that were so heavy and metallic to the touch. The body itself was less terrible to me then than the sight of that canvas bag, and as I stared at it, appalled, I heard Darcy, behind me, say, "How do you know she won't go?" And I knew he hadn't understood its significance.

"She told me—just now. She's staying with Laroche." I said it impatiently, for my mind was on that bag full of nuggets so carefully buried with the body—like a sacrificial offering. And there was that tin can full of them that Darcy had found on the grave. The man who had buried Baird had given to the dead all the wealth he'd picked up; a gesture of abnegation, a madman's attempt to purchase absolution? "My God!" I thought to myself. The irony of it, to want it all for himself and then to die alone in the midst of it!

Darcy plucked at my arm. "I'll go and talk to her," he said.

"It won't do any good."

"No? Then I'll bring her here. You think she'll want to stay with the man when she's seen what he's done." He had got to his feet.

"Wait," I said. "You can't show her this." I glanced down at the dead man's face and then at the bloodied hand, remembering suddenly that Briffe's hand had been injured, too. "And if you did," I said, "she still wouldn't change her mind." I looked up at him then. "Laroche didn't do this," I said.

"What do you mean?"

"It was Briffe who went berserk."

"Briffe?" He stared at me as though I'd gone crazy.

I nodded, for now that I'd said it, I knew it was true; I could see how it all fitted in—the wound on Laroche's head, his decision to trek out on his own. And no wonder he'd been convinced that Baird was dead. How could he have expected any man to live with his head cut open like that? And then his determination that nobody should find the place, that the search should be abandoned and Briffe given up for dead. He'd been prepared to go to almost any lengths to save Paule from the truth.

But even when I'd explained all this to Darcy, he didn't seem to grasp it. "I just can't believe it," he muttered.

" Then what about this?" I said and thrust the canvas bag at him. " And the can full of them you found on the grave. It was Briffe who buried Baird, not Laroche." And I added, " You know the sort of man he was—you said it to Paule just now. He'd spent all his life prospecting, and this was one of the places he'd always wanted to find. She told me so herself the other night. Well," I said, " he found it." And in my mind I could picture the scene as it must have been when the three of them stood on the lake shore here and Briffe held that first nugget of gold in his hand.

" I still can't believe it—her own father."

" If we ever get out alive," I said, remembering now that first day in Labrador, " you go and talk to McGovern. I think he knows what really happened. I think Laroche told him."

He was silent a long time then. Finally, he said, " Well, see you don't let Paule have any idea what's in your mind. It'd just about kill her." And when I didn't answer, he seized my elbow in an urgent grip. " Do you hear me, Ian? You may be right. You may not. But Laroche is going to die here anyway. She mustn't know."

" She knows already," I told him. " She knew the instant you handed her the nugget."

He looked at me a moment, and then he nodded. " Yeah, I guess so," he murmured unhappily, and he crossed himself. " It's a terrible thing," he breathed. And as I started to cover Baird's body again, he said, " We'll have to bury him—up here beside Baird." And then he added, with sudden decision, " But we leave in the morning. You understand? Whatever Paule decides, we leave in the morning. We got to."

III

THAT PAULE now knew the truth was obvious as soon as Darcy told her we would be leaving in the morning. "We'll make him as comfortable as possible," he said, nodding to Laroche, "and then the three of us, travelling light——"

But she didn't let him finish. "Do you think I will leave Albert to die here alone?" she cried, staring at him, white-faced and determined. "I couldn't. I couldn't possibly—not now." And then she added softly, "I love him, Ray. I love him and I shall always love him, and I shan't leave him. So don't ask me again—please." She was past tears, past any show of emotion. She stated it flatly, and I saw that even Darcy accepted her decision as irrevocable. "You and Ian—you leave in the morning. Try to get through. I will keep the fire going as long as I can. If you have good luck, then per'aps you get a plane out to us in time."

Darcy shook his head slowly. "There's ice forming on the lake already. In a few days it'll be impossible for a floatplane to land here. And it'll be too thin for a ski landing."

"Then per'aps you get the helicopter."

"Yeah, maybe the helicopter could make it, though there's not much room." He eyed the narrow beach doubtfully. And then he said, "We're just going to bury your father, Paule. Maybe you'd like to be there."

She didn't say anything for a moment, and then her hand went slowly up to the little gold chain at her neck. "No," she said in a small, dry voice. "Bury him, please. And I will say a prayer for him here—with Albert." There was a little crucifix attached to the chain and she pulled it out of her shirt and held it, tight-clutched, in her hand.

Darcy hesitated. But when he saw she intended to stay there, he put more wood on the fire and then said to me, "Okay, let's get it over with, and then we'll have some food and decide what we're going to do." I followed him back to the place where we'd left Briffe's body, and as he stood over it, staring down at the emaciated face, he said, "I guess you're right. She knows."

He didn't say anything more and we carried the body along

the shore and laid it out beside Baird's grave. Then we covered it with stones and the black silt from the beach. It was a slow business, for we'd no tools but our hands. And when we'd finished, Darcy got his axe and cut two branches and fixed them over the grave in the form of a cross. " May God be merciful to you and may you rest in peace." He crossed himself, standing at the foot of the grave, and I murmured, " Amen."

" Well, that's that, I guess," he said, and turned abruptly away. " How much food you and Bert got?"

" I don't think we've any."

" Hmm. We got a little coffee, some chocolate and raisins, a few biscuits and some cheese. Hungry?"

" Yes," I said.

He nodded. " So'm I—Goddamned famished. But we sip a little coffee, and that's all. The rest we leave for Paule. Agreed?"

I nodded, though my mouth was running at the thought of food and there was a dull ache in my belly. " You've decided to leave them here then?"

" What the hell else can I do?" he demanded angrily. " She won't leave, I know that now. And another thing," he added. " If we do manage to get out, we don't tell anybody what we know. They were dead, just like Bert said. Okay?" He had stopped and was looking at me, waiting for my answer.

" Yes," I said.

" Good." He patted my arm. " It's a hard thing for you to have to do, considering what it was that brought you out here. But I think you owe it to Bert. He risked a lot to keep that thing a secret—and he'll be dead before we've any chance of getting him out."

When we got back to the fire, we found Paule lying beside Laroche, her head buried in her arms, sobbing convulsively. Darcy stood for a moment, looking down at her. " Poor kid!" he murmured. But he didn't go to her. Instead, he got the empty kettle and started down to the lake to fill it. " Leave her," he said as he passed me. " Just leave her, boy. She'll be better for a good cry." And to my astonishment I saw there were tears running down his cheeks.

Whilst he was seeing to the coffee, I went down to where the remains of Briffe's tent lay and searched about in the snow for the tools that must have been in that empty tool bag. There is no point in giving a list of the things I found there; there were his personal belongings, and Baird's, too—clothes, instruments, some empty tins that had contained emergency rations, an alarm clock of all things. They had salvaged what they could from the plane. Lying there, scattered about in the snow, rusted and wet and gritty to the touch, it was a pitifully inadequate assortment with which to stand the siege of approaching winter in this bleak spot. I found the axe, too. It lay bedded in the ice at the water's edge, its blade all pitted with rust, but whether he'd just dropped it there or whether he'd tried to fling it into the lake I didn't know.

The tools were scattered about under the snow near where we had found him, and as I retrieved them, I kept on finding nuggets. They were obviously nuggets he'd collected, for there was an empty flour bag that still contained a few and a tin mug full of them. The sight of them sickened me. I could picture him searching frenziedly along the lake edge, with Baird lying in a pool of blood and Laroche fled into the timber on the start of his long trek out, and I couldn't help wondering how he'd felt when the gold lust had left him and sanity had returned. He'd thrown the little useless hoards away in disgust; that much was obvious, for they were strewn all about the camp site. But how had he felt? Had he thought at all about the future and what his daughter's reaction would be, as he crouched over the set, hour after hour, trying to make contact with the outside world?

I collected the tools and went slowly back with them to the fire. By then Darcy had made the coffee and we drank it black and scalding hot, and it put new life into us, so that even Paule seemed almost herself again, though she didn't talk and her face still looked unnaturally pale. She ate what Darcy put before her, but automatically, as though the function of eating were something divorced from reality, so that I was surprised when she said, " Aren't you hungry? You're not eating."

Darcy shook his head, avoiding her eyes. " We got work to do," he said awkwardly, and he gulped down the rest of his coffee and got to his feet, glancing at his watch. " There's about two hours of daylight left. We'll leave you with as much wood as we can cut in that time." He picked up his axe and with a nod to me started up the rocks into the timber.

I hesitated. I wanted to get to work on the generator. But

I couldn't help remembering that message from Briffe. *No fire. Situation desperate.* The radio probably wouldn't work, anyway. Wood seemed more important, and I retrieved Laroche's axe and followed Darcy up into the timber.

It was desperately hard work. We were tired before we started—tired and hungry. Paule helped us for a time, dragging the branches down to the edge of the timber and tipping them over the rocks. But then Laroche cried out, and after that she stayed with him, refilling the oil can with hot water to keep him warm and trying to get him to swallow hot Bovril and brandy.

He hadn't regained consciousness. He was still in a coma, but delirious now, and every time I approached the fire I could hear him babbling.

Sometimes he'd cry out, " Paule! Paule! " as though he were trying to make her listen. At those times he was back at the point where she'd struck at him with the knife. At other times he'd be talking to Briffe or wandering on an endless trek through Labrador. It was just an incoherent jumble of words, with now and then a name cried out—Paule's or Briffe's, my own once—and then as often as not he'd struggle in a feeble attempt to take the action dictated by the wanderings of his mind. And the horrible thing was that, though none of it made sense in a literal way, knowing what we did, it was impossible not to understand that his mind was trying to unburden itself of a secret too long bottled up.

And Paule sat there with his head on her lap, stroking his brow and murmuring to him as she tried to soothe him, her face all the time set in a frozen mask of wretchedness and despair.

The light went early, fading into a sleet storm that chilled us and covered everything with a fresh, powdery white dust. We went back to the fire then, and when I had recovered a little and my body was no longer ice-cold with the sweat of exhaustion, I tried the generator again. But though the casing was hot to the touch, it was still damp inside. At any rate, cranking the handle produced no sign of life. By the light of the fire and to the intermittent babblings of Laroche's delirium, I set to work to dismantle the thing.

It took me more than an hour, for the nuts were all seized solid with rust. But in the end I got the casing off and with a handkerchief wiped the brushes clean. Fortunately the sleet had passed and after leaving it to toast beside the fire for a time and checking the leads and scratching at the terminals with the blade of a knife, I reassembled it. And then, with Darcy cranking the handle, I held the two points close together. When they were almost touching a small spark flickered into being. It wasn't much of a spark, but it was there nevertheless, and when I held the two leads gripped in my hand, the shock was sufficient to make me jump.

" Think it's enough to work the set?" Darcy asked, after he'd held the leads whilst I cranked.

" God knows," I said. It wouldn't be much of a signal. " Anyway, the set's probably out of action by now." It was over two weeks since Briffe had made that transmission.

However, we coupled it up, re-rigged the aerial, and after cleaning the rust from the terminal, I slipped the headphones on, switched the set to receive and, with Darcy cranking, went slowly round the dial. But I could hear nothing, not even a crackle or the slightest murmur of any static. I checked carefully over the set, trying to remember everything that fool of an operator at Camp 263 had told me. But as far as I could see I'd done everything I should. But when we tried again there was still nothing.

" It could be the jack of the earphones," Darcy suggested. " Suppose we give it a clean."

But I shook my head. " We could clean the jack, but we'd never clean the socket. Once we disturb the phone-jack we're done." I switched over to send then. It was long past the time I'd agreed with Perkins, but there was no harm in trying. The transmission might work, even if the reception didn't. " Crank her up again," I said. And then I put the mouthpiece to my lips. " CQ-CQ-CQ," I called, with the tuning dial set at the net frequency. " This is Ferguson calling from Lake of the Lion. Any 75-metre phone station. Come in, please. Come in. Over." I flicked the switch to receive. But there wasn't a sound.

I tried again and went on trying. And when Darcy was tired of cranking, he tried, whilst I operated the generator. But we got no response, and when we were both exhausted, we gave it up. " I told you the Godammed thing wouldn't work," Darcy said.

" Okay," I said wearily. " If you knew, why did you bother to go on cranking." I was tired and angry.

"You'd got the generator going. I thought you might get the set going, too."

"Well, I haven't." And because I thought this was probably our only hope, I added, "We'll try again in the morning."

"There'll be no time in the morning. We're leaving at first light."

"You can leave if you want to," I said. "I'm not going till after seven-thirty."

"That'll lose us an hour and a half, and we can't afford——"

"I tell you I'm not leaving until seven-thirty," I said obstinately. "I told Perkins seven to seven-thirty. He'll be listening in for us then. Ledder, too, probably."

"Oh, for God's sake!" he said angrily. "You know there isn't a hope in hell of your raising them. The set's out of action, and that's all there is to it. Briffe only managed to make it work once."

"Briffe started with a set that was waterlogged. He had to crank the thing himself, and he was exhausted and his hand was injured. If he could get it to work, then so can we."

"I think Ian is right," Paule said suddenly. "Per'aps my father only get the transmission side of it to work. But I think you should try, even if it means delaying your departure."

"That hour and a half could make all the difference," Darcy growled. And then he was looking at me, and the firelight on his glasses gave his eyes a baleful look. "Try if you must. I don't know anything about radio, but I'd say the set was useless after being out in the weather all this time."

So it was agreed and we heaped more wood on the fire and went to sleep. And every few hours during the night one of us would get up and replenish the fire, so that the hours of sleep alternated between intense heat and intense cold, and all through that endless night I seemed to hear Laroche's voice as in a nightmare.

At last daylight crept back into the sombre cleft of the lake. The Lion Rock lifted its black profile from the mist that lay like a white smoke over the water, and I went stiffly back to the radio set, checking and rechecking it in the forlorn hope that, by the mere fact of fussing over it, the damned thing would work.

We had our coffee and just before seven o'clock I squatted

down in front of that malignant, rusted box, put the earphones on and switched the set to send. And as Darcy cranked I began my fruitless monologue: "CQ-CQ-CQ. Ferguson calling Perkins. Calling Ledder. Camp 134—Can you hear me? Goose Bay? Any 75-metre phone station. Come in, please. Anybody, come in. Over." Sometimes I called "Mayday!" which I knew to be a distress call. Sometimes just Perkins, or Camp 134. But whenever I said "Over" and switched across to receive, there was absolute silence. Nothing. An infinity of nothing, so that I knew the thread was broken, the contact non-existent. And yet I kept on trying. And when Darcy was tired, I handed over to him and he tried with the same result. And at seven twenty-five, in desperation, I began describing our position—the river, the falls, the bearing and distance from the place where we'd crossed.

And then it was seven-thirty and I put the mouthpiece back in its place. "Well, we tried anyway," I said. Darcy nodded. He made no comment, but began quietly collecting his things together. Paule had disappeared into the timber. Laroche was asleep, no longer delirious. "What chance do you think we've got?" I said.

"Of getting back?" Darcy asked.

"Of getting back in time," I said.

He hesitated, staring down at Laroche. "We're in God's hands," he muttered. "But he'll be dead for sure." And he turned to me and said abruptly, "You afraid of death?"

"I don't know," I said.

He nodded. "No, I guess none of us knows that till we're faced with it. I only faced it once before, like this. I was scared all right then. Maybe not this time. I'm getting old." He reached down for his pack, which was barely half full. "All set?" And then he looked up as Paule came hurrying back to us. Her face had a white, frozen look of horror on it and her eyes were wide as though she'd seen a ghost. "What is it?" Darcy asked.

"Up there by that outcrop." She pointed a trembling hand towards a huddle of rocks that stood amongst the trees. And she sat down suddenly as though her knees had given way beneath her. "Where did you bury him?" she asked.

"I told you, down there where we found Baird's grave," Darcy said.

"Of course. It was silly of me, but I thought for a

moment——" A shudder ran through her. And then she was
staring at me with her eyes wide, and almost involuntarily, as
though she had willed it, I started up over the rocks.

I don't think I was surprised at what I found under that
rock outcrop. I think I had known the instant she looked at
me that I was being sent to pay my respects to the mortal
remains of my grandfather. He lay close under the largest of
the rocks, in a sort of gulley—a skeleton, nothing more. No
vestige of clothing remained; just a pile of bones, grey with
age and weather. Only the cage of the ribs was still intact.
The head lay beside it, quite detached from it, smiling a bare-
boned, tooth-filled smile at the Labrador sky, and the bone of
the forehead was all shattered and broken open as Laroche
had said. I turned it over, and there at the base of the skull
was the neat-drilled hole where the bullet had entered, and I
thought of the pistol that hung in my father's room. Had
my grandmother found that pistol at one of Pierre Laroche's
camp sites—was it the very pistol that had fired the bullet into
this poor, bare skull? I stooped and stared in fascination, and
then I heard Darcy behind me. " Funny thing," he murmured,
peering down at it over my shoulder, " I'd almost forgotten
about that earlier expedition."

" I suppose it is my grandfather?" I said.

" Well, it isn't an Indian, that's for sure. You only got to
look at the shape of the skull. No," he added, " it's James
Finlay Ferguson all right, and there's not much doubt what
happened."

" No." I was thinking of the man we'd buried the previous
day, and I looked at Darcy and then past him, down to the
sombre lake and the black rock standing crouched in the
middle of it. " No wonder the Indian was scared of the
place."

He nodded. " It's a bad place all right. And this isn't going
to make it any easier for Paule."

" Well, we can cover it up," I said. " And she needn't come
up here."

" Sure. But how would you like to be left here alone with
the body of the man you love dead by your own hand and
those two graves by the shore there and this lying up here?
Nothing but tragedy in this place. And she's part Indian
remember."

"Laroche may not die," I murmured. But I wasn't any happier about it than he was.

"He may not die to-day or to-morrow. But he'll be dead before we get out, and she'll be alone then. There won't be much incentive for her to go on living after that." And then he said almost angrily, "Well, come on, we got to get going."

We covered the bones with handfuls of wet earth and then went back down to the fire. "We're going now, Paule," Darcy said.

She was crouched over Laroche and she didn't look up. "He's conscious now," she said gently. And when I went nearer, I saw that his eyes were open. A flicker of recognition showed in them as I came into his line of vision, and his throat moved convulsively, as though he were trying to say something, but no words came. "Don't try to talk," she whispered urgently. "You must save your strength." And then she got suddenly to her feet and stood facing us. "You've—covered it up?"

Darcy nodded. "Yeah. There's nothing for you to see there now."

She was staring at me. "It must be terrible for you—to have discovered what happened. For both of us," she murmured. And then, pulling herself together, her voice suddenly clear and practical: "You'll go fast, won't you—as fast as you can." It wasn't a question, but a statement. And when Darcy nodded, too affected to speak, she went to him and gripped hold of his hand. "God bless you, Ray," she said. "I'll pray that you get through in time."

"We'll do our best, Paule. You know that."

"Yes. I know that." She stared at him a moment, and I knew what was in her mind; she was thinking she'd never see him again. And then she leaned suddenly forward and kissed him. "God help us!" she whispered.

"He will," he assured her.

She turned to me then and held out her hand. And when I gripped it, I couldn't help myself—I said, "I'm sorry, Paule. It would have been better for you if I'd never come to Canada."

But she shook her head. "It wasn't your fault," she said softly. "We both wanted the same thing—the truth; and that cannot be hidden for ever." She kissed me then. "Goodbye, Ian. I'm glad I met you." And then she turned back to

Laroche, who all the time had been staring at us with his eyes wide open. And as we picked up our things and turned to go, he struggled up on to one elbow. " Good luck!" I didn't hear the words, but only read them through the movement of his lips. And then he fell back and Paule was bending over him.

" Okay," Darcy said thickly. " Let's get going."

We left them then, going straight along the narrow beach, past the two graves and the half-submerged aircraft, and up through the timber, the way we'd come. The knife with which Paule had attacked Laroche still lay where she'd thrown it, and I picked it up and slipped it into my pack. Why, I don't know, unless it was that I didn't want her to find it lying there to remind her of what had happened.

Neither of us looked back, and in a little while we'd climbed the slope above the lake and the wretched place was gone, hidden from view by the timber. It was a bright, clear day, but by the time we'd crossed the river at the lake expansion, the wind had risen and was blowing half a gale, with ragged wisps of cloud tearing across the cold blue of the sky.

We were travelling light and we didn't spare ourselves, for our need of food was urgent.

An hour before nightfall we were back at the lake where Laroche and I had left them, and there was the canoe and the tent and my pack and all the things they'd abandoned to make that final dash to Lake of the Lion. It all looked just as I had left it, except that everything was covered with snow and only the two of us now.

Darcy collapsed as soon as we reached the camp. He had let me set the pace, and it had been too much for him. And as I cut the wood and got the fire going, I wondered how we'd make out from there on, with the canoe to carry, as well as the food and the tent and all our gear. But he revived as soon as he'd got some hot coffee inside him, and by the time he'd fed, he seemed as full of life as ever, even managing to crack a few jokes.

As soon as we had fed, we turned in. It was the last night of any comfort, for in the morning we decided to abandon the tent; in fact, everything except food to last the two of us three days, one cooking utensil, our down sleeping-bags and a change of socks and underwear. We ate a huge breakfast, shovelling all the food we could into ourselves, and then we started up through the jackpine with the canoe and our packs on our shoulders.

It took us six hours to get clear of the timber and back down into the open country of gravel and water, and by then Darcy was stumbling with exhaustion. But he refused to stop, and we went on until we reached the first of the lakes and could launch the canoe. His face was the colour of putty and his breath wheezed in his throat. And still we went on without a pause, heading well to the south of west in the hopes of avoiding the worst of the muskeg. The wind dropped and it began to snow. Night caught us still in the open and we lay in our sleeping-bags on a gravel ridge with the canoe on top of us.

It was a grey-white world in the morning—grey skies, grey water, white ridges. And on the lake ahead of us a dozen or more geese sat and called to each other in a little patch of open water they'd made in the new-formed ice. But we'd left the gun behind. We'd nothing but the fishing-rod, and we'd no time to fish.

There is no point in my describing that terrible journey in detail. I doubt, in any case, whether I could, for as we struggled on my mind as well as my body became frozen into numbness, dazed with exhaustion. How Darcy kept going, I don't know. It was sheer will-power, for his body gave out before mine did, and as my own energy diminished, my admiration for him increased. He never complained, never gave up hope. He just kept going doggedly on to the limit of endurance and beyond. It was this more than anything else that enabled me to keep going, for the cold was frightful and we ran out of food long before we reached the Tote Road and the line of the grade.

We were cursed with bad luck. The weather, for one thing. The freeze-up caught us and ice formed so thick that in the end we couldn't use the canoe. The compass, too, led us astray. It was probably a deposit of iron ore. At any rate, the result was that we didn't go far enough south and got into a worse area of muskeg than the one we'd come through on the way in. We were caught in it all one night, and when we finally made it to open water, still carrying the canoe, we found the ice too thick to paddle across and too thin to bear our weight.

A week later and we'd have been able to walk across the top of the muskeg and over all the lakes. As it was, we just had to abandon the canoe and struggle round the lakes on foot. And all the time we were thinking of Paule back there at Lake of the Lion. Twice we thought we heard aircraft away to the south, flying low. On the first occasion, we were quite convinced of it. It was on the second day—the only still day we had—and we were sure they must be searching for us. But we were in thick timber at the time, and anyway the sound was a long way off. " I guess it's just one of the air lift boys got a little off course," Darcy said when the sound had dwindled without coming near us. The second time was several days later. I can't remember which day. I'd lost count by then. It sounded like a helicopter, but we couldn't be sure. We were so dazed with cold and exhaustion and lack of food that we couldn't trust ourselves not to have imagined it.

We were eight days on that journey, and the last two days I doubt whether we made more than half a dozen miles. We were both suffering from frostbite then, and fifty yards or so was all we could do without pausing to recover our strength. By then we hadn't eaten anything for three days, and our feet were so frozen and painful that we had difficulty in moving at all.

We reached the Tote Road on the evening of the eighth day only to find it choked with drifts. Nothing had been down it for several days, so that we were forced to spend another night in the open. And in the morning Darcy couldn't go on. He'd come to the end of his strength, and he lay there, staring at me out of his red-rimmed eyes, his cracked and blackened lips drawn back from the teeth and his beard all frozen stiff with ice. He looked much like Briffe had looked when we'd found him. " Can you make it?" he asked, and the words came out through his teeth without any movement of the lips.

I didn't answer, because to answer required an effort, and, anyway, I didn't know whether I could. All I wanted to do was to go on lying there in the snow beside him, to abandon myself to the dream world that my mind was already groping towards, a lotus-land of perpetual sun and hot food where the warm planks of an imaginary boat bore me gently towards a horizon of infinite ease, without effort, without discomfort.

" You've got to make it," he croaked at me urgently, and I knew it was Paule he was thinking of, not himself, and I crawled slowly to my feet.

To make a fire for him would have taken too much energy. " Good-bye!" I stood for a moment, looking down at him, and I remember thinking vaguely that he didn't look like a man any more; just a bundle of old clothes lying in the snow at my feet. " I'll make it all right," I said.

He nodded, as much as to say, " Of course, you will," and then his eyes closed. I left him then and plunged into the timber beyond the Tote Road. It was still snowing. It had snowed on and off for three days now, and even under the cover of the jackpine, it lay in drifts and hummocks up to three feet deep. It looked pretty as a picture. It was virgin white and as soft and snug as a down bed. It was also as cold as hell, and at every step it dragged at my legs, my thighs, my whole body, until I lay like one drowned in a white sea, unable to go a step farther.

It was then I heard voices. I shouted and they stopped. But then they started again and I knew it wasn't a dream. I was within earshot of the grade and I screamed at them. And once I'd started, I couldn't stop, but went on screaming to them for help, even when they'd reached me; which was perhaps just as well, for the sound that issued from my lips was no louder than the squeal of a jack-rabbit caught in a trap.

They were two engineers, checking the levels they'd run through a rock outcrop due for blasting the next day. They had a tent half a mile farther up the grade, and between them they got me to it, handed me over to the bull cook and went straight off again to get Darcy.

My memory of what happened after that is fragmentary and confused. I was in some sort of a bed, and there was an oil heater roaring and faces staring down at me. I kept on asking for Lands, but none of them seemed to have heard of him. It was like a nightmare, for I didn't know who else to ask for and I kept on drifting off into unconsciousness. And then gradually the pain of my frozen limbs blotted out everything else, and the next thing I remember they'd brought Darcy in.

He was still alive, but that was about all. They thought there was about a fifty-fifty chance of him pulling through. By then, of course, the two engineers had guessed who we were, and when I asked for Lands again, they told me he was at Camp 290. " He's been there all week, organising the search for you," one of them said. I was given another hot drink then and they told me not to worry. We'd struck the grade way to the north of our starting point, half-way between the trestle and Camp 290. The man who told me this said he was leaving right away for Two-ninety on snowshoes. He reckoned with luck he'd get through by nightfall.

I tried to tell him how they could find Lake of the Lion, but they'd put something in the drink to make me sleep and before I was half-way through explaining it to them, I had drifted back into unconsciousness. And when I woke again to the throb of intense pain in my hands and legs, it was dark. But the entrance of the tent had been pulled back, and through it I saw lights and men moving. There was the throb of an engine and a tracked vehicle slid into view, backing up close to the tent.

" They're in pretty bad shape, I'm afraid," a voice said. A pressure lamp appeared at the entrance, the hissing white light momentarily blinding me, and another voice said harshly, " What do you expect, after a couple of weeks out in the bush. It ain't exactly picnic weather." That voice, so like a nutmeg-grater, took me right back to the day I'd first arrived in Seven Islands. " Okay," the voice added. " The sooner we get 'em loaded on to the sno-mobile, the sooner they'll be in hospital."

The light bobbed closer until its hissing glare was right over me.

" Well, young feller—awake, are you?" I could see them then, just their faces picked out by the light—McGovern and Bill Lands, and the man holding the pressure lamp was the engineer who'd left for Two-ninety on snowshoes. " We got an aircraft standing by for you," McGovern said. " Reckon you can stick a ride in a sno-mobile, or do you want a shot of something to put you out?"

" I don't want anything," I said angrily. " I just want to talk to Lands." And when he came to the side of the bed, I said, " Did you get my message—about Paule, and Laroche?"

" Sure," he said. " But you don't have to worry——"

" Get me some paper," I said. " I'll try and draw you a map."

" Take it easy," he said. " There's nothing to worry about. They're going to be all right." He said it as though he were talking to a child and it made me angry, for I knew every moment was precious. " You don't understand," I cried, forcing myself up in the bed. " Laroche was injured. He's probably dead by now, and Paule's been there——"

But he gripped hold of my shoulders. " I'm trying to tell

you," he said, holding me down in the bed. "It's all right. We got them both out the end of last week."

I stared up at him, barely able to grasp what he'd said. "You got them out?"

"Yeah. Four days ago. You don't believe me, eh?" He laughed and patted my shoulder. "Well, it's true, so you can just relax. They're both safe down at Seven Islands, and I got a report to-day to say that Bert's going to be all right."

"Then the transmitter was okay? They got my message." I was thinking we could have saved ourselves the journey. If we'd stayed with Paule . . .

"What message?" Lands asked.

"The morning we left. I was sending for the full half hour, from seven until——"

"Well, nobody heard you."

"Then how did you manage to find them?" I was suddenly suspicious, afraid he was trying to make our failure easier to bear.

I think he realised this, for he told it to me in some detail. "It was Len got them out in the end," he said. "The first day conditions permitted, Mac here had his Beaver floatplane fly in. But there was ice on the lake and though the pilot was able to drop supplies, he couldn't land. Then, two days later, though the conditions were bad, Len took a chance on it and flew Mac in in the helicopter. He got Laroche out that trip, and then flew right back in again and got Paule and Mac out. After that the weather closed in and we couldn't fly. Len and the Beaver pilot have been standing by, ready to fly a search for you the moment there was a let-up."

So Paule and Laroche were safe. It seemed incredible. I half-closed my eyes against the glare of the pressure lamp, and clear in my mind was the picture of the lake and Paule crouched there beside Laroche. We'd been so certain he'd die. And Paule—after all that lapse of time, we'd come to accept the fact that if we did make it, we'd be too late to save her. Neither I nor Darcy had ever mentioned it, but I knew it was what we'd come to believe. "But how?" I said again. "How did you manage to locate the lake?"

"It was Mac," Lands answered. "He knew where it was. He was down in Montreal——"

"Just a minute, Bill." The harsh voice moved nearer. "Would you take the others outside a moment. There's something I got to say to this young man whilst he's still conscious." I saw his face clearly then—the lined, hard-bitten features framed in the white hair. The other faces had receded. The tent flap dropped across the entrance. " First," he said, bending down and lowering his voice, " I owe you an apology. And there's not many guys I've said that to. Tell me, did you guess that I knew about Lake of the Lion when we had that little talk down at Seven Islands?"

I nodded, wondering what was coming.

" Yeah, I thought so." He paused as though to collect his thoughts. " I gather from Paule Briffe you know the truth now of what happened out there after the crash? That correct?"

" Yes," I said.

" Okay. Well, this is what I want to tell you. This expedition of yours—it's news. You're headed for hospital, but as soon as the docs give the okay, there'll be a score of newspaper men asking you for your version. You say your father was right and that Briffe made that transmission, you tell them the truth of what happened and you'll ruin two lives. That girl's had about all she can take right now. As for Bert—well, he came to me as soon as he got out and told me the whole thing. In that he acted right. I was his boss. He was employed by me. And because of that he was prepared to abide by my decision. He told me what had happened and what he'd done and why. He was thinking of Paule mainly, but the fact is that if we'd flown back in and found Briffe alive, we were certain he'd have to stand trial for murder. In the circumstances, it seemed to me Bert had acted for the best." He hesitated. " It was rough justice. But it was justice as we saw it. You must remember that Bert was convinced that he'd left Baird dead, killed by that blow from Briffe's axe." And then, after a moment, he added, " I guess you can understand now how we felt when you arrived at Seven Islands!"

" What do you want me to do?" I asked.

" Keep your mouth shut. Leave the world thinking Briffe and Baird were both dead when Bert left them at the lakeside. Okay? In return, I'm gonna call that concession the Ferguson Concession and cut you in for a share of whatever we get out."

I stared at him, remembering that he, too, was an old-time

prospector, like Briffe—like my grandfather. " I don't need to be bribed," I said hotly.

" No," he said. " No, I guess you don't. But if you're gonna save those two from a lot more misery, then you're gonna have to deny your own father. You're gonna have to say there never was a transmission. And if you do that, it's only fair that your grandfather's original discovery should at least be recognised. As for the share of what we get out, that's your right—a legacy, if you like, from old James Ferguson. Well?" he added. " What do you say?"

And when I agreed, too tired to insist that I didn't want anything more to do with the place, his face broke into that sudden, transforming smile, and he patted my arm. " That's swell," he said. And he added, " You don't have to worry about the transmitter. Neither of the pilots saw it. It was covered in snow. And whilst I was there I threw the darn thing into the lake." He turned towards the entrance of the tent. " Bill!" he shouted. And when Lands lifted the flap, he said, " Time we got going."

" He's agreed then?" Lands asked.

" Sure he's agreed. What did you expect?"

I saw the relief on Land's face as he bent over me in the circle of light, but all he said was, " Okay, we'll get you to the airstrip now."

And so, with Darcy unconscious beside me, I started on the journey back to civilisation. I had been only eighteen days in Labrador ; a very short time compared with the weeks my grandfather had spent in the country. And yet I, too, had got to Lake of the Lion, and though I hadn't lost my life, I had come very near to it, had been involved in both tragedies— the past and the present—and had suffered as much hardship as most men who have trekked into the heart of that inhospitable land. And if this account of my journey has been too much taken up with the conditions of travel, I can only plead that it is not my fault, but the fault of Labrador.

PART FOUR

ENDPIECE

It is five years now since I made my journey into Labrador,
and this account has been written largely from notes made
whilst still in hospital at Seven Islands. These notes were not
intended for publication. They were a purely personal record,
written in the form of a diary, and were prompted by reading
the meticulous day-to-day entries made by my grandmother,
her diary having reached me the day after I entered hospital.

However, circumstances alter.

From the moment Laroche was allowed to receive visitors,
he was plagued by reporters, and this continued through his
convalescence and even after he and Paule were married.
And when Ferguson Concessions Ltd. was registered as a
private company and the newspapers began running garbled
versions of the old Ferguson Expedition, the Laroches could
stand it no longer and emigrated, at the same time changing
their name.

By then Darcy and I had already made our escape. Darcy
had returned to Labrador, minus most of his toes and walking
with the aid of two sticks. But as he said, " A few toes won't
make any difference to the way the fish rise ; and I can still
paint." An indomitable figure, I left him at Seven Islands, for
I was bound for South Africa to work for a Canadian engineering company sub-contracting on the construction of a
dam.

With the departure of the four people chiefly concerned,
interest in the story subsided. But I suppose it was inevitable
that sooner or later some enterprising journalist should em-
bark on a full-scale investigation and should arrive at the same
conclusion, the same suspicions that had clouded my own
judgment of Laroche.

There had been a good deal of talk, of course. But it was a
chance meeting in a bar with Perkins that sent this man hot-
foot into Labrador. He was the only journalist to visit Lake
of the Lion, and he arrived just as the Ferguson Concession
company was dismantling its equipment, having dredged till
it became uneconomic and having failed to find the source of
gold. Nobody cared then that a stranger was wandering

around the concession. He uncovered my grandfather's remains and then dug up the bodies of Briffe and Baird, which McGovern had had properly buried. After that he tracked down and interviewed everybody he could find who had been in any way connected with the affair. He even got hold of the nurses who had attended Laroche and had them describe the nature of his injuries.

The resulting article, which appeared in a Canadian magazine, whilst carefully avoiding any direct accusation, was written from the standpoint of history repeating itself. " Like grandfather, like grandson," was the corny phrase the writer used, and he pointed out that Paule and Bert Laroche had both had shares in Ferguson Concessions. The implication was obvious; an implication that was far worse than anything I had ever thought Laroche guilty of, and it involved them both.

The article was sent to me by Laroche, and in his covering letter he said they had no desire to take legal action, but at the same time they had decided it would be better if the truth were known. He knew I had written what amounted to a journal of my three weeks in Labrador, for I had shared his room in hospital, and now he wanted me to send it to a Canadian newspaper for publication. " It is better that it should come from you," he said at the end of his letter, " than from any of those directly involved—least of all myself. You were throughout the inquiring stranger seeking after the truth."

This I have tried to bear constantly in mind through the long months of writing. And I hope that, in the result, I have done justice to two people for whom I have a great admiration and whose lives have been be-devilled by a tragedy that was not of their making. And in conclusion, I feel I cannot do better than quote the final passage of the diary of that extraordinary woman, Alexandra Ferguson:

And so, with God's help and the courage of the men I took with me, I have returned safe out of the Labrador, having been in that forsaken country one hundred and four days. I left my small son and my home in Scotland to search for the truth of my dear husband's death, and now in this I have failed. I shall not go into that land again, but shall give this record to my son on the day he comes of age, and may the good Lord guide him to that lake and to the truth, whatever that may be.

AUTHOR'S NOTE

The Land God Gave to Cain is the result of two journeys I made into the Labrador. The first was in 1953, just before the big freeze-up. At that time the "Iron Ore Railway" was still under construction, steel having been laid only as far north as Mile 250. I saw the whole of it, from the terminal at Seven Islands on the St. Lawrence to the geologists' camp of Burnt Creek, 400 miles into the interior, living in the construction camps and travelling first by train and track motor, then by truck and car and on foot, and finally by the bush pilots' floatplanes, and even by helicopter.

That I was able to cover so much ground, and see so much of a country that hardly a white man had seen before the railway came, was due in the first place to Hollinger-Hanna, the Iron Ore Company of Canada, and the Quebec North Shore and Labrador Railway, and I am greatly indebted to these companies for the exceptional facilities they gave me and for their kindness in insisting that I should be their guest in the camps.

Once having been granted these facilities, it was left to me to make my own way, and in this I was never without friends —particularly amongst the engineers with whom I lived. There were the pilots, too, and the radio operators, and the men themselves; without exception they put themselves to great trouble and personal inconvenience to give me as complete a picture as possible of this astonishing project. They are too numerous to mention individually, but should they read this, I would like them to know that I remember them vividly and with affection, for they were very real people. I would also like to make it clear that, whilst I have had to make use of certain executive titles, the names and characters of the men occupying these positions in the book, and their actions, are purely imaginary.

The second visit was made three years later when the book was half-completed. I was on my way up to the Eskimo country to the north-west of the Hudson's Bay and I stopped off at Goose—primarily to check up on my description of this isolated community, and also to work out a satisfactory basis for the expedition's radio link. Here, Mr. Douglas Ritcey of Goose Radio, who is himself a " ham " operator, was most helpful, and I would like to record that he has allowed me to use his own radio set-up as the basis of Ledder's.

Altogether I travelled some 15,000 miles in quest of the material for this book—one of the most interesting journeys I have undertaken. I sincerely hope that, in the result, I have achieved my purpose of conveying a picture of one of the last great railways to be built, the sort of men who built it, and not least of all some idea of the bleak and desolate nature of the Labrador itself.

Fontana Paperbacks

Fontana is a leading paperback publisher of fiction and non-fiction, with authors ranging from Alistair MacLean, Agatha Christie and Desmond Bagley to Solzhenitsyn and Pasternak, from Gerald Durrell and Joy Adamson to the famous Modern Masters series.

In addition to a wide-ranging collection of internationally popular writers of fiction, Fontana also has an outstanding reputation for history, natural history, military history, psychology, psychiatry, politics, economics, religion and the social sciences.

All Fontana books are available at your bookshop or newsagent; or can be ordered direct. Just fill in the form and list the titles you want.

FONTANA BOOKS, Cash Sales Department, G.P.O. Box 29, Douglas, Isle of Man, British Isles. Please send purchase price, plus 8p per book. Customers outside the U.K. send purchase price, plus 10p per book. Cheque, postal or money order. No currency.

NAME (Block letters)

ADDRESS